DRAGON EYE CH

STORY
OF THE
MANY

PART 1

ROSS HAINES

Copyright © 2022 by Ross Haines

All rights reserved. This book or any portion thereof may not be reproduced or transmitted in any form or manner, electronic or mechanical, including photocopying, recording, or by any information storage or retrieval system, without the express written permission of the copyright owner except for the use of brief quotations in a book review or other noncommercial uses permitted by copyright law.

Printed in the United States of America
Library of Congress Control Number: 2022909506
ISBN: Softcover   979-8-88622-277-7
          eBook   979-8-88622-278-4
Republished by: PageTurner Press and Media LLC
Publication Date: 09/28/2022

To order copies of this book, contact:
PageTurner Press and Media
Phone: 1-888-447-9651
info@pageturner.us
www.pageturner.us

DRAGON EYE CHRONICLES (BOOK 1)

STORY OF THE MANY

PART 1

story by
ROSS HAINES

For every beginning, there is an end, for every end is a new beginning. We are space dust, and we shall never fade from the miles we travel to learn the ways of our world. We shall listen and wait for a cried of all newborn in the vastness of the cosmos.

Proverb from the gods of stars

Acknowledgment of Supporters in Random Order

Artist of Book Cover

Interior and Cover Designs by Page Turner Press and Media

Editor

Editing by Page Turner Press and Media"

3D Modeling

James Coleman

Additional Supporters

Marc-André Poulette

George Dozois

Claude Lanthier

Charles Rouleau

The ones that gave a steady encouragement during the workdays and nights to stay the course during the many pages I typed.

A Special Thanks for the Support of Family Members

Claudette, my wife

Tara, my daughter

They each gave me a piece to unravel the jigsaw of thoughts in my mind of imagination. I am deeply grateful for their in supportive words throughout this project.

I hope you will enjoy the adventure

In loving memories of my sister

Janice Clermont Haines

CONTENTS OF THE BOOK

CHAPTER 1 **THE MESSAGE RECEIVED** 1

CHAPTER 2 **THE DARK WORLDS OF THE ELDERS** 19

CHAPTER 3 **THE REBIRTH OF LORD ID** 38

CHAPTER 4 **THE ECHOES OF THOUSAND YEARS** 44

CHAPTER 5 **THE RETURN TO THE FORBIDDEN ZONE** 61

CHAPTER 6 **THE CHILDREN OF THE GODS** 77

CHAPTER 7 **THE SINGLE LIGHT OF HOPE** 97

CHAPTER 8 **THE UNSEEN SHADOWS WATCHING** 117

CHAPTER 9 **THE CRISIS ON HYPERION ONE** 137

CHAPTER 10 **AN OLD FRIEND AND THE CHALLENGE** 157

CHAPTER 11 **THE CAPTAIN CHOICES** 175

CHAPTER 12 **TEN YEARS AFTER THE NEPTUNE INCIDENT** . . . 185

CHAPTER 13 **CHILDREN OF THE LIGHT**
           CHALLENGES THE ENTITY 212

CHAPTER 14 **THE IMMORTAL WAR** 228

CHAPTER 15 **THE STAR CHILD** 236

EPILOGUE **THE LOST BEING** 243

Characters/Players

Child of the Light

Sabrina Light	Azurian	Leader
Katrina Topaz	Azurian	Healer
Eris Grey	Fairy Azurian/Human female	Healer/Life giver
Gabrielle Red	Azurian/Human female	Warrior/Healer
Ben Diamond	Azurian	Spy

Shadow realm of the Elders

Krell	Elderian/ forest Male	Leader/Teacher
Ru	Elderian/female	Caretaker
Id	Elderian/child male	Listener
Emerald	Elderian/Forest nymph	Green Witch

Myra clan

Eltross	Myra/Jung zee	Creator
Sleeping Queen	Giant Beetle	Creator
Old one	Myra/ Human	Telepath/Peacemaker
Tenguard	Multiple Clones	Mage/ Servant

Jung zee Race

Helen Nightshade	Human Form Changeling	Spider Queen
Lord Id	Jung zee/Myra	Creator
Ru-Tava	Human Female Jung zee	Creator
Entity young	Human Child/Jung zee	Death walker
Entity old	Human Female/Jung zee	Collector of souls
Ru/Tava	Elder Giant Spider Humanoid	

Dragon Eye Crew

Mrs. Hellen Nightshade	Multiple clones	Telepathic Level 10
Marvin Patterson	Human male	Captain/telepath

Mega Corporations

Samuels Gray Sr.	Human male	President/ Gray mega corp.

Hyperion 1 Crew

Miles Oboe	Human male	Captain/Scientist
Snead Winters	Human male	First officer
Tava Pane	Human female	Second officer
Nicole Ravenhawke	Human female	Lieutenant/pilot
Ian Ross/Nigel Bruce	Human male	Dept administer/spy
Iran Pane	Human male	Scientist
Mack McKenzie	Human male	Mining engineer
Susan Chow	Clone/child female	Telepath level 7
Elizabeth Pane	Human female	Doctor/Psychiatrist

Construction Crew

Timor Smith	Human male	Commander
Lisa Thomas	Human female	Telepath/engineer
Heidi Stumtrum	Clone female	Telepath/engineer
Frank Thomas	Human male	Electrical engineer
Stanley Wolfe	Human male	Robotics/ androids
Miguel Rodriguez	Human male	Sergeant

Hyperion 2 Crew

Lawrence. Bertrand	Human male	Captain
Gerald Ashton	Human male	Lieutenant
Beatrice Grimes	Human female	Lieutenant

Alpha Prime Confederation

Kelton Skelton	Human male	General/ President
Marcus Cobbs	Human male	Captain/ retired Colonel
Bert Cobbs	Human male	Captain/retired Colonel
Aaron Frost	Clone male	Captain/General
Charles Blackstone	Human male	Lieutenant/ pilot
Eris Styles	Clone female	Lieutenant/ pilot
Maggie Redkill	Clone female	Telepath5/Lieutenant
Marvin Patterson	Human hybrid	Telepath level 3
Ito Lee	Human hybrid	Telepath level 3
Stella Neptune 6	Clone female	Telepath level 6
Marc-André Poulette	Human male	Lieutenant/ pilot
Mira Langford	Human female	Lieutenant
Olivia Nightshade	Human Female	Telepathic level 10 with telekenesis
Marvin Patterson	Human	Pilot Navigator
Bertha Blackstone	Humanoid/Immortal Being	
Damiene Nightshade	Human Teenager	Telepathic
Thomas Savage	President of Alpha Prime Confederation of the 12 galaxies.	
General Edward Savage		
Sheila Winters		Nurse
Doctor Styles	Healer/Scientist	Medical Biology

Prologue
Message from the Past

Somewhere deep in the vast cosmos an unknown spaceship speeds along the edges of two large galaxies. One of the crew waits for a radio message from their home planet to proceed with the start new variant flux of timeline The two old humanoid clones had spent a lifetime preparing for this day. The male is at his workstation, writing his daily logbook of their adventures. The other crewmember a female had a hardened look as her eyes glared at the ring galaxy from the bridge windows.

She mutters many curses of her life's failures from the paradox that had come back for the third time. Her thoughts were dark and cruel to many of her kind. Being from the future, she detests time travel; more then once she declared it the ruination of all intelligent life. She presses the com. channel to recall the other to the bridge. He responds quickly with a sharp grunt, "Okay hold your horses." He goes back to his last paragraph to read it over. His thoughts hope that it will make sense to the next one that returns to this place and time.

> *I the Captain of this living ship leave the diagrams to build the ancient probe that will bring the first generation of humanity. Your future as all other races will depend on the next million years. We await the signal to start the short journey that will have long lasting memories for the children in three time zones. The past, the present, and the future must be in line to end the paradox. I Captain Ito Lee and my wife Stella Neptune 6 have failed three times to end the paradox. We now stand at another beginning to reach the fourth generation, the hope of all intelligent races, which live across the cosmos. This shall be the last attempt. If I should return or any others listed in the final sheet, the orders are to self-destruct code name omega fire. Yours truly Captain of the Dragon Eye.*

The voice crackles on the open communication channel with anger ....

"It is time to go in the stealth mode or the evil beasts shall see us," snarls the woman.

"Calm yourself woman, all is ready we have done these three other variant flux of time with great success. This will be no different than before," the captain barks a reply and mutters his annoyance under his breath.

Ito leaves his workstation to the bridge to check on the sleeping guests. He hears a steady beep from the bio tubes. Curiosity took the better of him as he steps deeper into the cargo hold. They are resting well and secure, thought the Captain. Ito then turns to leave for the bridge, the com. channel beeps once more. He ignores it as his feet pick up speed towards the bridge. Just as Ito enters the bridge, the transceiver beeps the code both audio and visual of a silver faced humanoid with glowing red eyes.

"Commence fourth protocol and depart immediately for Azure. Prepare to battle the Entity."

The old woman releases her anger and curses loudly.

"Krell you foolish weak creature, now it must start all over again and we live the long pain and suffering of three races," snarls the woman.

"Do not blame him alone, many are at fault. Due to the lost of memory every time we used the time jump it always occurs. I warned Sabrina that would happen. Now let us launch this probe," hissed the old man.

"I completely and heartily agree with you old man! I want to go home. I am tired of this ship and living in fear that the paradox will finally close on all of us."

"Speak for yourself old woman. I love this ship. I would hate to see it destroyed. It will be some else, not I."

Within minutes without a second to waste, they launch their probe to the pending target. The spaceship slowly arches away on its impulse engines away from the two galaxies. They activate their jump engines and set the navigation to the planet Azure. The unusual, shaped sphere rises over the top of the ships canopy. The orb begins to come alive glowing and expelling great amounts of energy, large electric discharges burst away in all directions forming a bubble of charge particles. The energy collapses inward and flashbacks to complete darkness of empty space.

Only the discard probe moves slowly, uncurls its array, and in lines itself to transmit its data to the far-off planet. Through three transmitters, it starts to photograph the pending target at the lower ring galaxies where it picks large amounts of energy. Out of the dark space, the giant red sun reflects light on it to reveal the number and the name of the craft - NASA Voyageur Deep Space Nostradamus 8. The captain sends his last message to his probe

Somewhere in the present time this message from the past shall reach its destination, God speed you little one, grunts the captain.

CHAPTER 1

THE MESSAGE RECEIVED

Dragon eye log
Book one entry
Star date AI1E3Ap15:21

In the present on Earth, year 2535 man has reached the stars. They have survived wars, plagues, and evils that came by man's dark side for greed and power. The competition between big companies on the technology was furious and fusions with smaller business increased their expansion to reduce the number of players. Three mega Corporations have taken over the operation to explore the stars around their own solar systems. Due to the lack of resources on Earth, humanity spread out inside the solar system with great speed, by the highly advance Artificial Intelligence, accepted in their life. The slow growth in computers came with many breakthroughs by greedy corporations with a cost of many human lives from a trial by error. Due to the human beings, greed and power made their fast and impatient body of scientific techniques to reach for control of the world at any costs. During one occasion two great powers on earth had a computer melt down, which started the third world war, when the computers exchanged lethal weapons at each other and in peaceful countries millions died instantly.

The government slowly recovered in a new world body and joined private industries on September 09, 2109. They made standard protocols and safeguards to prevent such disaster. They applied their knowledge and expertise to build an advance AI system, for only space exploration to manufacture the rich resources through mining and colonization of the moons that orbit our solar system.

Earth slowly rebuilt with the Corporations help. The humans wanting the return of lost ones embraced cloning methods in the new order and accepted the used of highly enhanced artificial brains. In simple words, the computer core ran their spaceships saving the original humans on earth. While clones and androids-built cities and terra forming Mars and other moons in their solar system. A giant leap of technology came with the cyber link and the advance helix cube for the clone's mind to retain and increase the intake of knowledge and experience of the original human.

The most successful in cloning and cyborg technology were Dark-Lighter Tech, Tananaka Corporation, and Gray Mega Corporation. Dark-Lighter-Tech is on Mars they used clones to help settle each moon that orbits Saturn and Neptune for terraforming, mining, and manufacturing tech industries and weapons. While Tananaka Corporations office and factories are on the moon of Io. Their advance robotics with cyborg technology are the first place to used human child within a cyborg suit to live and work on moons of Jupiter and Uranus and the Pluto cluster. Gray mega corporation is run with original humans and clones in rebuilt world of Earth that controls the moon Mercury and Venus is what they control with mining industries they also have space platforms for mining the Astro belts between Mars and Jupiter. Each corporation are rivals all three spy on each other in hopes to steal or take advantage by brides or even murder to keep one step ahead of the other. Each corporation knew they would pick their top scientist picked to lead their take the world spaceships and claim the Arial system under the corporation's name. Dark-Lighter-Tech carried over one million children clones with a secret device called helix cube, created by two Doctors one a brain surgeon, Edward Bain, the other a computer specialist Claude Lanthier. Devise was the first name of the cube. Their invention was the first steps by a single microbe chip with optic fibre as thin as a spider string. The microchip had a power pack and processor about the size of a book. They used it on patients with brain disorders example retardation, epileptics and mental disorders like Alzheimer. After many deaths, the first success May 6, 2189, one hundred patients were cured of all their handicaps. Which became the first steps to raise the intellectual and physical capacity of mankind that help alter and raise the life standards by the large population turning into genius's push their invention in robotics and cyborg technology work force.

Many believed that the Dark-Lighter Mega Corporation were the ones that improved the second generation they named crystal cube. They found two large meteorites embedded with energy crystal. On June 2, 2299, Major IR Lewis a military Doctor devised a newer model in large numbers by removing all power packs and processors to the microchips with a rewiring of the human brain. This caused increased cognition by twenty percent with a large memory sensory and an increase of the human emotional state called blood lust. "The new technology improved military services significantly. More space troops were deployed to guard and control each terraform moon. There were also more space pilots and other crew servicemen for all their warships and starfighters."

So, each corporation had built their own armies that included pirates that would steal from each other for the control of the growing population. However, at the end of the war came a trial against Major Lewis for his inhuman methods. The new Alpha Prime government took control July 10, 2302, of colonizing after Grays Mega Corporation revealed the death total on two others colonizes. During this cause, a mini war between the corporations lasted ten years. The young son of the Dr. Ross improved the Helix Cube 2 with safety protocols February 29, 2312. As a result, many celebrate the leap year. The Government passed a law that all children born after this date will have this device implanted to control the minds of violent tendencies. Everyone knew the model number of the newest helix cube developed by Ian Ross; he named it Helix 4d. Only a few selected insiders knew its purpose, based on the past failures and many deaths. Grays Mega Corporation were the first ones with government approval base on all the safeguards and improvement in life receive permission to colonize all the moons of Alpha Prime. This new device however brought a new wave of slavery controlled by those two mega corporations. They stretched their resources to keep ahead of each other.

The two new corporations rose out of the ashes on Dec 2, 2210. The scientists created a Cyborg race with humans and computer enhancements. These first humans chosen were badly injured or near death. They offered them a second chance to live in a new form of advanced warrior. Most were highly aggressive clones made to live and fight wars and used for the far off reaches of space. Some had increased strength, agility, and wide range of information stored up in the portable matrix brain. For any covert missions, government protocols, and policy set programs for the cyborgs to follow. Their bodies had built in tools attached to human flesh.

They knew little about the military scientist who wanted it to record the minds of their best skill warriors. They planted them in their recruits, which became clones and Cyborgs. This improved their military war machine during the first planetary war between earth and mars.

These perfect soldiers designed by the military with enhanced weapons such as lasers, ion rifles, stealth shielding and highly advanced sensory equipment for analyzing their environments. First used during the planetary war years in the twenty third century between earth and mars. In the year 2215, two-mega Corporations purchased the Cyborgs that had survived the war. With reprogramming, they selected them as a security force and a go between for human clones and androids now used in large groups for mining exploration.

A big push out of the solar system for humankind became a new quest to feed the hungry corporations by going beyond their system. Only Grays Corporation had the edge with their secret projects to leave their home Earth system. While the other two remaining corporations, planned long-range flights with their AI and Cyborgs. The government of Alpha Prime planned a great celebration of two hundred years of peace, on July 10 of the year twenty-five thirty five.

The ruling government called Alpha-Prime was the planet that Earth had colonised in their solar system with Mars being the Headquarters. Jupiter with four main satellites as well as Saturn, Neptune, and Uranus satellites that they had terra formed. Each Mega Corporations mining and colonization controlled three more technology companies for special design probes in search for resources with money spent on probes to the far out stretches into deep space. Their quest for great riches towards the future, and the advancement of technology and humankind to rule the cosmos.

Grays Corporation, one of the mega companies received in secret, information from a lost probe sent out five hundred thirty-five years ago from NASA. The probe sent information and photos of a solar system with three different stars within one solar system that had hundreds of planets. The printer starts to drop information in numbered sequences into a scientist basket.

The two Scientists on duty concentrated on an experiment on producing the first artificial gravity well by a special probe on the outskirts of Pluto and Charron. When the old NASA probe started to send photos of the planets, the scientist realized at that time this was a single planet with an atmosphere three million years ago. Future tests confirmed the lost atmosphere. Some unknown disaster splintered into two rocky out crops confirming to a lower status. The cost of sending more probes were forgot until the big expanse. The computer test showed some great news. They knew this could open a new outpost under Grays Corporation in the start of 2529. While it would be the furthest out reaches to the rich field of meteorites. They heard the sound of an incoming message.

"Dam I will not have time to finish this work before noon. Miles, can you check it out for me? I am busy with that thing. I still need a minute."

"Yeah, all right, take your time."

Miles Oboe walked to the printer's tray that was already half filled. He took the pile and started to read as his eyes open wide.

"Come over here pal! Drop your glass tube for a minute."

The assistant joined Miles; he knew when he woke up this morning the day would end very late.

"What is so funny," said his assistant, as he tried to read over Miles's shoulder.

"Give a look at this pal its great."

The printed document amazed the two scientists of Grays Mega Corporation. If this printout is all true, it will jump-start this company on top of the competitors. To prevent the two rival corporations on this race, Miles rushed to the interphone to call his supervisor for an emergency meeting.

They called a high-level meeting to examine the data of the lost probe. The pictures showed far off and away across the cosmos large clusters of galaxies shape by their orbit and speed since the big bang class spirals with two strings of energy and a million zillion stars. During the meeting, they began naming planets and reference points of interest to the mining engineers.

"Welcome my precious contributors to this presentation. Please have a seat by your nametag. I am Snead Winters the executive assistant and I hope I will find your interest on this undiscovered galaxy"

"We focus on one system that is odd and completely different in its look and structure. The center is a perfect sphere of suns dying and reforming new ones. Outside the sphere are two rings in a perfect circle mix. Between the rings is the dark matter of space dust and ice particles, which absorb the energy of the stars. They interact with each other in odd orbit between the three suns. We named it the Beta system. The four giants gas planets range in size from one hundred fifty thousand to three hundred thousand kilometres across the equator which circle the red sun. Each giant gas planet has rings of age. Over twenty to two hundred planets ranging in size from one hundred ten thousand kilometres cross the equator. The two other suns have four atmospheres with oxygen and water."

"This old NASA probe what model is it, how can you be sure it is original, not false image of old data one sent by your competitors," hissed the dark suited man with a deep challenge that sneered across his face.

"Our company purchased all the records from the defunct NASA long-range probes" Snead Winters quickly responded. "I see the interest in your eyes for our project and I do not have pretension to know everything that is why we have specialists to work for us," Snead Winters smiled to the audience. "I delegate my best specialist to explain in detail. At the end of this presentation, we will answer all your questions." He waved at his scientist to continue his presentation.

"Sirs, I am Miles Oboe, and I will try my best to paint the clearest picture of what our company thinks of the century's greatest discovery. Each one is completely different in its basic makeup due to the density of life form animals and bio life of fawn and forest. Because of its large oceans and unique lands mass, this shows the diversity of climate from Snowcap Mountains to forestlands and grass plains to desert topics to wide range of islands make this an ideal first planet, called Terrain 6. In addition, it has a cluster of five moons that can be terra formed in the future."

Many of the group mumbled loudly interrupting his presentation as four men wanted to cut to the bottom line, they shouted repeatedly.

"How many light years will decide our involvement of money?"

"We do not have this information at this moment but as soon as we receive more details, we will inform you. Now please let us finish we have lots of scientific proof to give you," grumbled Snead. Miles, face turning beet red, took time to drink a glass of ice water to cool his impatience.

"The further planet out is ice dense with clouds and storms. Its long orbit cuts cross the three suns. When it nears the red sun, it gives it heat that changes the season and quickly increases the sudden burst of life that lives under the ice. As its moves between the yellow snows the temperature begins to cool as the temperatures lower to mild temperature. Then in the last circle, it bypasses the dwarf sun and falls back into the ice age. This planet we named Zlotoo has no moons," claimed Miles.

He glances about to gauge the long stares; these moneymen are hard to reach a thought cross his mind. Has he turned the page to continue his presentation about the next points of interest?

"The third set planet named Beta 5 is similar size and has four moons that orbit in different angles and distances. Each moon varies in size with many there are over twenty planets that range fifty to one hundred ten thousand kilometres that cross the equator.

"Each planet orbits into the atmosphere of two large giant's gas, which we named the Beta twins. We found exact make up hydrogen, helium, and methane atmosphere pressure. They have the same high winds that bring the matching colour bands that give them their unique make up. The ice bands give us our first clue to the wealth this system has to offer. The corporation probe receives and collects the crystal from the dense pressure and speed of their storms. The new probes dangerously close orbit to record the energy reactions between the two giant planets. The probe attempts to reach one of the planets, which cut along the edge of the giant gas planets. The twins are both about two hundred thousand kilometres across the equator. They have two powerful magnetic poles that cause massive aurora electrical plasma that shoot across each other. This releases great amounts of ice crystals that bombard all the planets during the winter months. They react to the atmosphere by the speed they enter and melt into rainwater that replenishes all the three main planets with the life force that lives in these worlds."

"This is all good speculations and seems viable only I want. No, I demand to know the distance and costs to this wild solar system. The Tananaka and the others are heading for the Arial system that might be a lower cost," quotes the dark suited man. Has his hands played with his jacket pressing a secret device in one of his cuff buttons on his coat to immediately transmit the information to other sources.

"Dear Sir, we are coming to the most important part of our discovery. This will put Grays Corporation on the leading edge for the next thousand years with great financial returns. Please let us continue without any more interruptions," pleaded Snead, with an additional warning to the money lenders.

"They have spies watching everywhere."

His thoughts wander if a spy had filter into this meet by the consent interruptions. Espionage in the modern times is at its highest as they battle for new resources. Dark-Lighter Tech Corporation is more advanced in technology than his competitors are, and they used more robots' androids; half human and half machine, which mine only colonies with clones based on the poor atmosphere of their planets they have established. The spy control room from the two-rival corporation had already received from a contact in Grays Corporation, an intercepted administration meeting that they recorded on a transmission link. The two console watchers rushed out with the media cylinder in the administration meeting room. As they enter, twelve administrators froze in action.

"What is this interruption all about," said the vice president of Dark Lighter Tech Corporation as twelve heads turned to the opened doors?

"Sorry to interrupt your meeting, Mr. vice president but you must see this right away."

The vice president raised a hand to voice his disapproval. A console operator inserted the cylinder in the video control and turned on the big screen. The twelve administrators started to complain that they have no time for interruption.

"We shall be late on scheduling our deep probe to Arial solar system."

While the big screen shows, a Grays Corporation interview of the new solar system recently discovered their mouths dropped down with a gasp. The vice president stands up so fast his chair crashes against the near wall.

"Contact the president! If we win this race, Dark Lighter Tech Corporation will be the first company of Earth to own a new galaxy."

The other rival is Tananaka Corporation from Mars had also learnt of it and had one advantage of being months ahead of the other two corporations. They built a new generation of star ships, bigger than all done on Earth. The overall structure has the capacity to carry a thousand humans for an unlimited travel with the new city ship called Black-Moon-Wind. They were making plans to reach the nearest solar system called Arial a similar dwarf star. The construction was two years away.

Tananaka Corporation was not blind at all, on what just happened at Grays Corporation. They had intercepted the information on the well-kept meeting as the news hit the airwaves showing the new discovery of a new solar system code name Beta system.

The meeting with the Grays Corporation and the financial bankers agreed to back up their launching program. Knowing other Corporations received the data at the same time. The other two took up the challenge. The race had begun to claim the planets for their own company. This started accelerations towards building a spacecraft for mining and colonization.

Miles Oboe ran the meeting as he explained the photos and data, in a deep echoing voice. The scientist looked at the photo in this far off star system with twenty planets of various size that orbited two large giant gas planets similar too Jupiter. The scientist spent hours studying the outer ring in the lower quadrant of the giant red sun. The outer ring had a bright yellow sun five light-years away and a dwarf sun that crossed the orbit of the others but ten light years from the larger sun

"We named them Beta and Corvas, they orbit the red sun. We found an odd planet that has a breathable atmosphere, which orbits Beta. We call it Beta 5. It is unique because it hides from the shadow of both giants' gas from the red star. It receives light from the dwarf sun, which develops the planet to conclude it is an Earth type."

The meeting erupted from a visiting investor, demanding more proof, Miles face flushed red, as he slams down.

"If you let me finish, you will have all your data."

The executive assistance Snead Winters stepped forward with his hands raised in the air to silence the group. Miles continues,

"The planet has a wide range of rich minerals for mining. In addition, we can colonize quite quickly. There is one greater find, a mystery substance in which the data state a new energy source. Just a tablespoon of this material could power our spaceships across the galaxy and beyond to higher effusions of ninety six percent in speed and distance. Cutting our travel time from years to months, our scientist Ian Ross calls it the white crystal."

Miles pulls out the graphs with the breakdown of the chemicals that match the current fuel. His right-hand points to the orange stripe indicating the purity level. Miles's voice rose with an excitement with the next words that claim the secret news.

"That is what every engineer calls the holy grail of power. Everywhere the stars will open at our feet. We need more money to send new probes through the new Star-gate portal code name, Dragon Eye 4, to complete the data and get a clearer picture while also retrieving a better sample. With this in mind, we will be the richest in the world." The meeting was over as Miles left the room with his fingers crossed.

Five hours pass as Miles paces the floor in the waiting room. His executive assistance Mr. Winters rushed in with a big smile and a cigar in hand for his boss.

"All the investors have signed in, with an additional one billion in gold each, for the mining colony to build a city ship."

Miles lit his cigar and inhaled deeply to release his stress. His thoughts filled with happiness of his accomplishment. The view screen beeped on his watch. He answered it with a happy tone in his voice. She was his co-worker a scientist named, Tava Pane.

"I have some bad news; this new star system is three hundred light years away from Earth."

"Are you sure of that affirmation Tava?"

"I am positive Miles; I ran my calculations three times to the same conclusion."

Miles cursed loudly, as he broke his cigar in half.

"Let's keep it a secret until the other probes confirm it. I will talk to the president."

"Ok sir you are the boss."

Miles called the president to tell him the news; somehow, he already knew the secret. With a wave of his hand, he dismissed it in one sentence. Miles made a sigh of relief but wondered how the president knew.

The president ordered Miles to send out the probes immediately through Grays Corporation new transport device.

"This is a secret project, Miles! Do not tell anyone. I will call it a looking glass project."

It is one of many private projects, the president built, from his own funds.

This self-made man was a successful scientist in his own right, a physicist engineer, twice winning the Nobel Prize for his discoveries. In addition, a history buff of Earth's failed experiments, including the Philadelphia Experiment and the particle beam chamber which he incorporated in his own experiments in the corporation. At the time, this cost millions of dollars. They cancelled the project after fears of damage to the Earth's atmosphere.

The Star-gate Portal is one of the president's discoveries. It is a huge open door that gave access to ships that travel."through the galaxies was used as a boost to launch probes and supplies to the outer ice planets. It orbited the dark side of Neptune.

He never sent humans through it for fear of any odd effects. Six months later, the probes sent by Grays Corporation reached the Beta system took position, deployed their long solar captor panels, and started to collected photos and information related to that system. The probes rotated on their axis and pointed to the planet of their origin and a new program started to send the information just collected.

Grays Corporation received the probe's transmission and informed the government. A wide range of tests confirmed the Beta 5's data sent from the NASA's lost probe.

Both Dark-Lighter-Tech and Tananaka Corporations learning of the existence of a Star-gate portal, attempt a joint attack to take over Grays Corporation by buying stock from investors and murdering key stockholders.

An open attack on the Star gate portal caused small skirmishes between the three groups.

During this time, sudden urgencies caused the three giant companies to rush to build their city ship. The Tananaka Corporations rename their ship Sol 1 to appeal to the population of Alpha Prime. The corporation is ready first to orbit in a space pod around earth's moon.

The ruling government took control by force and blocked any attempt to take advantages by either company. The Tananaka Corporations feared war between the supports that extend wildly among the satellites of Alpha Prime. Grays Corporation seized the moment to request a meeting with their rivals and the president of Alpha Prime. The rivals meet and exchange many threats to prove there could be no agreement. Miles Oboe following his boss's instruction offers a peaceful settlement.

"All three ships can enter the Star-gate portal in order, by pulling a straw the short one goes first the longest one goes last."

The Tananaka administrator scoffs.

"Why not count ten paces and shoot each other for the right to control."

Dark-Lighter-Tech administrator giggles.

"Your boss is certainly from old school, but I accept because our ship is a few months behind completion."

The president accepts the offer of Grays Corporation and threatens Tananaka Corporation with severe penalties and taxes.

"If the Corporation do not accept the offer of peace than I president of Alpha Prime will cut government tax incentives, plus investigate all spending and purchasing for the past six years income tax. This of course will slow you down, cutting margins to your investors, and I will eventually disqualify your company on all space expedition in the future," said the President of Alpha Prime.

Tananaka Corporation bows to the pressure for the lottery. The government sets the rules so that no corporation takes advantage. The three Corporations will all build a star ship in similar fashion with strict governmental standards holding 100 hundred thousand embryos and complete supplies for ten years. In addition, the ships will carry farm gear, mining gear, plus a tool shop to manufacture and repair equipment and emergency shelters to cover any disasters of environmental changes to the extreme.

The following year all three Corporations' ships left their respectful orbit and headed to the Star gate portal. Grays Corporation ship named Hyperion-One will be the first city ship to enter the Star-gate portal by pulling the short straw, then Dark-Lighter-Tech Corp's Dark-Ace; then Tananaka Corp with their ship Sol-One.

After a few murders of other executives from smaller corporations who had a shared interest in the Stargate and wanted to add their spacecraft into the exploration of Ea space. They bowed out for fear to lose other members of each corporation. Miles feeling after so many deaths wanted to tighten security around all the leading members that are to join him on Hyperion. He wants special force to guard all his group and met the Grays' administration to take control and organize the voyage. Using his organization skills to collect the best of everything to ensure success at all costs while using his sales force to promote a commercial enterprise in the center of the main ship. He incorporated some stolen system from another corporation as the central computer core to run the ships. He employed at least five thousand military types to handle the safety of the scientists, the engineers, and their families. He included a religious group to satisfy their spiritual needs. He programmed the computer core with historical data and educational tools to teach the future children. He gathered books on poetry, classical stories, movies, and copies of art works.

Grays Corporation's president insisted on installing bio tubes consisting of a sealed single bed for life hibernation to protect the humans from radiation once inside the Star-gate. He based his theories on the data from the Philadelphia experiment, the loss of lives, strange burns the crew had suffered in addition to the two missing soldiers that never found.

The Mega Corporation groups made sure each embryo had all the updates, which attached to their frontal lobes that will only start the cloning process once they reach Beta system on the other side. Dark Lighter Tech installed secret instructions in the AI brain that were preset to eliminate the other two ships from reaching the new solar system. This raised their percentage of success by eighty five percent of being the only corporation to claim ownership. The plans are set as they rush to complete the ships on schedules.

The three huge city ships reached Neptune's orbit for their rendezvous. All passengers were at shuttle and watched the Star-gate enlarge on their view screen. For the first time under military control, a massive pentagon shape stepped out of the Neptune shadow. The star gate portal was twenty kilometres side to side in the shape of the pentagon, a five-side structure with each point is a two kilometres particle generator that points to the center of the Star-gate. Escorted by two-defence fleets, one squadron from Neptune and the other from Saturn the fleet consist of thirty battle cruiser, one hundred blast boats and three-hundred-star fighters. In addition, a wide range of personal crafts from a space skiff to a large passenger cruiser. This being a historical moment many took the best view to watch the Star-gate and film the moment.

General K. Skelton, assigned in charge of the Star-gate's defence, walked onto his ship's bridge, and watched the three approaching in a tight formation. He sees something is wrong and orders a communications link of the city ships. The old officer back stiffens in his seat and complains

"This is all wrong. I want to communicate with them."

The com-officer leaned into the microphone to call out.

"This is Neptune's defence. Come in Sol-one, Hyperion-one, and Dark-Ace please turn on view screen General Skelton wishes to set the rules before the start of the particle beam."

They all acknowledged the communications, as the screen appears showing a middle age General with white hair, stone cold brown eyes with a deep frown across his forehead. He clears his voice before he speaks.

"You men are supposed to be obeying orders of the lottery and be a one hundred kilometres from each other. I do not need to remind you that I will not activate the gate unless you comply with the peace agreement."

"Yes sir no problem," hissed Miles.

The other two ships answered with a grunted yes. The two ships banked a hard turn to set up to the agreed distance from each other. General Skelton smiled at his success, wished them all the success in their future endeavours, and ordered to start the generators. The officers complied quickly as they hit the thirty switches to recharge the Star-gate. General Skelton watched as the bright lights turned on along the edges of the generator field.

On the Hyperion-one, the phase's preparation to hibernate had started. The passengers stepped in the bio tubes for a deep sleep. Tava Pane a flight navigator was kissing her parents for a good sleep on their journey. A quick kiss and a long hug is all she got when Miles Oboe called her on the interphone to report on the bridge. She hopped into the freight elevator.

She quickly took her station at the navigation board and spots a red flashing light from the last probe telemetries of the Beta system have gone offline. She chews her lips, as she does a system check on the clear error made by someone on the ship. Miles turns to the navigator with a deep concern he whispers.

"Can we make a lock-on to the Beta system, without telemetry to the probe on board computer?"

"Of course," replied to the navigator, "I have studied all the orbits for a year at every reference point in their orbit by the narrowest margin by point zero one percentile."

"Good, get a lock on the calculation and feed in the computer core, you got only ten minutes," barked Miles.

"Yes sir, should we report this to General Skelton and the other two ships," muttered Tava who pushed back her long red hair and waited for Miles's answer.

"No why bother them. They are only androids and half humans; besides they have experts in that field. Even the military must be receiving the same information." Miles grunted with a wave of his hands.

The computer voice broke to silence on the bridge with a warning tone.

"Ten-minute count down, all bridge crew to the bio tubes final warning."

Tava saw her wrist indicator as well as Miles started to flash. She got up to leave to her bio tube. Miles took hold of her hand.

"Go down to the auxiliary bridge and make sure that all backup computer systems are set on telemetry and on target to the additional probes that are currently in Beta system. I do not want to be scattered into atoms across the cosmos."

The navigator's eyes spread with fear thought she would not have time. It is an order from her boss. She swallows hard and gave a nervous nod, walks away to the elevator, and presses the floor level of the secondary bridge, watching the smirk on Miles Oboe's face. Just when the elevator doors closed the view screen of the star gate burst in swirl of stars that stretched out like a brief mushroom before imploding. Miles eyes froze to the wonderful creation of its energy as it pixel into multi colours of energy before the white clouds began to swirl in a counter clockwise motion. General Skelton stunned by the power output, ordered all non-military crafts to retreat another thousand kilometres. Recalling the star fighters to ensure the private ships followed his orders. One of his bridge officers reported a lost radio signal from the probes but added the old NASA probe is still transmitting in a lower frequency. He waved his hands in acceptance as his eyes adjusted to the brightness of the star gate. He could actually see a strange shape forming in the center of the white cloud as if a window opened to a new world. He sees a red star coming into view. It sends a strange aura spreading throughout changing the colours into a band of rainbows. The navigation officer confirmed its location was on target. Miles Oboe gives the signal to the two ships for final approach. Three bridge ships replied with final goodbyes to all of Alpha Prime.

Tava reached the secondary bridge, locked down the heavy-laden doors as she preps the spare bio tube. While she turned on all recordings, she was in awe by the Star-gate as she transfixes in the diamond shape window and the red star filled the center. She turned on the rear camera of the two ships and noticed something odd when the alarms rang final warning a three-minute count down. Tava called out to Miles as she goes into the bio tube. He answered with irritation in his voice.

"Yes, Miss Pane is everything secure."

"Yes, but I am getting high radiation level from the Dark Lighter corporation ship on our stern and bow, sir."

"I see it, oh god have mercy; AI computer, now raise shields full impulse now."

Tava tried to object but the sleeping gas made her body go numb. Only her eyes could see the horror as a rocket appeared at full thrush heading towards them. She felt the ship lurch and spin into the Star gate; she smiled thinking that General Skelton had activated the gate in time. She felt a cold chill from the other two ships that reflected two bright yellow shapes. They looked like a pair of evil eyes appearing on the left side of the gate. In her mind, a great premonition grew that a disaster was about to happen, before her sleep takes over.

Miles quick action saved the ship from total destruction. He looked behind and saw Sol-one takes a direct hit on their bridge, causing the ship to spin out. He screams in panic as the shock wave implodes inside the Star-gate, striking the second ship, seem to spin out off control towards his ship. Miles looked down from his bio tube control panel, giving his last orders by cancelling computers control and hits full power to his engines before his body goes numb, hitting his head at the sharp edge of the tube. His blood pours out from the wound and he fell unconscious.

General Skelton was relieved when he saw Hyperion one move in the Star-gate and thought peace had finally come to the three-mega corporations. The alarms went off as the gunner reported the sightings of two torpedo rockets that Dark ace had fired.

"Open fire, target those rockets" yelled the General.

It is too late, he thought. *You have killed us all*, muttered the general. He hits his emergency jump to control their escape as his crew pass on the warning to the fleet and gave orders.

"Prepare for emergency jump! Withdraw now. Recall every craft to the bright side of Neptune" ordered Skelton.

He watched the direct hit to the bridge of the Sol-one. It blossomed one kilometre in a perfect round fireball. The forward motion started a wild spin to the left side of the Star-gate. General Skelton fingers froze as he went to shut off the power and watched it strike one of the power generators before it absorbed in the pure energy.

The sudden release caused a large energy wave that blossomed a hundred kilometres wide and a thousand kilometres in length. It destroyed three satellites killing a hundred million people and sliced right through Neptune equators splitting the cord and releasing a second wave of radiation. It affected the other satellites washed over by radiation and charge particles electrical energy. Even the military post shields fail and cause all the warheads to explode. He quickly sends out a code red alert as a wave of deadly radiation blankets a huge cloud of debris, which poured between the inner and outer planetary moons of Neptune.

CHAPTER 2

THE DARK WORLDS OF THE ELDERS

Dragon eye spaceship
Logbook one
Star time 00:01

The old captain guides his ship to watch the strange event that he knew would appears within this timeline is the start of the variant flux. He wanted the first recordings of beings from another dimension entering our universe. He knew that his universe was young, and the energy between two dimensions will help these beings to crossed over. It mixed basic chemicals formed by pressure and electrical discharge. Interaction with the gaseous clouds of atoms it became aware of its existence.

Mostly tiny atoms of dark matter congealed into awareness of a conscious mind. With basic neuron, it begins to learn of its existence and searches for the meaning of life.

Attracted to the far distance lights it sets its journey for discovery. It grew older and developed a great consciousness slowly multiplying within itself for the search for perfection that drove it across the galaxy. At first, the creatures were curious of the hot colour gasses that formed a separate solar system. They searched further and found planets formed in a wide range of size and structure. They found the giant gas planets near giant red stars gave them vast amounts of food to stimulate their growth towards vast knowledge.

They realized that their bodies were stronger in the vacuum of space and their movements followed the currents from solar winds. Like children left alone, they started to feel the purpose of their existence

The creatures learned by trial and error. They joined in a cluster copying a distance solar system to learn to power the energy and the direction to travel across the stars more efficiently. They learned shapes and built floating nests of space dust rocks closer to their food sources. They grew large as if a large cell life heart veins a single eye and mouth, mostly made of water and gases which filled the inside of their membrane form.

Their shapes vary in sizes but all were a perfect sphere when traveling across the sky. Overtime their body changed to a diamond shape with a single eye in the same design. Their mouth with wide silver teeth, a hollow tongue with large brain cavities pulsed with wide plasma energy moving across and down the brain stem to the transparent heart

Their homes grew to a planet size that wandered between the stars fed by energy protons from the stars. Their favourite food came from the radiations by the red sun, or brown dwarfs stars that orbited freely in the cosmos. Their numbers increased until the oldest realized that their bodies changed form female to male during certain cycles. Being the largest of his group he gave himself a name in his old language call Krell. He became leader and teacher to his group of beings that he names the Elders. Their purpose is to collect great knowledge of the cosmos. Since he knew their beginning, he calculated time and distance travel. He is the first of their kind to understand the secrets of their existence and the group proclaimed him a great leader.

He calls his race the elders. They became aware of the different sexes between them and everyone thousand a few changed sex to profligate their race. They plan to return every ten thousand years to the unseen world to double in size the living cells. Their brains grew continuously with thoughts of the stars among them.

The older ones following the ways of the first leader became teachers of their kind and finally found ways to gather and collect the correct amount of energy to sustain their race, by absorbing radiation from wide ranges of stars. Over eons of time the elders mind continued to develop a mass of scientific information of the cosmos and maps of every star. They spread out to learn the ways of nature. Their shape never evolves beyond gasses of energy atoms in a circle of dark mist with a pale blue center.

This started a debate and new vision among the old ones. The young adolescents pushed for more knowledge about the cosmos. All races spoke in their own language and thought processes in telepathic language developed by the oldest elder to improve communications among its races.

"Is this all that I am, is there more then this spoke, the oldest of the elders. No, we must search for others of our kind or beings different from us in hope to teach them the secrets and knowledge with wisdom between chaos and balance."

The elders all cheer the new vision to search for other intelligent beings. They found other groups of living creatures from the further reaches of the solar system. They set a plan to study the creatures whose minds were full of emotional thinking.

The oldest elder suggested small groups of five children led by two elders to explain the differences in the galaxies to their offspring. Regardless of distance, their minds connected to each other. It took over a million years to find living creatures plus five million to measure the intelligence of the different living creatures.

The beings watched and learned from the reactions of each individual mind. Their self-development became slow and deadly crumbled by the greed of emotions foreign to their logical minds and marked them as mindless creatures. Not satisfied by what they had found, the oldest elder recalled a gathering at the next mating ritual. He found that inside each small group a female had developed within each cluster. This brought astounding news of revelation to enlarge their race. The oldest elder took it as a moment in history that would guide their race beyond infinity of the expanding cosmos. This in time would increase the elder's race for the search of equal intelligent life forms like themselves.

The debate went on, during the mating every female gave birth to a cluster of ten spheres all in various colours based on the energy the mothers would consume during the growth period. One set had ten red spheres unique since the red colour would represent the old ones. This troubled the oldest leader from some unexplained vision in his dream state. He is shocked to hear the children were already singing old songs of their history not been taught. The youngest of the ten spoke up about this debate in how to measure intelligence.

"The creatures of intelligence must have families and home structure their worlds in a combination with the natural order in comparison to our ways of law, order, and logic. In addition, they must have the necessary skills of math and the knowledge of probabilities. This is not part of the brain patterns. We are space dust our home is infinity itself."

Upon realization of the child words, the elders cannot exist on the same dimension or plane of existence. They made an oath never to interfere or copy the single minds. Elders became watchers. They still had a hard time understanding emotions. The elders looked at over one hundred billion stars in every direction to find and study what kind of life forms were being created. They needed more room among their kind. With the success of more females, they devised a way to spread their races by giving smaller groups one elder and a caretaker female to watch over the young ones to teach the ways of balance and chaos. They continued to send out watchers with children over large sections of space. Over time, they started to measure life forms to their own standards of thought process. In hopes to one day pass on the knowledge of their race in different sectors. The constant chaos and balances learned all occurred in space for the young ones.

The children of the red sphere were the quickest learners, pushing the elder and the caretaker with questions that even the elder did not have the answers. The old one broke the group up and mixed them with other normal spheres. The last one was the most talkative to the oldest elder as he takes the little one to another group. Over the years, the elders harnessed energy crystals from their food sources. They discovered these crystals gave them energy to travel long distances at great speed. In time, they created a portal to travel in inner space.

Each elder carries a minor crystal to open the windows of a young universe as the small ones gathered and learned what basic structures formed the Electro magnetic radiation wavelengths from matter to antimatter. By studying the distributions and temperatures of the cosmos, they watched how much space squeezed to form the entire clusters of stars.

One caretaker broke tradition by pointing to a star system, which she named Ea as the beginning of their awaking of self-consciousness. The elder hearing her words punished the caretaker for naming the place as if it was a possession. One of many laws written by the elder council passed to continue the wandering race. With an unemotional expression, he sent a telepathic message to the caretaker.

"You will fast for a year. Until you declare your error among the elders," hissed the teacher.

Her eyes were red with anger and she muttered a few choice words.

"I will never give you that satisfaction and rather die for my own beliefs."

The weeks and months passed, she grew very weak and unrepentant. As time went by, the elder continued the lessons on probabilities of interaction and reaction of the smallest microbes to the birth of distance suns. In addition, deaths and re-creation were one of many subjects passed on to their offspring. Elders also taught logical problems and mathematics that would lead them beyond infinity.

Only one student became concerned of the caretaker and her faint cries. He would pull away from the elder to comfort her. He thought that elder showed no emotions towards the caretaker. This surprised the elder as he sent a mind link message to expel the student with the same punishment. The elder felt he should share the pain with the caretaker, as she would continue to teach the youngling. These actions of punishment will instil that he learns more of the universe in a direct inner action.

Another small group of elders chose to visit the same solar system to educate the young ones they had visited a thousand times before. This time the race has abused their planet. It is dying. The planet is slowly drying up killing off its atmosphere. There remain small groups of alien creatures clinging to life in a small valley.

The caretaker mind sees opportunity to save these beings and steps forward to help by repairing their atmosphere and gave them better chances to evolve. The two leaders of the small groups show their disapproval of her action. They linger at the edge of the alien shelter with the children watching from the mountain edge. All could hear from across the galaxy the caretaker's blunder.

"You have broken two laws of the council, one your interference with another race that had no proof they were intelligent," snapped the oldest elder.

He points to her error of healing touches and the transfer of knowledge to alien race.

"These creatures now consider you a goddess. The laws forbid them to interfere with the natural order," hissed the younger elder. "The young ones pleaded for help" muttered the caretaker.

"You are careless female, stay with the laws of our race or suffer the consequences," hissed the young elder.

Her single eye turns a bright yellow and she bows obediently, knowing all too well that everyone is watching and have already passed judgement on her actions. The only thought to escape the punishment was to steal the time crystal. Her heart went cold with a dark feeling she had never experienced before that brought a deep purpose within her. She takes the little one with her. They have grown close during the rest period. She slowly sneaks over and grasps the crystal away from the startled elder. The caretaker evokes the power key to open the dark doorway to time and disappears in a blink.

This leaves behind the elder and the others as the world shrinks to the beginning of time. The two open inner space and then suddenly bounce away light years into the past, there they hope to begin a new era. The caretaker used the same race to prove to the elders that they can teach the lower alien race new methods.

These aliens worship them as gods of the unseen world. The rogue caretaker and the child teach the young version of the dying race and change their path with the knowledge of many secrets. This single act alters their ways and helps them to escape their doom in the future. Their future will bring the dark side of power to expand, control and enslave other races.

The news of their interference caused a quake through out the elders and young ones across the cosmos. The elders gave chase in large numbers when they saw energy quake across the dimensions and crumble the dark matter. The eldest knew about being to close their infinity.

The elders swarmed the planet in large numbers attacking and devouring every life form from animal to intelligent beings nothing escaped not even microbes. No weapon could harm the membrane of the elders, nor the telepathic powers the alien creatures had developed. The leaders of this doomed planet attempt to surrender to gods of a higher power. Instead, they where erased from existence at the same time capturing the caretaker and child for interfering with other life forms. The caretaker and the outcast child imprisoned and brought to the council of the unseen world. The rogue caretaker refuses to repent claiming aloud.

"These laws of the elders are outdated. We have evolved beyond any race, which has crossed our path. There is a way to extend and help develop an equal to us. We can control their growth with the knowledge passed on. It was working well until your interference," complained the Rogue.

"Enough of your heretic ways woman, they went vicious in the future destroying other planets and peace loving races. All for greed and hunger, they stole the planet's resources and enslaved the other races."

"I had not known this, a few adjustments could correct the electrical impulses of the alien's brains," mumbled the rogue.

"It does not matter you broke our laws and judgement must be declared against you caretaker with the little one to share your punishment. From this time forward, you will be planet bound. Every ten thousand years during the mating season, you will have the chance to repent these sins against the elders. The choice is your my little Ru", snapped the oldest of the elder.

He walks away in disgust followed by the elder's council. The Ru rebel snarls wildly and curses loudly the supreme elder" name. "Krell you are a fool by this decision." The two guards activate a golden sphere that engulfs the two prisoners. When the sphere rose up from the council room the two look at their race with hate and vanish from sight. The older leader knew where they were going on long journey into the past near a black hole. They would return every ten thousand years. He hoped silently that the caretaker and child would repent their crimes against the elder race. The punishment lasted for fifty thousand years. During those long years, the two plotted to take total control. They plotted to crossbreed a prefect race with their own make up of DNA. *These plans will take time to develop,* thought the female. She shrugged it off and muttered thought, *this means nothing to a god or immortal being.*

The two repeated their pledge for perfection, a more desirable form with a wide range of mind gifts creating a new race by only thought. They agreed to create balance and symmetrical bodies with a single mind to control all life forms in either dimensional world. Their nature was that of curiosity; however, they had to stay close to their food source.

While the elders would search the cosmos, study the universe, and watch the expansion grow and spread across the infinity. The caretaker needed the time crystal not the one they stole from the youngest elder but the oldest eldest who wore it as a crown on his head that connected with all. They plotted revenge on the elders for their interference.

On the next gathering, thought the caretaker, during the mating season shall be our time. She refused four times to plead for forgiveness among the millions of her kind. Finally, she repents and groveled for mercy. It had great effect on the eldest one that took up the cause to have her reinstated to shadow core group as a teacher.

The council agreed, after much debate, to give her back full status. She can mate with whom she chooses on the hour of the ritual breeding partner dance. The child also repents but weakly worded that the old ones notice quickly.

The council decides to start re-education with another to teach and correct his ways of thought that flows against the natural way of their teaching. Both bow to the wishes, which seem to please the populace. They all accept them back into the fold as they started to sing their way to the planet's altar. WordThe females call out the names of their chosen elders to mate within hopes to engage the reproduction cycle of the elder clan. During the mating ritual, they call the name of any elder. This rule existed since the beginning of time itself. The time came for the once disgraced caretaker to stand among the peers to call out her mating partner.

She climbs the narrow path to the lone mountain of hallow caves in a random order from pervious mating. Through the race existence, the mountain has ground one hundred thousand kilometres in width and sixth thousand kilometres in height. Each new birth must add to the mountain structure. They spent the early years repairing and enlarging the base up to its peak. The children would learn the basic songs of the elders and caretakers. From their basic beginning of their first moment of life, they became aware of the cosmos.

The rule of mating had become more of a tradition then a law of the council. Being immortal, they are somewhat ashamed of the basic need for sexual encounter. Their large minds would rather spread out cross the expanding cosmos to find life in far off worlds. The elders would offer the great gift of knowledge to a single race that is equal to their intelligence. Without hesitation they would pass the great wonders of the cosmos as a gift to the aliens.

It is their destiny to fulfill that push across open space. The caretaker thoughts had reviewed the ways of her race. Now she will use her sexuality gift for revenge on those elders that harmed her. She steps out at the narrow ledge to call his name.

The female looks down at her race of a million males. Her eye focuses on the one that stands alone that she wants for herself. She finds him further from the pack still in council talking of their encounters. The voice of the caretaker calls out the name not once but three times Krell.

This silenced the crowd of onlookers who all turned their heads towards the leader of the elder race. He must respond as all eyes were on him. The traditional response was calling her name and he knew the names of his entire race and even the ones not born yet. He moves away from the council of elders, which all murmured angrily from the break of tradition. To him this is unnatural for their life cycle, which requires three males to ensure the success. His mind stretches out to touch her mind. He feels the purity in purpose with gratitude of his speech to release her back with her people.

"I cannot refuse her" muttered Krell.

He calls her name Ru also three times to balance the change in tradition, knowing this would cause waves of desertions among males and female alike. He sends out a message throughout his people through his crystal crown.

"This caretaker is beholding to me for my kind words, she has blundered, but as you all now she has not mated for fifty thousand years. We must keep our ways true between each other and our faith for the balance of all."

The races of his people all respond positively and gave way for him to enter the cave entrance on the inside. The children clustered around with dance and laughter. He removed his crown as he entered the pool of water to purify his outer shell.

In addition, inner thoughts replaced with lust, from a drink of thick gold colour liquid, to raise his passion. He transforms into a sphere and floats up to the inner chamber where Ru the caretaker waits. This will be the first encounter. She washes and takes the same liquid. In addition, she called his name through a mind link.

"Come let us dance among the stars and share our vision, dear lover. I do want your essence Krell of the shadows," hissed Ru.

Her words echo through the hollow mountain causing a stir among both females and males all ready joined in the mating ritual. Ru's words drowned out the others who called out the males' names to enter the lower caves and start a new ritual.

These creatures never experienced emotional bonding or pleasure that other races had shown. The elders had study this interaction without any conclusions in their wandering travels. The knowledge the caretaker, Ru learned from the last encounter of the secrets of chemical response within the liquid form of DNA discovered by the alien race. She stands on the inner edge of a deep hollow opening cut in oval with smooth sand stones of various colours. She waits for Krell to appear. All around her, the ground trembles with a roar from the passing spheres sparking electric discharges along the spiral of crystals within the mountain.

The groups of males and females watch the colour spark out a light show. Ru's membrane cracks open and starts to leak in a pool of gentian that slowly drips into the cave opening. It falls endless as it reaches Krell's body where the basic impulse rose within liquid form. His membrane hardens, crumbles, and shoots up together while parts of her liquid form mesh with his.

This causes a chemical reaction to change his body chemistry to a hormonal response. He gathers electrical energy and his body glows as bright as a red star. The light darts out of the hallow caves so bright the many look away. Krell gathered Ru within him as he passes the cliff where she waited to become one with the liquid form of the elder.

The secret she discovered must be time right, as they swirl and gurgle within themselves and gather up the energy within the crystal. The old one had stop mating five hundred thousand years ago. His mind dictated to be a watcher throughout the years of watching other races mate. He begins to understand why they enjoy the act and though it was sinful to experience the pleasure. This is when they chemically release the male essence within the female. This cuts a large hole within the mountain core. It causes a slight advance of rock and dust particles to rush down the north face of the mountain. Ru releases the other chemical that instantly causes pain within Krell. He screams as his body colour turns pale yellow and tiny spheres erupt around him. Ru pulls away and then reforms in a sphere as her membrane hardens, she laughs with her final message.

"Now old one you will experience motherhood for the next million years. While I do my destiny, I shall bring forth perfection, Krell through your crystal. Since I carry your essence within me, the time crystal will obey my wishes," laughed Ru.

"You foolish female you will kill our race all that we were and what we might become."

"You cannot create perfection the probabilities point to failure and chaos through the cosmos," groaned Krell as his voice squeaked and he cried out for help.

"They cannot hear you since you became a mother, I am the new leader of the elders," claimed Ru. She then calls out the little one to bring the large crystal.

"Come, little one it is our time to leave for our home, you will never find us old one," replied Ru.

"No Ru you will destroy all the cosmos, I shall stop you to the ends of time," claimed Krell.

"Idle threats and false ideas will cause your end old creature. The change has begun. Foolish female take your children before I engage the time crystal" muttered the young one.

He appears out of the dust and debris with the large crystal crown above his shapeless head. The caretaker floats down to grasp the time crystal. Krell takes his only chance to stop them with a large shrill cry. Sudden cracks appear in the crystal that had broken in half each one held a piece. Krell sets a challenge with words he hopes to cause dissention between the young one and the caretaker.

"Your next words will cause your doom, even if it takes a million years. The evil you start will only give you pain and failures to your vision. The children of the light will end your reign, foolish female thing," hissed Krell.

Ru still stunned by the broken time crystal is slow to react to his words. She wanted to examine it first and escape from this world. Her thoughts wonder if it would work to bring her home to Ea. while the young one still holding the other half snarls a response.

"We do not need to search for intelligent beings. We shall create our own perfection in one place that will conquer all into one mind. You and all your followers may join the children of the light for you will never win against our perfection."

Ru heard the young one's words as both crystals reacted to the words of the young one and Krell. She cries out to undo the challenge.

"No little one, I will not accept that only evil may kill evil for the righteous will restore the balance of the four generations.

"I accept this as a challenge let these words bind us to the great adventure," Krell muttered darkly.

He then rolls back his inner eye and disappears with the children that cling to his membrane. The mountain and the planet fade away as did the stars and became completely dark and empty around the two remaining elders. Ru curses the child and strikes him hard with a mind force. He squeals in pain and pleads for forgiveness. His membrane cracks from the pressure and leaks out in the dark space as small bubbles of liquid floated around his body.

"Your foolish words of accepting his challenge gives Krell hope to stop us with other beings called the children of the light. We must hide for now and for your error, I should kill you to end the challenge."

"No please do not kill me, I have shown you my loyalty through- out your ordeal. Please, I will do anything you ask caretaker," the child mumbled weakly.

"Then drink the blood of Krell's essences, so you will know where he is at all times and that you will stay as a child so he cannot find you."

"Yes, caretaker I will prove my loyalty and protect you at all cost. We shall be one in this quest," replied the child.

"This I shall accept what you drank will slow your growth in the mind but in truth, your body will grow five times the size of a male elder with strength to battle anyone that challenges us. I will keep your pledge to protect me" claimed Ru.

"Enough, little one come and embrace me so we can travel the cosmos with our time crystal," replied Ru.

Their minds meld quickly together as Ru focused home where she was born in the Ea solar system. The images form a ringed solar system and guide the young one to the three stars. The crystal brightens as they beam open a hole in space the two floated inside and faded into the darkness of deep space.

"We must hide so they cannot find us."

Meanwhile, Krell slowly regained his senses. Confused by the suddenness of his departure from Ru, he took in the dark surroundings. He blinks several times to adjust his eyesight. He heard the moans of his children but no other voices or thoughts from his brethren. Using his mind gift, he tries to right himself; something is not right came a grunt within him. Hunger and thirst took his thoughts away from the weird sound.

I need energy to recover and destroy Ru plans if the time crystal accepts my challenge, thought Krell.

A sudden flash of light crosses his path. He jostles his body and wonders what it was that flashed across him. The dark thoughts of despair crept through his conscious. He knows now the elder race is lost for all time. He wonders if more of the elder's race had survived the broken time crystal.

He must break his laws to find altered alien beings with the same gifts of his old race. Krell thoughts became clearer. He suddenly felt a presence near him and feared harm for his children. He focuses all his mind energy to see what approaches. A strange voice in song rang out of the dark cave.

"Well hello, elder of the shadow world, what brings you to my home?"

"Sanctuary, I hope" stunned that he could hear his words.

"You are the second one to visit. Are you what they call a caretaker. I see you brought children how delightful. Oh, my, you have let them wallow in the mire of deep mud. It will take hours to clean them. Come, I shall feed you and bathe the children," replied the unknown creature.

"I would like that but I cannot see where I am or even who you are. Are you male or female of your species?"

"I am both. You sound like the first one that visited us long ago. I am a peaceful being, my shadow friend, and I can see you face is covered in mud. Take my hand and I shall guide you to water."

Krell had no choice but to accept his fate. He wonders what the creature meant by give him a hand. His body struggled to move out of the unseen mud and he wondered how he got there. He finally felt a strong grip that was warm to the touch like the stars he would feed on in his travels.

What kind of being are you he asks telepathically. No answer came from the alien.

Why am I going freely with the unknown being?

His senses were not sharp for some reason. The food and care from this alien sounded appealing to the old one. He still struggled with what had just happen to his race with splintered memories of their destruction and was learning to trust a stranger. This was all new to him when his mind plays back the elders laws that helps defines his race to the ends of his day. Strange sounds became louder that scared him as his children muttered their first words.

"Caretaker of the light you are very bright, and the warm food is good."

Do not eat yet, it is being generous, wait so I can finally see where we are.

Yes, Caretaker we obey, they answer in a choir of thoughts.

The first clear image enters his mind, from the children, of a blue sky with two small suns. The land space fills with colourful objects gently dancing in the breeze with a sweet smell of energy. He sees the pool and shudders as the memories of Ru's betrayal is fresh in his thoughts.

"Now, do not be afraid of this water to wash the mire mud from your face. I know of your mating ritual from the other who visited long ago. This will not harm you because you and your race have passed over to our dimension. Your body form is quite different in our time. I guess it is a leap of faith to trust a strange being. Take your time and breath the rich atmosphere it will reinvigorate you," replied the voice of melody.

Did the shadow give its name came a voice from him self deep and haunting startle him so.

"In our world, we let the other races find themselves in a place of balance and harmony within the life cycle. Your race is unique but a little restricted in matters of emotions, of course, it is only an opinion and not a correction to your beliefs" replied the stranger.

"Then let me wash this mud so I can learn and see what you truly are kind host," Krell stammered.

He was not sure of the meanings of his thoughts. The water rushed down and large chucks of mud fell away. The brightness of the sun was sharp as he looked up, wincing his eyes. He moves his body deeper into the pool finding it quite pleasurable to wipe the mud off. His vision cleared and the change to his body shocked him. Fear rose within when the image of his children focused on him. Through their mind gift, he saw himself as small in stature with white hair. His hands shook while one of his hands stroked his hair. He assumed that the green skin was natural colour of this race. It was like watching one of the many aliens he encountered on his travels through the cosmos. He remembers the pain from Ru; he cursed her name in silent anger.

"What am I, this is not a body of an elder of shadows."

"Yes, I forgot that this is your first visit to my world. I do apologize that the other of your kind did not mention my world named Azure and the children of the light."

"What did you say," while wiping his eyes from the grime off his face? Stunned by the figure that faced him which sparkled like smooth glass reflecting the sunlight

"You arrive in the dimensional world of the children of the light," mumbled the stranger.

"What kind of creature are you," Krell stammered warily.

He steps back to study the features of a giant and instinctually gathers his green-skinned child. Humanoid features with two legs and arms covered with round edges of silver reflecting the sunlight. It stood eight feet tall with a round oval head, deep eyes sockets, small mouth, and a narrow nose with lights fluttering across its chest. It arms moved with a faint hum which spread apart as a basic signal for talk.

"Oh dear, I frightened you. I am sorry. Let me see what words would ease your mind caretaker" replied the silver creature. It rubbed its chin, stepped back to the edge of the pool, and sat on a large rock.

"Trust, earned by time itself following the endless path to the true light across the stars and within your balance will be found from the others that visited our world a long time ago."

Krell dropped his jaw the words were his and part of what he taught his race. His muscles relaxed somewhat as the children swarmed around him demanding food. He quickly sent a message through his thoughts. He moves closer to the silver creature. The sunlight reflects off her crystal form which begins to glow a soft radiant warmth to Krell's children has he sent a telepathic message to his children.

"Not until you are properly clean will I give you food."

"Caretaker, can we eat the stranger now" barked another group of children.

"No, it offers open friendship and kind words. We do not harm intelligent beings that could be an equal to our own ways of logic," Krell answered sternly to the children.

He turns back to the silver being it had shrunk to a height of three feet. It is holding a tray of colour spheres in assorted colours. His nose smells the energy off the tray and he steps out of the water stiffly then drops to his knees. Krell uses his hands to prop his new body up.

"Do you require assistance caretaker" it inquired with a deeper voice.

"The atmospheric pressure is quite high, that is why your body changed into a solid form," the alien says softly to keep Krell subdued.

"So, I can return to my other state at a latter time," his eyes spread wider with an expression of hope.

"In time, but now you just arrived, the others never discussed what we are to your people I would like to pass this on to your race through your children," requested the silver creature.

"You have the advantage on me. You know everything about the elders. However, I never heard of you and this world," sputtered Krell.

"Then may I show our world caretaker as a guest of the children of light."

"I have pressing troubles in my dimension that need quick response normally I would be honoured."

He takes a brown sphere and sniffs it before he pops it in his mouth. The odd color food had a odd effect within his mind. That brought a torrent of memories, and realize he knew these beings name which pounded his head and mutter sadly.

"I have failed Sabrina the variant flux has already begun by Ru."

He dropped to his knees and wept. The children rushed to his side to comfort him. The silver creature backed off as her eyes turned a red glare. She looks up into the blue sky of her planet and presses a button on her wrist. Two antennas appear from behind her skull as she sent a single sentence to a distance place in time.

"Commence fourth protocol and depart immediately for Azure. Our first battle with the Entity is about to begin." She repeated several times. Sabrina had always kept secrets but she knew this old man well enough that he would do his duty to the end of his days.

"I am so sorry I failed you and the others, when I return to my dimensional time all of you were a distance dream. When I saw the children of the red sphere, I had a brief flash of danger, but I could not speak as if someone was shutting down my mind," mumbled Krell.

"I gave you a difficult task. Many others could have never done and endured so much. Tell me all that happened to you the past one hundred thousand years," replied Sabrina.

The hours went by as the children took equal portions of energy spheres for food. They eat quickly and listen to their father's story of the ways of the elders that were broken. The mating ritual of their race, the true betrayer named Ru the mother that she was to them. The added pain of their world totally erased. They are now in a new form not suitable for open space but trapped on a planet. The children weep for the great loss of their history.

It is time to come in my home to a warm shelter, say our password through your mind gift caretaker.

He looks up confused, realizes it is a test and frowns heavily. His mind focuses to find the answer, when a clear thought appears in his mind of three rings of pure energy.

The circle of life is in constant motion within it past, present and future. The power is natural life evolved from the beginning to the end and from the end to the beginning. Open the fourth protocol!

A low rumble underground shook, startling the children that rolled into the flowerbeds. They watched along the edge of the small pond as a whirlpool appears. The children step closer and watch the water disappear as a cylinder rose up and a stone path marked a path to the door that opens wide before Krell. The silver being's face gave a look of despair, and the lights of its eyes went dim.

"However, it is you returning in a female form with your entire race, Krell, hanging at the edge of the abyss. It is a pity old friend that you did not kill the children of the red spheres." She steps along the path, waving her arm to invite them inside the cylinder.

"We never take a life of our own race. I was prepared to do it but a vision shook my very being, until the youngest spoke, it seems to overpower my mind. I did punish them in the end," grumbled Krell.

"It begins again to the fourth and final generation," whispered Sabrina.

"Ru said something similar, until the rise of the fourth generation the final battle for the cosmos," replied Krell.

"The battle lines are drawn. Now let us renew our bonds of friendship, rest assured your race is safe for now," whispered Sabrina.

She handed him and the children black robes, which shimmered with energy and a wide belt with a jewel crystal. Once on his new body the energy renewed him and quieted his mind. New images flashed across his mind. He did feel more himself as his children went silent.

"What will happen next since I have failed you," Krell hissed sadly.

Sabrina touches the switch as the door closed tightly and the lights rose to a soft red shade, which reflected off her silver form. She touches the caretaker on the shoulder. Her eyes grew to a pale blue. For the first time Krell, felt a strong connection between them and his mind perceived it as love. While her words at first confused him, the walls of the cylinder open to the inner world of Azure that made him feel like a small helpless child.

"Many preparations are already in motion Krell now leader of the shadow world and mother of the forest people You must my lord reacquaint yourself with your new world," stated Sabrina.

She watches the caretaker's reaction upon seeing her world of the children of the light. *It is always breathtaking when one comes for the first time or returns,* thought Sabrina; she clears her throat with the final words.

"We now must wait for the first Entity to arrive."

CHAPTER 3

THE REBIRTH OF LORD ID

Dragon Eye
Logbook 2
Star date AI2EAS.000019.01

*R**u and the child* had now surpassed nine thousand years without any contact from the elder or any other intelligent beings that could be a threat. The young child proves his worth many times over to the caretaker. His growth stretched close to one kilometre wide and three kilometres in length. She stays her original size of six feet width and thirty feet in length. He travels at great speeds, which gives her the time to study the two broken half's of Krell's time crystal. It held many secrets of the cosmos, which would frustrate her to no end. The child would ask many questions or endlessly chatter of things that were not important. The child would always be obedient and strangely suggestive of what to do next in their travels.

What made her angry is that the solar system that she thought was her home became somewhat of an illusion because the star had shrunk into a quasar. The energy would sustain them for a short period. Her thoughts were of her home the Ea solar system. The young one went exploring and found a great place with everything they needed to start their testing on building a super race. He points to a better location with three stars that had large amounts of food similar to the energy crystal forming in the twin gas giants. She grudgingly gave acceptance to the child's point of view and acknowledges his contribution to find a home. She accepted the need to have a home base to operate if they were to keep the secret and achieve the goal of perfection. She knew grudgingly that this is right idea and relented to follow him into the three star solar systems.

The child guided Ru to the solar system on the outer edge of the galaxy ring then she had never been before this moment in time. The caretaker thoughts of the solar system impressed her mind that she insisted this is her home. The elders had played a trick and named it the true Ea solar. They proclaimed in a deep voice that sound more like Krell.

"We shall make new life in perfect symmetry and intelligence to a single mind all connected to its mother to reach across the galaxy and beyond infinity to rule over her own creations and control their destiny." The child cheered being her first subject to yield to her will. The caretaker, with her teeth grinding hard, glared at the child's single diamond shape eye that flashed red. They circle it several times. On the outer area of the solar winds is a wide range of charge particles. They feed off the dispel energy of the solar winds; she knew this place is Ea.

This place shall be a great house, Ru thought.

The child reacted to Ru words of her thoughts with enthusiasm by a swirling dance and joyful words. "Yes, this is my home too, shall you give me my rightful name has a caretaker of the elders, since I found this new system,"

"Quiet little brat, you are beholding to me and do whatever I command," growled Ru, while releasing energy to move the elder body closer to the new system.

The energy barrier from the three suns caused solar winds, which had an odd affect on both the caretaker and the child's physical body. All around the group of elders, the sun released super charged particles, which pulse energy when hitting their membrane skin. They had to join their minds and life force to the maximum point of their balance in the energy field. It was not working until the child tapped into the crystal with his mind gifts to increase the shield into the solar system. Ru watched the child elder body glow in a wide array of colours and felt extremely weak under the belly of the giant child elder. The caretaker used her mind to scan for the nearest planet with suitable energy to renew their strength. Her minds eye finds a nearby surround with a wide range of asteroids floating in orbit on an icebound planet with atmospheric methane clouds of violent electrical windstorms crossing its equator. Ru had no choice in the matter the child cried endlessly. A sharp object struck his eye as his blood leaked all over him, causing him to lose the crystal in his mouth. She barks at him for his error and foolishness. She steers the large child to the nearest planet.

They landed on the first world, which she names Zlotoo later in years. Using their powers in a mind meld, they heal each other and feel a strong connection and a need to survive. However, the injured eye reveals that the half crystal struck it. Ru had no choice, but to use her telepathic ability to remove it. Since stealing the crystal from the older elder, it had tripled in strength. His blood leaked and stained the crystal that was wedged in his eye socket. Ru focused her remaining strength of the mind gift and with a great big pull, the crystal floats out.

The caretaker steps back to avoid the gush of green blood, which sprays over her skin and onto her crystal. Both broken crystals react to the child's blood when it released a vortex of energy, wind, and clouds. All swirl down around each piece and cause a minor discharge of plasma energy. The force combined in a thunderous sound throwing the two wonders back into the deep snow. The two broken crystals were now floating as one without any blemish or crack. They floated over as it pulsed above the two elders. Ru completely surprised and puzzled studies the crystal as it hovers above them. They moved ever so cautiously and felt a strange, tingled wash over her elder body. The child struggles to find the caretaker. The sub-zero temperatures instantly froze the wound and blood onto the barren rocks and ice patches between. Unbeknownst to Ru it made a prefect circle. He repeatedly called her Forbidden name while struggling in a staggering motion. His wound bled on the snow-covered ground. Annoyed by using her secret name so openly, she spun the back of her tail and barked at him to be quiet. The bloodstain is still warm on her body and some accidentally sprayed on the crystal when she slapped the giant elder child who wailed loudly in anger for the first time.

"Let us keep our oath that the two are one until the two races arrive for the joining of perfection. Yes, crystal of time heals us and unite our powers, so that we shall begin as one." hissed the elder child.

Ru is in shock to hear the child cast a spell on her that she had used on Krell in reverse to divide his powers from the crystal. She puffs her cheeks, with her single eye-changing colour to a sickly red glare. Her mind tries to counter the spell, knowing that this is the first sign of male adult hood. Another dark presence presses his thoughts onto Ru as she feels a more powerful mind larger than Krell and hers with one thought.

"I can only serve one. I choose the child, since you must change into one being, the elder race have evolved and so shall you be a life force of the all knowing eye, until the first mating ritual your mind shall be one with no body. Your cause is good for the shadows honour the dark master of the inner dream world. Live well and fulfil your destiny of perfection. The creator shall be reborn within the one, by his name, Lord Id."

"No, I am the oldest as elder, I must still be the new leader, all what I did is for perfection," wailed Ru.

"The transformation is about to begin the spell is cast the two are one."

Ru panicked when the winds return swirl high into the sky gaining strength from the crystal and gathering dust, ice chunks and rocks into giant storm surge. She struggled to escape. Her strength already drained by helping to free the crystal from the child. No words came out of her mind to attack the child, with her own powers. She had learnt through travels, which mind gifts are singular in controlling the key elements. She looks down to see membrane start to leak from the sharp rocks and chards of ice. Her last glimpse is the child's blood circle on the ground as it floated above the fulcrum point of the crystal.

"I will suffer this pain once again, Wait the tide will turn, and all will feel my revenge."

Suddenly an eerie laugh echoes all around her last conscious moment as her form raises up into liquid to join the child's body and both continued to feel the unnatural power from the crystal. As if all new life is, the end of ones life and the spirits transfer into a new level. The crystal rose to the center of the liquid bodies as the child and the caretaker join as one.

It releases a cataclysmic effect which started when the planet core erupted, splitting the planet and disbursing streams of lava, water and steam with a great release of energy blast which fused the last two elders into a new form of a three-ring sphere white crystal black ring and a red sphere. They floated above the ground, altering the planet, creating fertile soil from smashing mountains into dust. Their voices became one and their sound punctures the atmosphere pushing the asteroids out of orbit. Their minds still struggle to separate as a dual conscious.

Both are prefix on the future of a new race in their own image of perfection. In the coming days they survive all the planets using the crystal to see across the cosmos and far galaxies. With many plans to go over, they start the long process to lure the chosen race with the endless tests of trail by error. She realizes it will take time to do it right. In addition, with the help of her other it would be a small matter to guide them to their world. They finally select two weaker races for the ease of mind control.

The planet best suits the subjects to teach the new race the ways of perfection. They had to learn traditions, laws, religious beliefs, mating ritual, and level of intelligence. This included engineering skill for buildings and scientific ability with the laws of nature along with improvements in medicine, techno skills, and horticulture to travel through space.

How to gather up the right species became a constant debate with her equal partner. Through the power of thought, she had slowly convinced the weaker beings to reach out to the stars for the great gift. Within a short time, they lure two races of insecta life forms, something that appeals to Ru's mind. The child prefers looking further and deeper in space. They felt like creators and destroyers from all the changes they did to the surrounding planets. He believed they could house five races to build a new generation. The first off spring is created within the next ten thousand years.

While they wait for the creatures, they build an energy conduit to hold their forms and hide from Krell and the children of the light. Ru feels this threat as part of their journey. She is committed to that task of working on contacts out in space through the new powers they had both gained.

The child prefers to be unseen by any aliens or elders. The other plan is to sleep a twenty-year cycle to save their energy. They had agreed to appear as gods visiting their test pets offering them enlightenment. Their telepathic powers can let them appear has would appear in their natural state like angels. In hopes so desire to help pass their own DNA and their secret knowledge of the crystal to the develop a perfect being. Ru stir with a vision has her thoughts floated across her mind with satisfaction. *"This was the only way to keep ahead of Krell."*

She also wanted to be one-step ahead of the unknown beings called the children of the light. She wonders what kind of beings they are, and then went into a dozy sleep. However, child spoke his last thoughts, that surprised and annoyed Ru with his over confidence, and swaggered attitude.

"They are coming the first ones will arrive during our sleep period caretaker. I have made a nest on Zlotoo that is visual from space" he muttered darkly.

She giggles and returns with uncaring words and went deep to escape his presence from her conscious space.

"What did you build? Let me guess, a giant circle with an x. In the past, this showed very little success, foolish child."

CHAPTER 4

THE ECHOES OF THOUSAND YEARS

Dragon eye
Logbook
Star date AIA000081.4

Far off in space to a distance galaxy named Corus blocked by the pillars of time. One hundred young star clusters around a giant black hole in orbit of a yellow sun lay the planet Auriga. The home of a warrior race named the Jung zee the last living creatures on a dying planet. It recalls the instruction of their god to travel to a new home. They launch themselves high in space using the right speed and angle of trajectory. All six made the turn towards the ring galaxy.

Just as their sun falls into the gravity, the pull of the black hole causes a super nova, scorching Auriga to a cinder of scatter dust. The queen's outer shell holds tight the cold vacuums of space in hopes to save its generation. Their food supplies to rebuild their new home. They move like a meteor but in perfect formation as they leave the Corus galaxy to the ring one and their new home name Zlotoo which is named after their queen of the new age. They are the first to make contact with a god like creature name Lord Id.

They follow the methods to achieve space flight with the new power source of light speed, which took ten generations to collect. The Corus galaxy at the time of the exodus was 83 light years away with a direct flight. One mistake and they would be lost in the darkness of space itself. The medical instruction from the gods on chemicals required to induce deep hibernations gave a safe and secure way to protect their race. All six spiders were on target to the ring galaxy.

An unknown spaceship suddenly appears behind the sleeping spider queens. This crew of the dragon eye is on another mission. The captain stays the proper and swirl around each spider. Their eyes are hollow and empty of life. Their large eight legs cross over each other in a tight formation as to share the inertia.

The captain of the dragon eye studies their flight plan and sees they are off course by six degrees. That would add thirty light years and destroy the timeline they had just set. Stella barks at the other for his lack in following orders.

"If you came to the bridge on time, we would not be these seconds off our appointed time. You waste too much time on the logbook old fart," snarled Stella.

"I am only one point two seconds off. Stop sniping old wrinkle face." snap Ito has he gives a bow and a short wave by adding a deep smile, he improves his opinion.

"I might add that we made up time by warming up the tractor beam, which is online now to correct the angle of the flight plan to Zlotoo," voiced Ito as he hits the switch.

A soft blue beam scatters softly across the six spider queens are different in size and length. With eight legs round shape heads small pinchers and sharp fangs. Their body had three sections Head, thorax, and lower abdomen most have black hair with colorful edges of blue and red stripes across the lower abdomen. That had a sharp stinger that leak liquid that the captain, think it is a dangerous poison. So, he floated towards their leader being the largest to focus on its large round head with eight eyes all the spiders are in deep in hibernation. He knew the spiders are unaware of his presence. The woman monitors the brain patterns of the queen to ensure their safety. Within an hour of correction to add speed adjustment to the giant queen spider, they are back on target reducing the distance by eight years. He checks his clock, calls out his computer to read the exact time. He gives a wilful smile at the old woman.

"Next stop we visit the sleeping queen beetle of the Myra clan."

"She is not on our list. We must steal all the embryos, destroy two of the human ships, and adjust Hyperion 1 all inside the vortex. You will place Azure and Sabrina in danger from the Entity itself, silly old fart" growled the woman.

"I gained five minutes; she will be the new player. I know her children could help us close the paradox. My guts tell me it to be true this move into the light will help us" claimed the male.

"What did Sabrina say when you told her of this great plan," came a sharp rebuff as the woman twisted her lips.

The old woman knows that he does not have approval. He shakes his head as he stares at the giant queen spider. He hits the engines to start the power to open the doorway to folding space, which engulfs the ship. The return of a dervish smirk appears on his face, the old woman has seen it to many times to understand its meaning and a deep fearful sigh escapes her breath, as he whispers a dark twist to their fate.

"Look at page seven hundred and six, paragraph four for Sabrina's words that give me the right to change plans. You know that very well. We shall encounter a time advent that will alter us."

"Shut up, you twisted human. I despise what I have become and suffer from those three other times I went through this agony. The people I kill for my own enjoyment and hunger still shakes me inside. I am not that person nor do I wish I could be someone else. Even a small rock can be at peace for a billion years. Let us stop now please," wailed the old woman.

He gets up with his arms apart to jester a peaceful solution with a softer tone to calm her troubled soul.

"That is why we must go to the sleeping queen. She is someone that has played with the dark force. Never cross over the one that is true to the light. Although it is a glimmer, you must see this will turn the tide my long-time lover."

"Oh, you remember our love to persuade me to this unauthorized action without Sabrina's approval", hissed the woman.

"I never lost my love Stella, but we are the product of our world altered by aliens. Only our true love connections guide us to the fourth turn. I knew the other times she would be the link to end the paradox and release us from this nightmare."

"Ito my dear we exist in this paradox too long. I see just another desperate attempt to adjust the end. The thought of another alien is a reckless gamble," mutters the woman whose face softened the angry edge she had portrayed from the start of her journey. Stella reaches out to touch his wrinkled face with a tender touch and speaks through her mind gift to reach him one more time.

"The advents will begin so enough without the change you wish. She passed by the last three times when the darkness returned her eye sight and moved on to another dimension with her children Stella sighed heavily as their eyes lock for a long moment."

The computer AI crackled to life with a warning.

"Long-range scanners report three anomalies have appeared ahead of the flight plan. Do you wish evasive manoeuvres, commander?"

"How far off are these anomalies?"

"They are proximally 6.8 light years. They are all coming at different angles toward us," quoted the AI.

"We still have the chance, darling, it will be close but we have done it three times before," smiled Ito.

"Yes, without seeing the sleeping queen," hissed Stella. The thought of three life times, flash across her mind, killing innocent beings from the three races from wild blood lust and uncontrolled rage. Could her lifetime lover be right? Only time well tell its fate.

The time variant flux is about to repeat the same disaster, presses heavily on her mind.

"I need you on my side Stella for all our friends and enemies," Ito hissed sharply.

Stella only nodded her approval the words failed to come out of her lips. Knowing the Black scorpion space craft with the first encounter of Ru and a human female name Helen. and different version of another Dragon eye spaceship ship is real a echo of time. Stella's minds accept it has a anomaly has it approach their last location close to the probe. She feels the effect and shudders by the intense chill of death. He sees this, takes navigation controls, and activates the escape through a dark time vortex. The fabric of space opens like a small tear and swallows the ship. It causes a small quake as a wave pushes the six spiders at a higher rate of speed towards the ring galaxy.

The other anomalies rush pasts them at different angles. All had a different purpose in being. Their interaction had a deadly effect on the six spiders causing a bigger wave of energy. Each ship scans the objects and only found the wide choices of carbon particles that make life's forms in the early years of the solar systems. They move on in their search for a place in time. They repeatedly send a radio beacon at different frequencies that echo out in deep space. None knew of the other ship due to the time excursion of arrival and departure all different by a few minutes.

"This is Black Scorpion space craft we are here on a rescue mission for Hyperion 1. Do you copy? Please respond and lock on our beam at frequency mega hertz 3452 station 4."

Only one flew directly to the ring galaxy all three had no idea of each other's existence. Each ship is a duplicate of the other with minor changes on its outer skin. Two ships turn towards the Corus galaxy at different angles again unseen and unnoticed by each other. The additional energy wave spun the six spiders in spiral motion inducing friction as their plate shields buckle and left a white vapour trail from the lead spiders. The conscious mind of the young queen begins to feel the strain and she cries out for help to their gods.

Inside the hidden location, the child's mind hears the cries. He attempts to wake up his partner, but she is in a deep sleep. Her conscious mind is so far away that he cannot reach her thoughts. The chosen race had somehow reached the edge of the solar barrier earlier then anticipated. The child thought they are going too fast and unless he does something to stop the destruction. He calls for the crystal to help wake Ru's mind. It floated in his present form of gases state around the inner chamber while he murmurs a prayer for assistance. The crystal glows as it spoke through the child's mind hauntingly.

"The day has come to cross over into adulthood I shall give you extra powers, Lord Id. You must embrace me, and then step out and save your race."

He felt the sudden change into a solid form of bones and flesh growing rapidly within his center as a separate being from Ru's control of a child for ten thousand years. He is freed by the crystal and developing into a powerful immortal like the supreme elder name Krell. With the awaking power, his thoughts went *I will have the edge to bring perfection. I need a name crystal of time* mumbled the child. The crystal glowed and engulfed the child has telepathic words enter his thoughts

"Yes, I shall give you your name only if you and I become one being," echo the Crystal. The child with all its on innocents quickly pledges his allegiance and fealty. The crystal seems to laugh endlessly and finally spoke. "Then your name is lord of dreams, the lord Id, is your name of power and you will hold all life accountable to the new order. You shall become a creator."

Outside the hidden nest, he stretched his form with giant wings to accept the electrical plasma striking his new appearance. He hears the cries and turns his brightly lit eyes to glare at the distance streak of white vapour. With the crystal in hand, he focuses his power to slow the speed of the falling spiders with a counter energy wave. It is working but fears of the solar winds turbulent nature, he decides to leap at the edge of the solar winds to ensure their safe entrance into Ea. He brings two injured ones to Zlotoo and the nest he had made for them. He gave each a circle within the large volcanic ring with one path to lead to the center altar. Ru with her gift would adjust their DNA to improve the mating ritual. He heals most of their burns and sings a song from his other life. The six queens were most impressed. They kept their head down in respect. Id sends a message through his thoughts.

You have arrived too early to receive the gifts of the god. Later when the next cosmic storm comes is when you will receive the gifts. Do not venture out of this circle until the other god appears.

We shall obey great Lord Id; all we ask is that our drones be allowed to feed and groom their bodies from our travels, muttered all six in one voice.

I have no objection if it is within my protective circles

We will obey wing god, muttered all six in one voice.

He feels a great peace and understanding among the female spiders. While placing the crystal across its wide chest he transforms to his other form of a black sphere and vaults away into deep space and heads for the hidden nest. He joins Ru inside their nest. She is still asleep. Anger plays within him as to why she did not hear the queen spiders and asks the crystal to tell Ru when she wakes from deep sleep. The voice answered the child with a strange explanation.

"She is gone to study the other race. Hers mind is intrigues by these beings"

Lord Id's face frowns with a puzzled expression as the crystal sparkles as if to wash over the black sphere. He feels the drain from the exertion of his efforts and quickly falls into a deep trance. He wants to ask another question but his mind fogs over in mid sentence.

"I must go to her."

"No, it is her adventure. Sleep it is your time to rule alone", whispered the crystal.

The outside edges of the solar system circle a spacecraft on a voyage to rescue a world ship. The computer reported the odd sightings and the interaction of alien creatures floating among the highly charged particles of the solar wind. The female commander follows at the safe distance for study. The computer makes an interesting statement while matching the planets inside the unique solar system that shares three stars.

"We are here at the wrong time; this is supposed to be where Hyperion 1 should arrive in a thousand-year Commander Nightshade."

"Blast your navigation Marvin", grumbled the young woman.

'I told you our numbers were off, that it would be suicidal to do a wild jump," Marvin expressed flatly.

The commander's eyes glare once to the scar faced young man. She reaches for a wristband and presses it. The man screams dropping to the floor while electrical discharges race through his body. He pleads for mercy between his screams. She smiles darkly and stops as she sees the shadowy figure turn for the twin gas giant planets.

"Computer full scans on all planets in this system with the full spectrum on all three suns also. I want this planet below us to get priority, while we stay in stealth mode."

"I have already downloaded a preliminary study enclosed is an example of a level three model. It is rich in mining material beneath its crust but has a high atmosphere in turmoil with storms and winds close to three hundred kilometres per second. In addition, plasma discharges would be harmful to our ship."

"There is a strange spot along the equator where oxygen and methane pockets do not belong. It also has water modules both in the atmosphere and deep within the ground. I am also getting the same reading from that group of meteorites in those pockets. For more it will take a few more hours, commander."

"Based on the data, can this planet be transformed to earth conditions," hissed the commander.

"Yes, It needs higher magnetospheres to lower the raging storms about sixty percent," crackled the computer.

"Continue your work. Deab1 with additional probes to send out to collect biomaterial in that air pocket," ordered the woman.

"Yes, shall obey," came a static sound off the speakers of a warning to the young man, who had recovered from the woman's attack.

"What you are doing will kill us all before the bell rings at the top of the hour you lunatic," grumbled the young officer.

"Marvin you will do what I say or I shall torture you repeatedly," snapped the woman studying the view screen of the planet below.

"Death I would accept more willingly than to be your slave," Marvin mutters weakly.

"That would be an easy way out, but your little helix cube would bring you back to life. There is no escape from me since I transferred it to my own system. Instead of a stubborn crew, I would have an obedient drone. I may still do it," hissed the commander.

Marvin lips twisted lightly with eyes glaring defiantly at the dark hair woman his fist clenching tightly. He turns to his workstation as he took a few deep breaths surrendering his anger. Only time may give him the options. He went to the charts to formulate the next course. His thoughts were of home with his young wife Maggie.

The commander transfixed on the readings, gave a small gasp when she saw two-foot creatures moving inside the dormant volcano. *I must have live samples* came a thought as her eyes focused on the odd creatures. A sudden chill crept up her back. She jumps and turns to check on Marvin. He looks at her coldly from his workstation and then went back to his work. Echoed voices enter her thoughts suddenly.

What creature are you that come to my planet of Zlotoo.

The sharp pain along her temples erupted. She bites the inside of her mouth as blood mixes with her saliva. The anger rose within the woman.

"My mind is my own. Stay out or I shall harm you," muttered the commander.

Come to the planet, let us embrace, we are sisters of the old clan.

The pain eases as her thoughts became singular with another conscious being. It could be the 1 that flew away or the other two on that planet, who were contacting me telepathically. She must respond in the same manner. They could give her the right information to save Hyperion 1. I must focus all my strength on those beings on that planet name Zlotoo.

"No, I must rescue my people first, if this is your home I shall leave it in peace. I am searching for other life forms with understanding of sharing our ways with the creatures on your planet."

"You confuse me with too many objects of your desire. Are you male or female?"

The commander scratches her head and refocuses on the screen at the worm like creatures. The sexuality between genders is the basis of all scientific study. She wonders what level accepted a gender as a leader of its people. Coming from ape form it took women thousand of years to be equal to a male figure. The words suggest that this being is far more advanced than what she is.

"Are you male or female are my first questions," it whispered again.

"I am female", grumbled the commander, "leader of my ship."

"I thought so. Your anger intrigues me. Come join us in the circle of life," it whispered softly.

"No, I have too many questions to ask you before there are contact between us. We could be harmful to each other without proper safety precautions," barked the commander.

"I have no time to play with small minds; although you have gifts you are weak female," growled the unknown voice.

"I am sorry. Although I feel a connection to you, I wish to be cautious. I will not be pushed or controlled," snap the commander.

"Then it is a test of wills," giggled the unknown voice. "We shall be one. Commander Nightshade" hissed the creature.

The sudden pain returns like a pair of vice grips across the commander's head. She screams while holding the sides of her brain. Marvin is slow to respond, while the computer gives a warning. The commander is rolling on the floor, arching her back as blood leaks from her ears and nose.

"Kill it, kill the thing outside," moaned the commander.

"There is a strange object hovering close to the ships starboard side," crackled the computer.

"Increase shielding and fire ion guns now," shouted Marvin.

"I obey Lieutenant Patterson."

He pulls out a medical kit to administer a sedative then leans down over her body to keep it still. A strange smile from his thoughts wonders if the god has finally answered his prayers to be free of this witch. Her energy form had time to transfer some of her will, as did the Commander Nightshade. However, when the ship strengthened its shields and fired the ion guns it caused instant death to both human and energy form. Marvin is stunned as the death expression fixed on Commander Nightshade. A strange glow pulses in the center of her forehead. He cursed, knowing what was about to happen and shouts to the computer.

"Is the helix cube activating for Mrs. Nightshade."

"Yes, sir but I am getting strange brain readings," quoted the computer, then added, "I will need further study. Her rebirth shall take the normal human time intervals. Emergency departure from this system immediately," hissed the young man.

"I have not yet completed the survey and the samples I have collected. They will reach us within an hour. I must complete my last orders of the commander," crackled the computer.

"I think it is best to leave before the other creature returns. If you insist to risk the new life of the commander, she will know by these recordings," Marvin challenged. The AI brain went silent for a few minutes.

"I will leave when the samples arrive. Then we will depart Mr. Patterson. You must set the correct navigational course."

"Yes, I will comply, Deab. What of her body do I have permission to depose of it immediately."

"I will take care of it. Bring it down to the docking bay and aim it toward the red sun when we leave," hissed the computer.

Unbeknownst to Marvin and the AI computer is they were still alive within each new form. Although the adult body is stiff and cold the energy of Ru is, still inside as it is within the rebirth of the commander. The ship launches and leaves the floating body as it goes to the sun. Ru suddenly awakes in a strange form very puzzled. She has lost some of her memories. She uses the power of the red sun to energise her powers to the floating sphere. The human part is transfixed on returning to Zlotoo to recover from the strange interaction in hopes to return to her ship. She sees the ship soar away from the ea system. Tears form the human part of abandonment. Only Ru scents their missing part. Ru becomes somewhat interested.

I must know this secret, weak female to immortal living you have discovered, Ru demands.

I will never tell you creature of hot air. My body is radiated I shall die soon enough, argued Nightshade.

That is where you are wrong. Listen we are being reborn. Moreover, we shall learn all your secrets; I am a god of creation. You are now one of my pets, whispered Ru.

No, I will not give you that satisfaction, snaps the commander.

The sphere landed on the altar inside the circle. Nightshade kept pressing her will to push the creatures away. She was also fighting the cold atmosphere of the planets. High pitch chirping surrounded the human form. They swarm like angry insects towards the human form. Ru sends out greetings but only anger and rage as they attack her new form tearing her flesh into pieces. The lone cry wakes Lord Id from his slumber. The crystal sparkles in front of the dark sphere.

Now you are alone for the first time, whispered the crystal.

Lord Id blinks and feels the lost of Ru emptiness deep inside him wails a mournful cry.

I need Ru to complete our perfection of the new race of beings that shall own its rightful place among the stars.

I Lord Id of dreams, will hold all life accountable to the new order. I shall become a creator of this new form. If you wish her return, she will return in the next generation. The creatures named the Jung zees are yours to mould. As the next race will arrive, the Myra will also follow you under another name, he will also be a creator. There can only be one God to control the crystal.

Lord Id took these words within his mind, he became curiosity took the better of him to check on his pets. The door would not open until he swore his quick return. Parts of Ru flesh is spewed over the altar. Only anger swelled within the new god who remembered the oath with Ru. He kept his word and worked to bring her back by eating her flesh and ravage the spider queens sexually deep angry that he must not fail Ru. Lord Id guided the offspring for. Eight hundred years have passed from the original spider queens lay million of Jung zee spread quickly to the four planets. The Myra arrived with a new being Name Eltross and the sleeping blue beetle That Lod Id felt a strange connection to Ru so he let them Stay on the blue planet closer to the dwarf sun in the last hope that Ru would appear soon. He had to wait for the next generation will be his testament for his caretaker Ru.

A thousand years from the arrival of the original spider queens had passed with many generations of insectoids name Jung zee and Myra beings had hatch by the spider queens multiply in large numbers and died off when each old queen pass away. These groups had built society by following the laws and rules of their creator. Since the death of Ru, he would follow the plan of perfection. Lord Id never satisfied and only hopes for the rebirth of Ru within the special eggs to the next queen to be born has leader.

With Lord Id's next awakening after a thousand years of waiting for the generation of Ru. So, he focuses on opening the doorway of time with the crystal as the tiny dark mist receives the initial energy and forms into a tiny dark cloud. Huge electrical storms increase from the two large giant's gas planets as their orbits crisscross passing within one hundred kilometres. The Earth probe orbited around this sector, recorded the colour display of green, yellow, and blue arc across each other.

This caused another white-hot energy to form into a round ball. A tiny dark sphere ejected from the center and streaked cross the atmosphere causing a quake wave of ice and dust particles in the high upper altitudes of the gas planet. Thousand of electrical tendrils came deep from the planet's core rising up with a direct hit to dark sphere. Two glowing eyes opened to feed off the energy, that is taking in the cycle of its return to this black sphere own solar system it had named Ea. He had left from a twenty-year travel.

The new spider Queen echoes a long high pitch sound to announce its arrival. In its mind, it reviews the long history before first contact of one of its pets to reacquaint other life forms of its return in this galaxy. Being highly intelligent, he absorbs great amounts of information by a single touch.

He recalls the elders' race when they became aware from the big bang that burst through his unseen universe of no form, a floating energy. Highly evolved minds led by the holder of the Seeing Eye found they only exist near the three suns of the young system. In addition, the white crystal contently renews its life force. The dark sphere is the last of its kind that escapes the doom of the inner world.

Over one hundred thousand light years it stretched his mind through all galaxies for any intelligent races and traveled time to time with his seeing eye. These gains were a gift from the old one, which it calls caretaker before premature death. Based on its two brains it can mind travel endlessly throughout the cosmos beyond the furthest reaches.

It being an immortal in a liquid mist to subatomic structure of atoms has the ability to transform itself in any life form of this system. It believes that its race is the first ones of intelligent mind, which awake from the long sleep of a dream world in the vast cosmos. It considered that this galaxy was the first to be the raised from the big bang that stretched out like a living tree. The sphere's mind sees the deep root of his past to widen the branches of tiny bright spheres of energy that its race used to collect all life forms to study. He comes back every twenty years looking to bring an existence in this cosmos because the inner world is shrinking, and dark matter is absorbing into another dimension of the nothingness. Its goal is to exist in a new race, a perfect one to rule the cosmos, with no concept of time only that it is what it is.

The dark sphere was aware instantly of intruders nearby his planet. He sends a burst of microwaves to the probe. The probe suddenly saw the complex patterns in its radio waves as it took time to understand what it was. The sphere changed direction to a ninety-degree angle. The probes camera lost sight of it as it spins to relocate. The dark sphere moved closer to the gas planet to gather electrical plasma into a round ball and then release it toward the probes and they exploded into multi rings as they faded into dust particles.

Thinking it was a tool from the elders to entrap its essence. He makes his rounds through the solar system to the planet on the outside rim. The dark sphere descends like a falling star. The creatures see and hear the sonic boom of its arrival. The sphere glows to a pale blue as it enters a temple to a stone statue with empty eyes with its arms raised up to the sky. The tiny dark sphere drops into its appendages. It is anxious to continue its work on astrobiology or exobiology on his pets. The change over to a new form is quite difficult. As the transfer begins, his worshipers appear all around the statue and grovel at his feet. Many scarify their lives for its blessing. Their voices rise in a song blessed by its return. The senseless killing for favours irritates it. It sees no new hatchings. Normally they are the first to arrive. It grumbles loudly as the ground shakes with its anger. No answer came from his pets as it felt fear within them. Someone whispers out its true name that only his caretaker knew. One that it knew well it calls out. It would take time to transfer his mind in the statue. Its empty eyes began to glow absorbing those that wish to sacrifice themselves. It took them in as food and helped to bring him into a life form to rule over its pets. It can hear the voice clearer as its mind is forming a matrix from the other creature.

I am reborn as Queen Ru of the Jung zee I can feel the flaws of imperfection. I went on a murderous rampage killing the old queens and my sisters. I apologize to you little one for my rash actions. I only live for perfection.

Yes, my old caretaker, it is good to have you return to me. I hope to accomplish perfection with these new hatchlings. It is all that I live for, whispered the dark sphere.

I am sorry this feeling of rage transformed the older adults to kill their offspring a few weeks ago. The new light forming outside EA space added to their fear. They claim new gods are coming the next twist of the prophecy is to begin, claimed the Queen.

Do not worry about wild claims; I shall punish them. Luckily, only this nest destroyed. When I transfer over completely, we shall start over my caretaker. Now that you have awakened, claimed the sphere.

No, you cannot. I am imperfect based on what we learned by our trials and errors. We need another race to succeed. The carnage is everywhere my young one, the strange light in the sky cause this harbinger of death and destruction, which I fear has spread throughout the other planets, Queen Ru mumbled to the statue as a aura sparkle around it.

I must see for myself, it hissed angrily.

The stone head turns upwards to the distance gas planets the glowing eyes seem to brighten; its mind stretches outwardly and moves quickly to the five inner planets that have an atmosphere. It is a rock desert world with only two seasons' winter and summer. It gives out a throaty rumble in a strange language; no answer came. Eyes now see a large impact crater had decimated its nest, empty of life. It wails in anguish as he quickly drops to examine the destruction. Within its mind gift, it feels the echoes of a scream from the past. His mind uses his gift of insight from the dead. It hears other voices not in greeting but with wails of pain and anger.

The pain of loss is so great; he soars up to the next planet with a long red streak of anger and revenge. Its eyes are so intense; they suck the life force of all the living pets to complete his energy transfer into the other form. Each planet it visits is a carbon copy of the same destruction to recover the others. His pets were vague of what caused the destruction and pointed to the new light that from an evil eye caused panic. Sphere minds looked at the strange formations rolling wave of energy in blue and red dust clouds with a yellow and a white centre forming a new star. Tired and sadden it returns. The stone statue breaks free and crumbles into a dust cloud obscuring the view of his followers.

It claims in a deep voice to his follower.

"I lord of dreams, Id, have returned, and will hold all life accountable to the new order." The new form steps out of the small dust swirls revealing his new appearance.

The creature who had a large round head, sharp glowing horns, and perfect round eyes of ebony gave a deathly chill to anyone who gazed. The creature was small in stature with a strong mind presence. It had large dark wings that stretched out and fanned the dust clouds away. His muscled forearms stretched out with a loud roar as its four sharp fingers and toes stretched from its long sleep. The sphere made a slow turn into a mist as it concealed his new body in a black cloak with only two pairs of eyes of death that only a few had seen.

"Once again, wants to rebuild a new world and begins the next generation that will bring the end of all stories from his past race," quoted queen Ru. The large eyes of Lord Id glance up to take in the creature, which bows low in a respectful manner and whispers in a low tone.

Our hopes are renewing with the rebirth of its caretaker to the beginning of a new world.

The giant spider with multi eyes steps forward slowly on all eight legs. She lowers her odd shape head and releases the broken time crystal to offer it to Lord Id. The only weapon needed to wipe out and absorb life to the beginning of time.

He amuses himself as his two brains see the great use of its power by the red giants sun to reflects its energy on the planet like a laser flash a bright yellow beam, which cause the planets to rotate, causing a great pressure which crushes everything The planet implodes into a fireball then fades to dust. His eyes blink when he hears the Queen rumble

You may kill me for overstepping our agreement I do not feel perfect, death would be a great gift for me my Lord Id.

No, tell me again what has happened to my children before I do anything-old friend.

You are so kind to the old caretaker, little one.

We have the same goals do we not, perfection is what drives us regardless the time that has passed, hissed the new form.

She begins the long explanations of the strange lights and the large, odd shape orbs that have circled their space of Ea. She hinted it could be the elders and was one of her reasons to destroy the nest. However, she felt a strange presence that raised her curiosity. The strange beams of light that descended from the night sky spooked our pets into killing their offspring.

Once again, the creature looks up at the sky recalling the mechanical mind that came too close to him in his altered state. She brought another device to show him what she had collected. It is an odd flat disc of ancient symbols, which describes a new life form.

We must join our minds to see if a new race is approaching us and whether they are of any use to us in our quest of perfection, hissed Lord Id.

Yes, let us find out if they are worthy to be part of our perfection replied to the giant spider.

She lowers her head to the stone floor of the temple. He raises his hands open palms revealing sharp claws and a mouth, which hissed out in a forked tongue. He presses his hand and bites hard on the spider's head. They both moan as their eyes glow to a soft yellow tinge. Two colour spheres one large red, the other a tiny dark sphere joined and grew together into a larger sphere, which rose up into the sky towards the edge of Ea space, in search for the truth and their quest for perfection

CHAPTER 5

THE RETURN TO THE FORBIDDEN ZONE

Marvin Patterson is in a panic has he takes command of the Black Scorpion spaceship. He had no choice the sudden unexplained death of Helen Nightshade while orbiting the odd solar system name Ea space. It was Helen's idea because of strong readings within a three suns system that had assorted exoplanets. They found this odd solar system is rich in mining materials of rare metals to building advance space craft. However. this not what brought them to this solar system, but a strange radio frequency had attracted Helen attention to investigate this odd solar system.

He recalls Helen angry and insistence to save her husband and child. It started with reports of an alpha prime capital ship being loss after it drops off new settlers in a nearby system of Corus. She tries to press the government of Alpha prime to send out search parties and rescue ships. They show interest until the computer points her husband spaceship had enter the forbidden zone. Base on old laws dating back thousands of years and pass down to every generation that had built the planets core population in a peaceful modern environment that all so advance by the technologies. They had lived in peace for 4000 years no enemies, no wars just natural growth to advance and share the wealth for all the people of alpha prime. The only rule is to never venture into that area of space. For warnings this could be their end of their world would come about by a great disaster of the dark void. Helen laughs it off thinking her husband and newborn are more important than one old law written by dead ancestors long ago. She believes her planet society is on such old fears by the modern technology.

Marvin knew all this and was trick by Helen and her two young friends that stole this special medical ship name the Black Scorpion. Their first story was to drop off medical supplies for a plague that struck the planet named Primo Prime. Marvin help take the ship out until warships chase them for several days that when he found out Helen had stolen this spaceship. He wanted to surrender to the authorities, but Helen telepathic powers force him to obey her every command. He had no choice and used his skill, and they escape with ease through Astro belt. Helen kept her promise and drop off the medical supplies with Doctor Styles and his nurse Sheila Winters to the native beings on the planet Primo. The leaders accepted their help while Helen took Marvin to search the forbidden zone. They receive a broken radio message which convince her that is where her husband and child are alive with running out of supplies on their damage space craft or desolate a planet in the forbidden zone.

Marvin Patterson wrote in the captain's logbook details of Helen's death and medical details ran by the ship's AI. He took the time to read Helen's entries found she had felt guilt harming Marvin. He shrugs shoulders with a deep sigh, while he closed the ship's logbook. He turns to his flight station and starts to set course to pick up Doctor and his nurse at the planet Primo prime in the Kreek solar system. His Ai takes over the general operation of the spacecraft, but it needs a pilot to steer the spaceship through vastness of open space between the twelve galaxies that is part of these thousands of worlds. His focus is to get back to alpha prime and to surrender to the authorities quickly hoping they will be lenient, but he knew Helen's father and mother will be first to blame him for the death of her daughter. Ai is first to report odd statement. "Stage one is activated and subject wishes to have privacy all units are secure no entry is allowed in the bio tubes."

Marvin gave a puzzle look has his eyes are focus on his last calculations to enter the Kreek solar system and line up the orbit to Primo. "Hey Deab what are you claiming I have done now," snarl Marvin.

Ai Deab did not answer him, and it seem to shut down her computer system in the flight controls turn on to manual control. Which angry Marvin because it will take longer to set the course to primo. He also knew Helen had all the codes to run this advance medical spaceship that can save and cure people within the special design bio chambers. He also knew it's had been kept a secret for this ship Ai is very independent to human control. He just got free from Helen control he did not want a computer to boss him around. He will be happy to pick up Doctor Styles and his nurse Sheila Winters within the hour of flight time.

This spacecraft had a unique engine speck for interdimensional travel at trans wrap 10.5 that would take years to travel down to hours within the ship's matrix. He checks the spaceships navigation everything is green and running perfectly that he thought that a short nap would relieve his stress in loosing Helen Nightshade. His goals are simple with only a few other worries of being a thief to the eyes of Alpha prime. His eyes turn to the Ai console and tap on the button has he express his wishes to go for a short nap. "Hey Deab please take over flight control I want to rest before we reach planet Primo." Strange voice buzz to life it almost sound like a familiar laugh of Helen which gave him a chill down his back. Marvin snarls back. "Hey, stop freaking me out Deab just take over I am tired." The AI answer with a deeper voice. "Yes, I agree little human it is your rest period I have a place for you to sleep my little tommy boy I grow tired of your mistakes you are a glitch that must end quickly, but I shall restart your life from a new beginning," came dark laugh.

Marvin burst out in angry while struggle with every word has, he felt death nearby him in deep loud noise coming from behind. He tightens his grip on the flight controls, just has his words fumble out. "Deab what are you talking about you have except me to run this space craft back home." Deab is silent before she answers. "Marvin notice the oxygen levels are dropping to critical" has a deep voice of Helen answers his last question. "Oh yes that is correct Tommy boy, but my new master is hungry, and you are the only food she can devour so be a good boy' She is sending her cyborg's suit to pick you up bring it into the specialize bio tubes for rebirth. I have decided to change your name to Thomas Patterson Knowing him to be more like you in weakness of character and will become my little pet." echo laugh.

Marvin tries to move off the Captain seat but the lack of air to breathe made him collapse onto the bridge floor. His eyes see the oversize Cyborg moving towards him. He mutters no and tries roll over to an escape hatch however his strength is wading when he tries to turn the hatch door to open. That when he realizes it too late and surrender his fate to be a slave of Helen Nightshade.

The Black Scorpion Ai made sure the body of Marvin Patterson is secure and took sample of DNA to restart life. The AI watch its Cyborg place a syringe into Helen's embryo with long tube into the dead body of Marvin Patterson drain all fluids to help speed up growth. The Ai is totally satisfied it is following her master's orders and completes her latest task by ignite its engines to enter inner space. At wrap speed. The Ai had activated her robots to run the ship to the Kreek system to pick Doctor Styles and his nurse on the planet Primo. The computer knew she need the doctor to save Helen Nightshade at all cost that is why she had to take the life of Marvin Patterson. Thinking logically, he can start life over again in alpha prime nursey for clone children The computer's goal is to protect life. Since it's a where of the laws to respect all life and protect it she had to keep Helen Nightshade alive and hope the doctor can save them because of the odd DNA now surrounding the embryo of Helen. While the ships are traveling, she watches over the bio chamber to help monitor the serval newborn embryo multiple arms and camera's she keeps them all in health mod all the lights stay green. The Ai knows they will have a higher chance to survive if it reaches the doctor in time. She checks on its eternal clock noticing it needs to hurry. So, it adjusts the fuel mixture to get more speed out of the engines and hopes to shave off more time to save Helen.

Meanwhile Doctor Styles and his nurse Sheila Winters had their hands full with government officials of Primo and the military general from Alpha prime. He had come to arrest them for the stealing of the Black Scorpion space craft. Doctor Styles ignore the General's demands by staying silent while he treated beings of primo. Most are human form, but different planets have different physical changes due to the atmosphere and environment conditions and food sources. Primo has been terra form it's been 1000 years with great success until now has the Doctor treats a new patient that had a growing parasite across her sender body has, she moans and mutters. "Doctor burns within my soul." Oh Sorry, little one I got medicine that will help you, just relax. He takes the syringe from Nurse Winter's hand while a group of government officials hover near by with the presents of General Edward Stark look on glaring at the doctor to obey his requests. Doctor Styles had experience and delt with strange illness from other worlds before with success. However, this virus is more deadly and spreading rapidly across the whole planet at an alarming rate. The woman skin color is pale blue natural for this planet base on the giant yellow star and the thicker atmosphere. Her parasites react to the medicine slow disappear, however the woman started to complain of chest pains the moderator started to show her heart and blood pressure rising at a alarming rate. Styles whisper softly to the young woman. "It's okay little one I have another needle right here to ease the pain you must give the drugs time to spread throughout your body."

Nurse Winter gave a calming smile to girl has she adjust her pillows and whisper into her ear. "You be fine in no time. With the last shot give the young woman fell asleep quickly. Doctor Styles turn to face a large group of men and women. Okay gentle beings of Primo prime you may disburse the drugs after I have samples of this new parasite, before I give approval of this medicine vaccine, I have is safe for all the inhabitants of your planet Primo, explain Doctor Style.

Government leader step forward with a concern expression and voice his opinion. "Can we not use these drugs now to save our race dear doctor surely it is the cure." However, the general had enough of Doctor Styles ignorance and wave his soldiers to arrest both him and Nurse Winter. Sudden eruption of voices from all the government officials and the general staff. The leader raises his arms for silence. He steps in front of Doctor Styles and face the general with angry across his face spoke with a growl. "I told you this doctor and nurse is under my protection you may have them after the cure no sooner."

General Edward Savage scoff at the blue face humanoid with contempt step right up into his face." I have the military force to seize this planet and lay it into a wasteland for your attempt to interfere in Alpha prime business." The tension rose high by the silence in the room. However, another voice from the back of the room seem to deflate the tension instantly. "That is enough Edward these beings are related to us and they have a need for Doctor Styles stand down Mr. Warmonger." The government staff moved out of the way has a woman dress in a black cyborg suit step between the general and the government leader. However, the general face went pale and gasp out her name. "Blackstone what are you doing here."

The middle-aged woman long white hair that run down her back show her deep purple eyes that seem to penetrate anyone with a challenge. Everyone looks up at pale skin face tall and slender frame of seven feet tall. She gave a hearty laugh before answering. "I want my spaceship back the Black Scorpion and not harm any peace-loving beings that you are doing cousin. Now step back and let me handle this, Edward." The general growl step back red face and muttering to his men. "Release them go back to Omega four spaceship right now." His men salute and step away quickly out of the room. The leader of planet Primo gave a warm smile with a bow at the tall woman and spoke softly." I am honored to meet such a beknowing being that has pushed all our humanoid kind throughout the twelve Galaxies."

Mrs. Blackstone return the same jester with her tight smile and gentle nod and spoke crisply. "I want this doctor to help save your planet, but he must answer my one question first. Where is the hell is my ship Doctor Styles"

Nurse step closer to Doctor Styles and whisper in his ear "I guess we must tell them whole the truth now." "Sheila be quiet," snaps the Doctor has he look at his watch. Blackstone eyebrow rose slightly and whisper a telepathic thought directly into both Doctor Styles and Nurse Winter both went pale has she saw the images from their minds. The answers she got from images only added more stress to both the doctor and nurse. However, has the young woman stir in her bed and whisper "father. I had a dream of darkness over our world," and shouted, "doom is coming". Leader one, rush to his Daughter's side to comfort her has tears pour down her face, Blackstone snarls and waves her right hand to erase the image of the young girl's mind and spoke softly. "My dear child calm yourself it's only a dream young one" who then went silent in her father's arms. "Now tell me now Doctor I want leader one to hear it from your only lips." hiss Blackstone.

Doctor Styles clench his teeth together and punch his fist against his side of his legs and blurt out the truth. "Helen Nightshade and Marvin Patterson went to search the forbidden zone since this area is the closes to where her husband ship had disappeared."

The room fill with angry, and cruses from all the government employees has Blackstone knew this would happen because of the history of Alpha prime forefathers' secret knowledge. The leader one face went to a different shade of blue and spoke crisply. "I expect you to save my planet but what you friend Helen Nightshade has doomed the twelve galaxies."

"Please gentle beings, and Mrs. Blackstone your ship is coming back within a few hours. I have been monitoring the ship locations and they did not stay to long in that forbidden zone to do any harm, snap the Doctor and went on with another claim. "Yes, I have recorded all the updates and location by this information center on my wrist, tied to the Ai name Deab."

"Give that device to me now, it belongs to me Helen stole that from my home," snarls Blackstone.in a demanding tone. The leader wave his assistant and gave private orders which the assistant nodded and left quickly. He then turns his attention to Mrs. Blackstone with a cold tone in his voice. "My security will guard the doctor and the nurse you may have the device. However, They must finish the cure for the people of primo prime first. Has for the Black Scorpion you may have it and please leave our space in peace if not we shall fire what weapons we have to destroy that ship."

Blackstone step forward to take the device from the doctor and mutter, "foolish child." The doctor gave a harden smirk while handing the monitor willing, but his words are full of angry. "You and our government hold all twelve galaxies with false fear of the forbidden zone." Blackstone gave a haunting laugh has the doctor and nurse left the room while she walks away in the other direction only to be stop by a young red hair woman in a white space suit with a large group of children blocking the way of Blackstone. "Well, what did they tell you auntie about my daughter Helen," snap the woman. Blackstone roll her eyes with a deep frown and mutter her annoyances. "I told you to stay on my ship no one must know you are here especially your children, what if your husband finds out." The young woman eyes darted about and then step back little out of camera view. She waves and sends a silent message at her oldest daughter who nodded a yes started to push her sisters back to the spaceship. The woman raises her hood to hide her features then spoke harshly to Mrs. Blackstone." I want my daughter back and you want your silly ship I have already transferred millions of dollars and shares to my corporation, so stop stalling and tell everything."

Bertha Blackstone knew this day is coming with deep sadness grew within her soul and took the first steps towards her spaceship while explaining her point of view. "Yes, Olivia I know everything about the Nightshade cruse, dear sister. You and I have done a lot to prevent it but we both know it is destiny that we can never change it without Krell intervention. You know he is far away from our Alpha prime timeline looking for his lost children. it's just us that must face this danger, Olivia." She started walk up her ramp to her spaceship while Olivia began to weep blood tears. Blackstone last words had cut deep within her heart and soul within the younger woman. "We made a mistake not telling Helen about this paradox and its to late.

Now we must hurry to intercept the Black Scorpion before she enters Kreek solar system You know the laws of the Twelve Galaxies it must be destroy before it touches any of our planets within the twelve galaxies." Olivia froze while she looks up to watch the Alpha prime warships and Omega 4 world ships jump into warp drive. She knew they are going to capture the Black Scorpion and possibility kill her oldest daughter. She turns away to her spacecraft and mutter angrily," Sister will you help me save Helen or shall I kill you and everyone who tries to stop me protecting my oldest daughter."

"Olivia do not be foolish I am more powerful than you," snap Bertha. Her eyes flared red with a deep sign and then went on to say. "However, I promise to help you but if we are to late its is you that must kill your daughter if she is infected by elder clan." Blackstone raised the ramp Olivia heard the wining of Blackstone's spaceship saucer quickly rose from the space dock and sped away into space. Olivia started running towards her ship, while calling on her other oldest daughter Damiene startup the engines to leave this planet Primo. However, no answer came back which upset the young woman more so and she wonder if the dark effects have reached her children. Olivia focusses her telepathic powers to reach her children and was relieve they are on board the shuttle craft. Although Damiene is outside the ship talking to a security force that seem they want to inspect her ship. Which she is refusing entrée because of sanitation issues from the Planet Primo is in quarantine

Olivia arrives and joins into the conversation and waves her daughter into the ship to prepare their spaceship for liftoff. The lieutenant and his crew are insisting to inspect the ship by the laws of Primo government. Olivia had no time left to waste on this conversation. She knew if she gives her name the lieutenant would back off being the wife of the president of Alpha prime confederation which this planet Primo is part of would only start another diplomat problems.

"I must insist you step aside to let my crew inspect your ship immediately Madame," hiss the lieutenant and brush pass her gently tries to walk by her. Suddenly a burst of electric tendrils appears to block his way has his team step away from it. The lieutenant slowly turns to face the unknown woman that is floating before him with her arms apart which spew out wave of electrical tendrils of energy all around him and his crew. Olivia spoke in deep voice that bought a chill down the lieutenant's spine. "I have no time to play with silly rules little man. I suggest you and your crew go play childish games with other gentle beings right now." The lieutenant's eyes seem to go blank and started to jump and skip away with his crew that gave roar of laughter.

Olivia turns away and floated into her ship. Just has the engines lit up and lifted quickly off the docking platform and sped away into space. Once inside her ship she started breathing exercise to calm down not wanting her children to see her dark powers. The voice of Damiene clear the dark images of Olivia's mind that have been appearing more often. "Mother I place the children in the bio chambers if we are going to warp speed, I just need the navigation requirements to set a course." Olivia studder her words at first when trying to bring down her telepathic powers. "Yes, I be there in a few moments for now just follow Auntie Blackstone flight at impulse drive." "Okay Thank you mother, I will follow old Bertha," giggle Damiene.

Olivia did not like the old joke from Damiene about to correct her, when she realize that was the name of her old sister's special spacecraft name, Old Bertha. A sudden smile form has her past dealing in good times fill her with happy memories. She knew this always makes her chase the dark images and started to feel better has she went to check on all her children that are place in separate bio chambers. The smile broaden they are all asleep went to get some warm drinks for her daughter and herself while she slowly comes up with the right solutions on how to save Helen and keep all twelve children safe from the effects of forbidden zone. Olivia steps out of the elevator and heard voices in the cafeteria, has she steps forward to find Doctor Styles and Nurse Winter drinking coffee. Olivia went pale and mutter in shock. 'What are you doing here on my ship." Before anyone could answer her question, she is interrupted by a panic voice. "Mother we have a dozen Starfighters coming up fast want us to return to the planet," cried Damiene.

Olivia face went red and snarls "I will not protect you for what you done doctor with your nurse. If my children are harm, I will tear you apart." She turns to the bridge and shouts to her daughter, "Stay calm and stay on course, I am coming my love raise shiels" "Yes, mother will do," snaps Damiene.

The doctor followed with his nurse while he explains that it was his daughter Damiene that invite them on this ship to meet Helen on the Black Scorpion. Claim doctor Styles and went on to explain Damiene reasons. "she needs our help for medical emergency after all its Helen's idea to look for her own family is this not what you are doing Mrs. Nightshade." Olivia is stun by the revelation that Damiene is telepathing with Helen, has more question form in her mind. Damiene call out for help once more. "Two starfighters have fired missiles at us mother I am eluding them I has I speak to you."

Just has Olivia enters the bridge she sees one of the missiles wisps by the front of their shuttle craft and explodes. "Wow that was to close mother," remark Damiene. Just has she press down on the control arm to a sharp left turn to face the starfighters. Luckily Olivia reaches the copilot seat and turn the communications with the primo starfighters. "Hold off your attack right now because you are going to start a needless war against the President Savage's wife. She hit another switch which gave a operating code of her personal spacecraft." The starfighter lead Captain scoff at the code and claimed. "that is fake code turn around or be destroy is my final demand."

Suddenly a burst of bright light flash all around the six-star fighters has all the radios call out to the Captain. "We are surrounded by three Omega world ships." Starfighter Captain bark out to his flight crew, "shut up and stay in our attack formation. We have our rights to defend our on planet," it went quiet has the captain look at the Omega two open the large docking bay and release twenty more advance starfighters to circle the primo starfighters.

Just the radio buzz alive with one deep voice that made the captain turn to pale and sickly expression. "This is the President Thomas Savage of the Alpha prime confederation. You are requested to withdraw and escort Omega 1 and three to your planet because We are carrying your vaccine. So do not waste time with idol threats. Do you want to be a hero in saving the planet or die right now in cold space."

The starfighter captain stumbles with his words has he answers. "Yes, Sir Mr. president we will be honor to escort Omega 1 and 3 to our planet primo. All primo starfighters ships turn 20 degrees to starboard and form up to accompany Omega 1 and 3."

Damiene is cheering and dancing about while Olivia looks away with fear. She had been followed by her husband and wonder how much he knows about his daughter Helen and the black scorpion space craft. The radio crack to life on the bridge. "Hello, my sweet love come aboard my ship with all our children it will be a better and more comfortable. My ship has everything you need my darling love, plus a lot of medical equipment you may need in the future. The stress level shot right up within Olivia, and the sudden pain came from the planet Primo by her telepathic images of both Omega1 and 3 fire all their weapons across the planetary landmasses. While Alpha prime starfighters attack circle escaping spaceships which fell back into a blazing planet Primo."

Olivia sent a private telepathic message to her husband mind; you must stop this destruction these are peaceful beings my love. "She already knew it to late has she watch the destruction of the planet Primo start to fall part into itself has large chucks floated off into deep space. Her husband voice came alive once more with three sharp words. "Come aboard now." Just has three different loading docks open and a tractor beam engulf the shuttle craft to pull it in. Olivia is in panic mod just has she fought to keep control of her blood tears that her husband had turn into a murder of worlds. She felt the anguish cries within her telepathic powers has if it was food to feed on such a violent loss of one world. She knew then that she must sacrifice herself to save all her daughters lives from the evil of the elder clan.

Doctor Styles face drops to the floor and shaking his head in disbelief, but he did remember Helen's last warning that we may all be killed. Nurse Winters is crying with deep wails of pain within her soul. Just has Damiene dance and prance with joy the nurse slaps the young woman's face and took hold tightly with a shake screaming at her, "This wrong to cheer the death of millions you have sin against all gentle beings. Olivia step between them and order her daughter to go wake up the kids' father is here." She then growls at nurse Winters "Your foolish woman all my children are telepaths power of the mist they are all connected to each other they would or could cut you to pieces with a simple snap of their figures. So, I warn you now never touch telepath in that manner." "I know its wrong, but she is only a tall child ten years old not a woman. I am keeping her calm so stay out of her way from now on Ms. Winters."

Sudden thud echo throughout the shuttle at the same time the shuttle craft entrance ramp opens wide to let in a swarm of Cyborgs rush through the ship with their weapons drawn. Several of them circle both the nurse and Doctor Styles started to search their body for weapons and then place handcuffs. The sergeant orders them to get on their knees for execution. Olivia objected loudly, "No wait I need information do not kill them." Another voice cuts through the air only to raise the tension and stress within Olivia soul. "Why do you wish to save criminals that threaten Alpha prime, they already destroy the planet Primo you and your sister Bertha Blackstone know of the forbidden knowledge from Ea. Space has started rumors of destruction of Alpha prime and the 12 galaxies." Olivia step forward to face her husband slightly older in years but still a rugged shape of a tall man jet black hair with deep brown eyes and long sharp nose with a square jaw that seem harden by the beauty of his wife words. That seem to touch him deeply has he chews his lower lips. "You are mistaken my love my only goals are to protect my children at all cost I think you should not be involved in this dangerous adventure. I am pregnant once more with twins my love not wanting sheik responsibility to our marriage," claim Olivia.

Savage gave a broken smile call on the medical team to take care of his wife. He then looks at the nurse and the doctor has he wait for conformation from the spaceship doctor. Who then turns and nodded yes, and voice is slight shaken with his words. "She is Mister president ten weeks". He slaps his hands greedily together then order him place his wife in the bio tubes for safekeeping Olivia refuse which seems too angry him that made him growl out his words in a threating manner." I am your husband you do what I say or do you wish to be executed with this nurse and throw you both out of the docking bay."

Olivia was about to object but it was the doctor that jumps in with harsh words to her husband." I can save your daughter with my nurse she is empath by just her touch she can heal anyone and read anyone's body emotions you need us both for I have the coordinates for the Black Scorpion locations.

Savage walks towards the Doctor Styles and grasp his hair and pull it back to face Nurse Winter. He then activated his laser sword place across the doctor's throat and then made his demands. "Okay empath tells me if my wife is carrying a male newborn." Winters blink several times has her hands shook in fear but could see this man lives for power and greed and mutter," I can do it but please do not harm us."

Savage scoff and then hiss out his words, "I make no promise just do it or there will be blood spill today on you if you do not do what I say right now." Olivia stomps her foot down spoke harshly, "I am not in the mood to play your game Thomas. They are twins and they are boys I will not be in your little bio tubes, when my daughter Helen needs me now."

Savage release the Doctor and place his dagger back into it sheathes. He step forward to look deep in Olivia's eyes breathing heavily she could smell the dark rum, and strange smile form across his face. His words were slurred has he hug Olivia tightly. "You finally fulfill my request but know you wish to risk your life and our future for a selfish daughter that broke our sacred laws of alpha prime. No not ever going to happen, I must keep you safe."

Olivia tries to pull away, but Savage held her tight with in his arms. He then waves his soldiers away and point to the two prisoners with orders to the captain. "Take these two idiots to the bridge immediately." He turns to look at the doctor and gave his final threat. "Doctor Styles tell my navigator the coordinates to the Black Scorpion instantly or I shall have a test subject at the nearest airlock for Nurse Winters."

The doctor nodded to the president and briefly look at Nurse Winter sadly knowing their pledge they made to protect Helen at all cost only if her father gets involve. Now this truth has happened and wonder if Helen saw this in a telepathic vision. Being strong with telepathic powers is part of the Nightshade persona is a level 10.

Olivia and William are alone which seem to raise some fear within her, because of his single-minded demands for male children after having fifteen years of girls only added to the stress between each other over their careers. Their love has always been true to each other, but the acceptance of the presidency opens the old wounds of past deeds from the Nightshade family corporate actions on all living beings within the Alpha Prime confederation. William final knew the president secret knowledge of the forbidden zone. This is what change everything they both once cherish together. Helen has jeopardized it to a dangerous level between them right now. Olivia will do anything to save her Daughter and William will do anything to save Alpha prime at any cost also. Her thoughts are random, but one started to form in her mind. While she took a deep breath and kiss her husband passionately. Her telepathic thoughts came out clearly. "How do I escape him I need a faster ship I wish my sister Bertha had waited for me and the children."

Suddenly she heard a familiar voice. "Oh, my sister you do know how to kiss a real hard man in hopes to a calm his anger. Now put him a sleep I taken care of his security team and let's go," snarls Bertha. Olivia laughs between kisses that confuse William tries to pull away knowing his wife may try to trick him and demand she tells him right now, "What are you scheming my dear wife." Suddenly the room fill with his eleven children all demanding his attention especially the youngest name Mira with warm hands touching his face gently. Who held him so tightly that his mind felt a heavy and drop to his knees before he fell into a deep sleep.

Olivia slaps her hands together knowing Bertha's plans to escape. So, she scurries the children to an escape hatch that is connected old bertha's spaceship.. However, Mira decides to stay and place everyone in a deep sleep to give some time for her family to escape. However, Olivia wanted to object but it is Damiene who push a darker idea to kill everyone with a single thought before escaping to have a clear path to the Black Scorpion. Olivia quickly calm Damiene with touch of her telepathic powers and found the image is from Helen's mind. She pushes her thoughts you must respect all intelligent life forms and be at peace. She kisses Mira and mutter softly." Stay safe daughter, father does love you. Mira answer quickly while pushing her mother through the escape hatch."

"I know mother I have a different path to follow," and turn away quickly while shouting, "go and find Helen. I hope you save her sweet mother."

Bertha had gathered the ten children and help Olivia place the children in the bio chambers. Damiene is the last one although she complain endlessly that her dreams have been dark of late. Olivia felt the deep fear in her all her children of late, but Damiene had most fear of them all. So, Olivia use one of her many gifts to immediately cast a spell. The energy flow between Olivia's fingers and wave them across her daughter's body to build an energy field around the child younger mind in hopes to end the dark dreams.. This alone instantly reach Damiene and the other children fell into deeper sleep. This is when Olivia realizes Helen is already lost to the ancient evil of the elders. She decides to cast a spell on the rest so no harm will come to them when she faces her daughter Helen. She then joins Bertha on the main bridge.

Bertha saucer ship look ancient but is far advance then any alpha prime spaceship. Has old Bertha seemed to fade in and out of time by great speed by this special Ai. Olivia knew this spaceship had travel to the forbidden zone undetected in the past. Just has Olivia enters the main bridge controls of old Bertha, the AI announce their arrival to the last edge of the forbidden zone. Olivia looks out the view screens saw only the blackness of space and the far-off galaxy of Ea. She is confused and muttered to Bertha. "You sure it's here that your Black Scorpion spaceship will come out this dark zone."

Bertha sitting in her command chair, while press several buttons has the spaceship fired a string of energy plasma into the dark zone and spoke her thoughts out loud. "Yes, my sister takes a go look of the choices we must make at our darkest hour." Olivia could only watch has the energy plasma burst reveling what is waiting for them in the forbidden zone. She gasps at the first sight. Hundreds of thousand dark warships of many sizes, just has each flare exploded reveals more ships with only one moving around and darting and jerk around other ships. Olivia final spoke to Bertha. "Who are they dear sister I have no memory of text that explain these ships. Bertha final gave haunting laugh, just has she explains. "These are the Jung Zee a lost tribe of insectoids highly intelligent and dangerous, they lost their world 10,000 years ago by our forefather's cleanings war. They wait for their new queen to invade our space and conquer the 12 galaxies."

Olivia panic stepping closer to her sister." You know this already how come you never told me we need my husband to protect this border from invasion." Bertha laugh loudly pointing to the left of the view screen has she went on with her words that seem to shake Olivia with fear. "This the paradox sweet sister looks at the next flare it will show you everything claim Bertha in truth dear sister this is our fourth attempt."

Olivia shook her head no but step closer to view screen her mind repeated no this not real. However, Bertha words kept explaining the story of the forbidden zone. "For we are daughters of Krell, and they are related to Krell also so this a family affair. We are part of the paradox and the vortex of time. Every culture on every planet in twelve galaxies are tied to this giant vortex."

The last flare exploded to reveal the vortex of a large spinning hole in space its swirling dark energy seem to pull at her soul. Just has thousands of voice echo in both Olivia and Bertha's mind. Olivia screams out her words." No, I will not accept this I rather run away with my remaining children." Bertha mutter softly, "only you can stop this claim Bertha has she pause to look at the black scorpion is about to enter our solar system. You must listen Olivia. These vortexes are connected to every solar system across the endless galaxies for we came from another earths name Alpha prime and in truth it was destroy by your Helen future life. Olivia went slightly hysterical once more. "I do not believe you she keeps to good side of telepaths she never hurts anyone.

Bertha shrugged her shoulders went on explaining while they both are watching the screen and the voice of the ship AI is announcing four large ships have just appear on their Radar. Bertha gave a deep sigh and tried to convince Olivia that Helen had turn evil. "You forget she lost her husband and first child, but I know they have been killed by your grandfather General Edward Savage. When Hellen finds out she will lose her mind. who will be one of the new spider queens that is being created by the evil elder name Ru. Their DNA are infused and its only you that can stop all this Olivia you must kill your daughter I am sorry for this burden but this the truth."

Olivia went silent upon hearing the last words of Bertha has the image of her sister accepting a bribe from Edward to keep quiet about the death of Helen's husband and child. Her telepathic powers erupt has an invisible force, reached out and attack Bertha with a choke hold while raising her off the metal floor. You betray me and my daughter so you can watch our family die a cruel death. In addition to your own greed, you plan to start the destruction of Alpha Prime confederation for money. While you hide the truth from me, thus making Helen be alerted by the elder poison. I will kill you myself you are the true monster, Bertha Blackstone."

"I had no choice in this mater" squealed Bertha, has struggle to break free from Olivia death grip, and on to claim the truth. "I follow the rules of the children of the light they are adjusting time itself I am sorry Olivia you have no choice." Bertha eyes pop out of her head and glugger her last breathe before her body instantly faded away

The Ai continually announces the distant the large world ships and warning that missiles have been fired on course to the Black Scorpion. Olivia is saddened by the grim resolve knowing the truth she sends message to Helen warn her off. "My darling Helen stay back and fight the urge to change into Jung Zee Queen. I now know the truth my eldest daughter it was grandfather "General Edward Savage that kill your husband and child. He is on Omega 4 world ship there I will permit you to take your revenge but go no further I beg you do not force to kill you, my sweet daughter."

"I am now calling myself the entity of time, it is to late mother with the help of my sisters we shall multiply and conquer all," came a dark haunting voice. Olivia burst into blood tears when she heard all her children joining Helen has, she feels the hate and words of revenge to all Alpha primes. That all humanity will be wipe out and then I shall claim all the twelve galaxies for the Jung Zee race. Olivia had no choice, knowing she had lost everyone even the two unborn twins all must be destroy. She steps forward to the command chair and sat down to steer the ship into the vortex. While arming all the ships weapons aim at the Black Scorpion. She can hear her husband calling her come back that he had little Mira. He feels her pain, just has he sees what about to happen and cries out no. Old Bertha spaceship fire twenty missiles and laser cannon fire at her Daughters ship. The energy released by the missiles also effect the vortex that burst out brightly and engulf across the 12 galaxies.

CHAPTER 6

THE CHILDREN OF THE GODS

*L*ord Id looked down and saw the massing of his two pets who wanted to pay homage to him. He was pleased the Myra had not killed its hatchings, has done the Jung zee. He whispers to the new Ru of all what he had done during her absence. She shows interest, while the two travel towards the new light. He reviews their history and their ways as to control the insecta with his god like powers. They are my children as well as yours since we are considered gods, that we created perfection with a few adjustments. Ru amuses herself with this adult version of the child she befriended long ago. She still struggled with the memories of her demise and waits for Lord Id to finish his long speech of what he did to the Jung zees.

His caretaker's choice was an insect race called the Jung Zee hordes in the Corus system from a planet named Auriga. Their world was a rich jungle planet with forests, wildflowers, and an abundance of water. Insects are a large group of arthropods of large portions sizes. Their species range in many forms Ten thousand dragonflies, two thousand piranha beetles that were the main predators, twenty thousand types of grasshoppers, one fifty thousand flying true bug, two hundred thousand wasp, bees, ants and three hundred thousand beetles. They ranged in size from a small seed to giant boulders. Before the rise of the Jung zee hordes, they lived deep in the dark foliage of the living forest small to blue dragonfly equal to a leaf eater. Like all insects, they are pre-programmed by their mothers or queen based on the colony. Insects possess segmented bodies supported by exoskeletons, a hard outer covering made mostly of chitin. Their body is dividing into a head, a thorax, and an abdomen Jung zee head supports a pair of sensory antennas, a pair of compound eyes, and mouthparts. The thorax has six legs and the abdomen made up of eleven segments some of which may be reduced or fused has respiratory, excretory, and reproductive structures. Design for speed and agility to escape or attack their enemies. Their nervous system can be dividing into a brain and a ventral nerve cord. Jung zee adults, during a select by the new queen, grow a set of wings located on the second and third thoracic segments. Insects are the only invertebrates to have developed flight, and this has played an important part in their success. The winged insects and their wingless relatives make up the subclass Pterygote. Insect flight is not very well understood, and they rely heavily on turbulent aerodynamic effects. The primitive insect groups use muscles that act directly on the wing structure. The more advanced groups making up the Neoptera have foldable wings and their muscles act on the thorax wall and power the wings indirectly. These muscles are able to contract multiple times for each single nerve impulse allowing the wings to beat faster than would ordinarily be possible. The young queen hatches and flutters away. She leaves a hormonal scent for the winged male Jung zees to follow. This marks the success of the nest to spread across its world in great numbers. Once the queen selects her new location, the males build the nest and fill it with food. The best hunter and builder of the nest are the ones selected to mate. After mating, the queens eat the warrior for the chemicals inside which help the eggs to survive and hatch a new colony.

Most insects hatch from eggs but other queens brought more ovoviviparous or viviparous eggs, and all undergo a series of moults as they develop and grow in size. The inelastic exoskeleton necessitated this manner of growth. The Jung zee moulting is a process by which the individual escapes the confines of the exoskeleton in order to increase in size and grows a new and larger outer covering. With some insects, the young, called nymphs are similar in form to the adults except that the wings do not develop until the adult stage. Insects showing this incomplete metamorphosis are termed hemimetabolous. Holometabolous insects show complete metamorphosis, which distinguishes the Iniopterygian and includes many of the most successful insect groups. In the Jung zee species, an egg hatches to produce a larva, which is generally worm-like in form and divided into five different forms. The natural way of the Jung zee consists of a drone or worker pushed by the warrior clan before the great change into the next level.

"The first queens' follow your instruction saving DNA of other species which I used as cross-reference to natural bees and ants. Jung zees practice their skills for hunting and fight for every morsel of food to stay alive. It is awaking into a higher conscious level which came from visitors from the sky based on the stories passed on by the queen of the Jung zee," giggled Lord Id.

If the nest is too big, the new queens chose the larva and gave it a blue liquid of fermions to be fertile and the liquid placed into the princess chambers of the hive. The sudden attack of piranha beetles causes a great panic in the nest. Amid a battle came the brightly coloured angels from the god of light.

New queens became aware of a new destiny as they released a chemical toxin, which kills the attacking piranha beetles, and any other predator attracted to the blood and gore in the coming years. The toxin spread with the winds affecting all the planet species of insects. With only the Jung zee left, they begin to moult several times into larger forms eating the dead bodies of fallen insects for years to come. With this strange sudden development came their first awaking to their worlds around them and changed their ways to save their race. Their brains grew large and the skills of building a better nest and tools improved their harvest of resources in their world.

This race lived to prove its worth to the Queen to mate and bring forth a new order by passing on the knowledge learned from generations. The Jung Zee evolution has a twenty-year cycle life where they hatched from eggs and learned more each generation. They formed into larva for the next twenty months. They harden into pupa and step out into nymphs' form. They range in size from one to three feet. Overtime the food had vanished. They turned on themselves. During the mating season, their face glows red, they would fight and kill each other to mate with their new Queen.

The history of the Jung zee is long past a million years, which begins the exodus from the planet Auriga in the Corus system. Their dim sun gave off an orange colour as it rose from the east the queen mind stretches out the signal for time for the mating season to bring the prize worthy of the new queens'. They massed in great numbers to hunt other life forms. She gave orders that their resources must be refined, machines repaired, and energy banks recharged to escape our worlds doom.

A million years ago, it slowly became aware when they defeated their rivals by a strange plague, but we both know that was our influence. With your help and the illusions from the gods of the light the Queen was warned of the time their planet's destruction by the eruption of their sun. They collected every item on their planet in two and placed them in their living ships with vast amounts of food for the trip to find the gods.

The Jung Zee race took the challenge to the stars to escape the doom, recalled by a musical voice and the promise of a new world passed down the generation in song in the being of their awaking mind. The crystal and you bind their fate to us. They were to join and be one with a living god of the three suns and enter EA solar system. Twelve young queens of the Jung zee raced across the vastness of space. Only six made it to the far planet and transformed into a glowing Jung zee warrior. The queens instantly believed that he is part of their ancient god passed on by the pervious queen. They all called me Lord Id god of warriors. The queens believed your story, if they mated with me, by a single touch, they will inherit the cosmos of time.

The image transferred into the mind of Ru by Lord Id's mind. It had grown quite powerful over her absence. She had stated that they were imperfect, maybe it was harsh words. The memories of the drone's ripping at her flesh are still sharp in her mind.

"One thousand years have passed since your death caretaker. I have no clue of what happened. The crystal would not speak of it," mumbled Lord Id.

"My mind is still in the fog, please continue with the history of what you have accomplished these long years," hissed Ru.

"Very well, caretaker as you wish" whispered Lord Id, the mind refocuses and transmits the images once more.

Out of the six large spider queens, only three survived the mating exchange of essences. The total of eggs reached ten billion. His children, in larva form, developed the skills of mathematics and shapes with which they built his temples to honour Lord Id and Ru. On every planet is a temple that praises us.

The changes occurred as they reached nymph stage. They hunted for prey and offered it in prayer to the living god. In adult form, they fought each other to claim the new queen for mating. Since gasses cloud, superior mind would wait for the last standing warrior then possess the last warrior and proclaim him Lord Id.

The new race came from the one of the dark spheres. They plotted to use the insect form for a more violent and a sharp increase in intelligence. Lord Id continues to mate with the new Queens from the second generation. They mate several times because of the multiple birth chambers within its lower abdomen. The lone gases sphere plans for the return of its partner the caretaker to continue their plans for perfection. It is never satisfied during the third generation and wipes out the nest by the millions as its restarted the tests for perfection.

Thousand of years of many generations had risen then fallen in a murderous rampage with some results. The Entity altered the meaning in the message to promote a more purified race from each queen.

By altering her atomic structure for a perfect race their message also altered the destruction of any race that encountered the next generation. This modest change increased their skill of building structures and tunnels and portals to travel from planet to planet in the Ea solar system, in leaps and bounds to dominate other races.

The formless beings tried desperately to lower their violent nature and change their thought patterns to build the perfect race. The gaseous sphere thought by giving himself a permanent body to rule and be the single challenge of a living god named Lord Id. He had almost reached his goal when another race killed the caretaker. Lord Id quickly blamed the Jung zee who wiped out their drones and three large queens except for three, which he placed on other planets He made each queen, eat all the energy of his beloved caretaker in hopes to bring her back in another form. It did raise the essence of her chi over the next ten generations, which multiplied quickly.

"I see the truth. You felt emotions for the first time of rage and despair over my death. I am deeply touched, but it was not their fault but the other two-legged creatures that did most of the damage by killing the larger queens and their drones. Much of what we need was in their blood. That is why I feel something is missing," whispered Ru.

"Then I failed you caretaker," growled Lord Id.

"Well at first, I thought so. Especially the young grubs, which developed faster in form of structure and organizing skill based on one mind, appeals to me," muttered Ru.

"In addition, your emotion of anxiety mixed with anger plays with their thoughts that a success in mating with this last cycle showed promise of my return for which I am grateful," hissed Ru. She continues with a deeper apology for having destroyed much of the next generation.

"The next generation gives me hope. Now that you have returned, with our combined efforts they will develop faster in their stages but completely different in form and intelligence. Even the new queen like you gave promise after a thousand of years and many generations had become more powerful although they lost some of its history," mumbled Lord Id.

"I have changed the history of each queen for a joining with a future race. I have influences to alter the queen's atomic structure to what he considers a perfect race. I altered the message to destroy any race that comes in contact to the next generation of Jung zee. With you we can start to right our own stories."

"Yes, your modest changes over the years increased their skill of building structures and tunnels and portals to travel from planet to planet in the Ea solar system. The hope of our offspring will spread over seventy planets that orbit the red sun of Omega." He garbled his thoughts "perfection in life is my existence, for it is in me that I must pass on to a new race they will inherit this solar system."

"I am glad you agree that this message planted deep within the brain of the Jung zee primed their hunting skills to perfection. With strict rules and order, they ensure the purity of their race," hissed Lord Id.

"I do disagree to start a religions sect towards us as a god of Ea, Lord Id and goddess Ru of fertility. We built temples to honour the old ones and their transformation into superior beings. You must remember to keep it hidden for they will hunger to steal the crystal from us," implied Ru.

"I did not see it that way Ru, when I encountered the Myra race that is very religious and traditional in many ways. The sleeping queen is a perfectionist also and not swayed with my powers of persuasion, so I created a brother in Myra form that has brought her around to my way of thinking."

"I do not like her, she laughed at my warnings and threatened to kill me if anyone touches her nest," snapped Ru.

"She is very independent that way, but I must wait to see the hatchlings before I do anything in haste," mumbled Lord Id.

"Then enlighten me with your knowledge great one," sang Ru.

"It is my honour to show you the origins of the Myra race that you had also selected caretaker."

"We shall wait here as they reach the other edge of the solar winds" quoted Lord Id.

Ru's mind gathers the images once more from Lord Id. His words troubled her when he said that she had selected a beetle race. There was some truth but the image did not match what she had thought was the chosen ones for perfection.

The second group of beings named the Myra clan were wanderers of space more connected to building blocks from other worlds of natural life forms. This group collected and naturalized the energy source of the array. The Myra clan, from their beginning, came from the first galaxy in the cosmos in the far off reaches of deep space. Born from a dream, as their story goes, by their first queen trapped inside a molten rock that explodes to form its original planet named Jadgaea. Their ravenous hunger for energy to eat more vegetation, protein, and minerals inside the rock core of the planet destroyed the planet.

The children of the light saved them and gave them a new purpose with a special gift to satisfy their enormous hungry. The first queen agrees to remove her eyes so she may dream of a new beginning for her race. They made a promise to mate with the next generation among the gods of light and darkness and create living ships moving form solar system with her children planting and altering planets into a living paradise. So goes the legend, her offspring develop into many stages from eggs to larva, pupa, and then a bluish beetle in a twenty-year cycle. She selects the choice ones to be the high guardian level and gives the beetle a special drug altering into higher and more intellectual insect to a cross over with biped features. They had an oval head with large ebony eyes flat nose and a wide mouth. They have soft colour fur from the back of their heads down its back and chest area. They also have four well-built arms with a three fingered hands and large legs muscles for agility and speed.

Their race became aware from the big bang that burst through their universe energy, which brought them a goal to prepare the coming of the chosen race that shall inherit the cosmos. Myra beings are highly evolving minds that exist to fulfill their own prophecy of balance. This was given to them long time ago by the gods of light when their living ship neared the three suns of is young system. Their hearts burst with joy finding the white crystal. This alone renews their faith of the coming life force promised in their ancient books to escape the doom of the inner world, which collapsed into a black hole.

Over one hundred thousand years they stretched across through out all galaxies. The Myra race traveled in three living world ships. Their sleeping queen felt that Lord Id was the god foretold in their ancient books. This makes him a god of creation. Her mind had no understanding between good and evil. The religious group of the Myra race tend to adjust to the environments around them on the planets with other races. Their goal is to travel to the next system from time to time. Lord Id powers drew them into Ea space with his seeing eye that he gained from the caretaker before her premature death. He believes these beings are more like his beloved caretaker. He wanted to use their methods to spread out his children to control the cosmos. He believed the Myra race were meeker and more dedicated to the peaceful ways of nature. They were a wandering race whose purpose was to create breathable planets with floral and fawn, forest produce and wild life to every solar system in the cosmos.

"I was right she is dangerous to our cause. We must eliminate the animal as soon as possible Lord Id," hissed Ru.

"Why do you say that caretaker, she had done much to bring life to many of the planets that both races share," snarl Lord Id. His eyes challenged Ru; she lowers her head and mumbles the first reason.

"You forget our first change with Krell, you cast a spell as did he, It is you that quickly accepted the challenge, before he disappeared with the elders. This left us alone to travel endlessly until the crystal came alive. Do you not remember," challenged Ru?

"Forgive me, the thousand years I waited for you were long and lonely ones, the sleeping queen helped me as well as most of the religious sects," Id explained with a slight annoyance in his thoughts.

"Krell claimed the final battle with the children of the light to challenge us and stop our perfections to rule the cosmos. If she were here, I would kill her and drink every ounce of her blood," growled Ru.

Lord Id shakes his head, and then begins to explain.

"I probed her mind; no such creatures were encountered since the first generation when the first queen gave them a blue planet named Azure. These creatures had never left it. Alternatively, they cannot exist outside that dimension. There is no threat, and the sleeping queen pledges herself to my brother."

"Then show me more to ease my fears, my long-time brethren," grumbled Ru.

The imagery begins once Lord Id's words fade as she sees the open cross section of a Jung zee queen and warrior. Base on their drive to look for the chosen race, Lord Id uses the power of its two brains and lures the wandering race into Ea space. He offers freely, to the high priest and the sleeping queen, six planets to rebuild a breathable atmosphere and end their travels in the Ea solar system. Lord Id used words of the Jung zee to cross-reference to the Myra holy book of truth to bring in a connection. He used all his tricks to take control and direct the two races for ten generation.

The Myra kept to their faith while the war like Jung zee pushed the violence as they fought with each other over their beliefs on whose prophesy was correct. The superior being who the Myra believed was the first god to guide them made a peace treaty to ensure the time of destruction related to the maturity of the new queen in both races. The mating methods of the Myra were quite different from the Jung zee.

Lord Id greets them nine hundred years ago with opened arms when he touches their living ship. Their gasses creature learns of the same prophesy which matches from each word to Jung Zee horde legend. They travelled the cosmos to find the living god of the mist to travel the endless space. He finds the sleeping queen only relates to him as a ghost. The Lord Id transformed in the remains of one of their dead high priest that they honour within the holy shrine of the light. He is over joy that his caretaker's choice of Ea solar system gave him his chance to rule over the cosmos of the one single mind.

Lord Id showed them the greatest gift by giving the newcomers eleven planets to terra form to a living planet. They dropped to their knees and opened their chest to reveal their true love and praise him. They named him after the dead high priest. Lord Id proclaims himself as a dream master of the Myra order.

He watches and learns many secrets by spending time with the high guard of the Myra race. He sees the twelve distinct Myra leaders with six others; the warrior cast, agriculture cast, religions cast, the element cast of earth, wind, water, and fire the next mating ritual priest of the ancient text with the sleeping Queen. The method of mating from the moment of conception of a single child slightly disappoints Lord Id and he thinks twins or more would be effective. He studies for years their strange ways.

The sleeping queen deposits a child yearly on each of the eleven planets. Has the child grows; it alters its makeup it deposits small eggs in the soil across the planet. After time a small blue beetle stepped out in large numbers to fertilize the soil and rearrange the landscape of all the planets. At the end of the year, they went into a pupa state for a long sleep. They emerged five years later has winged creatures, blue in skin tone with red eyes, white hair, two arms, large hands and feet with sharp talons. Lord Id found them quite attractive.

On a moonlight night the high priest initialize the slow change and one hundred thousand Myra walked the planet from North Pole to South Pole four times to awaken the seeds of life. There they cut their arms several times and summoned the wind for the old ones to give new life to complete the circle. The winged creatures devoured the flesh of the dead elders and spread the excrement across the planet. After time the wings creatures died giving birth to the final stage of the Myra child and the rebirth of the planet from the seeds. The child slowly gathers up the new seeds to restart the journey into adulthood of a Myra. Only the sleeping Queen stirs up and chooses the mate from the young pool of Myra that took many generations for him to mate with the Queen.

The sleeping Queen would awake every twenty years for the mating season. She would choose the elder that carried the next seed of life to the planet. Lord Id had to learn their ways. He would attempt to mate with the sleeping Queen. She was more a ghost of the Myra form but more of a sightless blue six-legged beetle in a physical presence. This was his first time that he had to divide himself to take over the body of a young Myra, which the sleeping Queen named Eltross of the light. His fur became long and curly. He was smaller in stature than a normal Myra. He knew the scriptures of the holy book and the added knowledge he shared with Lord Id. They could not co-exist on the same planet, so Lord Id went back to the planet Zlotoo. Overtime they would share their knowledge and power, like equals being one of the same within each other's chi.

The day came when the Jung Zee crossed paths with the Myra and both queens suggested an exchange of males for a peace ceremony. The high priest of the Myra argues that the custom of eating a male is against the traditions of the nest. Lord Id wanted to join the mates of each species. It took many years before he could cross breed. They were hoping that this was the next generation to become one race of their perfect world. Eltross finally mates with the sleeping queen on the eleventh generation. The eggs were about to hatch at the same time of the Jung zee hatchings but now due to the chaos of the Jung zee all is lost on one generation.

The new forming light outside of Ea solar system caused the disaster. Ru fidgets in the sphere with her thoughts heavily on the sleeping queen and the bright light that lay before them. Ru had a burning sensation with her thoughts of the sleeping queen and blurted out her first thought.

I wish to mate with you when we return, I want to start the prefect race without any rivals, thought Ru. Lord Id grunted an answer, *yes of course I shall be honoured to share my essence*. Ru then request, "I want to see your long voyage before you return in this body of a queen spider."

By his expression and last words, she felt a cold chill in explaining her absence for a thousand year. Ru explains, her first encounter of the dark hair woman name Mrs. Helen. Nightshade, who mind had telepathic powers above her own. During her time in the sleep chamber, she felt a probing mind not just one but eight equal to her mind gift and that of an elder mind and thought process. They were all merging in one spot outside the ring galaxy.

"I was alarmed to see each ship interact with the spiders. My mind travel too far to return; when you came to the rescue me it was too late, and I went into a deep sleep. The other part of me stayed in the human female mind, I felt trapped but curious to learn it secrets. This what intrigued me to stay close and read her every thought and memory. Until I took over the human side of emotions for revenge that started the quest to take control of the 12 galaxies.

"She was a complex being whose mind surpassed even me. I thought that she was one of the children of the light, yet she had a cruel side, which I fed on to get closer. Some how she felt my presence and I thought I could control her. My first attempt I tried trickery by bringing her down to Zlotoo. I failed then we fought but that is when the ship attacked me. I found myself split in two with the alien being. We shared two bodies one old and one reborn in a strange tube. The man slave carried the old body of the commander out to the loading dock and cast it in space. This is when I become confused for, we continue fighting on a spiritual plane. The reborn moved away to travel the stars in folding space.

"Our minds melded then splintered into pieces. It is hard to explain by the imagery, for I appear in many tiny life forms. What I have become is a child of many females and a single male. I stare at one child the chill struck us. When I struggled to awake back into the human form, I found that I was floating in space and the other was still with me. We floated freely for some time. The heat from the red sun burned my human flesh. The human side that had struggled with me gave in wanting to return to her ship. I awoke feeling like a child from the space and burning by the heat. I summoned all my powers of my mind gift. When her ship took off and left our solar system, I felt the strange emptiness that I still have trouble within my mind.

"The sudden pain weakens my attempts to capture the ship. I look down at the burns and blood blisters, which dribble, from my human body. I descend to our planet to heal. During this time, I tried to free my spirit and energy from this human body. The commander seems to know that she is dying and uses her last strength to hold in that body. I did not now that she had angered the spider queen that was my blunder. I underestimated her powers. The mind gift she had was equal to mine, but since we melded, we both became one being. The drone worms and the queen spiders attack the human but after I spoke to them that I was Ru, they only provoke their rage and started to tear the human flesh of Mrs. Nightshade. It gave me satisfaction that I had beaten this two-legged creature, but I was deceived.

"The spiritual world opens a door. She smiled and floated away. Fury took me as I gave chase, only to be lost in a maze of a giant forest of trees. I spent a lifetime searching for that female and I had to endure a life span of a human. Her memories are within me, but it feels as if a heavy curtain blocks my mind. Three times, I thought I had the answer. The fourth brought me back to you when I became aware the new light could hold the answers my Lord Id. The shock and rage within me took many years waiting for revenge; it awoke my blood lust once again towards the female. I could hear the echoes of her laugh in my mind from her challenged words."

Lord Id visualized too much to articulate what she had experienced for a thousand years. He did however feel the emptiness and the hunger to eat and drink the blood of the creature that had done this to the caretaker. It gnawed deep in his emotions that he was helpless and then understood the blood lust that she had killed so many while he slept. All warriors started the battle to mate with the only Jung zee queen. The drone worms deep inside the planet crust would come out and fight to be the new leader. He did not mention this since their focus was on what had caused this new light source. With only the Myra children about to hatch, they would be the first children of the gods in the second race. His thoughts went to the religious sect foretelling the third race of beings. He wonders could this two-legged creature be the third host and the catalytic to one-day rule over the cosmos. He was about to ask the caretaker this question as if she had felt his thoughts.

"This female is not worth to be part of our plans; this is why I killed and destroyed the nest. In your rage, you force fed the flesh of the dead alien to the three queen's spiders."

"The human DNA is within the structure of the spiders DNA I felt her spirit in them taunting me. They are only good for food and fertilizer to grow our fungus to supply our next generation. They will never come here; I will kill them with my poison bite," hissed Ru.

"I can see by the imagery that you portray your personal irritations and frustrations, but it was the crystal instruction to ensure your rebirth. I have kept my pledge to you but now I alone have the final say my brother as well. You cannot do anything with out my permission," snapped Lord Id.

"Why did the crystal split in half once more my Lord Id," inquired Ru?

"It happened when I divided myself into Eltross; he is my new partner since your sudden departure."

Ru was about to bark a thousand curses when the dark space before them exploded into a rainbow of brilliant colours. They absorbed the energy of the small wave that rushed pass them. My curiosity made a decision to take a closer look at a wide angle before making any dangerous moves. Somehow, the energy from the blast caused several colour rings. This nagged at Ru with something from her deep memories that the presence of the female was nearby laughing at her. She felt safe with her child that she had nurtured and guided, although some pain came from it, he had kept his word to bring her back to Ea.

Dragon eye
Logbook
Planet name Azure
Time 99999.09

The explosion of the planet Azure shook across time and space from its north and south poles. Even their sun felt a flicker of solar explosions spewing out energy, disrupting communications and surface power supplies. The leader watches from her office the reports of the minor injuries. Sabrina was thankful no deaths had occurred, even though none had died before. She presses down on the com channel.

"To all planet leaders please report to the council meeting."

This announcement spread to the under-ground complex in several languages. Krell in his forest realm was quite annoyed to be call back to the main terminal to meet the other beings. The news of his failure was well talk about with blame laid on the Elders, this weigh heavily on his shoulders. Only Sabrina gave him a little hope and comfort with their advance medical experiences she had separated the female DNA by adjusting his chromosomes. Their energy crystal washed over his body and returned to a male form. He became his true self with all the memories that he had from the first visit.

In his heart, he asks if the female version can remain. He loved life in general, adopted the female child, and named it Emerald so it can live within his new world that Sabrina freely gave the new race called the forest dwellers.

The entire elder race of one billion were altered similar to Krell's green skin, white hair, and wide range of height in both sexes and ages. His people quickly adjusted to the new life faster then Krell had thought. He still had problems with his speech. He prefers to send messages telepathically. All accept his ways and authority. Not one elder or forest dweller would blame him for Ru's betrayal of their race. This alone pleases his mind and eases much of the burden. Overtime he became sharp with other skills such has healing by touch and master of lightning control of wind and water. He loves his knew world. It had life and gave balance within his spirit. Krell hated to leave it for council meetings. It took a while to understand the nature of the Azure planet, and the children of the light. He found so much similarity in his teachings and beliefs were all the same except for the idea to measure intelligence. In the last visit, Sabrina expressed and showed examples of emotion in some races that push the strength of awareness to a higher plane of wisdom and knowledge. That any failure is in part one of the learning tools to many intellectuals' beings.

His small group of leaders from his old council were at the portal waiting for his arrival before entering the chamber of the circles. The group walks through the shimmering light and appear in a loud chamber of voices full of languages he barely understands yet he could feel great anger, despair, and fear. Sabrina explains that he did not need to speak but could express his thoughts so all would understand him. This is his third meeting within two years since his arrival. The chamber was a simple room with a perfect circle. Each race had their own entrance; all were equals in this chamber. Sabrina floats down from her private chamber to the center of the room. Her body is back to six feet tall, completely sealed in a silver metal form. Her eyes expressed the mood she was in at this moment of time. The chamber went silent. Her eyes blazed a deep red.

"Time has come the wars are about to begin. All of you had a part in this that had caused the paradox. Blame is not on one race but all. We attempt to hide from far beyond time itself. The sleeping queen especially builds our world to save all of you so that you may live in harmony within the worlds of your choice. Our paradox shall find its way to influence us here like a twist of fate." Sabrina stops to let her words sink into the councillor's minds. She slow spins to face the wide range of beings.

"You may bring in our prisoners while I explain the charges of genocide of humanity and two other races to be judge and settle our next move in the continuous battle of the dark entity."

The floor opens as the figure rose from the depths surrounded by the child of the light; the chained figure was a transparent creature with empty eyes. Her hair was yellow with skin tone had a shade of blue color that went from her arms up to her face while her lower half-covered in dark gases mist.

"This female creature destroyed a planet of three different types of beings two insectoid and one biped they lived in peace and had shared natural telepathic powers. She must be punished by our laws, the usual penalty is to be erase from time and space, or long-term sleep," claimed Sabrina.

"I am not guilty," wailed a female voice. Krell noticed her tone the feelings were strong of innocent.

"Quiet the child of the gods of Ea we have proof of your dark deed of genocide, snapped Sabrina.

"I am not a child of Ea; my mother is the sleeping queen. It was her orders to end that timeline and start again. They shall all be reborn within one woman she alone will carry their new seed of the three races."

"Yes, that is what you claim," snarled Sabrina as she slapped her metal hand down hard on a table. Krell felt fear of the silver woman to silent the prisoner's wails.

"It is a fact leader of the light; my mother, the sleeping queen passed on instructions to destroy the evil festering and growing on the innocent. The dark Lord Id gave a set of eyes that brought a vision of great disaster. She left messages for us to follow that are to destroy the evil before it would spread. It saved many worlds, no one race should dominate the weaker ones until they learn wisdom, knowledge of the ages; harmony, love, and balance," claimed the ghostly figure.

Krell is quite impressed with her commitment to her beliefs and that the words she stated carried an emotional connection. Many around him stir and complain almost the same thoughts that he clearly felt. Sabrina eyes glow a softer colour of red has she tilts her head.

"We know your mother well. This planet is one of her gifts that you are in Azure she made for us. To hold true the ones that have achieved the great levels that you claim that is in you. The poison is you that wipe out all life without mercy and compassion. These beings will never reach us," Sabrina snarls.

She points to an empty section in the chamber and the crowd whisper in agreement, Krell became confused. His memory in the council chamber was more emotional than this thought Krell. A new voice leaps over the whispering.

"How did you measure your evil among the innocent nameless prisoner!"

"I do not understand the question" all thought the voice is vary familiar "is that you Emerald of the forest people."

Krell was completely stunned as she had only existed a year. She never left his side. What is this all about? He stands up stiffly and glares at Sabrina while he moves towards the prisoner. His mind gift reaches out and washes over the ghostly figure. The images all came to place even the appearances of the sleeping queen had to face, one he recognizes instantly and loudly stated for all to hear.

Ru eyes were on the sleeping queen this one had been fooled. He sees the trickery; his eyes darken with rage and barks out his anger to the prisoner in normal speech,

"My mate fooled you; she possesses your mother spirit through the evil eyes. You have sinned by ignorance little one."

"Father please, she see what you see the tempest that had infect the innocent to feed her hunger," whispered Emerald.

The prisoner weeps heavily and wails loudly which echoes around the chamber. Sabrina caught off guard by Krell's way to find the truth. He projects in all the minds within the chamber ended this trail. The prisoner became repentant. Emerald returns to the prisoner, she studies the ghostly figure vary closely, trying her best to remember when they became friends. Her short life had no connections.

"When and where did we meet," grunted Emerald.

"On Terrain 6, I was looking for my mother to get the last instruction. You taught me the ways of the forest until someone killed you. I grieve for you. It is good to hear your voice again," murmured the prisoner then giggled with another strange comment.

"Your last words to me always puzzled me until now."

"What did I say that amused you unknown prisoner," Emerald flatly remarked.

"You said no one really dies but are reborn to continue the journey of wisdom and knowledge. You begged me not to revenge your death," garbled the prisoner while her voice weaken as the memory of her death blossom in the prisoner's mind.

"I am not who you think I am, for this is the first time I met you. I do feel your pain and I ask this council that we correct this error and learn more of the world Terrain 6," suggests Emerald.

"Undoing time is not a quick fix. There are many dangers as we speak a great danger with the Entity that will soon arrive. Born from this prisoner the destruction of Terrain 6 it speeds straight to us destroying all the worlds that once were yours."

Krell stood, realizing that Ru and the child had unleashed an evil from the past to the future. Sabrina eyes change colour of a pale green, she had guess his next large suggestion. Emerald steps back respective to her father authority. She already knew what his mind and heart thought about life in general.

"It is a dangerous just to wait for the end. I myself have learned this in my failures. I wish to take on this task and fight through time itself to keep our ways true for all. I have thought of nothing else but a chance to redeem myself towards the living cosmos," claimed Krell.

"You already know of this variant flux of time and the death that approaches us. If you wish to fight it will take this battle from our future, to the present and beyond the past itself," barked Sabrina.

The crowd stirs with an open discussion over the two choices of fighting and accepting the end. Suddenly a voice spoke out to break the silence. To most, it was incoherent in the chamber. They realized that it came from the once empty seats. Krell, at the same time as many others, turn to see a two legged being dressed in white with pale coloured skin, piercing blue eyes, broad shoulders and bulky arms. He was equal in height to the silver being. He glances at Krell and bows his head slightly. Krell felt a strong familiarity to this being. The chamber whispers many names but mostly what he heard was the captain of the dragon eye.

"Yes, my friends, I have returned in time. I believe to hear the words of a great leader. He is right; we must fight and push this evil back. The other three timelines we accepted our fate and let time reline it only to begin once more our journeys. This I always believed was wrong and now I have proof," claimed the Captain in a strong voice. Sabrina being a leader floated over to the captain.

"You are too late to discuss your proof," snarls Sabrina, has she added to her words for all to hear. "A planet quake rumbles across the chamber." The crowd shouted in fear as many stirs among the alien groups.

"She is almost upon us!"

The captain waves his arms to subdue the chamber as his voice translated in the many tongues of all the cosmos life forms. Krell is intrigued and supports the two-legged creature. Emerald joins in, Sabrina eyes change to a lighter green and clapped her hands to calm the chamber. Emerald speaks out from her heart.

"The sleeping queen has seen the trickery passed on new instructions of balance and chaos to her children. Her children will truly measure the beings on Terrain 6 and most importantly to protect the fourth generation at birth. Teach them the ways of the cosmos by seeing and feeling the powers of both light and shadows. I ask all to support her cause while we push the evil back to terrain 6 for the final battle."

"My god she is alternating time as we speak," Sabrina gasped.

She glances at the prisoner who disappears as her chains drop to the floor. Hooded beings, which cover their features, appear around the captain. The ghostly figure reappeared with two small creature's one red the other blue hovering on each side. Emerald gave a yelp then quickly apologies with a nervous smile and curtsey to the new beings. Krell feeling a new danger step close to his adopted daughter and wonders what he was getting into with the children of the light. He wonders that this could be his only chance for revenge on his wife and son of the elder clan.

"We have a plan it is long and will be a struggle for all in this room. Many will choose both sides from darkness to the light; others will embrace balance or chaos. In the end the final battle will be at the waking of the fourth generation to end the paradox and total peace for all," claimed the captain.

The chorus of voice echo one word, "yes!"

Sabrina eyes turn to a softer blue and then moved to the center of the chamber. She turns to count the vote to fight or surrender to the darkness.

Krell felt a wide range of emotions within the chamber. Other children of the light entered the far door, dressed similar to the leader but in a wide range of sizes. They all gave the same positive answer to fight. Sabrina sighs, then clears her throat for all were silent

"You know that once we start the end must come at Terrain 6. Let us hope that we shall succeed. Go ahead Captain Patterson we are ready and willing to do whatever to have order within chaos and balance. Our children of the gods will rise up and judge us all"

CHAPTER 7

THE SINGLE LIGHT OF HOPE

Out of the darkness of space came a single spark, which blossomed into an electrical ion storm. It warmed the cold space to rainbow colours from super heated gases from blues, reds, and yellow to a white circling shape of a giant eye causing spirals of energy thousand of kilometres in a wide arc. Many dark objects ejected from the center of the eye storm. These inanimate objects moved at different speed but only one of them steered at greater speeds as it headed to an old NASA probe showing its age of the long travels in space.

The aged probe waited to greet the newcomers to Beta and Corus solar systems. Locking down on the moving craft it communicated a binary code in three languages of greets. No reply came from the fast ship. Suddenly, behind the craft, three other objects appeared out of the swirling clouds. The NASA probe repeated the same greet binary code. The three newcomers were small rockets. They made contact and then exploded in a fireball and disintegrated into space particles. The great energy released reflected a light on the other objects as the wave pushed them apart on different angles.

The Sol one ship from Tananaka Corporation is adrift. The ship has a large gash in the cargo hold that expels a string of debris. The backup computers of the auxiliary bridge regain basic control, set a course to the Beta system, to lock its new target to the nearest planet of Zlotoo. The scientists programmed the drive computer core to complete the ultimate mission at any cost to reach the Beta system. Since the accident, it had saved the lower stern upper floors of the bow sections. The androids frantically repaired the impossible damage.

Dark Lighter Corporation was not any luckier like the Dark ace ship it spins wildly, a dead hulk, sending an odd message of greetings from its computer core to the NASA probe. This caused silent sparks, which ignited a huge fire from a fuel leak. It super heated the interior and destroyed the entire machinery and computer control; personnel who could not take control of the situation died in flame. It became an empty shell and floated towards the Corus system aimlessly.

Grays Corporation ship was unfortunately the only survivor of this great disaster. The Hyperion 1 slowed to a crawl it had spent its fuel to escape the holocaust in the Star-gate. Mostly intact, except for some scouring along the front section with no hull damage. The transponder lights began to flicker on as the main computer core responded to the NASA probe, and then its sensors picked up the explosion. Realizing the danger the computer core stopped and awoke the main bridge crew. Without any response from the main bridge, it selected the next human in charge of the list; this was Mr. S Winter's executive assistant and Tava Pane scientist in astronomy and the most important first navigator.

Both were in deep sleep, which took eight hours before they could respond to the computer. The main computer core ran an emergency program to maintain life inside the ship. It executed a complete shut down of the main engines to keep the reserve of fuel. As it begins to explore the new outside environment of the Beta system the computer core sent a wide range of specialized probes to find the best planet for the first colony in this new system. It also sends a message back home to Earth, but found the ion storm caused too much interference. The navigator system activated air thrusters to move the ship toward the Beta solar system by the inertia of the ion storm to raise its speed to half impulse. It fell right behind the glide path of the deadly ship Sol 1.

The navigation officer's mind, Tava Pane, became clouded with the strange images played back repeatedly of two glowing lights rushing towards her. She felt cold hands and shadows all around her, touching her mind and body. They spoke in whispers and echoed in her mind. Tava began to shiver wildly. She shouts angrily.

"Get away from me; we came in peace"

The sudden appearance of Miles Oboe face with his overconfident smile seems to drop her anxiety. He gives her some water to reduce the pain in her throat. She tried to ask a question. He held his finger up across his lips to quiet her down. Tava blinked endlessly as Miles face became younger in age then blurry. She hears his voice speak oddly about an error.

"You are the beginning of the adventure; Have fun with the children of the light. They are here to help the future of humanity as well as the cosmos. We shall be here to rescue you at the end of the fourth generation."

Tava's head began to spin once more as the fire in her throat became more painful. She tried to call out for Miles to help her. Only a shadow drops over her as she struggles to wake up from a strange nightmare.

She felt and heard a presence with a high pitch voice, which helped focus her mind. She tried to flutter her eyelids to clear the vision, which increased her anxiety.

"Stop struggling Miss. Pane the blindness is only temporary, you are on a slow wake up module from this bio tube, and it will take another hour to stabilise completely. Calm down, it's me Snead Winters."

"What has happened, did we make it on the other side. Is everyone okay? I must speak to Miles," Tava muttered in a weak voice.

"I will answer all your questions once you are out of this bio tube. As for your concern for your family, they are awake and waiting for you down in the medical center. All I ask is your patience," replied the executive assistant.

Tava nodded silently as tears filled her eyes, which made them sting from the salt contact. To keep her mind occupied she recalls the recovery time from the bio tube control panel, is four to six hours. Her uniform soaking in gelatine covered her whole body. She recalled how human cells lower the body temperature into a deep hibernation state for ten years.

Her brain was cyber linked from the hibernation from computer life support to her subconscious, in a virtual reality. She felt the hands of the executive assistant as he lifted and placed her on a gurney. She suddenly started to shake wildly from the chill. He noticed her shaking and placed special heated blanket to raise her body temperature to a comfort level of warmth. Tava still tried to force herself to stare at the shadows moving around her. She wanted more answers from Snead.

"Is Miles Oboe recovering in the medical center also? I must speak to him immediately. I want to confirm we made it on the other side well across the Star-gate portal."

"No," replied M Winters, "he is stuck on the bridge with Ian Ross and your father for navigation duty. For being on the other side, yes but the computer core has not confirmed our location yet. Just relax and let your mother and the Doctor fix you up. We will keep you up to date when you feel one hundred percent. Now calm down," hissed Snead.

She felt the motion of the car elevator drop down. Fifty floors below, the elevators opened into the medical clinic. They were in utter chaos by the sound of so many voices only fed into Tava fears. The authoritative voice of her mother cut through the chaos. Being a medical Doctor and scientist on astrobiology and exobiology made her one of the mission leaders.

"Bring her in cubical twenty-three, so I can prep her in a quicker recovery. We need her now that Miles Oboe is dead," in a tight voice.

Mr Winters snarls a retort angrily.

"I see no reason to bring him up when she is not recovered from the hibernation syndrome."

"It is you that caused this entire mess by waking up the whole crew," Dr Pane snapped back.

"What is the true status of our ship Snead," Tava interrupted loudly.

"I will leave you with your mother to explain. I must report to the bridge as your Doctor suggested. She will brief you on our situation. We shall talk later when you have recovered."

Tava heard the door close after Mr. Winters left. Her mother cursed the administrator. She felt her mother hands touching her face as she gently removed the gelatine off her forehead. She felt the warmth of her mother's touch. She hums one of the old classic tunes from the past. Dr. Pane administers vitamin booster shots to bring the blood circulations back. This leads to a large pounding headache for her patient. She follows up with a second needle and eye drops to improve her vision and remove the fogginess in her mind.

During the recovery time, her mother revealed the horrible accidental death of Miles Oboe. She relates Mr. Snead Winter's error when he hit the total recall of the whole crew, because of one man's accidental death,

The navigator had many flash backs of daily meetings with her boss. He was sometimes a demanding fellow, but he had all the best qualities of a great leader. At one of those meetings, he discussed deaths in the crew and explained the chain in command. To her surprise, she realized she was third in charge of this space ship until they landed at the selected planet. Once they landed, the scientist in addition to the mining engineer will take over the whole operation of colonizing.

Tava vision was cleared and focused on her mother's face. With short black hair, deep brown eyes of a middle-aged woman and a professional manner expressed by her overconfident smile. She looks younger then forty-three. Her unusual slim body in her white Doctors' uniform covered her pregnancy Tava finally sat up as she stretched her body with some yoga exercises to untwine the tightness in her body. She gave a smirk in hopes to change the subject. She gentle touches her mother's stomach feeling a great kick. Which even surprised her mother who broke out in a giggle?

"I see baby brother is still quite active."

"It is your baby sister," replied her mother.

Her mother's eyes sparkle as she rubs her stomach and coos softly as she expresses her thoughts aloud to her daughter.

"Yes, the little one is quite active; I forgot how demanding a newborn would be. You were a dream come true for me when I had you with your father."

Suddenly the speakers came on. Dr. Elizabeth Pane requested to the emergency room thirty-five. She got up with a deep sigh then turned to suggest an idea to stimulate Tava's body.

"I think you must hurry along and go take a shower and I shall bring you some energy bars and a new uniform, little one."

Tava nodded as she got up to take her few steps alone to the shower stall. This pleased the Doctor who then leaved to respond to the urgency. Tava felt quite foolish being at the age of twenty-two and as helpless as a newborn, she pressed her will to make the necessary moves. The sonic shower hit ever corner of her body. She felt the steady warmth pulsating to every curve of her body. Miles face reappeared in her mind and his words echoed deep through her ears.

"You will have fun with the children of the light. I promise to rescue all, within the fourth generation."

She shook her head to chase away the echoing dream. The voice of her mother returned with a somewhat strain in her words. She gave her fresh towels to dry off while holding her new uniform, which is a bright red suit with military ranking of Captain. Tava Pane blinked thinking that it was what Miles Oboe was wearing when she left the bridge.

"Do not be silly, it is the spare uniform. It is unique technology equipment. When active it connects directly to the main computer core, which handles bridge control and every cyber link human as well as the clinic, bio dome, auxiliary transport room and a wide range of probes. For protection, the world ship has three squadrons and four blast boats for defence purpose," quotes her mother.

All in one touch of her arms control and the VR screen received on going data. Tava touched the coarse fabric of the automatic environment suit from deep space.

"The council all agreed that you were more reliable than Mr. Winters, based on your overall abilities in problem solving. He reacted poorly to Mr. Oboe death, and he awoke the whole crew for one man's death," stated her mother.

"Those two men have been close associates for over thirty years both sponsored by Grays Corporation like child prodigies as you and father were too," replied Tava.

"In this business of exploration, death is part of the life. We all could die in a blink of an eye. We like you always focus at our job in hand," stated her mother coldly.

Tava sat down on the medical bed and frowned heavily and felt Snead Winters pain.

"I would feel the same way if unfortunately, I lost you and father. I think the council overreacted to Mr. Winters," replied Tava sadly.

"Well maybe so, but he did admit his overreaction to the death of Miles, and he recommended you be the Captain of Hyperion one to complete the mission and that is a compliment to you," replied her mother.

She paused to touch her daughter's knee and continued to speak in a frank tone.

"You must take control of yourself. You are the best in your field as I am in mine. Now get dressed Captain T. Pane, they desperately need you on the bridge."

Tava nodded with a deep sigh. She studied the special suit filled with three linings from head to toe. The suit started to react to the young woman's body and natural shape forms tightly around her thighs, hips, and narrow waste line, around chest and shoulders like a second layer of skin. The suit started to beep as new data from the main computer core came online, as she placed the head set on. The computer acknowledged the new Captain with a verified code to pass on the bridge control and other functions, which appear as a list of various responsibilities on the view screen.

"Alpha Prime date, December 20 of the year twenty-five thirty-five, local Neptune time twenty-six hours zero four minutes passed the hour. Captain Tava Pane announce the take over control of Hyperion 1," she heard on speakers.

"I have recorded 101 mission profiles to review Capt. Pane," came a mechanical voice from the small AI computer.

"Give me a complete readout quarter speed" order Tava.

"Will comply do you wish print out with visual display on screen Captain" Computer voice replied.

"Yes, that will be fine" Tava replied.

The probes that were sent out by the computer core on emergency procedure followed the Dark ace ship and transmitted on bridge screen their video also captured Sol 1 path towards the Beta system. Capt. T. Pane saw the debris and checked on her speed which is at steady at one-quarter impulse.

"Send out a salvage crew to gather the material from the other ship," immediately ordered Tava. With her other eye she saw a distinct irritation from her mother's expression. The computer answered,

"Will comply, passed on orders. The crews alert for salvage is on standby launch in one hour thirty minutes Neptune time."

"I will be at the bridge in four hours for a staff meeting bring all issues to the meeting. In addition, I want a follow up on the Dark ace and Sol-1," ordered the captain.

"Yes, will I continue the data stream to you Captain," replied the computer voice.

"Yes," replied to the captain as she gave a long look to her mother as she chews on her energy bar. Her thoughts swarm by her mother's expression.

Just then, Dr. Ian Ross and Mr. Snead Winters entered with a long look of dissatisfaction. He is respectful to the young woman who just took command. Mr. Winters saluted her in military style with a smug look. Dr. Ross's file appears like if on cue to give her firsthand knowledge of his specialty as administrator of the leading council members for all engineering and science programs he will take control upon establishing the first colony. Tava Pane now saw an odd site that sent her pulse up when Mr. Ross became too familiar with her mother. He saw the cold stare, backs off a little, and then clears his throat, to speak his mind.

"Do not make the same mistake, like our defunct Mr. Oboe and Mr. Winters. Our goal is simple, and the council wishes too immediately colonize the first planet in the Beta system."

Tava looked at Snead who shrugged his shoulders as he eyes Dr. Ross. Tava raised her hand to stop Dr Ross from speaking then typed on her own visual control pad a playback of the death of Miles Oboe, which gave a specific read out.

Function: Playback video.
Location: Bridge.
Time: two minutes before entering Star-gate portal.

She gasped at the site of Miles Oboe bio tube filled to the brim with his blood, which shorted out the system. His flesh shrivelled up. She heard the anguish cries of Mr. Winters who continues his duties. It was Dr. Ross and her father that interfered with his job. She then looked at Dr. Ross.

"I will follow standard protocols of the laws of Alpha Prime, which clearly state to give aid, or salvage ships and help ourselves to ensure our safety. Until then there will be no short cuts into that system, our first duty is to perform a wide range of tests," quoted Captain Pane.

"See here, as head of the council goals are our first primary function, because of Mr Oboe's blunder all our fuel reserves are seriously low, if it was not for the computer core that cut down the main engines and used air thrusters, we would have fallen back into the eye of that cosmic storm. The only way is to drain fuel from our entire small ships and place everyone back in hibernation," replied Dr. Ross.

"I am wearing this command suit now and the answer is No that will never happen on my watch you may bring it up at our next meeting on the bridge. I will follow all protocols before I step into the Beta system, now if you excuse me. I must go to the bridge. Come along Mr Winters we have lots of work to do," snapped Captain Pane.

They left the room and the clinic leaving her mother and Dr. Ross alone in cubical twenty-three. His irritation is clearly shown on his face has he mumbles under his breath an insult to her daughter. She raised one eye with a smirk across her face.

"I warned you, Tava is by the book person, she knows the rules of Alpha Prime and Gray's mega corporation. She is like her father when he has a backbone. You should use more of an opposite approach instead of confrontation," voiced Dr. Pane.

Ian's mind took in her beauty ignoring her advice and looked at her in hungry fashion. He steps closer to fulfil his need to control women. His hand moved so quickly and he wraps his arms tightly around her body. She quickly forgets her words, breathes heavily, and whispers softly in his ears.

"It is too long since our last embrace, this child in me is yours as well as mine, kiss me Ian kiss me hard so your lips will linger for the rest of this long trip that we shall suffer the long separations," replied Dr. Pane.

"Liz, I will not deny our love any longer. We shall get to Beta system quicker then you think. I went and sent out a mining and construction crew to build our first mining base called Star point on the sixth planet on the outside of one of the Beta twins gas planets. Just before your daughter took control, I knew she would object. To me it is the best atmosphere with oxygen," replied Ian as he presses his lips against hers. Dr, Pane is lost in his embrace as she softly echoes in deep moans of delight...

"I do not care as long you are with me. I want more of you now then ever before."

"Then you must support me in the council meeting in four hours to force the issue," whispered Dr. Ross.

"I will do anything for you Ian," in a teasing tone; she opens her blouse revealing her breasts and places his head between them. He smiles wilfully as his head drops down between them and kisses them ever so gently.

The computer called Dr. Pane for emergency to cubical hundred nineteen repeatedly. She pulls away to leaves her lover sadly and stepped away to continue her duties.

Dr Ian Ross left alone to plot his next move. His contacts on the Dark Ace ship destroyed. Who betrayed him; luckily, he knew the protocol keys to override the other ship moments before its damage hull. Now all alone this is his chance to become a great leader of men on a new world. This fed his hunger for power. He rubbed his hands greedily; he could name any price to the rich fuel reserves back on Alpha Prime,

"No one will stand in my way," hissed Ian as he walked out of the clinic.

Meanwhile later in the bottom of the hour Neptune time. Captain Pane had a full briefing from the computer core with a new assortment of photographs and special graphs to the properties of the target planets. Mr Winters quickly formed a good working relationship with the other bridge crew that took over their post.

They were a few light-years away from the target system. The main computer had done its job to keep the ship moving towards its prime target. This pleased Tava although she will be in her late thirties when they reached the planet by her own calculations. Mr Winters suggested a one thousand kilometres search for any material for fuel. She sent out one squadron to do the visual search. The salvage crew hauled in large amounts of equipment from the damaged ship, Dark Ace and Sol1. The chimes rang to announce the council in session for all updates must be discus immediately. She steps in her meeting room to glance at the department heads, Tava eyes bulge as she lock on a six feet 3 inches tall will muscled man name Mac McKenzie a Canadian born adventurer who specialized in mining equipment with androids and giant lasers.

This is their first meeting he is the last-minute replacement of the sick engineer at the Mar's head quarters, before they lift-off to the Star-gate. He was very polite and friendly, with a strong independent feel about him. Twice Dr. Ross pushed his idea and Mr. McKenzie put him in his place voting down his proposal. The others saw that safety is more important. With most of the items settled, they move to discus the possibility of having children that could be born on the flight to the solar system.

Dr. Pane recommends using the bio dome since it is close to planetary conditions that will help the children adjust to the environment. Ian Ross grumbles his disappointment that it is a waste of time to give children any hope that they should reach the planet at all. Tava was about to give him a lecture based on her calculations when the computer called for medical assistance to the main docking bay. They had found survivors in bio tubes from the other two damage spaceship.

The Pane family with the other council members rushed down to the main loading dock. The engineer McKenzie immediately recognized the cloning tubes, somehow became active the children ranged from an infant to thirteen years old. They were a mix between males and females, almost a hundred of them Tava eyed each tube as the words of Miles Oboe rang the loudest in her brain.

"You will have fun with the children of the light. A promise has been made all shall be rescued within the fourth generation."

She walked a full circle around the device, rubbing her chin. Ian suggested ejecting them out in space because they would drain the resources of the ship's food supplies. The engineer scoffs at him with a sharp insult that made Captain Pane giggle. She looked at her mother who already knew her daughter quite well enough to see in her eyes what she intended.

"They could be our test subjects to the bio dome where we can monitor them in an Earth atmosphere to see if our children could adjust in the future," quoted Dr. Pane.

"The power supply is low in this unit. We must release them soon or they all die," muttered Tava's father who seem to be following his daughters ideas.

"They are substandard humans their bodies must be adults if you take them out now, we must teach them the skills in our society that will drain us, this is waste of time," snapped Ian Ross, and walked away with a harsh resolve in his last words.

"I want no responsibility on that part of this calamity."

Tava went to the panel as their computer analyzed the locking codes to release the clone children. She looked at the thirteen-year-old female her white hair matched her oval face.

The Canadian brought out his dark rim reading glasses and quickly types on the keyboard and broke the five-digit code. This caused the liquid to drain as the mist washed over the children. The thirteen-year-old female drops like a brick but somehow Tava caught her before she could injure herself. The girl's eye opens slowly with unintelligible words.

"Mother of the light your children have arrived. Praise the gods of our heavens to the turning of time."

The captain stunned by the strange words went slightly pale. Her father questions the statement with a little grunt.

"I always thought you would be a great mother; I think you have inherited one hundred and three children in a single hour."

Dr Pane giggles also as she administers booster shots of vitamins to bring the blood circulations to the children. They used several skiffs to haul the children into the bio dome. The words of Miles Oboe still haunt Captain Pane. She types in her request for information on the meaning of the child of the light.

"I must find the truth in his personal files," Tava says in a tight voice.

She placed the thirteen-year-old on the skiff moves back her long white hair to see her face; her eyes flutter open as she smiles warmly. They had a new mystery to solve first before they would ever start a colony on any planet in the Beta system. A strange thought crosses her mind they could be an outside influence.

A few hours later, almost at the end of her duty, back in her Captain's quarter Tava performed a daily status check on all online working systems. She found through read outs, orders from Dr. Ian Ross and Mack McKenzie., to send out three construction ships with six hundred construction workers. The captain ordered their immediate recall. However, their radio frequency does not match with the mother's ship. The captain's face flushed red has she stepped out of her office.

It will take a few more hours to find out.

Her eyes fixed on McKenzie as she thought of ways to confront him for hidden treason to Alpha Prime. He was a strange fellow; twice he voted down Ian Ross plans to go direct voyage to the solar system. In addition, he spared the children lives and volunteered to care for them, she scratched her head.

She waved Mr Winters for a private chat as they transported the children to the bio-dome. She is shown read outs of the missing ships and their location on the outer rim of the red suns solar winds of dust particles and charge radiation fields, which gave her an odd feeling.

"I have a long history of McKenzie as the best computer hacker and trouble-shooter to getting the jobs done. He sticks to protocols like a preacher and never wavers. I think if you show him that his name is use illegally, he will go ballistic" warned Mr. Winters.

"We both know who went behind your back; it is Ian Ross," with a cold voice of hate.

"Maybe so, I have never heard of this McKenzie," snapped Captain Pane.

"He worked for the Grays Corporation president in secret," whispered Mr. Winters.

"What did you say," gasped Tava as her eyes looked at his square jaw lines, roman type ridge nose with thick eyebrows, piercing green eyes and short crop blonde hair.

He seems to be having a good time with her mother, while holding onto two boys keeping them warm in their thermo blankets. She returned her gaze back to Mr Winters who seem more nervous as she watched him chew his lips with regret on his face for mentioning it to the new formal Captain. He then leans over to finish what he desperately wanted to explain what he knew of this man name McKenzie.

"We knew that the other corporation wanted to take control of this system at all costs. We may have saboteurs on board or one that will take control and funnel the resources into their corporation. He is here to stop that nothing more. He refused the captain post when the president offered it to him three months back. I suggest letting him be."

"I need those ships recalled or better yet ask McKenzie to take over Sol-one computer program. There could be more survivors that will need our help," replied *Tava Pane* whose eyes searched for other injuries on the little girl. Mr. Winters nodded about to go talk to him, his new Captain shook her head with an edge to her words.

"It is my job description when we get to the bio-dome I will confront him alone."

"Be careful he does have a wild temper," mumbled Mr. Winters.

Mr. Winters nodded his approval to the captain. He held two small infants they look like newborn children. They were quiet and gave the impression that they were imprinting on his face, he could not contain his enthusiasm as he made silly faces, and they in return matched his look.

They finally arrived with emergency staff that followed her mothers request for shelters, beds, clothing, food bars and showers. The small children under five went into cribs while the others went for showers and received clean one-piece jumpers. Tava's father took charge of the boys as her mother took the girls. They followed without a question or confusion.

Mac McKenzie step back with admiration of the loving couple of a tight family group. He lacks that in his life when he lost his parents in accident while they were building the city ship Hyperion 1 and 2. During the meeting, he never thought a woman could handle this ship with such poise and strength. The young woman sticks to the principals of the corporation policies, which are one-step forward two steps back.

Study all aspects before entering in a new system. He was lucky to have awakened in time for the first meeting. Thanks to Snead Winters, he would still be in the bio-tubes of a deep sleep. He wanted to introduce himself, but his pulse rate was running high when she came into view with the red electronic command suit. It stirred something deep inside him that he could not explain in words. He reached the last skiff to help unload the child he offered to carry the thirteen-year-old girl. The captain accepted the offer with a tight smile, as her eyes seem to glitter in his presence. The little girl raised her finger to bring both Mack and the Captain closer.

"Now, with father and mother of the light we have completed the first circle."

Her hands touched both Tava and Mack's hands. A strange but brief glow crossed over between them. They gasped as both shared a dark vision. The tall McKenzie brushed it off with a loud laugh. He brushed death countless times on all his jobs. The captain saw it more different than his wild laugh, she is responsible for the lives of the people on this ship. The young Captain called for medical assistance as the girl passed out and her head drops back onto Mack's shoulder.

Dr Pane step between them with a heart stimulator as the nurse went to work on the little girl. Mack moved to assist them, but Tava cut him off.

"They know what to do. I need to speak to you right away on something more important."

He gave a dark look as if it were a challenge to a fight.

"In which capacity as a woman or a Captain of Hyperion 1," came a sharp retort!

Tava's face flushed red.

"Captain of course, received your authorization before I took office to send a survey and construction crew with construction androids to build the first city called Star point. This is against Alpha Prime protocols; ensure that we do not contaminate the planets environments," claimed Tava Pane.

Mack's face went three colours of red.

"No, I have just awoken one hour ago so someone used my name, this may help you to recognize my intentions by the code reference."

Alpha Prime assignment code, red ball bounces once. Her computer in the suit buzzes so loud, she had to disconnect her earpiece.

"I need your help to recall those ships; you know we must first adjust our shielding to the radiation released, by the red sun. Especially those ships whose shield generators are weaker," pleaded Captain Pane.

"I do things my way if they know I am here too soon they could self-destruct the whole ship then let Grays Corporation take the special fuel. I am sorry but I am very independent in handling crisis," replied Mack.

"Then you just killed six hundred people and lost three good valuable ships, I should put you under arrest," snarled Captain Pane.

"Hold on there, daughter of mine. If you wish to punish someone I, your father, used his name to get a head start in the Beta system. I do not want my son to be born in the vastness of space."

"Mr. Iran Pane I have killed for lesser crimes against the Corporation," hissed Mack.

"I am the captain here if punishment is given it is by my authority. You are under house arrest. Your assignment will be to teach these children human values and team spirit."

"That is a fair punishment," replied Mr. Pane.

"I say you got off easy, I would have at least thrown you out the air lock," hissed Mack McKenzie.

"Give me the radio frequency to recall the ships father," pleaded his daughter as she stepped between the engineer's threat and her father's guilt.

"Iran be quiet you must not give our daughter the radio frequency. I will share the blame with you, but we must trust Ian Ross he is right, and our daughter is wrong. You know I must have this child in an Earth type atmosphere. The Doctors have said so repeatedly."

"Elizabeth please, do not add to the stress of this moment, I realize our daughter is right to protect six hundred lives to one child that is not even mine," answered Mr. Pane.

"You two sure shatter the image of wholesome family units of Grays Corporation; such betrayers to each other as well to the Corporation you both represent," replied Mack with vehemence in his words.

The captain growled as she spun around with an uppercut to the jaw of McKenzie. He sensed the danger and leans back but Tava got him on the chin just the same. The command suit doubles her normal strength as she presses forward with her sharp words.

"No one speaks to my family in that way, you muscle bound airhead."

Everyone was stunned to silence. They saw the engineer fall to the floor and giggle as if to brush it off.

"I might have deserved that for family honour not from any Captain who cannot control her emotion," replied Mack, as he rubbed his chin with sharp eyes staring her down.

"That is for my family honour, and this is to correct their mistakes." She presses the button on her right arm for computer input.

"Computer voice command online what is your request Captain Pane."

"There is a security breach of protocols. Until further notice, the following personnel suspended from duties and privileges interment to the bio-dome. No computer access and all files locked down and only released by my voice command."

"You would not dare to do this to your own mother," hissed Dr. Pane.

"Waiting to enter names and file numbers" crackled the mechanical voice.

"Dr. Elizabeth Pane Med. file number H00101, Mr. Iran Pane file number A00100, Ian Ross file number MP000001." She then turned to look at the engineer who slowly got up with his hands down to his sides.

He seems to show some respect towards her from his eyes. He knew what she wanted him to do. He points with a peace gesture to the screen and outlet in the hallway to help her communicate with the three ships to recall them back. Mr. Winter's follows him a few yards back as she passes the captain with a smug look and whispers.

"Well done, Captain," she nodded with a sad smile.

"Initiate Neptune time top of the hour, which is 00:01."

"Comply," cackled the mechanical voice. Two beams appear to downturn all electronic devices on the parents. They stepped back inside the bio dome with the cyborg children. Her mother let loose her irritation towards her father and daughter.

"You do not know what is involved; you will kill your baby brother if he is not on a breathable planet. If he dies, then I curse you to suffer the same fate."

"Please, Liz stops she is family I am glad it is out in the open, darling, this child is the second generation of telepathic powers, and it must be born on the terrain clusters in the Beta system. If you promise to help us I will give you the frequency freely," Mr. Pane replied sternly.

"Father there is too many tests to cut short without a high risk of loss of life. You will die as well as mother and the newborn," quoted his daughter. Tava's mind runs through the obstacles to overcome for a safe colony to be disease free.

"How much time do I have mother if I take short cuts," muttered Tava.

"Four to five weeks, my little brat," hissed her mother, who turns away to join her nursing staff.

"Honey she is still our daughter and always will be our little one," snapped Mr. Pane.

"I cannot promise but I will give it my best effort," replied Tava.

"That is good enough for me," as he threw the paper with the frequencies, they both said their goodbye.

Tava went to join Mr Winters and McKenzie at the computer console. McKenzie was busy pressing the keys at unbelievable speed. She passed the frequency to him with a grunt of irritation in his voice.

"You know I always get even with those who stand in my way."

"As Captain Pane, you may do what is your right as the lawmaker on the planet we colonize, on this ship I am in charge. As for striking you, it was family honour only," explains Tava.

"Then accept my apology for my rash words but be warned what Ian Ross has on his agenda I will not intervene if he attacks you," sneered Mr. McKenzie.

The screen beeped endlessly with a short brief message; return to Mother ship.

"It will take two hours to reach the ships due to the interference of the red sun," replied to Mr. Winters.

"I only hope it reaches them before they cross over," whispered the captain. "Thank you for your help, Mr. McKenzie." She walked to the elevator shaft to head for the bridge.

"Well mother of the light you are heading the wrong way, these cyborg children need you imprinted on their minds as their true mother. Your parents have shown a dark side to their personality. The white-haired girl told us that we are their parents now we should go together to spend at least two hours with the children. Mr Winters is capable to start the tests from the probes sent out. I will forgo my revenge if you join me now;" quoted Mack.

"Yes, I would rather have a good friend then an angry enemy," replied Captain Pane.

Her parents with their daughter re-enter the bio-dome, spoke to each child with children's stories, and lullaby songs. Tava thought by shaming her both parents, that had to follow bad advice from a dishonest supervisor. Their fear push them to protect their newborn Tava sees and understand however, if they live on a safe world, it should have been their home planet of Mars. Tava had no choice to restrict their computer access and place them in the care of the cyborg children. Iran had reached his wife finally with an understanding to be more patient in this environment.

Meanwhile Ian Ross had monitored the captain's computer request realize that she had found out about the three survey ships. He had trick Iran. Pane and his wife to forage the documents to release the ships journey into the red a solar system. This is his corporation goals to be first and knew where the four earth type planets are to calm for the Dark lighter Corporation. In addition his partner Talwoolt is the first to claim the planets under there corporation. Ian Ross being a spy for the Dark lighter Mega corporation had fought Mack Mackenzie over fifteen years. This is chance to kill him finally but right now must change his identity He quickly changes all his electronics to another man's identity with fingerprints, swapped retinas, shaving his beard and removing his headpiece. He instantly became Nigel Bruce as the main computer scanned the room and shuts down all electronics belonging to Ian Ross. The computer passed over Nigel Bruce without a care or interest. He was relieved with his thoughts not to underestimate the young Captain. He went to a computer outlet and punched in Nigel Bruce's operating code. He must seal off the smaller bio dome that is his special laboratory in human DNA and gene repair. Two female twins answer in French dialect in a nursery rhyme from ancient story. He replied in kind and gave instruction to raise the barrier until further notice. The two nodded in agreement just as the main computer tried a scanning wave and bounced away in less then a second. Mr. Bruce was relieved that his timing is a little slow. He bangs his hand on the table and barks out new orders.

"Move all samples to the escape ship and bring sample AN00099-1 to level thirty-six-East wing room thousand one seventeen."

"Yes, will comply Minister," replied the two twins as the screen went black.

His entire plan abandoned because of Captain Pane and that new engineer; this man also had his own agenda that may not follow his orders from Dark Lighter Corporation. However, he is still one-step head of the captain. He will regret killing Dr. Pane and her newborn but thinks it is best for all to start a new world without people present with old human standards of laws of Alpha Prime. His dream of a new race under his control is but a few hours away once he eliminates Hyperion one from his existence. He turned off the computer outlet on the main hall as employees scurry out of their sleeping quarters for the change in shift. He blends within the groups and causally walks among them to the elevators. His features are change to a more youthful looks of short blonde hair and dark brown eyes with a round face of a basic maintenance personnel. He expresses a board smile and friendly demeanour to anyone who makes eye contact.

CHAPTER 8

THE UNSEEN SHADOWS WATCHING

The two entities were mind traveling to the outer edge of the Ea solar system in a large sphere. The two superior beings were curious of the new light they considered as a new sun forming in the dark matter of space. Wanting answers to the claims of the Jung zee race those new gods were coming to reason; they had run amuck killing all their offspring. This only antagonised the mind of Lord Id with his caretaker powers to rejoin in a different form of a mating queen of the Jung zee name Ru. The two were the most powerful aliens in the whole galaxy next to the elders of the inner world trapped in another dimension. The supreme Elder Krell fought the caretaker Ru and the young one name Lord Id who stole the time crystal. He had gathered the broken pieces and share to control of this system and all life forms within Ea space.

The Entities reached the edge of the solar winds of the giant red sun. They found the presence of these minds more chaotic than the organized thought compared to their pets. All accept the mechanical brains of the on-board computer. The noise of many voices seems to irritate Ru who wishes to silence them all. These seem to intrigue Lord Id to study these new animals more closely. He openly whispers his thoughts to calm his new caretaker who acted with tendencies that are more violent.

"I suggest that any creature that finds their way to our space is worthy of our attention, after all is it not our goal to create a perfect race based on the Jung zee and the Myra alone who have given us their complete loyalty."

"There are too many minds in chaos, and they seem to be neurotic with the edge of madness," mumbled Queen Ru.

"Then let us focus on the individual mind, for example the lead ship of three. We shall search each mind in this ship. Let us entice, and hope this one mind will bend towards our point of view in perfection," replied Lord Id.

"Why so, they are not insect type you could risk contamination. Have you not listened to my encounter with the other," hissed Queen Ru?

"We shall take samples and lead them to a planet were we can watch them. Our time crystal power can obliterate any life form that enters our system. Have you forgotten Ru," whispered Lord Id.?

"All right let us learn more from these beings, but I feel they are better if returned to the dust where they came from," snapped Queen Ru.

"Now let us find a suitable subject to control, we shall split up our minds search from the bottom of the ship to the main bridge," suggested Lord Id.

Their minds float in a circular pattern around the lead ship has it dips low before entering the lower loading doc. They study the strange looking crafts loaded with construction material, androids, and robots. The place looks deserted until they saw two humans completely different from each other. One with black skin six feet tall in a green jumpsuit with a wide tool belt and the other white like snow look sickly, short and stout in a white jumpsuit with three blue stripes his voice crackles with age, thought the small shape sphere. The old one complained to the young man about the lateness of his maintenance duties, if they were to enter the new system.

Ru felt anger from the young man at the same time it seems to draw her mind to feed off his thoughts. She lands on his back while her inner eye stabs the back of his head to absorb his emotions. The black man felt a chill creeping up his back and jumps with a yelp of pain. This confuses the other man as he steps back to see a strange red glow behind the young man's head. Ru now felt his fear and dug deeper into his brain as blood dripped down his jumpsuit. He froze in place as his eyes went back into his head. This even attracted Lord Id attention. The energy released gave them great insight to these creatures, which could be a food source. He went to touch the other older looking one as he transferred into a black mist to encircle the man. He reacted as he felt a sharp sting in his feet. He tries to move as he looks down to see a bubbling pool of his own blood and screams in panic. He takes a desperate attempt to reach out with his hands to hit the emergency button.

However, Ru had finally taken over the black man's mind. His face soaks with perspiration. His eyes changed to a deep red while his arm yanks out to strike the older man hard across the face. The pain gave the chance for Lord Id to take over the old one's mind. The old man's hands shake as they lost control when Lord Id touched the blood of his face. It tasted like wine. The two bodies collapsed on the floor as they absorb their life and memories. Their flesh disintegrated to dust quickly much to the disapproval of Lord Id. These creatures had no compassion for life, their hunger is endless. They felt more satisfied with these newfound energy life forces. They now absorb the complete knowledge operations of this ship in mechanical robotics and android.

"Let us absorb a few more of these creatures; I had never enjoyed so much life in one being it is intoxicating," whispered Queen Ru.

"Yes, they were different and gave me a strange taste, but I saw something that is comparable to both my pets of Ea. They are both war makers with a great history of blood lust, they long to be peace markers, they are great builders, and they are healers. I must learn more. We shall use these minds to find more truth then just kill for food," answer Lord Id.

"I am still hungry," hissed the Queen Ru.

"You will do what I say. I am the holder of the crystals," whisper Lord Id.

"Of course, I bow to your power," replied Queen Ru?

"Now, let us bring back their forms so that we can use their tools and learn their ways," ordered Lord Id.

The two energy forms took their memories to reform into the humans under their control. The black man reformed with no hair on his head, one diamond shape eye, without a nose and swollen lips. His body grew wider with an extra set of arms and hands. Ru became puzzled when the black human spoke Jung zee.

"This is not what they look like when we absorb them. The shape of his eye looks like the old ones of our past." The other man returns as a small boy with a swollen head completely covered in wild hair. "We cannot completely rebuild these beings without absorbing all the medical information," whispered Lord Id.

They boy slowly turns using the humans mind and vision to familiarize himself to the ships environment and spots a large table with many objects. He recognizes a computer with keyboard on a workbench. He sits down and slowly hits some of the keys. The small boy uses the computer codes for Frank Thomas and Lionel Wolfe. This opens the vast history of earths past, present, and future goals. Lord Id eyes speed through the information.

The two entities absorb all including their flight plans. His mind picks up the wide choice of languages. They had just received a recall to stay out of the system because of a second asteroid belt. The scientist approaching the solar system in the advance spaceships, named Hyperion 1. The first human ship slows to explore the outreaches to enter the solar system. Humans are alarmed to see four giant gas planets so close to each other. Many believe it is a young system more dangerous to predict for safety. They plan to spend five years mapping the system and gathering information confirming the crystal has the energy source to power the ships. They find three breathable planets and four others similar to the atmosphere of Mars in their own system. Their target is Beta 5 the two gods see the schedules for hundreds of probes and robots to check the planet minerals. The humans appear to want to establish new colonies under several different corporation Each ship carries equipment and people with different experiences and skills build the first city call Starpoint.

They come to embrace our new world, thought Ru. Lord Id begins to study all the humans and especially their children. His mind flashes with an idea as he picks a small planet with an atmosphere and starts the long processes of perfection. He spent a few more minutes studying the different languages and communication skills. They are the first step to what he believed could be the chosen race. His first group of tests will be on children. These intrigue him for he can easily alter their young minds. Each child has a different colour of hair, eyes, and skin tone. They differ from their parents, yet they have the same internal structure single heart, blood rich in iron, lung capacity, and agility. He thought he must find a way to control them through cross breading.

He looks back at the history of humans. They came from a planet 300,000 hundred thousand light years with a long history of many cultures and religious beliefs that go back to the pagan times and even further back to cave dwelling. He studies them to find ways to control his test subjects. The Entity sees religion as a control of his new pets. He knows this is his only opportunity to bring a perfect race through crossing breeding. With access to the human's history, he takes notice, which brought these humans out so far by the images of the fourth and fifth war that almost wiped them out. He sees their solar system of nine inner planets with four outside planets on wide orbit. He studies the sun classified a grey star completely different from his other captors.

Queen Ru points out why these humans came here and explores the reason and found a depressed society. Lord Id's point of view differs. Watch a history of the modern age is the title from one of computer disc he finds and watches with interest. Their race spread out in space slowly as they seed the next plant named Mars. He watched how they seeded a living planet. They found ways of using a magnetised shielding to exchange the carbon to oxygen. A sudden burst of exploration to expand to the other planets that orbit the gas giants increased the population to one zillion souls. He sees strange rituals of kissing and affection between the many ages of life a pattern becomes apparent, which he thought disgusting and went on to other films.

Three Doctor of Science that he found in the history disc were the ones he believes help made a giant leap in technology. One is a cyber link to each human connected to the main computer to increase the resource of ideas. The other clone's perfection with the helix cube that stores the past knowledge of each human life's experiences and enables the exact duplicate of the individual. He stops the tape to rewind it and repeat their words. It had some merit. He thinks he could use the helix and the cyber link to watch over and correct the problems immediately.

He lets the tape continue their work. He wondered if he could duplicate their steps with his other pets instead of their killing ritual. The two entities disagree as she points out the many copies doing endless routine. He finally understands why they wish to escape their home world. A thousand beings doing the same exact work gave an imperfect world, thought the creature. Queen Ru cut him off with sharp hiss.

"This is the food source that will make us stronger into finding perfection thinking that they would be great food resources. They have a similar taste to the other but a weak mind."

"Maybe so, I would like to get a closer look at the helix cube before I agree to eat human flesh"

"If this helix cube has that much power, we could use this on other pets," replied Queen Ru.

"I like to see their children if the are truly, what they look like. I do not like this hair all over me. Moreover, what is this small object between their legs," quoted Lord Id

Queen Ru grunted with an insult but held back her words in a softer tone.

"Have you forgotten the mating rituals of the Jung zee that have multiple ones to penetrate the egg chamber? These humans are different they have no queen to mate with they are all individual beings who choose their life mates with an emotional binding. I saw his life mate in my mind; we must find her if you wish to know about their children," whispers the queen. Lord Id spoke through the alter human in his native tongue of the Jung zee. "I do not have time to test her; she could be anywhere in the ship there are over two hundred beings on this ship alone. We must speed up their entry to our space."

"I suggest we study their flight plan make them fall into our system," snaps Queen Ru. "Yes, let us do that, they could be our beings, which might be what we require to complete our perfection," grumble Lord Id.

Meanwhile, on the bridge the communications officer's name Lisa Thomas had one hour left on her shift. She is monitoring power usage with her husband's code. His shift ended an hour ago but the fact that he has not called or returned her messages annoyed her.

"Wait until I get my hands on him for fouling up our off time."

Commander T. Smith a twenty-year veteran in construction ships could not help but hear Lisa Thomas words. He was already disappointed with the recall from Hyperion 1, turned his ship in slow wide circle while all scanners scanned the solar system. He always dreamt of being a first pioneer.

Like those of the western United States in the early1800. Now he was hearing a woman whispering over her husband. He stares at her for a few minutes he could see the tightness in her face. Moreover, her eyes flare at the communication monitors. He wonders if all women get that way once they are pregnant. Only two women had passed the physical to allow them on this voyage. They altered the special bio tubes and hibernation chamber to protect the unborn child inside them.

He looked at the clock with forty more minutes to go he did not want to be involved with a family squabble on his bridge. He thinks everything is on automatic. The last message is a bitter pill that depresses everyone in the three ships.

"You may leave early Mrs. Thomas your replacement always arrives early anyway. I think it will best for you and the little one," quotes Commander T. Smith.

"Thank you, commander, I must report the over use of computer time by Mr. Thomas and Mr. Wolfe in the docking bay."

"After the recall to return, everyone does odd things. Log it in your report, they will have some extra duty time," remarked the commander as he waves his hands to send her a happy thought.

"Now leave maybe you can cheer him up."

"Yes, sir, thank you once again commander," Lisa quoted quickly as she hits the switches on auto recordings and leaves the bridge.

She passes her replacement coming out of the elevator the youngest on this ship sixteen a child prodigy at five. Highly decorated engineer normally very shy nodded her head in their brief meeting. Lisa taken by surprise when she mentions her sons name Frederick in a verbal greeting, Lisa felt sudden movement in her womb. She was stunned and wanted to know how she knew her son's name when she had decided only a few moments ago as the elevator doors closed. She presses the button to go to the loading dock. She went in a deep thought while she rubs her belly to calm the unborn child. She steps out on to the foray; she glances at the indicator remembering that Frank is in the blue sector section D level one.

The two entities felt the occurrence of another being coming towards them Lord Id returns to his gasses state, while Queen Ru stays at the monitor and feels a familiarity to the one approaching. Lord Id grew annoyed and whispers to the queen not to harm this one. She hissed back with a little irritation. Lisa enters the docking by unlocking the magnetic door and steps in slowly, she calls his name repeatedly, and Queen Ru whispers her name to lure the being from the door. Lisa barks angrily as she steps forward Lord Id slams the door and locks it tightly.

"I do not like playing silly spook games come out Frank Thomas, now!"

Lisa steps towards the humming sound of a computer terminal she sees the shadow of her husband with his back to her, walks crisply up to him. Lord Id eyes seem to see high-energy aura around the midsection of this being. It knew that queen Ru would scare her. He started to change into a tentacle creature, from the early days of the Jung zee. Lisa yanks and pulls the seat to face her. The single diamond shape eye and head throb with its jaw split open has two sharp mandibles hissed out. She steps back and screams her lungs out. Lord Id wraps her up in his tentacles. She garbled wildly at the creature that once was her husband.

"Please do not hurt my child; I will do anything you wanted," shouted Lisa. While she weeps for her husband. Lord Id not wanting to kill her took blood samples. Then he took a sharp needle to connect to the frontal lobes of her brain. She did not feel the puncture. She hears a low whisper in her Africa language.

"We will not harm you; take us to the medical units. We wish to repair your husband we accidentally touched him." *answer the creature.*

"What did you say; who or what are you, what have you done to my husband" as she weeps and shakes with fear. Lord Id moaned in delight as he absorbed the energy of the woman. He growls back and explains his story using the image of her grandfather to calm her thoughts.

She had no choice but agreed as the words came from her grandfather the tension and fear disappeared. Her husband looks came back to what it was although his uniform had turned black. She also notices that her uniform changed to a shimmering black as it tightens around her body. She repeated her request.

"If, I agree to your demands you will not harm the child in me."

"Yes, take us now to the medical unit before I change my mind," hissed Lord Id.

Lisa pointed the way as the doors unlock, queen Ru wanted to stay and study more information she had plan to contact his alter being named Eltross to make the official contact with these beings and to invite them to the white planet. Lord Id answers in his own language to the Queen Ru that sounded full of hate. Lisa eyes bulge by the pressure of this creature squeezing her.

"If you want me to help you, stop hurting me, if you honour your words that you are peaceful. Then show me what you are," mumbled Lisa.

"I am a life form of the unseen and entities of energy, to be physical I had to share parts of me with other pets this is all I will say until we reach the medical center of this ship," replied Lord Id.

Lisa tried to ask more questions, but he cuts her off and makes her body move into the elevator and press the section to the medical. They step into the medical unit passing by the nurse's station to the examine room. The nurse tries to question her follows her into the medical room. Lisa lies down on the bed her uniform disintegrated showing her naked body that is eight months pregnant. The black form wash over the nurse's body ripping her clothes off. She screeches but is easily overwhelmed as a shadow figure forms in front of her the face of her departed mother. Lord Id learns everything about the helix cube in those brief seconds but does not totally understand its purpose. The Doctor on duty rushes in, but freezes at the sight of the black mist, which wraps around the nurse who gives a childish smile. He is fascinated as it changes form into a child s face. He reads volumes of books gaining great insight on humanity basic chemicals DNA structures to the very beginning of the human experiences. The mist pounces on top of the Doctor and encases his body in a tight vice grip.

Lisa could only watch the doctor glow a blue hue and notice the helix cube protruding from the skin of the doctor. She looks desperately to fight this creature and then spotted a tray of the doctor's tools to reach a scalpel at the edge of her figure tips. She hears a warning form her grandfather. The dark mist saw the device inside the forehead of the doctor it feels his fear and strength to fight him. Lord Id sent a telepathic message to the human male using imagery to one of his teachers from the doctor's past.

"Therefore, you have the helix cube attach to the mind tell me the purpose of it. I want to process its power and knowledge, give it and all the ones in stock to me." The Doctor instantly replied, as if he is a student in class. "Yes, it gives me all the knowledge of every medical research to keep our workers healthy. There is no evil purpose to the betterments of the human life cycle." The man expression changes from clam to sudden dread of the darken image in his mind.

"I will trade you for the lives I have taken plus the ones I plan to liquidate on this ship. If you do not give me what I want to learn," hissed Lord Id. The human male smirked and responded rudely. "For being so powerful, take my life and rip it out of me." Lord Id snarled, "yes, I will for I am a creator of life and death."

He pulls his crystal out of the black mist and points at him. White energy sparkles around the crystal. It made a narrow beam and hit him in the stomach hard. He falls back against the wall, while his cloths burn off. He begins to shrink into a small boy screaming in agony while his life force absorbs into the crystal. The helix cube falls off his forehead. The baby cries endless. He suddenly feels the anguish of the older nurse that walks in from the child's cry. She had been hiding ever since they appeared in the medical center. He takes her into himself absorbing thirty years of her experiences altering her physical make and knowledge of the Jung zee language. Her mind surrenders for the hidden love she had for the doctor, only wanting to hold him.

"You will be his mother the beam hits her the same way as the other," Lord Id commanded. The nurse drops down on all fours and bows speaking a different dialect. She changed into a younger woman of fifteen years with only one thought to care for child that was planted in her mind. She crawls to him and places him in her young arms. He quickly becomes quiet as he buries his face in her chest. Lord Id steps closer to the helpless children and giggles out his first human words after absorbing the doctor knowledge.

"I will learn everything, and you will be my new little pets."

Lisa stunned by this act of cruelty, blindly panics. She tries to escape the examine room. She only makes a few steps as her legs weaken, dropping to the floor and hears the creature cold voice wash over her.

"I told you to trust me I have a need of you, I will keep my word to not harm your child, and I will not even harm you, well just a little. I shall even give back you husband and this old man I took and even send you back to Hyperion one but the rest of the three ships are mine to study," barks Lord Id.

Lisa hears this in her grandfather's language as he summons her to return to the table. She knew there is no way out of this trap the creature is a god that creates life and feeds off the fear to increase his powers over her mind. The creature seems to be absorbing her energy and she loses her strength to resist. She surrenders and returns to the table and listens to the strange language while he talks to the young girl. Lisa focuses on the baby that clings to the nurse's breast. She nods then leaves briefly and hands him a box. They are soon joined by her deformed husband and four other naked children.

"I follow your orders Lord Id the ships are turning back in our system. When you used the time crystal, I was able to absorb all their memories as well as their life force. No human can stop us now. All have turned into children aboard these three ships. I have absorbed all their adult life force in me," grunted the queen. "It was a most satisfying meal I enjoyed in my lifetime. Only the bridge crew of this ship show resistance I would need your powers to control them. The have a mind gift similar to the other," hissed Ru.

"Yes, they will be a great food source, but I think they could be the ones that the others are waiting for. We will study them, and invite them to our system," replied Lord Id.

"I guess you were right my little one, but they are not exactly the other that attacked me a thousand years ago. I feel something familiar with this one," whispered Ru as she points to Lisa. She waves her arm seeing that Lord Id was not amused and changed the topic back to what he likes.

"There is much to learn from these pets. Once they are in the small form, their minds less cluttered, they shall become obedient to our ways," quoted Queen Ru.

"I agree but we must have more of them to experiment on," explained Lord Id.

"Eltross will join us once he guaranties that the Jung zee will not attack his nest," whispered the Queen.

"That is good to hear we shall make plans but first, we must keep our word to the female Lisa Thomas," replied Lord Id.

He summons from within the human form the old man, which came back has a hairy beast in a small boy. The mist swirls over the head of the boy then split his skull open to remove the helix cube in its forehead. He watches the creature shrink into small-unborn baby. The mist then floats over Lisa's womb; she feels sharp pain. He places the helix cube inside, Lisa moans, tears flowed down her face, and she wails not to hurt the child. She watches the queen follow Lord Id and starts to alter her husband back to the man she had married. Then in a flash he changes into a teenager, and a boy of five, to a baby, finally an embryo placed inside her womb. She weeps for the great loss of her friends and family. She now carries inside her the unknown future. Lord Id takes control of the boy that was once the Doctor, at the same time as the queen Ru takes control of the nurse.

"You will have these children in order, but you will send a message of hope to the Hyperion 1," Lord Id commanded.

Lisa responds in her grandfather's language. "Yes, I will do anything I always obey my elders of my tribe."

Her memories begin to swim backwards. In her mind, she sees storm clouds with range electrical sparks altering her perception of her life. She hears a voice as her body floats up to the glaring eyes. She repeats yes repeatedly until her throat hurts and her lips parch. This brings a vision when she became ill while living in South Africa with her grandfather before she enters the Grays Mega Corporation at the age twelve. She had high marks on quantum physics and electronic engineering. Her grandfather had pushed her to success at all costs. He said that she would never age with great knowledge that gathers in her mind. You must always accept the powers that come your way, even if it is bad or good. She passes out as her mind goes quiet into a dark void.

She suddenly hears the familiar voice of Commanders T. Smith. She tries to ask for help but her voice is gone. Her eyes open to a strange sight of a bright star coming at her. She screams endlessly as her body changed to a child of twelve. She recalls the horrors still fresh in her mind of the dark mist that reveals his form. She remembers his message to the people of Hyperion 1. She looks back to see her ship and the others enter the solar system. She begins to sob at being left behind and drops in despair. Lisa Thomas had lost her son, husband, and comrades in a blink of and eye by trusting the unknown aliens. The escape capsule booster rockets kick into warp one. Lisa cries out her mother's name, "Claudette help me!" The two beings watch the capsule head back to the mother ship.

The dark mist had placed all its human children in a deep sleep. He takes over the body and mind of Commander T. Smith. He decided to take all the memories slowly absorbing his life forces. Queen Ru prefers the young communications officer; she freely accepts the oddity doing exactly what the queen wishes. She found a great calm and orderly mind requesting to bring the other ship with the cloning machines that Lord Id wanted. Her mind held a secret desire to kiss the commander. Queen Ru intrigued whispers to Lord Id the request, in hopes to dwell deep in the young woman's mind.

"No wipe that thought from her mind, I have other plans and many tests to do on these new pets. Turning them into children is brilliant idea from an immortal standpoint. Once I knew their genetic code and absorbed their chaotic life, I found their minds quite small. Now we shall teach them the ways of Jung zee and the Myra culture. If they or the others are the ones to inherit the cosmos, they shall be under our control with one mind forever," stated Lord Id.

"You have lofty goals which I admire Lord Id, since our beginning, these beings are only food nothing more to me I thought but this one is already at peace and accepts my presence. I will not interfere but watch your brilliant mind at work. This young woman has a stronger mind but bends to my will without question, yet she still longs to kiss that body under your control. Would it not be right to see and feel the human emotions that have satisfied my hunger to the highest heights," Queen Ru requested with a sharp plead.

Lord Id steps closer to the young woman with the oval face, long reddish hair tight up in a bun, soft pure complexion, and small button nose with ruby lips. She looks up with wanting like a dare. He notices the two colour eyes, which convince him she is a special child. He shakes his head and walks away as the girl leaps at the commander's feet to grasp him.

"What is the meaning of this as he swipes her off," snarls Lord Id.?

She rolls to her feet, while queen Ru stunned by her the strong will, quickly apologies and claims.

"She is quite attached to that body."

"I accept it, if she completes what I want. She may have whatever's left over when we land safely on the sixth planet of Ea," muttered Lord Id weakly to Ru, and then adds another statement that intrigues the young woman.

"This one is strong like the other but different my lord. Yes, my lord she agrees to it, but prefers that you go to Zlotoo where Eltross awaits you," suggested Queen Ru.

"How does she know of him," snapped Lord I?

Eltross is with me claimed the young woman, and then adds.

"We joined in the mind link through this woman. I do not now how but he is here now and wants to speak to you; Lord Id," quoted the young girl.

"He is of no importance; I rule this solar system," growled the Ru.

"When you arrived, I felt your aura through my mind gift it has been searching for alien's life forms, but you are a dark force. I found him guarding his nest; we joined our minds and connected. Eltross is the one protecting me, when you released the time crystal. That is why the crystal told me of what I must do. In hopes that did not change us, and I have done it when I offered myself to the Queen Ru, body, soul and mind. She hates being a spider," smiled the young woman then spoke her last words telepathically.

We are slowly exchanging ourselves Ru will be a female human and I shall be the spider.

"No, I am the creator of life. I even made Eltross. His job is to mate with the Sleeping Queen of the Myra does not interfere with my plans with my new pets," growled Lord Id.

"That is your error Lord Id. You must realize that he is your equal when you brought the Myra into the solar system and now, he is on this ship with the Sleeping Queen," giggled the human woman.

"Now, I will keep my word of my sacrifice, her hands play with the red mist that held the spirit of Queen Ru."

"No, do not speak those words, I order you Queen Ru to take this animals life force kill her now, absorb her flesh, I know you are hungry," hissed Lord Id.

Queen Ru became silent as she begins to swirl around the young woman's body. The mist caresses the skin finding perfections. She felt a door opening inviting her inside to a new form equal to Lord Id but more powerful. The same hunger for perfections was her goal long before she had made a pact with Lord Id. She enters and becomes one as the transferred spirit switched to a human and the spider speaks the language of the elders.

"Now old one you will experience motherhood of the third race for the next ten thousand years. While I do my destiny, I shall bring forth perfection across the cosmos through the time crystal. Since I carry your essence within me, the time crystal will grant our wishes," growled Ru and the young female.

The mind link broke between them with Lord Id. The mist changed colour to a light grey and left the ship to the queen Ru's spider body where she altered the blood red spider to a white shadow with wings and faded from view.

Lord Id screams the sudden lost of power shocks him as he falls backwards into a void and is draws back to his Jung zee form. He screams out his anger that echoes through the planet.

"I will kill you all this very night!"

Eltross appears to him in his youthful form of a child of the Myra with cruel hair of brown and silver, large round black eyes and small purple lips. He glows of bright colours of rainbow and holds the two-time crystal. He is appointed leader by the sleeping queen. Eltross reads their history, memories, and all their songs, which gave the clue they could be the chosen ones.

"I have found more information that only I can improve, while you and the rogue name Ru blunder about I read more into the human race. The humans that you turned the clock back all know you as an evil creature. They saw your form of the Jung zee. They think of me as the angel of the light. They will accept my presence spectre; these humans will eventually obey me. If the young woman had not reached out, you would have ruined our chances."

"Explain yourself," hissed Lord Id.

"I agree with you that we could train them in the pagan ways of their history with the Myra and the Jung zee ways. While we erase these humans confused and chaotic mind by their own technology. The helix cube and the cyber link would satisfy our hungry for thousands of years. We need a large amount of people to succeed the first six hundred. We shall isolate and alter them to teach the others our ways. We shall give them every opportunity to populate this system, while we search to find one male and one female from their DNA and genomes to bring the seed of our three pets into one race to this we need time," quoted Eltross who floated around Lord Id.

"I am no fool I know this," snapped Id as his wings fluttered with annoyance.

"Let our minds connect and see a different angle of your errors my brother."

"You forget I created you to serve me in cross breeding," hissed Lord Id.

"Calm yourself I am still part of you. Be still and learn the truth," grumbled Eltross. Lord Id bows and closes his wings to sit down on his haunches and work their problems out in a mind link.

"I do like the way you sent out the escape capsule to the city ship but I altered your plan to corrupt the ship through air borne disease by the children in Lisa Thomas. By making the adults age faster until they place a helix cube to reverse the disease, which we will have the controls wiping them into mind slaves at any time we desire," smirked Eltross.

Lord Id now sees the evil in the Myra plan is much darker then his own, with more control which could also spread to the other beings. The visual link shows Lord Id's errors.

His attack on the humans and his torture methods on capturing the other three ships, regardless that he announced his name and purpose has a god of life. All humans see him in their words of ancient demons of earth. He knows now by the other races had given him different names. This meant to him a powerful being to fear when he captured the other races in the past. They all believe it is ghostly monster that appeared out of the unseen world from one of the moons of the four gas giants of Ea solar system. He recalls the description in one of the human history readouts of a large round head, sharp glowing horns, and perfect round eyes of ebony gave a deathly chill if any human gazed at him. The creature is small in stature of a young teenager. It had large dark wings with four sharp fingers and toes, concealed in a black cloak with two pairs of eyes that were empty only a few had seen, but all were instantly terrified.

Once again, Lord Id's hunger envisioned the choice of what being will have one million generations to bring an end of all stories, to the beginning of a new cosmos. He now sees and hears the words of Eltross that weaken his hopes of perfection. He rushed to take control too quickly, like a mad hunter. He accepts that he does need Eltross's help to build a better world with the Myra leader and surrenders the broken time crystal to Eltross. It is the only weapon needed to wipe out and absorb life to the beginning of time itself.

Eltross feels the energy from the crystal at the same time as a vision of a far-off future. He sees the red giant sun shrink then burst the energy into a massive explosion causing a great pressure crushing everything in the solar system into dust particles. The planet implodes into a fireball. Eltross believes it is a clear defeat of Lord Id's methods. It shows his weakness.

Now it is Eltross turn to guide his dark reason that he finds too many imperfections in the three races. He takes part of Lord Id plan by repairing the black moon ship were they can have a permanent labs for experiments to select and establish a new race. With six hundred children, he will match with the Myra and the Jung zee. The two gods are confident they will succeed. Lord Id wants to start field tests in the coming years on isolated islands. They select the children of the three races plus animals and plant life for his new project. He brings Eltross to the captive ship and hands over all the memories he had stolen. He thinks more tests needed as he studies the human children."

"I will still need you brother while I go to build their first colony you will do the test on the select few that already have some mind gifts from the children you have captured. The bulk will come with me at the smallest planet that the Myra clan will create. Perfect planets that will suit their needs, while we steal the technology and entice them in with open arms," claimed Eltross.

"We share everything with a blood oath," hissed Lord Id.

"Of course," Eltross cuts his wrist, the same as does Lord Id but he speaks aloud to ensure his dominance.

"I take the Sleeping Queen as my bride to control the Jung zee since you encourage Ru to cross over to the human body," snarls Lord Id.

Eltross hissed at the words then quickly adds another spell to the blood oath to bind each other.

"Queen Ru will bow to me then this will keep the balance between us brother," demand Eltross? Lord Id gave a silent yes with a nod of his head.

They left each other as Eltross fades into a small sphere that floats up to the captured ship. Lord Id climbs to his altar and goes into deep meditation to review what he had learnt from the computers mind and the minds that he and the Queen Ru had stolen. *The next move belongs to Eltross of the Myra clan,* thought Lord Id. His only worry was his long-time caretaker is gone from him once more. He thinks Ru made an error, as did the human girl who wanted to kiss the older man. He realizes they are still connected and stealing each other's experiences. He recognizes an odd feeling when the vision came they had crossed paths from an adult form to a small child. It is love for the instant that the young woman had a connection being an orphan. Lord Id thought how foolish the emotions that humans carry and decides in anger before he goes deep within himself.

This I promise, all emotions will be purged!

Queen Ru mind dissolves into the dark matter of the caretaker. Her atoms increase the electric flow of brain impulses, which the human part uses one third. This gave the connection that the caretaker slowly awakes with a third of their minds. She now realizes that this young woman is strangely familiar to the first one that killed her. Now in the human form it is unfamiliar to her nervous system. She tries to move her hand to reach the commander to fulfill the last request of Heidi Stustrum. Ru stretch out her telepathic powers to find her own equal that she would absorb the human DNA finds something that connects to the first female Helen Nightshade the deep secret of the real human's name is Tava Pane with an odd identical twin sister, which is younger, on the Hyperion 1.

Ru feels the mind link to her younger sister from the cyber link, which she calls Sister Susan. She is pleased, responds, and freely helps her with the exchange in formation of both minds who share the power of the elder clan wonder how that could be. Its odd thoughts swirl in her mind when she was a rogue to the younger one has a secret name Tava. She freely helps her older sister connect with her body and awaken a sexual desire. Ru connection seems to give her mind a pathway to reach the younger man in his twenties to fulfill the young woman's request for a simply kiss of affection.

The young woman with the dual connection reaches his pant leg. She takes advantage with her hands and forearm. Ru spirit smells the sweetness of him when she reaches for his lips with her new body. He instantly accepts the warmth and tender touch of what he thought is Heidi, who breaks the connection with Lord Id.

Their passion erupted which sharpens the spirit of Queen Ru. Her instincts of the Jung zee mating ritual take over with a mighty roar and she bites him on the neck to claim him forever. She lets the wild passion of the combined Jung zee lust burst out. She rips off his clothes and mounts over his essence. The second mind link of Tava being so young confused by her sister sexual moment and quickly breaks the connection in fear. The evil intent of the Queen felt another surge of unknown energy. It pulsed through her human body as if Heidi wanted her body back. However, the queen's mind overtakes the human form. She then realizes a strange connection of the first human she had encounter long ago. That they seem to interact and become stronger all though her memories are vague she felt a strong increase of telepathic powers that made her hungry for more. She completes the act of cupellation, only to hear an echoing scream of her new name Queen Ru-Tava.

"Little one, we are now one; you are a queen of both human and Jung zee forever," proclaimed the Jung zee as Ru-Tava.

Eltross enters the scene with words of shock by such a display and angered by the act he uses mind force to yank her off and press her against the far wall. He aims the time crystal at the commander, which quickly blossoms into a shower bright energy turning him into small baby boy.

He picks up the baby, who looks confused, as he studies it. He sends it a mind message. "You shall be my second in command your name will be given from our holy and there you will earn the truth from the Myra clan." The small child smiled, "yes, I would like that," smiled once more.

Eltross turns to Queen Ru and sees the hate running deep in her eyes. They slowly turn red; he only thinks of aiming the crystal of time towards her. When she sees this, she quickly adjusts her mood and bows to him.

"I shall give you your little pet back. You may keep him for now."

He tosses him into her waiting arms. The baby grasps the crystal as he landed into the arms Ru-Tava. There became another transfer of great powers between the two of them with the energy flowing. She regains all her memories of the elder rogue and sees her death was no accident. Eltross quickly bows to her in fear and snarls a human phrase.

"Mother of all creation, I bow to your wishes."

Ru-Tava stunned by the human child that saved her from Eltross shook the very foundations in her quest for perfection. The darkness dismisses it when she sees the opportunity to have one powerful super race in the future.

"Let us proceed for I am not complete; I must have the other two in me to see the end of our quest. You may continue my son with all the plans," hissed Ru-Tava.

The boy's face changes from love to hate and rejects Ru-Tava. She laughs like a wild woman as she gives him away to a Myra servant. Eltross waves him and the child away. The ships begin to cross the barrier into the solar system of Ea towards the earth type planets.

CHAPTER 9

THE CRISIS ON HYPERION ONE

Captain Tava Pane had the hardest twenty-four period in her entire life, being thrust in command of Hyperion one after the death of Miles Oboe. Moreover, Mr. Winters had made an accidental error to wake the population from the bio tubes. The first of its kind a complete city of one hundred thousand humans from all over the Alpha Prime from the oldest aged fifty-five to eighteen, until she found children from ten years to five months from the damaged clone ship. She had spent four hours helping one hundred and three children to settle in the central bio dome, it was quite relaxing so many innocent faces she was amazed how they settled in their new environment. Being clones they are born at age thirty and preprogrammed to twenty years of hard labour. The oldest were twelve with basic skills in manner and protocols of language with math and writing skills. They were a source of cheap labour for the corporations. The government were addressing the rights and privileges to the clone race. Many tested for intelligence believed they had equal rights to the originals. Her parents were involved to give them rights at conference on the planet Titian. They pushed for better living conditions to have equality and safety. That is when things went wrong as everyone turned to the Beta project

She found more truth from her parent's adventure about the unborn child not being her biological brother but a hybrid who must be born on the planet's atmosphere or it will die instantly as claimed by Dr. Ian Ross.

He secretly attempts to undermine her authority on safety protocols when exploring the new solar system. With the help of an engineer named, Mack McKenzie who looked like a muscle-bound Viking with the brains of Einstein and the attitude of a street kid of old New York. He rescued the clone children from their bio tubes by hacking their computer codes. In addition, convince the three-construction ship to turned back away from entering the solar system and diverted them to the damaged spaceship of Dark ace and Sol1. She headed to the bridge; Mr. Winters was sleeping in the captain seat. She gave a short giggle as the computer came online to announce her arrival.

"Captain T Pane on deck," the mechanical voice crackles loudly!

Mr. Winters jumps out of his seat knocking over data chips from the recent probes exploring the Beta system. He bends down quickly to pick up the data as he muttered to himself. Tava Pane sees the deep worn out look of Mr. Winters. Her mother had mentioned he had lost his mind from the death of Mr. Oboe. She thought it was genuine grief that his best friend is dead. She moves closer with compassion shown across her face and takes the reports silently.

"You need some rest go and get some down time at least eight hours. I will take over and monitor the controls for the next shift. When do the other crewmembers come on duty," inquired Tava?

"Dr Ross prevented the pilots of the scout ships to awaken from the bio tubes at the lowest level he wanted the entire medical, scientist, and the engineer team ready to go. You might say that you cut him off good at the meeting," replied Mr. Winters with smug smile.

"Yes, I enjoyed that meeting but not the betrayals of my parents. Have we found him yet?"

"No, he vanished must of had advance knowledge of his arrest. There is only the lower chamber of level 101 section D rooms 1 to 500 restricted to Captain eyes only," replied Mr. Winters.

"I best get to work and find him. I will do it in a minute. I am curious who is flying the scout ships," muttered the captain. Her eyes caught six read outs from the radar and radio traffic.

"That's no surprise, it is our bridge crew. They volunteered and completed one third of the circle in search for any of those particles we can use for fuel," Mr. Winters mustered his words in a deep voice.

"Maybe I should go and help them," with enthusiasm voice as her eyes glittered slightly to fly an interceptor.

"No, you do not pull that crap on me. You are the captain you regulate but never do things on your own, especially in the command suit," hissed Mr Winters.

"Sorry I took enough courses to pass as alternate commander, you are right I should know better, you go and get some rest. The computer and I will watch the bridge monitors," suggested Tava Pane.

"Thank you, oh here are Miles Oboe files on the children of the light project," replied Mr. Winters who showed no interest.

Tava eyes widen as her ears perked to hear it was a project.

"You mean it is one of Gray's mega corporation projects."

"I do not know for sure, this is for captain eyes you can only read once for it self-destructs and you must be wearing the red suit so it will transmit to your cyber link when you are in dream state," stated flatly Mr. Winters.

"That sounds odd how will I remember what is inside in a sleep mode," inquired the captain. Winters shrugged his shoulders then went on to explain.

"No not really, Miles Oboe obtained a number of gadgets secretly like your command suit that fits this Captain chair it is a virtual connection to your mind, as you know. We all have a cyber link that was attached in our frontal lobes, once connected with the chair you become one with the main computer and can go anywhere in our city ship or any ship that is under our control. This gives way for quick command assessment to avoid danger and threats from outside or inside; be it a virus or insurgents of the third kind. When you see, secret material you wish to investigate just use the command words programmed in the machine for you."

"Miles was a gem he really wanted this to be his moment of glory. I will miss him," Tava sadly expressed. Mr. Winters gave a deep sigh and cleared his throat to prevent him from crying.

"I will go rest for six hours; the computer monitors everything. If you wish, take the seat, and learn the controls. The computer will help you in adjusting the

suit to the chair and you can check out those secret areas that I cannot access. That could be where Ian Ross is hiding."

"That would be fun, but I hope I do not fall asleep," giggles Captain Pane.

"You may think it is funny but our best work is done within our dreams young Tava Pane," replied Mr. Winters.

"Come again, that is wrong is it not dangerous to be taken over by any insurgents when you're in REM sleep," quoted the Captain Pane.

"Not really, the computer is your guardian it has its own power source number. One prime directive is to save and protect all life from harm especially the Captain," replied Mr. Winters. Tava moved closer to the well-cushioned chair and touched the surface of the chair with her fingers, while Mr. Winters saluted and said good night.

Tava eyes fixed on the captain's chair as she circles only to return the salute from Mr. Winters. This is her first moment alone since being awakened into tragic death of Miles, the surprise from her parents and Dr. Ian Ross obsession and the children of the light. *The answers are all in that chair of dreams,* thought Tava. Her eyes study the style and equipment attached to the chair. It is well cushioned in the back straight down to the seat and right down to the legs. It has the same cushion material on the armrests, which match her red jump suit. It had dollar size magnetic discs that aligned to her suit at the joints of her body for a connection to the AI computer. The headrest, a round shape helmet with wide visors covered her eyes to see inside the virtual world of the city ship through the computer. The voice of the computer broke the silence on the bridge, bringing Tava Pane back into being a Captain.

"I have found Dr Ross's DNA Trace to section101 level D; I lost him in the secret rooms for Captain Eyes only," crackled the computer voice.

"Send security force to arrest him," she coldly stated.

"They cannot go to the restricted area without clearance by the captain through the cyber link to enter that level. You must sit in the captain's chair to be able to pass on orders to the security force named the Black Watch from a late twenty century army battalion, most are androids with a few

Cyborgs that are still in hibernation. However, you command the androids Captain Pane through the virtual reality only in the captain chair please try it," suggested the computer voice.

Tava pursed her lips recalling her experiences of virtual reality on Mars she had countless lesson in these that always made her queasy Even though, it was frequently used in the context of entertainment by popular culture since the 1960. This illustrates the point that the future of VR gives emphasis into therapeutic, training, and engineering demands. Given that fact, a full sensory immersion beyond basic tactile feedback, sight, sound, and smell is unlikely to be a goal in the industry from the past to the future. She remembers the stimulating smells added to the realistic vision knowing it requires costly R&D to make each odor. This machine is expensive and specialized, using capsules tailormade to the user.

This more advance technology of Virtual reality will be integrated into daily life used in various human ways. Techniques devised to influence human behavior after the two world wars and the planetary, it open sharp sensors of the brain and improved cognitive skills. Many believed this was the cause of the human race plunging into violence from over stimulating the minds of millions. Since then several protocols were initiated and proof of two hundred years of peace came from it depressing the dark side of violence of the human race Tava took a bold step without reading the safety protocols. She wants Dr. Ross under her watchful eye before he could jeopardize the mission by rushing in without further study.

She recalls that through the history of Alpha Prime millions rushed to terra form the Jupiter moons of Ganymede, Callisto, Europa, and Io. As they were colonizing them, they found, new and strange bacteria causing plagues and in addition poor shielding from the radiation. It took twenty years later and close to ten million deaths to perfect the Vargas shield and drugs to combat and quickly multiply with the clones. The corporations fought over the other fifty-seven planets resources of gold, diamonds, and other great minerals. Alpha Primes new government quickly set rules and protocols for the safety of the colony and the people, which. Tava is determined to follow for this new colony.

Tava sits down slowly while her instructions to the computer let her get accustomed to the VR with a tour of the city ship. The computer replies in a cold tone. This makes her a little anxious when the sudden pull of each magnetic disc along her back and legs pulls and locks her in place. The computer asks two questions before joining in the VR.

"Do you wish the data of Miles Oboe included with your tour Captain Pane."

"Yes, that would be good idea" replied Tava.

"How long do you want to be in the VR program?"

Tava thought long she remembered she got sick the last time if she passed four hours, but with this suit she had all the available safety protocols online. She knew Mr. Winters would be back in six hours; she took a deep breath and speaks softly to the computer.

"Let me try Five hours and forty-five minutes."

"Will comply, clock is set, please place arms on the armrest and head back into the headrest so visor will animate the VR, Captain Pane."

Tava followed the instructions, her ears pick up the hum of the visor dropping down; she gives a silent giggle to dispel her fears. The main bridge shimmers in a bright light then fades away to view of open space. She bites her lip in fright as she found herself outside the ship; suddenly two small screens appear below the image in her eyes. The tour begins outside forward position to the slight damage by unknown material from the Star gate. She agreed to see it; the second panel gave a warning upon watching Miles Oboe's records require codes to proceed. She sends the code through her mind as well as tapping the invisible keyboard.

The Ai quickly acknowledges with a warning that this action my do brain damage upon receiving secret data. The mechanical voice requests a special code word for safety protocol to prevent memory loss to the captain. Tava quickly type her password Murphy laws 101, has a happy thought fill her mind by the strange sight of her spaceship Hyperion 1. She is intrigued by the patterns of the scoring on her ship. She floated closer and is amazed to see billions of little odd shape crystals imbedded in the spacecraft outer skin. The red sun made these crystals sparkle like tiny little stars that glowed with its own energy. She also saw debris from the other two ships floating by covered in the same crystal. Tava's mind of a scientist work on what these crystals could be and gave a sharp giggle suddenly had a flashback of what they really are possible fuel.

"I want samples taken to the lab before any repairs to the ship," ordered the captain.

"I will comply," buzz the AI.

She continues the tour outside as she looks at the other screen of Miles Oboe's file. It covers details of the command suit she is wearing. This gave extra information that it is a AI moulding device to enhance strength. It equally gives details about the computer link to all ships under the Grays Mega Corporation that also picks up the character of the user's traits in normal world. To Tava's surprise, learns that the command suit had built in weapons for defence and attacking. She brought up the lists of codes to activate all the devices and opened the first file using the password. Tava suddenly felt the tingle of a wave rushing on the right side of her face that increased to a pain level. She wants to touch it with her right hand, but it was locked down.

"Computer I have a slight irritant on the right side of my face please discontinue."

"Cannot stop time for five hours and four minutes, the irritant will stop upon the completion of battle codes, Captain. I could send you some medicine to ease the transfer, would that be to your approval," crackled a mechanical voice.

"Yes, please the pain is rising, and it hurts," hissed Tava.

The pain quickly evaporated as a surge of warmth came over her whole body. She notices that she had entered the upper loading dock where maintenance crews were prepping drones to gather the crystals samples. She also saw the damaged remains of a cyborg with human parts burnt to a crisp. The crew worked on deactivating the computer parts. She became concerned when the ship's crew made rude remarks of the dead cyborgs. She curses loudly as she calls out the names and gives out punishment. Both men stiffen to attention as they could feel the emotions through their cyber link.

"You are both fined one hundred credits and assigned extra duties to study the history of the cyborgs. You will speak in the plaza to the assembly on the new month of the first workday."

"Yes Captain, sorry sir we do apologies," quoted the young worker, while the other one just bowed his head in silence. The medical Doctors and engineers arrived to recover the remains of the human parts to study, while the engineers looked to salvage the computer parts of the cyborg. Mack Mackenzie is with this group. His presence gave Tava a slight flutter in heart as the man walks right through her VR.

She shook off the sudden surge as the second file of Miles Oboe came on screen with the same warning. She continues through the bulkheads to the core of the ship. She reaches the city centre. It was as small city like Slate Lake, or Rockland Canada, and the first city of Mars. It had a commercial center. They paid to have their corporate names of Hilton, MacDonald's, Lloyds of London, and many more who filled the city center of the world ship. Through human history from the late 1900, banks, fast food, clothing stores and other businesses were the norm. To her surprise, it was packed with the ship's crew all taking part of ongoing activities using their well-earned credits. She passes a few checking their identification and their personnel assignments. She could see why she must find Ian Ross. They were terra form workers waiting for the ship's departure in the new month with times and dates including duties under colony council. She was about to narrow her search to the secure areas that the computer suggested before she entered the VR.

Tava gasps when she sees a picture of herself when she was seven years old and focuses her attention to the number sequences on the left side. She begins to read the caption below her picture. It gave her parents name and her whole history from the first day to age twenty-three up to the date of the new assignment to the beta system. She saw sequenced recordings of the president of Gray Mega Corporation and pressed on to hear his words in the headquarters Mars central city. She recognizes Mr. Oboe and Dr. Ross with her parents.

"Gentlemen it is tough out there to get trained men and women to step into the cooperated world. We after all are the future of this world of Alpha Prime. Since the shortage of men and women, I do not want to follow the methods of our competitors but need smart hard-working crews on all our mining ships and colonies. We must go by the cloning method, like this child oh what is her name yes, Tava 3 her new name is Heidi with the usual background adjustments in her memory core. She is a level 8 telepathy. We will clone her several times and shall have different identities. They will not know each other clones and we will expect them to advance fast in ESP with great engineering skills different from to the original. Therefore, they never cross each other path is the priority. Many scientists suggested changing their eye and hair colour to prevent a complete copy of the original. I only want this project to be under code name children of the light. Only you Dr Ross and Miles Oboe handle this project 13b. The main reason I have consider this a priority is that you will never know when we need the two of you to go out and find other worlds. If the test works, we will try for the third one in ten years cycle. I want hundred thousand clones done each year for ten years. It starts today April 10, 2511. Gather all blood and tissue from all employee's adult and children who have extraordinary IQ scores."

"No, that is not possible; they would not do," wailed Tava. Then she sees her father stands up to offer his insight that this is morally wrong. We would be as evil and corrupt as the others are. However, her mother cuts him off with sharp hurtful words.

"We are talking tissue they have no value silly husband. Beside we are part of this corporation; we must adjust to survive against the other. I find no shame to keep this company expanding for the future at any cost. I as the others in this room know the true value of family," quoted Dr. Elizabeth Pane.

"Well put, I agree I would like to speed up the device we call the helix cube number 4d. Better than the other models as it records your whole life from three months to five years old and keeps the original DNA. In addition, it retains all its memories and skill levels obtained in 100 hundred years to the end of their life cycle." The president slams his hands on the table as the room went silent his words almost carry a hidden threat.

"You may use the Doctors and other important members but that is all. I want these cloned children to have a normal childhood so they can develop their ESP. See you stay the course, Dr. Ross."

The meeting is ended, and the screen went dark. She hit the pause button to clear her thoughts of mixed emotions as another dark event stunned her. They need to learn more of the helix cube became a priority. Medical improvements are part of the wave that pushes the human race out of their solar system. She clears her mind and asks the computer for a brief history on the helix cubes in general. The computer quickly answers the captain request.

"Created by two Doctors one a brain surgeon the other a computer specialist name Edward Bain MD and Claude Lanthier Md. Devise was the first name of the cube. Their invention was the first steps by a single microbe chip with optic fibre as thin as a spider string, with a power pack and processor about a size of a book. Used on patients with brain disorders example retardation, epileptics and metal disorders like Alzheimer. After many deaths, the first success May 6, 2189, one hundred patients cured of all their handicaps."

"Stop I know all that," grumbled Tava. The computer went silent instantly flashing a standby code. One of Tava abilities is that she recalls all human history by her memories. The computer is repeating knowledge she knows by heart. She decides to go back to the secret file.

"Please, return to the previous tape."

"Yes, I will comply," hissed the computer.

The next scene is with her mother she is walking into a white room dressed in a special suit with the younger version of Dr. Ross. The room is full of newborn children all in sleep mode except for twelve children. They are in another room and being watched by video cameras. Tava gasped as she sees herself much younger floating in mid air, her eyes glowing hues of blue. She swallows hard as she clears her mind to send a message to the main computer.

"Please, give me a read out on my helix cube three."

"Cannot comply due to disconnection sixteen years ago, "came a mechanical voice. Tava growled out her words. "On whose authority!" The AI gave a short answer, "DR. M. Pane September 9, 2315."

Tava's mind gave a long pause with one question why, while the computer ran on with other options and reports the scout ships are now halfway with no news. In addition, the construction ships number 4 has captured the Dark ace spaceship and returning to the docking bay slowly to ensure they secure the ship. "Do you wish to continue reading the file of Miles Oboe?"

"Yes," in a weak voice, *with hope for more answers* thought Tava.

Then came photographs and a bio read out of each clone compared to the original human. She found six clones each marked in code with different colour hair. The first one is a male with reddish hair, a wide forehead, and a square jaw line, *handsome* thought Tava. She then spots scores relating to ESP gifts. The second one had blonde hair about five years old. They all have a planted helix cube device. She now knows the third one is what her mother is carrying inside her. Sudden rage boils inside her for all the hidden lies. Tava Pane's must decide whether to keep it a secret or bring it out in open for discussion. The screen flashed three code words and a location in level D, section 101.

There she stands in the open foray with five separate hallways with one hundred rooms in each section. She passes through all the security clearance and disarms each one. After the report, Tava is not surprised to find the clone children playing a game of kick ball they seem to work like a team. It was symmetric in its form and style the ball never touches the ground as it bounced from each other with their minds. There out of the group of children Tava feels the little girl scanning her mind. Her eyes search and focus on a little blonde hair girl of five years old with electric blue eyes wearing a pink jumpsuit floating by her. This girl caused a wave of emotions in Tava. She looks to be in deep meditation and speaks with a sharp tone like her mother.

You are annoyed, you should not enter here with these emotions, came at little voice in Tava's mind. Caught by surprise she answers back harshly.

"I only want to see Dr. Ross, little one."

Everyone turns to the small child and shouts in panic as they run for cover.

"You have brought an original in our midst" the children echoed loudly in the play area.

"No, she is the Captain of Hyperion 1. Show yourself we wish to have a friendly greeting," rumbled the blonde child.

"Computer, please provide me with an image through their COM link," requested Tava.

"I will comply, but first you must choose Miles Oboe file code to end tape, which should it be. Captain Pane."

"Code word Gemstar we shall discuss this in the next meeting," mumbled Tava, as the file closed quickly. She felt a pull on the left side of her check.

Like magic, she appears in silhouette form in front of the little girl. The others came out to look at the aberration. Tava smiled and stood stiffly with arms out from her sides turning them back and forth to prove she had no weapons to harm the children. They all came around her to form a circle. The little blonde girl looks like age of five. Her skin colour was very pale and grey. *She looks underfed,* thought Tava. Her mind gave a sharp impression that the small one is reading her thoughts. She gazes at everyone to get an impression, but the children seem more curious about her ghostly image then what she represents.

"My name is Susan Chow we are all clones of our father Ian Ross, so how can we help you, he is not here at this time, Captain."

"My name is Captain Tava Pane;" she spots the eyes of Susan Chow flare by the recognition to the family name.

"I need to find him on a most important subject, to correct any misunderstanding between us, Miss Chow."

Every child broke into laughter like if Tava spoke another language, she then got the impression the other children were laughing at Susan. The little girl's face turns bright red, which gave a sharp clue that she could possibility be seeing her clone.

"In this place of our creation, we only use our first name or nickname among us. It is you, Captain that is disturbing the harmony of our group," snarled the red face girl.

"I am deeply sorry for any offence to your person. Dr Ross is what I came for," replied Tava who bows her head.

"He is in the lower docking bay preparing for our departure and a special launch ship called Wind Seeker," mutter Susan.

"Thank you Susan."

Tava is about to turn away to head for the other location. Susan read the captain's mind.

"I would be careful Captain; Dr Ross is no ordinary man to take lightly. He is committed to his goal by changing his name and appearances. I suggest you give him his space if we are to die, so be it. Is it not the way of humankind to stretch our limits at all costs," quotes Susan?

"Yes, that is in our history, but I hope to do it differently, can you give me his name," replied the captain.

Sudden alarms rang in Tava suit that she faded and reappeared on the bridge. The computer was shouting code red ninety-nine the three construction ships are under attack.

"Can you give me a feed and a better explanation," hissed Captain Pane.

AI computers click several times before it voice answer the captain. "It is verified data that alien attackers are on the three construction ships. But main computer bank shows no life from all its crewmembers. All brain patterns have been erased. There is no life aboard and I lost contact from the cyber link and all helix cubes locater confirms the disaster. Out of six hundred people, I find only three life forms. One is approaching from escape capsule on collision course to the lower docking bay of Hyperion one," sputtered the mechanical voice.

"All right, turn off warning alarms, charge up the ion canon at twenty percent impulse when it is in range. For back up, use our tractor beams to slow the advance of the runaway capsule," ordered the captain. Another voice of the scout ships leader name Lt. Ravenhawke ask to use her squadron to intercept the construction ships.

"Negative, I order you to pull back to a defensive posture cover our left flank," snarled Captain Pane.

Mr. Winters rushed in quickly to take command of the helm and weapons. He studies all the read outs to confirm the escape craft is coming in too fast. His mathematical mind quickly surmises that telemetry confirms it will miss us by five hundred yards. He reports this to his Captain. Tava rubs her chins; she thinks the survivors could be injured or unconscious.

"AI please, identify the humans and try to communicate to see if we can override the ship's system."

"Will comply," came the mechanical voice.

"What do you suggest Mr. Winters," hiss Tava?

"I am working on its Captain. I wish to check the navigation before I give you any options," gritted Mr. Winters.

"I identified the helix cube code is human. It is Lisa Thomas, bridge officer, upper management to the survey crew. She is with unborn child one of two that were given permission to have children during hibernation cycle." reported the computer.

"Can you take over the computer systems of the escape craft, requested the captain?

"Will try," came a strained mechanical voice.

Tava looked at the screen seeing the ship spin wildly and the long camera view of the four ships only minutes in passing the red sun giant solar winds. She was still in the captain seat. She looks at the time of the duration left on her suit forty-six minutes. Her eyebrow rose as she grunts a complaint to Mr Winters to hurry up.

"I can angle the plane so the ship will drop under the capsule, but we will be off course without fuel,"

"I have found fuel, I will explain later, just do it if the computer fails," mumbled Captain Pane.

Mr. Winters dropped open his mouth on hearing the news when a loud buzz from the computer announced.

"I have successfully overridden the escape capsule from the danger of collision."

"Her heart rate is in stress, and she is not communicating with the on-board computer. It believes she needs medical assistance" Captain Pane replied to the computer.

Tava pressed the communication switch to the medical center.

"Code blue medical assistance to the lower docking bay, with complete sterile environment complete shutdown of center and all assets to loading docks limited to command crew and medical officers," ordered Captain Pane.

"Yes, will comply."

She remembers Ian Ross.

"Oh, security arrest and contain anyone not authorized regardless of name or rank that includes Dr. Ian Ross and lock down the Wind Seeker."

"Yes, Captain Pane" came two acknowledgments from security and medical center.

Captain Pane moves slightly in her seat, while looking at the remaining time on her Virtual reality, which is forty-two minutes. She ponders if she can use her telepathic powers and tries to connect of the ships many computers. being in this cyborg suite gives her many options to save the three construction ships. She wonders if she could risk it to save 100 follow officers. The main Virtual reality computer crackled with static regarding that construction ship computer is now corrupted with a foreign substance. She continually plays with the idea, remembering that her Virtual reality is on every ship under Alpha Prime. She looks at Mr Winters and knows that he will demand that I have an escape route planned. At the same time, a voice on the radio kept requesting other suggestions, which she knew as the voice of LT. Ravenhawke She, is requesting once more to intercept the four ships.

"Scout one; please stand by for secret orders. Only you may head towards the three construction spaceships Lt. Ravenhawke do not cross into the influence of the red sun's solar winds, it could crush the starfighter" she said in a sharp tone as a plan form in her mind.

"Yes, Captain standing by," snaps Lt. Ravenhawke.

"Mr. Winters you have the con, I will be in Virtual Reality when this happens, I think I can turn around the three ships by altering the magnetic pull."

"That is too dangerous. You will have no back up" complained Mr Winters.

"I will switch to scout one if I am in danger," order Tava.

Winters cursed loudly, knowing she could be right to save the two ships with the dead remains of six hundred crewmembers. He nodded that it is her call and pleaded that she be careful. She nodded with one of her great smiles.

"S Lt. Ravenhawke proceed 100 hundred kilometers of our runaway construction number 1 spaceship and then stand by to pick me up in VR form," orders Tava.

"Will comply, Captain Pane," became the wary voice of the Lt. Ravenhawke. Tava had another plan in mind and bark out an order to the AI

"Computer transfer me to secondary bridge control on construction ship one and place me on standby to transfer to another location if I am threatened." The AI gave a short answer in a monotone voice.

"Will comply stand by distance delay five minutes."

"Good luck" was the last words Mr. Winters muttered that Tava Pane hears before she went in complete darkness.

It is black she did not even hear her breathing; all five senses complete shutdown. It felt like five minutes turned in to hours. A slow panic crept in her thoughts that everyone is dead. She swallows back the panic, finally her eyes started to see image of the secondary bridge come into view. Built has a backup to override the main bridge when attacked or destroyed. It was hard to get a clear look from the lowlights in the bridge. She knew there is always one crewmember on duty. Based on the low lights she knew it is sleep period for some of the crew. Tava prepared herself to see dead bloated bodies. What she saw next only puzzled her mind. She saw a little boy of three as he crawls out of a space suit. He could see her somehow and saluted. A very naked child Tava saluted back trying to show no fear she knelt to his level.

"Could you tell me what happen little one."

He spoke in Spanish with a shrug of his shoulders. His hands went down to cover himself up has he blushed. The main computer quickly translates.

"Sergeant Rodriguez stated a deep light wave went through the whole ship that is all he can remembers he wants to know where he is and wants to go home to his mother." Tava pursed her lips and in broken Spanish with the help of the computer.

"Tell him soon I promise."

She immediately goes to work on the computer to override the engines in a complete reversal and automatic shut down to prevent them to enter the solar winds of the red sun. The young boy watches intently and sings a Spanish song. Tava warn the child to be silent in case of alien takeover of her ship. Finally hears footsteps approach the door.

It opens as two cloak beings appear carrying seven children. The computer whispers to Tava the code to summon warrior weapons are standing by. She sent a message to be quiet. The boy cried in panic as one reached down to pick him up. Their faces were concealed no language spoken that she could understand only bird chirping. They gave him a small florescent tube filled with unknown liquid. The minute the liquid touched his lips everything changed. The boy pointed to the computer panel that she was working on. The two aliens chirp at each other then release the boy who shuts down the computer and locks it out. He gives a smile with his arms out to reach the hooded being. *The child look contented* thought Tava. Her eyes study the others; they all seem to be happy children. She aims her bioscope to analyze what is in the florescent tube that the alien is giving to child. The human side of Tava wanted to intervene with the attempt to save these children. However, parts of her scientific mind had to many questions that ran through her mind. Like how the crew turned into children and where are their helix cubes that contains the knowledge of being a human and technical knowledge that runs this spaceship. She wonders if they would attack her and Hyperion 1, she had to be careful do more research to understand what is really happening to her construction crew on the three spaceships. She decided to wait and see what these alien beings really want to hold back on any rescue.

The two hooded beings quickly left with the children. She followed them out on to the hallway to the loading doc. all eight children turn their heads and stare at her, while drinking the liquid. Tava quickly touch each one to check on their blood samples. The elevator opens to a teenager girl with a baby. She approaches the child to collect more samples his eyes spread wide open like if he could see her. He cries out as the child quickly buried his face into the young woman's chest. She snarls and snaps a curse in a language that Tava had never heard in her life. It is similar to the chirping of the other two cloak creatures but gives her a chill. Then the eight children point at Tava's location. The beings at the entrance loudly squealed that almost pierces her eardrums. She falls backwards in the other bulkhead and reappears in loading dock c. She checks all systems before she will go exploring. Tava makes notes and checks the time fifteen minutes remain on the VR.

"I must do something to save these ships," snapped Captain Pane.

A strange sound rustles behind her; she feels a strong mind presence standing right behind her. She moves in a slow circle to get a better view while her hands move to hit the escape recall to Lt Ravenhawke. She sees her mirror image, becomes puzzled while her eyes readjust to the poor lightening. Fear burst inside Tava as she shouts.

"Beam me out now," oh god she hits the control switch. The alien creatures swarm in a blue haze with multi legs three feet high and six feet to one foot in length. Two large round eyes a small nose with two small but sharp mandibles that flex and chatter with chirps. Their body is so smooth and mirrors the world around them. The beetles surround Tava Pane with an energy field that block out any transmission. She was their prisoner. The energy field even cut off all her weapons.

Oh, hello, I greet you with open arms of peace and tranquillity mother of the light echoed a booming voice within her head.

Who dares to speak in my mind with abounding strength show yourself, demanded Tava. It laughs before it answers.

We are old friends in another lifetime; my children and I will not harm you. You are holy to us, you are special to my race, and I wish to pass a gift to you, after all, it is you, who gave it long ago and told me to give to you when meet in this timeline.

What happened to my crew, why are they turned into children, demanded Tava?

That is another story I am not part of the beginning, old friend you well learn everything from the file tape, Good-bye, and safe journey.

The swarm of beetles moved away, and the last order given transfers Tava Pane onto the scout ship as a ghostly figure, which startles the Lieutenant. She hits full thrusters to her scout ship. Her mind shook from the surprise of the large insect and its army. The insect's size was beyond description, she quickly checks her recorder on the visual display to show the science experts on first contact with aliens. This was one of her favourite hobbies next to astronomy and navigations. She had a wide collection of insects in the special bio tubes to use as part of the terra forming. She looks back as it cuts across the bridge using all thrust power to escape the solar winds of the giant red sun. Tava checked the radiation level and noticed the sudden peak.

"Do you have the shields on maxim Lt. Ravenhawke," quotes Tava?

"Yes Captain I do, but I must say you sure scare me in that florescent suit."

She hit the arm display to communicate with Mr. Winters on the bridge. No answer came when she called. Tava look long at the disc while she was waiting for Mr. Winters to answer.

"Computer, locate Mr. Winters on his cyber link and order him to respond," with a slight irritation in her voice.

"Yes, which one we have him on the bridge and in his sleeping quarters Captain Pane."

"Oh, God no. emergency securities to the bridge send me to the bridge active energy field around my location."

"Sorry cannot supply securities due to the activities in the lower docking platform. Your energy field is too far from the spaceship to transfer." She suddenly had trouble breathing as she felt shadows coming after her.

The Lieutenant offered her a spare oxygen mask out of habit. Tava knew that she really needs someone to save her on the bridge. The duplicate Mr Winters giggles and whispers in her ear.

"I must follow my orders from Dr. Ross. The strange happenings to the other ships were not his primary responsibility, only killing the Captain and Dr. Pane. The crisis provided the best opportunity to eliminate the whole Pane family."

He knew her body would be all his in a matter of minutes. He reaches down in his baggy pants and pulls the electric cord. He knew that he had very little time. The other scout ships had landed in the upper docking bay, and they will report to the main bridge for extra duty time. They should be up here in another hour reported the computer. At the same time in the lower deck, the emergency was just reaching crucial stage. He steps closer to the captain's chair. He is curious to touch her body, she looks very attractive as he places her hair back a little so he can study her beauty in a natural sleep mode thought the duplicate. He wraps the cord around her neck and starts to press his strength. He can see the reaction in her body as she begins to shudder slightly. He mumbles to himself, wets his lips, and shows his teeth.

"Father will be so pleased of my good handiwork."

Tava through sheer will focussed to fight off the attacker. She waves about her arms striking feebly, the lack of air press heavily on her mind. The vision she is receiving of a death mask from Mr. Winters.

"You will die now little one," giggled Mr. Winters was the last words she recalls as her vision narrows.

A sudden shadow appears over the head of Mr. Winter's duplicate; Just has Tava looks up she see a giant fist smashing into Mr. Winter's face. The sheer force of the blow actually sent him over and across the captain's body. The sudden relief came to Tava and the image of Mack McKenzie strange smile. The duplicate hissed and snarled like a wild animal as it shook off the effects of the hit. Tava rechecked her locater to the Hyperion it flashes quickly in range ten seconds. She places the disc to be played back as she orders the transfers, the sudden darkness of an empty void briefly fill her mind. Her eyes saw the recorder of the strange object; she sat straight up and screamed as the decapitated head of Mr. Winters rolls to her feet.

CHAPTER 10

AN OLD FRIEND AND THE CHALLENGE

A huge insect four times the size of a blast boat rumbles in a deep and hollow song in greetings to the little ones. The swarm of beetles and larva move back to their mother. The beetle gathers her children. The high guardian of the Myra clan Leaders stood by a healer, warrior, farmer, peacemaker, and a wizard high priest of the old text. Dressed in coloured robes and the gold chain of office, he enters the docking bay with the small human children. They spoke as well as communicate telepathically, among themselves.

"Are they the chosen ones", echoes the queen to the six scholars. She already knew it to be true, but it would take time to prove to the unbelievers.

"We are not sure my queen they have been altered," quoted the high priest.

"We want more proof," barked another.

"Since they are children you will teach them our ways, if they grasp our ways is that not proof what they are as the two-legged race written in our ancient text," replied to the queen in a soft voice.

All six agreed in unison with a bow.

"I see you have started to feed them my milk," the queen replied anxiously.

"Well Yes, they are children they need nourishment," muttered the Myra farmer.

The Sleeping Queen wanted to ensure that her milk cared for the little ones. It had healing qualities that would give them time to readjust to their new lives in the Ea solar system. The three suns emit a high range of radiation which are deadly to soft flesh that she had seen upon her arrival with her larva's until she found the right combination to combat the effects. She follows the instructions of Eltross her new husband she had picked many years ago, in hopes that her race would move to the next solar system, a promise that Eltross had not fulfilled.

The prophecy of the arrival of a third race caused a great stir between the two-insectoid races. The Jung zee queen Ru went on a murderous rage, as did the Jung zee horde that kills all their young. This had a great outcome on her clan and the high priests, both torn in different directions, luckily, Eltross calmed everyone. The Sleeping Queen decides to take the children to a better atmosphere, without any Jung zee on that planet. The Sleeping Queen recalls the past that clearly confirms in her own mind that they are the ones. Memories of her long years of travelling through space by the hidden message of a nameless god to terra form the planets she encountered.

From a bright star of red, white and blue they will appear like innocent children, with great acceptance and love offered without question or demand. The mother of light will appear a glowing aura of peace and harmony. She being the oldest monarch to reign over the Myra clan reread the ancient text, finding the verse to confirm that they were the ones.

She remembers the first meeting she had ten thousand years ago in the far off quadrant. When she fell ill and a humanoid gave her the medicine to continue her quest in making living planets and searching for the chosen one. The Sleeping Queen recalls the final instruction of the first humanoid's request ten thousand years ago to hand over the flat metal piece back to the woman.

She lowers her thorax to have the children enter her body of soft cushion hairs that wrap and secure them while they feed on her fluids. She had gathered all the crews from the other ships at such great speed that neither

Lord Id nor Eltross knew of her plan. The last one a male baby responded with such open words of love from the mind gift that he possessed. She places him nearer to her head of the six hundred children. She rejected the young woman with a baby because she is under the influence of Lord Id.

"You must seek Eltross to be free from the other. You have chosen poorly little one. You must redeem yourself before I can accept you. Just like the one female whose passion for another blinded her to the truth when she gives up her body to the Jung zee queen and lost her soul to the dark side beyond my power," stated the blue beetle.

The young woman gave a sad and painful look as she bows, then walks back to the main bridge. The high priest began chanting a prayer to prepare the way to the sixth moon on the outer rim of the beta twins. The queen waits to pass the barrier of solar winds from the two larges stars. The large beetle falls into a dream recalling the first meeting of Tava Pane. She knows very well the fourth generation will rise regardless of what the gods do to them. Human minds are small and use only one third of their brains. With her formulas, they will slowly accustomed to the new worlds eventually. In a non-violent way, this she had seen in the eye of Tava Pane.

She tired of the Jung Zee ways they live for chaos and disorder pushed to the point, only the strong will inherit the worlds and the cosmos by the nameless god. Lord Id being a Jung Zee like always declared himself a servant to the god of chaos. The first thought of him gives her a shiver as the red sun light rolls across the ship. A slight vibration shakes the ship plates. Her six legs took the blunt of the shaking, the children never felt it and most seem to fall into a deep sleep.

"Go my trusted Myra leaders and take control of these ships. My husband waits you at the main bridge. You will absorb their experience," ordered the queen.

All six turn to each other silently then bow to her orders.

She steps to the opening of outer space to line up her body to the chosen planet. She summons the energy within her and the sharp tips of her mandibles began to glow. The creature develops a round barrier from an energy sphere. The beetle walks in the flow and vanishes in a bright blue flash. She suddenly reappears on the planet with a large sonic boom on a high mountain. She first looks about on this lifeless planet, at the time there was a full dust storm in the lower valleys of the desert floor. She releases all her children of larva and nymphs' beetles.

"Go and prepare the way for the new ones," ordered their queen.

"Yes, great mother," chirp the beetles as they scatter quickly and spread out in great numbers.

"Bring grass, trees, and spring flowers, babbling brooks to fill an ocean depth, to feed the youngling nymphs of the human race, to give a whole new world their playground by the time Eltross arrives," softly whispered the Sleeping Queen.

"We shall honour our human brethren into the light of truth," chirped the lead Myra beetle as the others started to sing their mother's praise.

The queen goes into the cave all six legs move in sync across the soft sand. The human children nestled deep in a trance like state. She begins a deep-throated song heard for miles. The insect children answer in loving praise to their mother, while the sun sets down. The Sleeping Queen feels the slight change in the ground, knowing a new world is about to be born from love and a deep promise to save the fourth generation. She reminisces of the old ones who saved her life and gave her purpose to establish a wandering race from extinction with the gift deep inside her being. She wonders how long it would take the evil ones to find she had taken their human children. The queen will challenge them in a way to bring the humans here, to prove they were the ones to join all three races into a single hybrid race. She wonders what it was like to be human as her mind taps into the children's subconscious. They were dreaming of their home planet earth. The queen related those images to her own children in an effort to duplicate the world of earth. *This would help them accept their new lives* thought Sleeping Queen.

Meanwhile the six Myra Guardians go to meet Eltross on the main bridge. They walk in give the message that they are here to take the knowledge of the humans to pilot the ships and build the construction of star point. Eltross barked and grumbled at them when he realizes what his queen had done. Queen Ru-Tava only laughs with the news that his wife took all six hundred children except for the one woman and child. Somehow, a jealous streak burst through Ru-Tava as she stares angrily towards the naked woman and child. Lord Id had possessed her mind and body to the dark shadow. *He chose this one for his own experiment* thought Eltross. The female drops on all fours and kisses the queen's feet in her new form, speaking Jung zee in the lower classes of their race.

"I am here to serve you and god of the light," chirps the woman.

"In our race there is only one female to have child of the Jung zee, horde little nymph. You are a reject in my eyes; the value in you is food for my people."

Eltross gave a sharp long chirp tone. "Queen Ru-Tava do not be so hasty in dismissing her after all if they are the ones we must learn more about them then eat them."

The woman suddenly wails at the site of Eltross who steps forward between the Myra guards. She drops flat on the floor and softly whispers a prayer to the glowing being.

"Mercy, the light of truth," she cried aloud and turns quickly to offer herself to him, much to the displeasure of the Jung zee queen and the Myra priest who swings his staff hard against her back then kicks her hard in the ribs.

"Heresy you lowly creature you do not offer your essence in that fashion nymph of human race," chirped the priest

The woman prayed as she accepts the beating by both the priest and Queen Ru-Tava.

"The heavens have opened to the light of your face; the search has brought us here to your true radiances. Praise the light I see before the true gods of all creation. I only ask to be touched and cured so I may join my brethren taken by the queen of passion."

Eltross intrigued by the fixation of the human woman's inner strength who has given him an ancient prayer of the Myra clan, while accept the beating from the Jung zee queen. The other five Myra circle the woman and hold back their anger upon hearing the prayer, and whisper that another proof is given that she recognizes Eltross as a god.

"You promised not to interfere with my plans on these humans Ru-Tava. She and her larva including the six hundred other humans are under my protection" grumbled Eltross, in addition has he turn to face her. "I must lure the world ship into Ea space."

Ru-Tava grunted then aimed the crystal at the young woman and child. She recalls all the humans' lives and medical information at the same time as the beam hits the two pushing them back as the boy fades inside the woman. The little girl cried for her baby, much to the pleasure of the Ru-Tava.

"In our world, only two queens allowed children. You can now teach the ways of the Myra she is a true nymph like the others now!"

"You fool, they are different even if we alter them biologically their mating is different to the ways of our two races. Even you in that body could have a human child from that encounter you had with the other male figure," barked Eltross.

"No that is impossible," mumbled the human lips in wary tone of Ru-Tava as doubts sprung in her thoughts.

The oldest Myra steps forward, now as a healer, picks up the little girl and whispers something in her ear that silences her wail. She accepts the blue liquid and then covers her under his cloak. Eltross takes a deep breath while shaking his head at Ru-Tava.

"We need more information on the humans that you stole and I must read all their memories stored in these crystal."

Confused by the suggestion that she has a human child inside her only hardens her heart to kill it. She only saw brief images of human pregnancy. The inner voice of the caretaker quiets the thoughts of the Jung zee queen with a whispered suggestion.

Go to the medical center to test if you are pregnant. You are tired from the great change. Give Eltross the crystal freely he knows it belongs to you, came a strange inner voice.

Ru-Tava's face changes from scorn to an expression of weariness. She hands over the crystal to Eltross. He bows to Ru-Tava and then turns to face the six Myra guardians. The queen walks away from the main bridge, silently to head back to the medical center. The caretaker suppresses the rage of the Jung zee, believing that she could have the first hybrid under her control if what Eltross had just claim be true. Eltross eyes expand with the energy in his hands. All join in a tight circle to mind link with the information it held of human memories. The crystal sparks a soft blue narrow beam reaches the frontal lobes of Eltross mind like candy he hungrily accepts the knowledge, which fulfills him deeply. All though something inside is missing, since the separation from the inner spirit of Lord Id. He passes the information of the three construction ships to the Myra clan. Each one receives their instruction then leaves Eltross to study all the information in detail.

He learns their history and finds ways to control them with his god like powers. He recalls the reaction of the woman when she first saw him in this image. He sees the many religious faiths recorded from the earliest history of man. Eltross sees religion as a way to control his new pets; he knows this is his only opportunity to bring a perfect race through crossing breeding. Eltross looks back further into the history of the humans many cultures and religious beliefs. That dates back to the pagan times and even further to cave dwelling. He wondered how they accelerated in such a short period to arrive at this far distance world. The quick awaking to explore space beyond their system is like a leap of faith. This could fit in his plans, and he studies more to find ways to control his test subjects. With so much information available to him, he takes notice of the reason they have come here.

What brought these humans out so far by the images of the fourth and fifth war, which almost wipe out the race of humans? The constant wars throughout their history intrigue him as compared to the Jung zee in rotating cycle of twenty to thirty years. The humans also had great advance in building temples to the gods plus the demands on their resources similar to the Myra culture that nearly wipe out their civilization before the wandering days in deep space. They terra formed countless moons in their solar system before they arrived in EA space.

Eltross now understands why Lord Id attacked and captured the crew of the construction ships. Lord Id appears in a sudden burst of energy that reacts to the human mind as an evil god. They all cried out demon so absorbed by the image of him in their words of ancient demons of earth. He remembers the other races stories of their first meeting with Lord Id who was referred to as a trickster or shadow fool. He tried to trick the Sleeping Queen to enter the Ea solar system. He believes this to be true when his mind envisions Lord Id's, large round head, sharp glowing horns and perfect round eyes of ebony. It gave a deathly chill to any human who gazed at them. The creature is small in stature of a young teenager wearing a black cloak. It had large dark wings with four sharp fingers and toes.

Eltross shuddered from the sight as he refocused back on the humans and ways to bring them into the Ea solar. He sees their solar system of nine inner planets with four outside planets on wide orbit, he studies the sun classified a grey star completely different from his ea solar system. Eltross breaks from the crystal to find ways to bring them inside the system deep within him. While he ponders in quiet reflection, the little girl's head came out of the Myra cloak. Her eyes were big and round. They reflect the souls of the innocents. The human children are happy when well fed by her milk.

"Oh, god of light may I have a blessing before I go to sleep with the others so faraway I feel so lost," she says in Myra tongue of chirps and whistles.

Eltross looks up from his deep thought with a strange smile. He steps over and touches the child's head. He feels the quiet mind inside her as a vacuum wanting to accept the gift of a god.

"Yes, I grant you insight and the return of your son, but you must be mindful to follow the ways of the Myra. Then all will be true to you little one," whisper Eltross.

"The others will learn if you would be more open with us," murmurs the child. She yawns and slips back into the cloak of the old healer.

"It is a better way then genocide that the Jung zee practices my lord," muttered the Myra healer. That makes him look up with a sharp glance, as the revelation came to him the answer so simple thought the god of light.

He turns away to clear his thoughts while he examines the ships contents. He sees maintenance androids picking up all the uniforms that lay about the hallways. He finds three books of poetry. He reads aloud the words but does not understand the emotional meaning. Hours go by as he reaches the medical center seeing the human female struggling with the equipment battling the Ru- Tava in her body. She had taken off her clothes he could hear three voices in the female. The one he fears is the caretaker, since it was he that had murdered her so that he could take more powers to influence Lord Id to be part of the Myra clan. It had worked but Lord Id reacted against the Jung zee for killing the caretaker not knowing the truth about her death. Ru-Tava finally shuts out the voices inside her and takes control of her new form. She evokes her chi with a powerful word in an ancient tongue that Eltross never heard before as he sends her a compliment.

"You are full of surprises queen of the Jung zee."

She turns to snarl a challenge at him. Eltross waves his hands in a peaceful way, to the Jung zee it means surrender to a Myra he wants peace, to a human Eltross head spins from peace to war. Eltross offers her the time crystal with a deep bow. She snatches it holds it tight to her naked breast. It begins to glow and seems to add strength and awareness. Her fingers brush the left nipple of her new body that rise up with a trace of white fluid appearing. The scent arouses Eltross as he suggests to the Jung zee queen.

"I see my claim is right that you have become pregnant in this human form. It would be interesting to study its development to see if it becomes a hybrid."

"Yes, Lord Id and you would be interested in that, but not I, unless she becomes the true ruler of every living being in the Ea space."

"I want the other two Tava females I will give you this thing in my body freely."

"I agree but you need to be patient. I l have a plan when we reach the planet where the Sleeping Queen has gone" hissed Eltross.

"I hear Lord Id is upset with her taking the six hundred children, have you not heard him scream in anger," barked Ru-Tava.

Eltross rolls his eyes back as he connects with Lord Id. His bright aura changes into a darken shroud around his small frame. They mind link as the queen watches with interest. She circles Eltross with thoughts of revenge but the other side of her the one she depressed surges up to cool her thoughts. She backs away and listens to the two gods talk to each other.

His mind travels back to the planet Zlotoo where Lord Id reigns over the Jung zee horde. He sees the destruction of the Jung zee nest and larvae forms, which spewed out and spread across the desert floor. He hears the cries of the Jung Zee warriors in a ritual form to mate with the queen. He realized the connection when Ru Tava changed itself it felt like the death of the queen to the Jung Zee warriors. It is in all adult males to fight each other to the death to be the only one to mate with the Queen. The sudden violence came as a surprise to Lord Id after the transfer of the two queens who were supposed to subdue the race while he quickly replace the children with new eggs. He blames Eltross and the Sleeping Queen for not returning here with the six hundred. He wanted to show the new beginnings of the prophecy but instead he watched over the battles that will reign for months.

Eltross arrives to see the carnage all around the lower level of Lord Id's temple. His mind moves up the long stairs to the altar. He floats by a dozen of the Jung zee warriors fighting each other. His authority causes a brief stoppage while they angrily curse at the light for stealing their queen. Eltross ignores their wails of hate and rage to reach the top where he knew Lord Id would be waiting. Lord Id final feels the presence of the light and jumps down from his perch with his wings spread open causing a large shadow over the stairs. Eltross sees his approach with a deep resentment in his eyes.

"Look what you and your queen have done to my best pets, you have not kept our agreement and now I want my pound of flesh," roared Lord Id.

"We have all made mistakes this day brother; do not add more to it. Your pets act this way for they are programmed to respond after the death of the newborns caused by the queen Ru's fear of the new beings," replied Eltross.

Yes, with a snap of his wings as he hesitates then closes his wings and lands a few feet to Eltross floating mind.

"My pets are now modifying the three construction ships and repairing the other for our lab to experiment on the new beings. With the improvements to the Myra clan, the ship will jump at the oxygen type planets in hours instead of months. Let us work together on this," pleaded Eltross.

"I would like that but the Sleeping Queen plotted her own way with my captured prisoners by protecting them with her life giving milk, like did the Jung zee queen, by disobeying my order. By taking over a human female and kissing the commander, waking her lust for mating changed everything," hissed Lord Id.

"Calm yourself little one, I am still your caretaker, but now my two sons you may call me mother" came the new female voice of Ru Tava.

"What is the word mother it has no meaning to me, if you are my caretaker then that is what you are," snapped Lord Id.

"It is a human word for caretaker," garbled Eltross who nervously blinked and backed away from the red sphere.

"Yes, that is true of the meaning, but since I am the oldest between the two of you, I claim it and demand that title," snarls the red sphere.

"Of course, I will call you mother," in awry voice from the god of light.

"I will not change my ways, and you can only be my caretaker," replied Lord Id.

"You are still fuming over my accidental death; I think it affected your mind in some ways after you separated into two gods," snaps the red sphere.

"Nonsense he has his powers and I have mine we work for the one race ruled by one mind, we are one in the same thought, mother dearest," replied Eltross.

"Yes, this agrees with the god of light, caretaker of the unseen world," hissed Lord Id.

"Very well, I will speak of it no more, do you wish to journey with us to the other planet," offered the red sphere.

"No, I must wait here to fight the last Jung zee. I demand you bring the Sleeping Queen here in three months time to start the mating process. Alternatively, I while create a new race from her larva," barked Lord Id.

"She will be there in time" grumbled Eltross he bows and fades away for he felt some urgency from his Myra leader that had control of the ship.

"Eltross plan is much more practical to ensnare the humans I have calculated I need a billion life forms to find the right connection to develop a hybrid race to follow our minds," giggled the red sphere.

"That ship only carries one hundred thousand humans, it would take more than a thousand ships to fill our needs caretaker," came a deep sigh from Lord Id.

"I found some odd connection, which I will investigate it could be the clue in helping reach that number. Let us sit back and watch Eltross trick and blind them. He has a gift to lure them in our space," replied to the red sphere

"Yes, you are right caretaker this time I will show more patience," stated Lord Id.

"Beside after the mating ritual you must leave this space to renew the energy of your alter state. Not like me, now that I have a permanent human body you should have joined me in that quest," replied to the red sphere, feeling the urgency to rejoin Eltross.

"The human sexual process is too binding to individual emotions with a single offspring. While both the Myra and the Jung zee give a great emphasis in large numbers. You are right the first time my queen they are only food source for us," snapped Lord Id.

"I am glad you see it my way but let us play the game with Eltross if he is right you must think of the possibilities. We could control one race to inherit the whole cosmos, that is our first goal little one," quote the red sphere then fades from his view.

He shouts and takes to the air as he returns to his throne on top of the tower.

"I will be watching and waiting for the news to feast on at my next mating ritual."

The red sphere rejoins the human's body feeling a drop of temperature in the medical center. Her cold body is not used to mind travel. She puts on a nursing uniform lying on the floor. It fits her well; she giggles and reads the name tag, Nurse Mead. She feels the strange sensation of the fabric; *seem to be a second skin* thought Ru-Tava. She quickly feels the tension in the ship and heads for the main bridge. Eltross faces his first challenge of the human Captain dressed in warrior uniform; it glistens with energy of her life force with the face hidden by a mask, with only her lips speaking harsh words.

"You have attacked our people and provoked an act of war by stealing our ships.

"I beg to differ on those two rueful words; we did not attack or steal. We came when we felt a distress from your people."

"Then return them for a peaceful solution," demanded Capt. Pane.

"That is impossible; they were struck by a temporal time plasma that shoots out from our red sun it caused a strange illness. We have grown accustomed to it with these special liquids. Once immune they will start their lives all over again. I took the responsibility to finish their goals and bring them to a planet that they have chosen to build the colony. My name is Eltross creator of the Myra clan."

"May I speak to my commander to confirm this story," insisted Captain Pane?

"I am afraid he is gone with the others. My Queen took them immediately to the planet; rest assured they are safe in her care," giggled Eltross.

Ru-Tava enters and feels the pull of energy of this well armed warrior on the view screen. She walks in towards the old Myra healer and takes out the little girl. She fusses in Ru-Tava hands her eyes flare to the child, which sent a clear thought that she would kill all the humans if the girl did not prove that Eltross saved them. The god of light yanks the child away from Ru-Tava, this happens so quickly that Captain Pane did not see it except for the well muscle man sitting in the communication booth who was playing with switches checking other monitors. He spoke to the little girl in his own language as he points to the image on the screen.

"You must tell the truth what had happened, but I remind you of your blessing," whispered Eltross.

She gave a nod and stood up on the work desk monitor to let the captain see her clearly. The completely naked child with a small round face, large brown eyes and messed up black hair shivered with goose pumps on her flesh.

"We creatures wear clothes for warmth and protection from illness, this one should have clothes on for god sakes," with hint of irritation from Captain Pane.

"They do not know our ways Captain, if they knew they would have given me something to wear, I was lost in thought looking for my child and my mother. This is all strange to me," stammered the little girl. She placed her thumb in her mouth and went silent.

Eltross removes his cloak and covers the child then hands her to the healer who whispers something to the god of light. He turns to see the tall male shouting in rejoice that they have found a living god. The god of light took it a little further as he reveals his whole-body shape. Luckily, the brightness of his body shorted out the view screen. Leaving only, the audio as both voices call him a true god of the light and ask for his forgiveness in speaking so rudely to him. This caught the alien by surprise that he could affect the minds of weaker beings. His presence seems to inspire him as he spoke human words once again.

"Come and join us to renew you lives in peace and tranquility of the Ea solar system," proclaimed Eltross.

"Oh, lord god yes you are our special blessing we have search long for to embrace new beginnings. Yes, we are coming with open arms," replied the captain with enthusiasm in her voice.

"You have them in your hands" snarl Ru-Tava.

Then the view screen burst into flames and fades disconnecting the link as well as the audio. The Myra crew scramble over the connections to correct. Eltross glared angrily but held his words briefly. The farmer steps forward and bows before he spoke. "The ion sphere is blocking the audio communications my lord." Eltross muttered under his breath a simply order. "Then let us proceed to the oxygen planet to join the others at jump speed." The Myra guardian called out, "Yes, sir engine starts in five, four, three, two, and one," suddenly all three construction spaceships flash way to their new world.

The ship rattled slowly to a violent shake and broke to a jump speed as it vanished from Zlotoo. The little girl counts the planets as the healer points to the planet where the others were living. "This should be called Terrain 6 the home of the human colony," proclaimed the little girl.

Eltross thought for a moment and agreed to name it Terrain 6. He quickly started to work on the structure of Star point. He feels the mind of his Sleeping Queen to hurry and complete the project.

Ru-Tava found children's clothes and plans to distribute them among all six hundred the children. Once they landed, they found the planet had completely changed from the last time Eltross was here on his honeymoon with the Sleeping Queen. He is happy to be around his children of larva, pupa, and nymphs. The older beetles had already changed into the pupa state lined the entrance to the large cave openings. They turn into adults of the Myra clan. Ru-Tava stays in the ship because the Sleeping Queen has a different view towards the murder of the nestling child of the Jung zee. Eltross steps out of the lead ship while all six hundred human children sang." praise to the gods of light.' He then releases the little girl who skip down the ships ramp into the crowds of children she speaks Myra tongue. She explains that this is our new world Terrain 6. They all cheer Eltross name. He raises his hands everyone went silent to listen to his words in human tongue.

"If you are the chosen ones of prophesy. I will share myself with you through our mind, body, and soul. The Sleeping Queen has waited for hundred thousand of years. I greet you with a loving embrace, as she is willing to the test for now you must build your home for the others. They will join you here at star point. You will be the leaders of the future."

The human children still drinking the blue liquid slowly gather around to cheer Eltross name. They all line up in six rows to collect their jump suits, shoes, and tools to help build the structure of Star point. They were now imprinted to follow the words of the Sleeping Queen and the six Myra guardian clan members and the god of light. Eltross touches a few children all were the same empty mind with a willingness to learn a new life. He walks up the path to the cave to see his Sleeping Queen. She would at least listen to reason for the test must also satisfy Lord Id. He knew this would be a difficult challenge. He hates this part to confront her about the error of accepting these beings as the three groups of prophesies without more tests.

He approaches her with open arms and greets her in a poetic song of love chirps from their first ritual of mating. The queen steps out in the morning sun his eyes open wide to the large size she had grown. The blue beetle stood one hundred feet in length and forty feet wide in the thorax with her oval shaped head eighteen feet wide. She had no eyes the only connection is with her antenna stretching another twenty feet as it swayed in the air. Her mandibles were clapping excitedly as Eltross approached. Her body lifts up to invite him to the lower abdomen. He sees her sexual cavity had turned red for mating. This is something unprepared to him since the agreement with Lord Id. He sits down on a small boulder and tries a mind link with the Sleeping Queen. Her words were unkind towards Lord Id and the Jung zee queen for the damage they did to the humans. She even accused her husband Eltross for betraying the Myra laws of the innocent; he listened as his anger rose.

"Even you did the unthinkable for a Myra, using the time crystal against a innocent human caught between mating and the possession by Lord Id.

Stealing his life forces is against the Myra clan ways and laws that we have in place for a hundred thousand years, my beloved Eltross," chirped the Sleeping Queen.

"I regret that action, but the ways of their mating disturbed me and I overreacted my love," whispered Eltross. He senses her mind probing his thoughts for the truth, as she gives a deep throbbing pulse to mate with her now.

"Will you agree with the test Lord Id & I must do to confirm these beings are the chosen? Lord Id thinks them to be a source of food," grumbles Eltross angrily.

The Sleeping Queen's wails a deep long sound as she envisions the dark future and the long road that is now paved in blood. She moves away from Eltross. Her insect body turns to line up to the far distance planet Zlotoo. She speaks aloud her thoughts

"You have sold my love to Lord Id for exchange of a murdering queen. May you reap the horror you have placed on the future generation. The fourth generation will rise up from the wrongs you have done this day. Their new form will punish you for the lack of faith to our ancient prophecy. The lack of compassion for all life forms has shown me your true intentions. You ruined our mating rituals for our new nest."

She calls her own children of larva and orders the nymphs and the remaining adult beetles to stay and guide the children of the humans. Eltross calls her back to discuss the fine points, but she ignores him. His pleads turn into rage as he wished to have the time crystal in his hands. It would weaken her will against his ways. She would bend more and be more understanding. She was gone when the queen Ru-Tava steps out of the ship to give him the time crystal, but it was too late. She is gone he could hear her wails of anguish, which harden his heart.

"You will have those two Tava females for that child in you shall be mine," grunts Eltross.

"Once, I have those two life forces are within me I shall gladly give you the unborn child to experiment on," Ru-Tava stated coldly.

"Then we have a deal mother of dark force," scornfully whispers Eltross.

Eltross watches the humans work on clearing the land for the first colony of humans.. Even though they are children, the Sleeping Queen had given then telepathic powers to move heavy objects without machinery. His lips curse the Sleeping Queen she had boost their powers beyond the level he thought they were, based on the knowledge from the computer. They are already changing the tests. He looks up to the shadow of the distance moons with thoughts he will need the others from the world ship. This time a new plan shall form in place on the other satellites away from these children. Eltross wanted to stay away from the construction as he went back to the main ship to the communication station in an attempt to contact the captain of the world ship. Somehow, the interference was worst then before. Needing rest, he sat down to clear his mind and fell into a deep meditation. He wanted to find answers that troubled his mind. The odd claim by the Sleeping Queen of the fourth generation danced in his mind.

Being both Jung zee and Myra gave him a slight advantage to the written prophesies of the two races. His other part was small the living atoms of energy in a gasses state created by Lord Id to get around the mating ways of the Sleeping Queen. Had he faulted in not mating with her in that giant state? A sudden vision burst in his mind on what kind of creatures hatched by her eggs if Lord Id mated with her. The red omega sun collapsing cause the great shock wave destroying all the planets while a giant round metal sphere equal to the size of beta twins leaves the system. He sees a human woman with blonde golden hair and bright blue eyes in a brightly coloured dress with a number four between the emblems of a Myra and a Jung zee healer. It speaks to his mind in a sad voice very familiar to the Sleeping Queen.

You had your choice now live forever in the shadow world.

No wait, shouts Eltross, but his mind trapped in this illusion goes on repeating the same vision. All clearer than the last one, that this is the path chosen. He tries to escape it and cascades back into a deeper trance state of a darker world.

The Sleeping Queen returns to the Myra nest on the planet Zlotoo. She starts digging a deep tunnel in the planets crust. The Jung zee unaware of her presence because they were in the battle to claim first mating rights. Since the Jung zee queen had faded from her station with Lord Id, never returned. The entire Jung zee male from the different groups went crazy and started a killing spree.

The Sleeping Queen takes this time for advantage adds her female hormones, which became a grey colour mist essence to release in the air to arouse the Jung zee in a frenzy of murder. She knew it would be Lord Id the last of Jung zee to mate. However, she had another plan and prepared for it by digging deeper into the ground. Her larva calls out to help in the digging, but she chirps a short message.

"I will release you when it is time to do so repeatedly."

CHAPTER II

THE CAPTAIN CHOICES

Hyperion 1
2 liht years out
@Ea solar system
Neptune time 46:15

Captain Pane had just recovered from her experience of seeing Eltross. He had some kind of mind influence on all humans. Luckily, Mack McKenzie had set up a relay in case they tried to takeover their minds like what happened on the construction ships. The special suit of the captain shielded most of the effects, however, when he removed his cloak to reveal his radiance. Mack moves away from his station, it cuts off the broadcast, thus saving them from another disaster. She orders a stop to the world ship to check the alien claims. The scientist's station was running overtime to find the temporal distortion. The disc that Tava had received from a giant beetle became the main topic to the council. It revealed that everyone on board was cloned with a helix cube number four D.A. With the death of the duplicate Mr. Winters by McKenzie and the disarming of a bomb, he found in the engine room.

The security force captured Mr. Bruce with Dr. Ian Ross's transport ship. The medical team did a blood test to find out who he really is. They found that he had two DNA of men with mechanical brains. He was a cyborg spy from Dark Lighter Mega Corporation. He reveals all his plans to take control of the colony by using the two clones within his body that would live for hundred years. His plan is simple to be the leader of the government and keep control by any means necessary.

It took Dr Pane several days to understand the new matrix of the helix cube obtained from Susan Chow. The little girl was forced into isolation due to a strange illness that affected her skin colour and breathing. Dr. Pane and her daughter took extra care for the little girl and offered a blood transfusion to bring her back to a health. All thought her mood was darker after the near-death experience she appreciated the kindness from Tava and Dr. Pane. Tava had a direct talk with her mother about why her brain device was off for sixteen years. Being her daughter, she had a right to know these clones existed. Dr M Pane kept her statement simple and unemotional.

"We all follow orders; we are part of the Mega Corporation. We give our company a chance to compete. We selected the clones of special children with high IQ and cognitive abilities. I had to disconnect your helix cube, we found that you and the copies would sense each other thoughts and feelings, and there was a strong possibility to communicate with each other."

Somehow, Tava had to accept the explanation, brought up under the company rules and regulations all her life; it took some of the bitterness away. The thought of having more sisters played in her mind, and maybe she could share some of her own experiences. In time she thought of only helping Susan, like an older sister rather then a Captain of Hyperion one.

In the coming days, her mother had Ian Ross's baby girl. He had assured her that his male sperm was humanoid not artificial, some how lied that it was a boy. Dr. Pane was deeply torn by his betrayal, and names its Ida Pane. She leaves the care of her baby to the one hundred and three clones. They accept to take care of the special child.

The loss of six hundred people brought the cold hard reality of space travel. The knowledge that their copies are still here on this ship locked in the computer. They had a prayer service for the lost ones. The only other strange news was Captain Pane had found enough fuel to reach the Corus solar system.

Lisa Thomas had three children two Africa boys and white baby girl. They are still in isolation for fear she carries a disease from the alien encounter. All could see her alter state in a younger age of twelve. She only speaks an African language. Luckily, the computer translates her story as the council sits to listen silently. She claims that the gods of Ea have given her the task. To go back to Alpha Prime and bring more humans to please the dark lord her eyes glow blue. Lisa tries to send a message through the cyber link to force others to follow the call of the gods. However, the ships computer blocks the message from the isolation chamber.

Dr. Pane regains her strength through the support of her husband. She listens to the story of Lisa's experience of deep torture. She reviews the service record about her grandfather who kept her isolated for years to keep the traditions of the African language and the traditional ways of her people. The council took a short break to clear their minds and decide their recommendations. They had three options go back to earth, or head to the Corvus system, and the last choice take their chances on Terrain 6 with dangerous aliens. Iran Pane had a simple plan to do all three choices at once as he tables a report. Captain T Pane gave a deep sigh and mumbled.

"This will be another long day to find a solution." Mack McKenzie hears her words, and giggles to the thoughts of spending time with her.

Tava Pane became attached to the brash young man after her rescue by the murderous duplicate. She had many boyfriends, but her career came first, this attitude always breaks up any relationships. She knew that Mack had his own independent ways, with ideas for both long and short-term solutions. He brings them out to a harden reality, without any regrets which she admires the muscle-bound man up to a certain point. He seems to want to show off his ways in doing things to impress her and always comes across to strong and arrogant to her liking. He did have a nice physique; she wonders how to change his attitude. He would be a good husband in the future thought Tava once they resolve the issue of direction to colonize or head back earth. Ultimately, she made the final decision while each councillor speaks the many options, they would press forward with many suggestions. The only one missing at the council meeting is Mr. Winters. He had left a text message that he will be late.

Ingram Pane had finished his proposal it had merit. She followed the disc recording suggestion; all thought Tava Pane had many reservations if they could survive on a planet full of aliens. No proof had come forward by the scientist on the temporal time flux. The exact location from the star chart was off by ten thousand light years regarding Alpha Prime's location. This was always a thorn to quantum theories, astrometry, and navigation used in star plotting and positioning to calculate their arrival and departure. The entire team of scientists of Alpha Prime knew the distance was thirty lightyears to the beta system over five million years to earth years. That is why the star gate was use to open folding space to cut the distance by sixty to ninety-one percent, with the bio tubes covering the rest of distance.

However, Miles Oboe had boosted the engines to maximum tolerance and spent the fuel escaping the destruction behind him changing the calculations and possible location. They were about one and half a light year from entering the aliens Ea solar at impulse, which would be twenty years. The Clovis system is 15 light years away, Tava wanted more proof, which added more pressure in the council chamber. Her father and mother supported the other scientists. Only Mack objects with his own reasons, like did Tava, needing Mr. Winters to even out the vote or carry the motion. He finally appears and enters with two young boys of eight years old their jump suits were oversized. Iran barks with annoyance to Mr. Winters.

"This is a council meeting not a nursery, you must vote on the right direction we should take in this crisis." Mr. Winters started to pace back and forth to plead his case. "Well, this is not my turn to bring my proposals in the council chamber. Mr Pane, my plan has a twist to it, if you hear me out."

"Oh, very well but make it as short as possible, if you are following my suggestions lets us hear the twist and vote on it before we all suffer the fate of the six hundred," hissed Mr. Pane. The captain jumps out of her seat and blurted angrily out her father. "It may be all right for you father, but there is no proof this disc is real or fabricated by those aliens."

"I have proof Captain Pane to all your questions and answers to the ones that you have not thought of yet. It is all there on the disc plus the formulas that the giant beetle called the Sleeping Queen had given to the six hundred and more," replied Mr. Winters with a giggle. Mr Pane twisted his head back in surprise by the statement of Mr Winters and waves his hand as if to surrender with a grunt. "Very well, I am interested; you may proceed." "Thank you Sir," he gave a warm smile and waved the two boys over to him. Something caught Tava eyes, and she gave a short gasp. The expression from the tall one's face with blue eyes added movement to his tight lips and down turned chin.

"I found these boys in Mr. Bruce's labs they were in a strange liquid but similar bio tube, but more a stasis unit. Let me introduce Commander Miles Oboe and Commander T. Smith of the construction ships taken over by aliens."

"You mean they are clones" hissed Dr. Pane.

"No, they are second generation of the helix cube number 4d an exact duplicate of the original and all their experiences up to their death. This tall one is Miles and the other is Commander Smith, he has a completely different story.

Everyone was stunned to silence only Mack McKenzie grunted and seem irritated to see the children. Dr. Pane jumps out of her seat seems anxious and blurts out, "they must stay in isolation!" She then explains the examination Lisa Thomas with her microscopes to the complexities of the helix cube. It had released strange micro nano bites in her blood stream. This is the cause of her physical change, which must have happened to the six hundred. The other interesting note she is broadcasting a radio signal. "He could very well be a clone, of a different kind restated as a true duplication of our Miles Oboe, but I need more tests with the right equipment to confirm. They are not the same as Lisa," stated Captain. Pane. Mr. Winters salutes the Doctor for her words an spoke startling news with his own statement.

"I have already confirmed this with other Doctors they have no nano bites or parasites of any kind." He points to the young man, that he named Miles.

Miles spoke first how he manoeuvred away from the torpedo rocket, then accelerated to escape the explosion inside folding space. He recalls luminescent beings that repair and activate the helix cube so I can pass on in this new form. Most gave him a sceptical look thinking he was merely a clone. Finally, Miles walks to Tava Pane and hands her a disc file.

"They gave me this disc for your eyes-only Captain Pane. It is the proof you require to understand the complexities of this quantum universe, I believe his name is Krell," he says in a nervous voice of the young Miles, with his famous crooked smile.

Tava Pane melted inside and gave an uncontrolled hug and a kiss that made Miles blush a little. Ingram Pane slams down his hands and curses loudly to Dr. Ian Ross, for breaking the scientist code of honour playing god over humans. Others join wanting to punish him severely for being a spy from dark lighter mega corporation.

"He will get his due when the time comes," muttered Mr. Winters.

"May I speak now, I have more words from the Sleeping Queen," voiced the young Commander Smith.

The meeting went on for hours with great revelations to the truth of a future history difficult to avoid. Tava went to her quarters to read the disc in private away from prying eyes. Mack McKenzie was waiting for her at the door of her private quarters. He gave her a big smile while showing a large bottle of champagne with the years vintage 1997.

"I thought you might want to celebrate the end of our existence," Mack snarls sarcastically.

"I do not need any more pressure from my trouble-shooter of Grey's mega corporation, besides you turn down this job any way," sputters Tava.

"The Sleeping Queen's advice is doable for me after all we are practically married. I must remind you we are parents to the children of the light."

Tava rolled her eyes back and with a deep sigh was about to bark at him, she instead pursed her lips in a pout as a thought flashed in her mind. She steps closer to press against his hard body. He melts his arms around the small of her back. She could smell his musk; it was sweet and made the blood rush to her face. She kisses him gently on the lips and whispers in his ear.

"This is all you get from me even if you are the last man standing in the whole cosmos."

She unlocked her door and slipped out of his arms into her room. He utters another word of protest and walks away slowly juggling the champagne bottle.

She is finally alone, without relatives and company for the first time after they wake her out of the bio tubes. Strange she was not tired. Mr Winters had explained the VR system place the body in rest mood. Her mind works through the operations of their ship. She had already agreed to release Dr Ross and all his equipment after she heard the plans of the Sleeping Queen who needs a doctor to go to the planet Zlotoo to protect the humans' rights. Tava could see the Sleeping Queen wanted to protect the humans from death and torture of these superior beings. Based on her suggestion this is the only a short-term solution; the Myra nest is a good place to start that the gods will never find them. In addition, the assurance that Dr Ross will suffer his own fate, seem to please everyone in the room.

The disc from the future plays in her hand wondering if she should watch it or let the future unfold naturally. With a deep sigh another thought crept in that is *if I do not look at the tape, I could destroy the future to a perplexing variant of time.* She places the tape in her forearm plays it. To her surprise, she saw the president of the corporation Samuels Greys a middle-aged man with short salt and pepper haircut, narrow set of eyes, strong hooknose, small lips and a trim beard

"I must apologize for the pain I caused you. Believe me if I had another solution, I would have done it. Playing with lives is cruel to any living being. We found ourselves in a variant flux of time to escape this; our only path is through the fourth generation. You are the key the child you will have will bring us to the edge and these children will be the hybrid of the future. This will bring us the freedom that we long have lived and died for throughout time itself. I will return for the final battle.

"Stop tape, computer scans my body for any additional life form in me" requested Tava with a slight edge in her voice. A beam of light fluttered quickly across with back-and-forth motion over her entire body and took blood samples form a portable scanner. The hours went by when computer buzzed to life in a mechanical voice with a short answer.

"Biological system is working found no life form, but you are ovulating on your Sixty-day cycle." This seems to ease the tension in her mind.

"Please continue tape," the image returns to the president.

"Now, for the difficult part you already know of the helix cube and its matrix control I will tell you the complete process and whose child you will carry." The door rang while Tava let the tape play on and went to open the door. It was Mack McKenzie again with a bouquet of wild daffodils and champagne.

"I know I come on too strong I am willing to adjust my nature if we could maybe start over and find a happy middle ground," muttered Mack with a weak smile.

Tava stiffened her eyes water slightly as she grasps his arm to pull him into the room. The door closes behind him. His smile gives way thinking the flowers did the trick. The tape had finished with the startling news; with one thought of the president last words. She guides him to her bedchamber.

Her hands punch the code to release the suit. His eyes pop out of his head showing awkwardness at her nakedness.

"You were right the first time let us work hard on knowing each other a little more closely, more natural state," whispers Tava. She pulls him down on the bed and kisses him hard and often. Knowing this will be his only chance with her, Mack quickly agrees to undress between the kisses while Tava turn the lights down low.

Mr Winters and the Commander T. Smith brief Dr Ross on his mission to redeem himself to the crew of Hyperion 1. He quickly agrees with the thought of escaping once inside the ship. The council used their only trump card; his two personal clones will be terminated if he tries to alter his fixed course that was pre-program to meet the Sleeping Queen within a year. In addition, the council added instructions to set out the special equipment from his lab. The queen is building a secret chamber for him and his equipment.

"How will you know it will be done correctly," gave a snide answer to Mr. Winters. He remembers his cruel word that embarrasses him. He purses his lips while the face darkens, and he shrugs his shoulders with cold and uncaring words. "I have scanned you pathetic body and found the item of the helix cube number four. You will be the first test subject for science." Dr Ross went pale shook his head and refused to go. Mr. Winters had expected this as he brought reinforcements to threaten him. He gives orders to the security force in front of him.

"Kill Nigel Bruce and Ian Ross in their special bio chamber these are their code numbers."

"Yes sir will comply," came a plain answer from the security drone.

"Captain Pane would not dare take a child's life," stammered Ian Ross.

"That is true, but she gave me complete control of this project", Mr. Winters muttered sarcastically.

"I do not see the aspects of death after all I am reborn with all the knowledge of what I was," squeaked the young boy who is the exact duplicate of the original Commander Smith.

Dr. Ross ignores the child's words. He reads his bio signature and knows there is no escape as he laughs his fear and tension off.

"All right, I will do it," hissed Ross.

"Cancel termination on clone forms named Nigel Bruce and Ian Ross," ordered Mr. Winters.

"I will comply with your orders Mr. Winter," stated the security androids.

"Escort him to his ship the equipment and supplies are all ready," ordered Mr. Winters.

"Yes, will comply"

"I will see you in the future I hope I have the chance to cut you in pieces Snead," hissed Dr. Ross.

"I feel the same way I like nothing more than to rip your lying throat out," snarls Mr. Winter. The three security androids escort the Doctor to his ship. The two men stare at each other silently until he took the elevator. *The evil men in history always die quick but live long in the memories of the many* thoughts Mr. Winters.

Elsewhere in the city ship, Dr Pane follows orders from the council for Lisa Thomas and her children. The computer gave Lisa Thomas a new goal to bring more people of Alpha Prime to Ea. They follow the Sleeping Queen instructions by giving the formula to kill any illness planted in Lisa Thomas body and her children. The liquid is quickly accepted by all four, which seem to subdue Lisa and the children. Still locked in the isolation room; they took a gamble to let her out to enter a drone ship for Alpha Prime. The ship has a hundred containers of the formula and four bio tubes. They launch the drone quickly to the bright cloud behind them.

"Thank you I will bring millions to touch the gods of light and darkness," Lisa Thomas stammered repeatedly on the radio.

She did not know the radio was disconnected. In addition, the warning lights flashed constantly that the ship carries harmful radiation. The AI computer sent out warnings to keep away. It is set for the sun of Alpha Prime. It carries messages and warnings not to come to Beta system because of a more advance alien race dangerous to human race. Please stay away. The passengers on the ship have a virus if they are released your only chance is the formula that is in the medical computer database. We have set this ship to self-destruct if they try to escape.

Dr. Pane felt the despair and anguish of Lisa. They became close being the only two females to carry children into the new system. She sees her alter state caused Elizbeth Pane great distress, that a being with so much power could be so cold and unfeeling. She watches the escape pod; the isolation and clone chamber eject into space. The council ordered the main computer to send a virus to the construction ships to wipe out its computer memory core. With tears flowing, she walks to the bio dome to hold her daughter close to her breast, wondering what the future will bring. Kissing her forehead gently, she whispers a silent prayer.

"I hope you will survive to the fourth generation, little one."

CHAPTER 12

TEN YEARS AFTER THE NEPTUNE INCIDENT

The sudden energy release from the star gate caused a large plasma wave that blossomed a hundred kilometers wide and a thousand kilometers in length. It destroyed three mining space stations killing one hundred million people while it imploded from the energy wave.

The wave of energy is unstoppable. It reaches and slices through the equator of Neptune splitting the core and releasing a much large second wave of deadly radiation of dust particles. The moons that have been terra form are Nereid and Proteus evaporate instantly while the moons that orbit Neptune push out from the energy wave. Triton with its retrograde orbit struck by two other moons the Galatea and Despina meld into molten rock. The magnetic poles of the planets increased its mass as it left its natural orbit. The melted ice and internal molten of the core caused mixtures of deadly gas clouds. They move in an arc towards the inner planets of Alpha Prime with the energy wave following behind it. A military space station lost all communications from the static discharge of the wave. Skelton and his Neptune fleet escape in time and rescued one complete mining population from the moon Larissa.

Only one ship survives from the Saturn fleet while cruise ships and onlookers from the press are killed instantly by the shock wave. The young Captain from the lone Saturn fleet makes a quick decision to fire his atomic warheads to explode a few feet to counter the energy wave in hopes to disburse it. The draw back of deadly radiation will be the by-product. His calculation would implode against the huge cloud of debris and deflect away from the remaining moons of Neptune. These were more heavily populated and had a level 10 force field, which could survive the energy wave.

The captain made a blunder as he attempts a back wave instead of deflecting towards the moon of Psamathe and Naiad. It slowly kills millions with radiation sickness and knock the triton moon out of orbit. The survivors of the initial blast of the star gate send out emergency calls for assistance. General Skelton regroups to disburse the wave but at a further distance to give time for more rescue attempts by other ships responding to the emergency. He immediately reassembles his fleet to plan the counter wave. While the rescue of miners and small communities fall under the medical emergency & rescue fleet.

With the sudden breakdown of communications, he goes to a telepath, which he had placed on all his war ships. With a plan made, he tries to come under the remains of Neptune picking up speed and survivors from the medical ships under his control. The military telepaths are trained to focus only on their partners but the distance cries of humans in death throws cause a quake in their minds. The general walks up to his telepath and see the tears flowing from her face.

"I need you Stella Neptune 6 to focus, we shall grieve later I promise you. We must stop it before it reaches the other systems of Alpha Prime."

"Yes, General Skelton I will do my job," she replied in a haunting voice.

The bridge crew cheer as they made the under pass to Neptune unharmed and picked up speed. The general gave a soft but sad smile. The radar man announces to the General some sobering news.

"I am picking up multiple warheads from a Saturn warship; based on the pattern he is trying a counter the energy wave sir."

"The fool is too close to the population of Naiad and Psamathe moons, do we have communications yet" snarled the General.

"No sir, but strange I have two corporations' ships one from Pluto and one coming from Uranus offering assistance and medical help" reported the officer.

"From which company," inquired the General. He looks over the radar chewing his lips, Gray's mega corporation. He looks at the radar screen that shows their location as the General, cursed under his breath.

"Tell them they are welcome ask if they could warn the population of Naiad and Psamathe of the radiation wave that just happened and start rescue operations there with the medical fleet."

"The Captain of Hyperion 3 will take that report to the communication officer." The General was relieved while he sat down in his chair to rethink his options.

"Well men and women of this war ship, let the hand of god guide us through these difficult times," proclaimed General Skelton.

"The other ship wants to offer their Gravity well probes to slow and angle the wave and stabilize Neptune," reported the officer.

"I will speak to them on my private line," ordered the general.

"Yes sir," shouted the officer.

The telepath steps forward and leans close to the general with some startling news.

"The Black Raven destroyer has fired on the Saturn warship it is evaporated sir," reported the officer.

"The blasted fool, we should not fight each other," as he slams down on his console. "I want you Stella to tell the other telepaths that Captain Norris is under arrest for murder. Give orders to the next in command to take the Black Raven and protect the medical ships with their shield generators."

"Yes, I have passed it on, but the telepath on the Black Raven is frightened of Captain Norris," stated Stella.

"I do not have time to baby sit all the telepaths to do the job required," hissed general Skelton. He gave a stern look towards the telepath knowing it would reach all twenty-one.

"Second in command, has killed the captain and is following your orders," gasped Stella.

"Now, pass on the medical ships their duty to do a joint rescue with the Hyperion 3 on the moon cities Naiad and Psamathe."

"Yes sir, they have received the instructions and are heading to the planets," muttered the Telepath.

The screen beeped as a young man appeared on the view screen General Skelton thinks he is too young to command a science ship. He had brown hair with matching brown eyes young face with hardly any hair on his smooth face and dressed in Gray's mega corporation uniform of a Captain.

"I am Captain L. Bertrand of the Hyperion 2, the four gravities well probes are ready to launch and activate at the dangerous points to contain the wave General Skelton."

"I do not have time to play with untested equipment not cleared by the government Captain Bertrand."

"We have done all our trials at Pluto cluster and I think you do not have time these devices will bring the wave back with all its radiation into the center Neptune. I can guarantee that, and we must angle at this moment to turn Triton, which is heading for Saturn as we speak General Skelton."

The general pondered his next move, being abreast on many science projects. He knew the gravity well could help, but the energy output required will surmount to a back hole, which he doubts a probe output could generate. Somehow, the young Captain knew what he was thinking and told him of what his ship will do to succeed. "I promise that we will self destruct before any chance of a black hole form general."

"That is a great sacrifice I will honour you by punishing those who have injured us, you may proceed," snarls the General.

"Thank you, General Skelton my crew and I will be honoured to save, Alpha prime," stated the captain.

The images freeze on Captain Bertrand as a man steps out of the shadows. The crowds cheer when he reaches the podium. With his hands waving for silence, the crowd hush to a low whisper. He clears his throat and begins his short and brief introduction of the coming scenes.

Ten years have passed with our great leader accepting the hand of Captain Bertrand and his crew. Their sacrifice in restoring the balance while it captures other moons like Titan form Saturn. Plus rescues other and reforming the balance to the gas planet Neptune into twin gas planets is a great moment in our history of the disaster and salvation. Although the lost of life was considerably high to surmount the worst man-made disaster of its kind has never been so deeply painful to all their survivors. You will also see tonight the last moments of the crew's great sacrifice on the ship, named Hyperion 2 and its Captain Bertrand."

The man stands back and fades as the screen erupts on the main bridge the speakers give a short explanation on how they had gotten to Neptune so fast.

"The scientist of Grays Mega Corporation with a new engine on their ship nicknamed a skipper or a war jumper open folding space and jump great distances in short spurts."

The navigator's voice is heard through the audio speakers at the same time as the screen went dark briefly. To a count down, to real space announced in three, two, and one.

The image of the bridge all working at their console and watching a large, odd shape of Triton moving towards them fills the view screen. Captain Bertrand hears collision alarm ands three quick solutions.

"Hard to port, raise shields and fire pulse ray at the rock."

The ship pilot and navigator rotated ninety degrees while the weapons blossomed into a sharp energy beam, which struck at the heart of the rock that shattered into dust. It sprinkled against the shield like fireflies.

"The captain calls out the pilot name Lt, Ashton prepare to release the gravity well probe."

Lt. Ashton sits in the VR console to deploy the probe in the best possible position; we must stabilize the moon Triton.

"Yes, sir," says the voice of a woman with a slight strain of tension.

"You are one of our best. Take the time to do it right but do it quickly," said the captain.

"Thank you, Captain, but I just want to remind you, Once activated we could be trapped in the gravity well," reported Lt. Ashton.

"I know that Lieutenant, but the computer brain will activate simultaneously, with our new jump engines," the captain replied confidently.

"Probe in the right position sir, I am ready for sixty seconds count down to activate gravity well," quoted the Lieutenant.

"Computer start count down a at thirty second mark be ready for jump at 0.001."

The crowds in the audience seem to feel the tension as whispers grew likes a wave across the large auditorium. The ships computer spoke mechanically unattached of emotions, with a simple replied. "Will comply, Captain at the thirty-second count down mark."

"All crews to stations and brace for a rough ride, we do this for our friends and family of the future," quoted the captain. Lt Ashton shouted, "mark, the thirty-second mark while the ships begin to warm up its engines." Sudden voices of the computer and the Lieutenant echo in the main bridge. With the last few numbers of three, two, one the screen went dark for fifteen seconds. Only the audio voice of the Lieutenant last words could be heard. "Initialize full power," before the eruptions of screams of agony and death throes added to the twisting sounds of metal deck plates. The screens return to show the captain's body twisted in odd angle. Both eyes open as he grunts with satisfaction, he hears the communication officer confirms and quickly announces.

"We have done it the probe has slowed down Triton but it's moving away from Neptune!"

"What is our status, Lt. Grimes?"

"My god we have moved inside the energy wave and inside" mutter Lt. Ashton.

This brought a great cheer from the audience. Triton started to slow and change angles to a new orbit approximately one thousand kilometres around Saturn, but undetermined of its new orbit that it would endanger other planets. The scientists of earth are all amaze by the sudden changes of orbits and destruction of moons between Jupiter, Saturn and Neptune. They kept a watchful for several years and use the technology to save many of the moons had swap around the three gas giants. The last moon to settle in orbit is the Titan moon around the newly form Neptune twins. This is the final report where we start to rebuild our lives. When earth scientist later confirms the orbit a year later that the moon of Titan had settle in orbit around the Neptune twins.

They were soon joined by rescue teams from the Uranus military who offered to search for the survivors of Triton. A Second Lieutenant answers the lead ship from Uranus telling them to be cautious at impulse power as it could affect the navigation. The captains of the other ships take the proper precautions, seeing that he is the only officer unhurt. He called for medical emergency to the bridge no answer came. He moves about to the flight crew. Lt. Ashton's face was burnt to the bone. The audience sees the expression of horror on the young officer. He checks the panel the other three probes are still on standby. He then notices damage from feedback. Energy from the probe is what causes the death and injury to his crew. He contacts the watch crew.

"Watch crew of auxiliary bridge control do you copy," while he approaches his injured Captain.

"Yes, we are on standby all electronics are performing well except for navigation" came a weak voice from the wrist band of the second officer.

"Do not touch me, Lieutenant Grimes just give me the status on the ship and our location to the next site Did we make it into the heart of Neptune," winced the captain. He tries on his own to sit up, instead falls back down with a deep moan of pain.

"We did change the orbit course of Triton The bridge crew six dead one injured badly and one survivor, the secondary bridge is intact the remanding gravity wells are on standby. I called for a medical team no response yet sir."

"We did save Saturn; now let us finish the task Mr. Grimes."

"Yes, sir however, I require transferring the navigation station to the auxiliary bridge to ensure we reach the target," complained Lt. Grimes.

"Then get with it get it done," came the strained voice of Captain.

"Your body is lying over the electric pane I must move you over to turn the switch on sir, I could kill you if I move you," stated the officer.

"That is all right Lieutenant we all been trained to do our jobs right to the last crewmember," with a tight grunt he tries once more to pull himself upright and fails. He looks at Grimes, notices the blood trickling down his forehead with a piece of a metal protruding on the left side of his face.

"Let's not waste time move me and transfer the controls to the other bridge we must save Alpha Prime this is my last order," replied Captain Bertrand.

"Yes sir, may I say it is an honour to serve under you," stated Lt. Grimes. He then places his arms and hands in the effort to keep the captains back in line with his head and shoulders.

"It was also mine," hissed the last breath of the captain.

Lt. Grimes lifts the captain away from the panel, has the lieutenant hears the last words of his captain who mumbles out." goodbye mother," Grimes then hits the switch to transfer navigation control and then hears the standby crew acknowledge the transfer to the secondary bridge control.

"We need a small jump of ten seconds to hit the mark," came the strained voice.

"Carry on Mr. Sharpe, make our Captain proud of his crew," came the last words of Lt. Grimes.

"Yes, sir will comply," and starts the count down. Lt Grime's feels the shadows of darkness close as the ship lurched, and the screen darkens. Everyone in the auditorium heard the weak voice of Mr Sharpe's acknowledgement that gravity wells were at full power of the main engine. The sudden silence from the screen as the images seems to reverse the flow of energy to fall back on itself. The audience whispered across the auditorium as the screen restarts at the bridge.

General Skelton's battle cruiser named the Wrath of God leads his fleet trough the rescue missions while he waits to see what happens to the gravity wells. Stella is visibly shaken with the sacrifice. She steps closer to the general with other messages from his fleet about salvage ships from both Mega Corporation Dark lighter and Tananaka appearing at the out skirts of Triton with the military medical fleet from Uranus.

"Sir, they are claiming full control of the planet, and they are preventing the medical ships to land to help the colonies," quoted the Telepath.

"I must keep my word to the Captain of Hyperion 2. Do we have communications back online," grumbles the General?

"No sir but we have twin corvettes with medium weapons and two squadrons of interceptors, they are on the outside of the black out. They seem to be blocking the other salvage ships," replied to the Com Officer.

The general looks at the telepath as she reads his thoughts of cold revenge on those that are responsible. He did not utter any words from his lips. Stella eyes widen in fear. She relents and silently nods to the general.

The two Captains of the corvettes were having a friendly chess game on their private screen before the disaster placed them on red alert. They watched with great pains while their home planet is being contaminated by radiation. With the Uranus medical fleet, they escorted them to Triton after the gravity well had begun to slow and fall back into a natural rotation and orbit now three times it s normal mass. Scores of salvage ships appear to blockade their way using the law to salvage first before rescuing. The two telepaths whisper as the four ways communication link resolve the legality of the salvage ships. The medical Captain of the ship named; Angels of Mercy seem somewhat agitated with the arrogant young commander of the salvage ship.

"I have no interest in machines, but the six cities of Triton need our assistance, their shield barriers are weakened," pleaded the medical Captain.

"I have my orders stand back or prepare to be destroyed if you come within our ten kilometres of our ship."

In unison, the two corvette Captains passed on a message to both.

The salvage commander and the medical Captain go back to their chess game to play the Sicilian defence. A loud laugh of victory came from the arrogant commander as the medical Captain gave a short, puzzled look as their words played in his head. The answer came to his mind. He acknowledged it with a dark smirk across his lips. The two Captains feel that the medical Captain understood their secret message and added a short warning.

"You may wish to stand back a little," echoed the two men.

"I bow to the best men I have ever met in my life." He orders his ship full reverse and turns off the view screen.

The young commander laughs and clenches his fist in victory to the screen at the two old Captains and his crew on the bridge He did not hear them give orders to attack. Squadrons of interceptors came upon them from the south and north poles of Triton. The close-range damage knocks out the six salvages ships in one pass. The young commander turns to face the attackers thinking another group is trying to cut in on the salvage. When the interceptors came into view, he, cursed them royally, since communication screens were still open. The two corvettes fire eight torpedo rockets and all their ion cannon with laser guns. The two last words were simple and direct to the long face commander.

Check mate.

Now a large hole in the blockade the Uranus fleet continues their rescue efforts to the damage cities the medical Captain reconnected.

"My crew and I salute you men of the Neptune fleet."

The two Captains bow and return the salute. The medical ships went to work in rescuing people. The two Captains look at the commander of the salvage fleet.

"You had better leave now, before General Skelton appears and wants to arrest you for the damage your company caused at the star gate."

"That is ridiculous I came from the ice world Zeena. My company never sent us here it is I who took the initiative for profit," hissed the young man. His face gave a pale look of anger as if he knew more.

"Well, we warned you. Now be off or we shall finish the job," quoted the captain.

"Yes, we will withdraw but I will come back with more ships to wipe you and your old ancient corvettes. My name is Commander Nedhami I always get even."

"I am Captain Marcus Cobb I will take this as another challenge."

"I believe so, Captain Marcus Cobb; May I give him another blast from my Ion cannon," quoted the other Captain.

"No let the little fish go."

"You old fools, sound the recall," as he turned off his screen.

The action froze once more while a young man reappears at the podium, dressed in military uniform with an Ensign of the Alpha Prime united space force. He clears his throat with a causal sip of water before the wide audience in the auditorium and across the Alpha Prime satellites. One camera zooms in waiting for the next words.

"I must say this is my best part seeing my two favourite uncles defending the weak and injured citizens of Alpha Prime. This is of course the first move against the Mega corporations who enslaved hundred of million clones and Cyborgs as slaves. Their poor living conditions became the catalyst for General Skelton and the Neptune fleet with the proof shown of the sneak attack that failed, and then erupted into the cascade of over one trillion dead and lost in space. This alone brought in other militaries that joined the cause to wipe out all mega societies into a more free and open market. I must give praise to a corporation that came to help us."

"Gary's Mega corporations became the leader for change and the first to surrender and embrace the edict of General Skelton. Yes, Samuels Grays had demanded changes years before this conflict started, more concerned for the people of the human race regardless of if a clone or Cyborgs. Only Grays Corporation's president moved decisively moments in the wake of the disaster. With their newest equipment from Pluto, they came to the rescue of Neptune and the remaining thirty-five satellites. This great leap of faith stopped the deadly scattering moons in our space saving more lives from Earth, Mars, Jupiter and Saturn with Uranus and the new worlds of the twin Neptune and Triton's larger mass."

"I give you Samuel Grays for his part must be reviewed and his contribution for the betterment to humanity to rebuild Alpha Prime."

The old man slowly walks to the podium while cheers erupt in the auditorium. The screen above reads out his brief biography. Close to his one hundred thirty-two years old reports of history database. Born in a Mars colony Pyramid city central, prodigy at age three in quantum physics, noble peace prizes at the age 11, 24, and 48. He is a survivor of many wars, diseases, and attempts on his life. He grew his business with openness and trust to the whole world during the rush to colonize the moons of Jupiter, Saturn, and

Uranus. With his great mind, he used failed technology from the past to the modern world of 26 century. This alone brought the rise of his corporation to its highest level. He searches for other child prodigies like himself. He waves his shaking hand in appreciation while the audience slowly silenced to hear his words.

"Good evening people of Alpha Prime" in a sweet voice almost child like. "This is the tenth anniversary of the Neptune disaster. I still grieve for the great lost of lives. The only hope is to never forget and learn by the mistake, prevent it from ever happening again. The hard work and sacrifice of the crew of all three ships give me deep pride. I only hope that Hyperion 1 did make it to Beta solar system their giant leap into the unknown. It makes me accept the sacrifice of Hyperion 2. Many newspapermen have asked me why one name for different classes of ships. The secret I shall reveal this night."

The crowd cheer wildly with standing applauses. The old man waves to acknowledge the cheer.

"It may sound a bit childish but at two years old, I drew four ships in crayons. As I looked up into the night sky, I saw the planet Neptune and thought of one name Hyperion. It had the basic chemicals of life frozen in time. I took this name, which I liked to represent the generations of humans who can travel the stars with my ships that will pilot them in the coming future."

Many laughs at the same time as the artwork is shown on the view screen behind Mr. Grays. He looks back briefly breaks out in a wide smile. The screen stops at the picture of Hyperion 3.

"This is the one that is led by my trusted friend Captain Wiseman in their efforts to save the people of Naiad and Psamathe moon six cities. I offer you the first glimpse of the crew's efforts in saving them through the highly charged clouds of radiation."

He turns back as the auditorium darkens to replay the inserts of the flight of Hyperion 3 the auditorium applauded once more and quickly hush as the bridge crew filled the screen. President Grays briefly states the basic information maximum human capacity is five million souls.

"It takes about ten thousand to run the ship. On that, particular day only engineers and flight crew were on a shake down cruise to test the ship's overall structure and safety conditions."

"Tape is on Capt Wiseman in charge since November 11, 2535, on a six-month shake down cruise, takes the realm of Hyperion 3 on the outer rim planets. He picks up medical supplies and the balance of the crew at moon Io, then proceeds to Pluto for a transfer of crew and supplies to the sister ship. Captain Wiseman calls out orders to the flight engineer to remove all mooring lines and proceed at half impulse."

"Aye, aye sir, mooring lines disengaged half impulse," the sound of a steady hum echoed of the screen. The tall, brown hair, clean-shaven Captain, as his eyes sparkle as his ship begins to move.

"We have a communiqué from the president of Grays mega corporation good luck and good journey, do not be too hard on the crew," stated the com officer with a hardy laugh. Wiseman grunts with a harden look to the com officer who almost swallowed his tongue.

"Sorry sir, I guess you want a private channel," muttered the com-officer who went quite pale. He nervously waited for a response from Wiseman. Wiseman then gave a slight nod while he studied the navigation to the outer perimeter markers of his flight plan.

"Number one, I want a few more fire and emergency drills before we start the jump engines."

"Yes, sir will comply to level eight tests on engineer and flight crew simulations," said the stern voice of burly stout man with a deep liking of drills. Wiseman looks down on his personal view screen, sees the president face smiling warmly.

"Uncle Grays it is good you send me off with encouraging words, I do appreciate it, Not to worry I will not throw anyone out of the air locks," giggled Wiseman.

"I do this with all my children," replied President Grays.

"Hyperion 3 will be the one that will break the mould of shipbuilding sir" quoted Wiseman.

"I am glad to hear that from you I was worried you were upset about being passed over on the first ship to leave our solar system" replied, President Grays.

"Nah, This one always intrigue me with its own particle beam built into the ship like number two. At least when we try it should jump intervals from five to ten light years. Beside you may send me out to bring supplies to our far out explorers," quoted Wiseman.

"Just, make sure you are wearing those suits to protect you from the radiation and plasma charges," snorted the president while his face gave stern look.

"Yes, sir," with off hand salutes and a slight giggle from Captain Wiseman.

"I will see you at Io to review all the scientific read outs, when you pick up supplies for number 2 good journey," replied the president as the screen went dark.

Wiseman looks up at the wide view screen as he left Mar's southern pole. His radar operator announced three large contacts are ahead of us Captain and I believe it is our sister ship Hyperion 2 and the others heading to Neptune.

The Dark Ace is warning us off replied to the com- officer.

"Navigator, Give them a wide berth, we do not want a political quagmire on our maiden voyage, and they would use it against us," mumbled Wiseman.

"Yes sir, turning starboard to exit 17a," confirms the navigator.

"All ahead full impulses," ordered Wiseman.

"Aye, aye Captain full impulses," confirmed the navigator.

The screen in the auditorium went dark as the lights rise up to President Samuels Grays still standing at the podium. He had a few tears running down his cheek. He dried them with his handkerchief. Murmurs rose from the audiences with concern. The young officer brought a chair and some refreshment that Mr. Grays quickly accepts. Now more composed he continues in this day of remembrance.

"On December 19, 2535, the initial tests were quite satisfactory as they arrived at Io they started to reload supplies and a full crew of scientist and medics to test the particle accelerator. I wish them well as they set their first test to the southern poles of Neptune. The next day is when the disaster strikes. I should remind you my corporation follows the laws and rules to assist anyone in need regardless of affiliation or race from original human to clone or Cyborg. We all come from space dust," stated Mr. Grays.

The crowd cheer loudly with a standing ovation, the old man waves with acceptance. They all sat back down when the screen went back on, in a count down to the true rescue of the two moons Naiad and Psamathe.

"You will now be shown the truth after ten years. This will answer all the hard questions that were never answered. Some of the scenes will be repulsive, those with a weak stomach should turn away now," mumbled Mr. Grays.

The crowd's murmurs with echoes, the old man waves his hands to silence the audience.

"When Hyperion 3 arrives after the jump, they angle their plane to a low orbit using their shuttlecrafts to reach Naiad first city central. They also took in other damaged ships in their lower docking bay to bring the injured. The medical teams used temporary platforms in the large bio dome to protect against the radiation released by the military. Wiseman orders the use of all drone ships to pick up and rescue survivors at the other two cities where the wave struck the hardest."

The images become real on the screen when the audience sees the tragedy of the radiation poisoning unfold before them; wails and tears broke among the audience. The image of women and children shows the deep burns across their faces, arms, and legs. In addition, volunteers went to help man the cities shields replacing the injured workers whose uniforms were melted into their skin. Doctors had to peel off large pieces of flesh and replace them with synthetic skin used more for cyborg repairs. Captain Wiseman shows his compassion to the cries of the people being pushed into rooms to wash the radiation. They strip down revealing the third to fourth degree burns across their bodies. He reaches down to his communicator in a tight voice.

"All personal not on duty report to the medical officer in radiation suits priority one in the main bio dome."

"Computer repeat message and confirm all staff on extra duty," requested Captain.

"Will comply, Captain Wiseman, I must also report Hyperion 2 gravity wells have trapped Triton and the communication blackout has spread across thousand kilometres."

"Keep me informed computer," ordered Captain Wiseman while inspecting the lower levels. He checks the shower area for stragglers to ensure their radiation levels have dropped. He sees a little boy who collapsed when he stepped out from the showers. He checks his scanner for the radiation indicator. Wiseman notices his radiations are still twenty percent over the safety margins. Panic finally erupts in Captain Wiseman while he shouts to Doctor Stark rushing the boy to him.

"You are cutting too many corners Doctor," in an accusing tone while holding up the child to him.

"See here, tough choices must be made we are dealing with millions. Not just one child I am using all what we have, until the other medical ships respond."

The Doctor examines the boy checking his eyes feeling his throat and listens to his heart. His face tightens and glares at the captain. He gives the boy an injection to counter the radiation sickness. Then waves the nurse over the Doctor gives her the boy and whispers instructions.

"Section 23 bio tubes deep sleep program."

'Yes Doctor," weakly worded as she stares sadly at Captain Wiseman.

"Let me give you a suggestion captain, please head back to the main bridge and finds me other ships to help us. Moreover, leave this to me I have the final say on all medical work it is in the company issued orders," hissed Doctor Stark.

The captain eyes bulge out and his lips purse tightly to contain his rage. His hands clench tightly at his sides. He steps closer to express his displeasure with a snort, while his finger stabs the shoulder of the Doctor Stark.

"I shall leave you to act as a god, this is a warning I am still the judge and jury if I feel you have failed in keeping with the corporation standards. I shall throw you out in deep space myself."

"Keep your threats to yourself; I am submitting all my work on the digital recorder, now leave the Bio dome or shall I call security," sneered Dr. Stark.

Beep, beep, broke the tense moment from Captain Wiseman.

"Yes, what is it now," with a slight irritation from the captain.

"Sir I have visual on Neptune ships they are coming around Psamathe moon. The lead ship is a destroyer class all weapons are hot and aimed at us," reported Number 1.

"I like to go on yellow alert ready our ion guns in case," suggested the weapons officer.

"No, do not provoke them leave all channels open. Our priority is the people I am coming up there now. Oh, find me a telepath so we can try to communicate with a military one he must have one on his ship," ordered the captain.

"Yes, will do," snap number 1!

Wiseman leaves as the Doctor turns his back to comfort a patient who was about to lose his left arm and right foot. He grumbles while rushing to the elevators at the same time as knowing the line-ups will increase to enter the bio dome. The captain checks his suit the radiation count has risen two points close to the danger point. He slowly enters the bridge seeing the full width of the destroyer come in to view. Number 1 introduces a small girl no more then eight years old. Only one R2 rated telepath on board named Katrina Topaz daughter of one scientist that he had picked up at Io when re-supplying his ship. Her head nods with a faint smile.

"Will you communicate with the other telepath on those ships that are approaching us?"

"Yes what would you like me to say to them Captain."

"Our normal friendly greeting, that General Skelton gave us permission to assist in the rescue of both moons we could use some more medical supplies to treat the injured," replied Capt. Wiseman.

Katrina took a few deep breaths and closed her eyes, Wiseman steps back and glances at the view screen, he sees the port guns are juiced and ready to fire. He thought the destroyer was coming in too fast. His right-hand figures nervously played with the switches to shield barriers of Hyperion 3.

"All but one had answered. They are requesting to funnel traffic to the three medical ships. The telepath on the warships is badly injured. The second in command is fighting a mutiny among their crew."

"Oh god, the destroyer might blast our rescue ships now that would be bad news," hissed the captain.

"Do the other telepaths know this also? They suggest you retreat to the dark side of the Naiad moon they will come to shield us from the destroyer," replied Katrina.

"Warn off all incoming flights to the docking ring full reverse and activate energy forward shields at full maximum number One on my mark. Computer control to all shuttle craft change flight operations to the Neptune medical ships, give a wide berth to the destroyer, please repeat my warning ever ten seconds."

"Will comply," echo a mechanical voice.

Katrina began to wail with flowing tears. Everyone turns to the little girl except the captain who sees the full spread of missiles coming. He hits the switches on his Captain seat to broaden his shields to protect the helpless shuttlecrafts.

"The mutinous crew murdered the bridge officers" reported the telepath Katrina.

"Sound off emergency collision shut down all blast doors this is not a drill. Helm sharp full forward on the downward plane," ordered Captain Wiseman.

The helm officer froze slightly in steering the ship. Number one pushes him off his seat to follow the captain orders. The lumbering ship drops then dives nose first into the artificial atmosphere of Naiad. The ship quakes from the sudden change of direction, which causes severe friction on the outer skin on the ship. Wiseman shakes in his Captain chair and releases counter measures to eliminate the enemies' torpedoes. His mind thinks of a solution, and he reconnects with the Doctor.

"Bring everyone inside the bio dome Doctor Stark quickly I have no choice but to do a particle jump, I will give you five minutes no more," grunted Capt. Wiseman.

"That is crazy and unwarranted, I need more time," grumbled the Doctor.

Wiseman looks up at the view screen the counter measures had destroyed five missiles. The explosion had struck two shuttlecrafts and three were still locked of Hyperion 3. The words of the Doctor became mute to Wiseman as he repeated his five minutes timetable before he commits to the jump. He shouts to number one commence evasive manoeuvres. Number one grunts as he uses air thrusters and retro rockets to junk and jive the massive ship like a small combat ship. They all could hear the unfriendly sounds of strain echo in the steel plates by the harsh stress to the ship.

"This not an interceptor sir we are too big, and the gravity will eventually win this battle."

"Weapons officer arm aft laser guns destroy those rockets," snapped the captain.

"Yes sir, already armed will commence firing."

Multi bursts crisscross the atmosphere striking one down a cheer came from the crew. However, shaking increased along the length and width of the ship. Its massive weight began to take a spiral plunge towards Naiad. Number one tried in vain to regain control. Suddenly the panel exploded in his face and he is thrown backwards into the air, crashing hard on the weapons console knocking out the officer. This caused the rear laser cannons to shut down. Captain Wiseman had no other options but to hit the jump engines. He sees one of the missiles about to strike the ship. He grinds his teeth and utters.

"This will never happen on my watch, mutinous scum, she is mine to protect."

With a simple press of the switch, the ship burst into a white light blanking the screen in the auditorium the audience heard tears and wails of pain. A large crackling sound and deep explosion vibrates on the floors of the auditorium. Five long minutes passed in silence before the picture clears. Doctor Stark face appears with his operating mask with a nurse handing him a clamp.

"Please do not move Captain I need you awake to reconnect the brain stem to a computer matrix. You will function in a few more minutes," came muffled words of Doctor Stark.

"What happened, are we out of danger?" His left arm and hand moves to touch the sharp pain in his forehead. He sees it is not his arm but a mechanical appendage.

"What is this you freaking idiot," wailed Wiseman as his heart rate shot up?

"You saved the ship and three million people! Only the bridge was struck you are the only one alive. Calm down while I finish the connections," snapped the Doctor.

"No, I do not want to be a cyborg, stop at once do you here me," complained Captain Wiseman.

"Disconnect power out relays and shut down for healing time and reaffirmation to cyborg program. You will thank me in the future Captain Wiseman the hero of Naiad," Doctor Stark proclaimed.

"No stop disconnects," ordered the captain. He utters his override security pass out in to a deep sleep. He hears distance voices from the main computer had taken over which gave him a glimpse of his escape and out flank the Neptune destroyer with a wide burst of ion cannons. They quickly surrender to a young Lieutenant in the auxiliary bridge. The screen went dead as applauds slowly filter through the auditorium the young military officer takes the podium once again. He waves to the crowd for silence.

"Before I introduce our next guest speaker, I wish to thank Captain Wiseman and his crew for their heroics of rescuing three million four hundred thousand people from both moons. The Doctor on the view screen was convicted for his unusual medical crimes. However, there were others deeply involved with this conspiracy to wipe out trillion of our human races. The large medical fleet from Uranus found more bodies that went up to one hundred million with a million injured and one hundred thousand survivors. The medical fleet was running out of space for the injured so the two Captains from the corvettes took the balance. They call for help repeatedly unanswered by the Alpha Prime government rescue squad, which was in Jupiter moon of Ganymede. Once again, Grays Corporation sent their entire fleet of old freight haulers with medical supplies they would arrive in twenty- one days."

"Tananaka and Dark Lighter Corporation in the wake of the disaster return with the large fleet to confront the two corvettes that chase the salvage ships away from Triton. They claimed salvage rights on all properties including all the dead bodies in an open radio announcement with a threat to attack anyone who interferes within eighteen days. This people of Alpha Prime are the work of an evil corporation that is full of corruption that has plagued us for over two hundred years!" His words echo in the auditorium to the silent audience.

General Skelton upon hearing this made two quick decisions. He sends out probes with a message pleading for help to the human race. He suggests that they all break free from the two-mega corporation who has prevented the rescue operation. "These companies treat all our people like machines stand up for your rights and help us save our race from this disaster was the message sent out to all of Alpha Prime."

With reports that the gravity wells work and seem to bring back the energy of Neptune back on itself. Only two energy waves about twenty kilometres wide and one hundred kilometres in length are angled on Neptune's orbit in opposite direction. At the speed they were moving the will strike the Kuiper belt that was part of the Oort cloud on the edge of the solar system. The Kuiper belt was mostly ice and rocks where meteors and comets would come from which increase the danger to the outer planets of Xenia, Sedna, and Quaoar This may knock them out of orbit, and they could collapse onto the inner planets of Mars and Earth. His fleet were closer to attempt fire breach to disburse the large energy wave to the Kuiper belt. General Skelton hopes the Jupiter military fleet would be the ones to handle the second wave moving towards the inner planets. He uses his telepath to relay instructions to the two corvette Captains to pass on the message to either Alpha Prime government or Jupiter military fleet. He repeats the same message to the all the people of the living worlds of Alpha Prime. They must handle the one heading to the inner planets. General Skelton continues narrating about other military men and woman of different groups that are part of all terra form moons.

He speaks of two other Captains' loyal to their general made a telepathic promise that is recorded in each Captain logbook. Has he repeatedly sent out his plead to rebel against the two-mega corporation. Direct warning of the inner wave to the Alpha Prime government and military of Jupiter must be stopped. With tough decision to make these men and woman made where unselfish commitments to save the human race for its own lack of direction. I am proud to introduce your leader of the new government called Unity Group. Mr. K. Skelton.

The audience erupted wildly with cheers and adoration to Skelton stepping out surrounded by personal guards and twelve telepaths in among the guards sensing for any violent tendencies. His face gave a cold glare with a fake smile. He was six feet tall, broad in shoulders with thick white hair combed neatly. His eyes were a deep penetrating blue that stared out to the audience. A clean-shaven look shows his square jaw line. He prepares his papers to speak he jesters for peace to the understanding audiences. Above the general, the screen reveals his humble beginnings through the military and all his commendations up to his last post as General of the Neptune fleet.

"I am here to honour the fallen and the sacrifice of the elite on December 20, 2535. Now ten-years has past, we have built this monument that is dedicated to the fallen on every planet and moon across Alpha Prime. Their names of the three ships that started the destruction and the ones that gave their lives to save us. This history will have countless stories of bravery and self scarifies with one goal in mind to save our children of the future."

The crowd's cheers wildly shouting his name repeatedly. He seems to sparkle accepting their admiration. The telepaths move about in the crowd, Skelton raises his hands for silence that came quickly in the auditorium.

"Yes, even my personal grief of my entire family killed at Naiad moon. This became my part to bring our first change of a new revolution for all the planets in Alpha Prime. Now for the first time you will see and hear what actions I took to save the outer planet and moon colonies. The record is uncut or altered; the truth will be revealed to those that love humankind, and the blind justice to the corrupted ones of Tananaka and Dark lighter."

The lights dim as the recording begins with the general sitting in his office with the telepath Stella Neptune 6 bright blonde hair, brown eyes, and small round face with a slender body in one size too big military jump suit. The general is listening to the latest data from the two Captains and their needs for more battle ships to counter the closing war fleet of joint Tananaka and Dark lighter.

"I will send you six more squadrons of interceptors and eight blast boats and four transports with supplies that you can convert to carrying more survivors," quoted the general. He took in a deep sigh from watching the energy wave starting to spread out into a string before he regains his thoughts and finishes his last words to the telepath to pass on to the two Captains.

The telepath repeated the message for help to promote the revolution to disrupt the mega corporations and protect the Uranus medical fleet.

"They must hold their position with their last breath of freedom," quoted General Skelton.

A dozen of Captains from his battle fleet enter the general conference room to complete the plans to disburse the wave. Using a magnet coupling and shielding to field align their engines and lighten their overall mass to reach one quarter light speed. Catching up and passing the wave in a matter of hours. The general holding his report of the Black Raven mutiny went out to establish his control over the fleet. All twelve Captains saluted and quickly said aye, aye, General Skelton.

"So far, only Grays Corporation has shown great support. As well, the Uranus medical team units are doing an excellent job. Still no answer from the central government or request to stop the inner wave," reported Stella Neptune 6.

"We must do the right thing for the outer planets," ordered the General.

"Why not divide the fleet to tackle both waves sir," inquired a young Captain of a battle cruiser?

"We could help black raven repairs and increase our potential strength with their warheads," said another Captain.

"No every atomic weapon is required to disburse the wave to save the outer planets," the general suggested firmly.

"They are only cyborgs and clones sir that would be a waste of our resources," repeated the older officer.

The general's face tightens with rage because his eyes study the veteran officer showing blind ignorance. He chews his lips but instead moves towards the young telepath. She turns on the rude officer by slapping his face as she yanks the weapon from the older Captain.

"Captain Frost is a traitor to Alpha Prime his thoughts of heading back to look for his parents, wife, and children instead of being here," hissed the telepath.

"Stella calms down we all have family back there on several Neptune's moons," hissed the General. He moves between them to break the tension. He takes the handgun from Stella and gives it back to the Captain Frost. With the tension rising in the room, he continues to explain his plans.

"I only want to stop one wave not only the clones and the cyborgs on the outer planets of Xena, Sedna, and Qusoar. It would prevent a disturbance throughout the Oort cloud, which would bring waves of comets, and meteors to destroy all life that we have sworn to protect in Alpha Prime."

"My apology," muttered Captain Frost.

"I accept it but let us get down to the plan our scientists have came up with Captains. We must set up in less then an hour and realign at one thousand kilometres apart in crest moon shape firing each ship releasing twenty atomic weapons. Force in to collapse on itself the only danger to the fleet is that it could disburse a magnetic storm. You must retreat further into the Oort cloud to escape the storm."

"I think sir it will be better if we stay in units of three in case we have to regroup and do it again if the wave does not break down," grumbled the older Captain.

"Very well, I agree to the plan that units of three ships must fire simultaneously. Most importantly, the navigation officers must work together on the flight plans," replied the general at the same time as others agreed with a nod.

Beep, beep came from the com channel. The telepath went to the communicator, that was flashing at the entrance way.

"Yes, go ahead with updated reports."

"We are getting reports of disturbances in the lower levels on a few ships it sounds like a mutiny."

The captains stood up upon hearing the news.

"Turn on a wide communication on internal com. We must end this quickly if we have a chance," ordered the General.

Each Captain enters the code channel. They spoke directly to the crew about what they are about to do and backup plans to join the other force to protect their planets. The General knew the crew wanted to know of their family members, he decided to give the list of survivors too quell the mutiny in hopes to subdue the crew. Each Captain had lost a loved one or a complete family.

"This must be done first we shall grieve later I promise you no one will ever forget the innocent lives taken this day," replied General Skelton.

The captains went to their battle cruiser and destroyers. They drop into formation of a crest moon. They time all their charges to match with the general's flagship the Wrath of God. They place additional weapons on line while the engines were tuned. The General sits anxiously in the seat watching the monitors and blimps of the atomic weapons spreading out in perfect telemeters. The weapons officers count down as the sensors pick up the first quake of the wave. The bombs floated freely towards a massive wave. They hope they can create a counter wave by correctly disbursing the explosives. As the five second count down begins, 4, 3, 2, ignition. Strings of pearls erupt and engulf the energy wave. The auditorium screen blanks out including the audio. As it goes dark, the lights in the auditorium brighten slowly. Mr. Skelton standing at the podium, smiles as the audience clearly appreciated his strength. Cheers went wild and they shout his name for the new president. Mr. Skelton waves his hands and quickly silences the crowds.

"The defunct government of Alpha Prime never responded. The people broke away from the bonds of the Mega Corporation and corrupted officials. During the time, we disbursed the energy wave. The Jupiter military led by General w Cummings disobeyed the president orders and left to destroy the other wave in a similar fashion. When it confirmed the first wave evaporated leaving a counter wave that curved towards the main asteroid belt that circled the inner planets between Mars and Jupiter. These asteroids have a wide range of sizes enough to form a large planet. Once free, no living planet or moon colonies and space platforms can withstand the wave of destruction. General w Cummings fleet is loyal to him for the long years of service which General Skelton wish to honor him. General w Cummings successfully stopped the first wave heading for the inner planets. However, General w Cummings and eight of his battle fleet ships were wiped out by the magnetic storm, which cause a reforming of a new planet. This had a similar result at the Oort cloud I lost two ships and these new planets also form into existence. The two new planets I named one Thor the other Odin due to the strange lightning storms and strong magnetic field that was created by this disaster. The people had spoke from various groups of humans, clones and cyborg join and took over the large fleet from Tananaka and Dark lighter. The group of freedom fighters turn on their ship Captain and the winners join in the rescue attempt on the moon of Triton. They had help from 100 hundred Grays Corporation ships had arrive with more supplies," stated Mr. Skelton.

The audience all rose in anticipation of the unveiling monument to the brave heroes of the Neptune disaster and their great sacrifice by the people of Alpha Prime. The hush spread like a wave waiting for his last words on the podium. Mr. Skelton sighs deeply has he searches the papers of his speech with tears forming in his eyes that he must fight off his emotions and spots Samuels Grays sitting off stage. Then he sent a telepathic message to Stella Neptune 6 to bring him forward to help pull the cord. Samuels Grays accepts his offer and moves forward toward the cover monument while General. Skelton begins his dedication speech to the large crowd.

"Thus, ending the disaster ten years ago now is time to grieve. This monument is forever breathing life across the planets of our Alpha Prime and will never forget their sacrifice. I am being a citizen of this solar system proudly unveil the tribute to our fallen families, friends, neighbours, and soldiers of the elite fighting military."

The lights rise up when Mr. Skelton taking the hand of Samuels Grays pulls the cord. "The wave of the future is back in the hands of the people." The old man blinks sadly when he sees what they used as a monument. It caused great pains in his chest. The remains of the star gate shatter in a circular heap with tall pillars with the names of the dead and injured for all to read.

With elections the next day, a new leader with the widest reform Mr. Skelton a front-runner takes control of Alpha Prime. His promise to clean corruption and give freedom to clones and cyborg brings about the resolution of giving the individual planets control of their resources. Shutting down all corporations under government control including Grays Corporation.

The two Mega Corporations were destroyed by President Skeleton on the quest for revenge. He steals the clone technology to repopulate Alpha Prime and replace the loss of life. He gains control of all their assets and quickly imprisons all management. He sentences them to death by firing squad to be televised in three days across the planets. His zeal of wanting to save his race came at high cost knowing that the human race must survive this utter destruction of humankind, gave the opening for the military to take control through the new president Skelton.

Now in charge, he takes over Saturn, Uranus, and parts of Jupiter satellites. The death of his family and fellow comrades did a great deal of damage to the general's mind. Over the next four years, he became a vile dictator. He selected telepaths to be in every sector of government from the elite council to directors, mangers, and military leaders to ensure the other groups stay inline within the new constitutions to the free market.

His constant nightmares about the energy wave he destroyed as he watched the magnet storm whip apart two escort battle ships. The dream state gives him other visions that point to a new beginning of a magical sphere hidden in the Oort cloud. His doctors proclaim it a dream state to form a perfect race, proclaimed by a new visitor and her brood of children. The telepaths close to the president join him in a sleep state confirming Drieson sphere that will bring a new wonder to the world. President Skelton is consumed by his dream to search for the mystery sphere. He leaves his elite committee of telepathist, in charge of running the government and military controls.

He enjoys the power over the weaker races and plots to find and destroy anything that threatens his controls. He promotes breeding in telepaths by natural ways or by cloning with altering drugs to boost their level for telekinesis. He also started a program to collect gifted children, rated their powers, and placed them above the other groups. The people of Alpha Prime are given to despair as more are forced into farming compounds and basic labour works. This brings darker days to the human race across Alpha Prime. The planets and moon satellites went into a free market with no controls to share the wealth of all the worlds. This left old wounds, hatred, mistrust and bigotry between the original, clones and cyborg. It became more difficult while the military tightened its grip on every resource of Alpha Prime.

CHAPTER 13

CHILDREN OF THE LIGHT CHALLENGES THE ENTITY

The planet Azure is equal in size to many gas giant planets. Its large 3/2 mass compare natural zones where life begins with large amounts of water, planet life and atmosphere is rich with natural barriers from all elements from space. It is located in a tight orbit of a dwarf red sun. The pressure of the atmosphere is greater than old earth or any other planets that came to mind. Filled with broad oceans and large landmasses wide temperate zones from long mountain ranges, rolling hills of forest, flat lands grass plains and desert area. The weather had four seasons, filled with life with aquatic, animal, insect and planets. The children of the light were one with their entire world. No city was on the surface of the planet with only wade stations and medical centers hidden in the mountain caves and forest campsites attuned for animal life. The Children passed on this information to all of the doom if they approached Azure. Sabrina works with others and Krell to setup the transfer of Azure life forms into various worlds. They also use a time portal in hopes to find new homes for all the alien guests.

Deep within Azure's crust is the heart of the children of the light with multiple cities and construction sites for world spheres. Chambers upon chambers contain a collection of gifts and knowledge brought from alien races. This took a billion years to be placed in the cosmos library. They reached the highest level of awareness to the verge of making its own creation by thought from many minds. Instead, the children of light gave alien races sanctuary from their own demise. Sabrina guards many secrets of each race that she had saved. Their efforts brought peace and security for all. She follows her great father's ideas, which he named the Babylon project; where many races found a new order dedicated for the betterment of the cosmos. Within Azure came the meeting place called the circle of life where they watch over younger races. Their efforts guide the races to survive the growth of wisdom and awareness and show them that they were not alone, each new being placed according to the levels of balance and chaos. Everyone watched the Entity spread its touch, the children save many from her deathly touch. They had faced her three other timelines. Each time they surrender, the two-forces cancel each other with an odd result to start all over from the beginning of the big bang.

All that changed with an open vote to follow the captain 's plan to set their worlds free across time and space. This erased all knowledge of the children of the light, until the final battle. If any would survive the travel back in time, all scientist of the many worlds works on finding ways to ensure that all would somehow remember their alliance with the children of the light. Only Captain Patterson and his crew of hooding beings gave hope, which they gave a special crystal to a male and a female of each race in secrets. When the time comes, they will search for the hidden world ship name the Drieson sphere. Their computer technology matches many races of the artificial mind each will carry all information advance knowledge and operation control by each alien race. All are set to activate the flight plan to the ea solar system. Sabrina visits the entire races on an individual basis in a ceremony of friendship. The captain wanders among them to select one being to carry the special crystal. Once done they leave the chamber, seal the door, and start the countdown of their departure. These visits seem to drain Sabrina each time she had to say goodbye to so many. The lights of her eyes would slowly dim from each world chamber she visits. Many of her kind committed to the captain plans spent hours and days rebuilding the time portal to ensure all ships would pass through moments to the end of Azure planet, with others above ground watching the sky for the black ships.

The oldest of the children work deeper in the planets core and special collectors to gather the red sun energy to power the time portal dropping the world ships and the Drieson spheres across space. Sabrina is often quoted in many speeches in the circle of life. Many describe her like an older teacher, which weighs over the dilemma of the entities brought to the silver woman from the other races. The room transforms into a mission control with plugs and view screen all locked on each of the chosen couple of each race. One of the Captain plans is to recruit and instruct new races to ensure preparations to join in the fight. Sabrina names it the sleeping eyes and ears of the cosmos. One million Volunteers from many races take part in the advance ship operations to watch over all the worlds inside the wormhole.

Krell and his people were the last seen by Sabrina and the Captain. The two enter the forest by the gateway with a wide range of animals, which bow to Krell and walk away into the forest. His clan prepare for the visit building a stage of rocks in half moon and fill the edges with assorted flowers and fruit trees with a small waterfall and babbling brook to set a special place where their race first met Sabrina to hear the leader of Azure for the last time. Krell led the way into the special place, which they called the first place of friendship. Sabrina shrank to be an equal height of all the dwellers. This brought great cheers that even surprised Krell. His daughter Emerald gave a short introduction. Sabrina floated to the center of the crest moon. She sang and old elder song which brought great emotions within his people. Her eyes were a soft purple colour with tears flowing in a strange colour of brown. Everyone had tears in their eyes and freely gave a cheer for her tenderness as she gave a small wave to silence the crowd and to speak from her heart.

"We are all one family we exist on one grain of sand. Life starts small and blossoms in many forms based on balance and chaos. I am your first contact when you reach the higher level to become what you are the protectors of the green and the balance of all life. I am proud to be your first contact in your new form," stated Sabrina.

The crowd cheered with applause; her eyes glowed warmly floating in slow turn.

"You are the chosen to take the giant leap and the first line of defence to guard and guide the awaking of the hybrid race between the light and shadows. Balance must remain constant to fulfill our goals. Many may die from this challenge or live without ever being involved in this battle. The fourth generation will need you to be their teacher. I only hope you show compassion and restraint not to harm any life form."

Sabrina eyes look over to Krell who sat in the first row among the tall trees. He listens intently picking up her emotions with every word. The little green man had grown some attachment to Sabrina, knowing that this would be one of her last speeches. He took her words deep in his heart not to take revenge against Ru or the child of his old race.

His mind would flash the pain of Ru's betrayal. His adopted daughter felt it and sent a message that washes his dark thoughts away.

You must hold tight when we met Sabrina, we were reborn to the next level. Is it not so that every newborn must suffer the birth to be born in a new world, this is it father and she is our angel?

Yes, you are right Emerald, we must be thankful to Sabrina.

The crowd cloud cheered and applause loudly breaking Krell's mind link. He blinks his eyes and sees the two fairies fluttering around Sabrina. He became curious stood to walk over and inquire what help he could offer. Suddenly the Captain appears to block his way. The captain's plans were being implemented within a certain timeline to match the invasion of the Entity. Krell 's heartache for the commitment of all the races for the time shift against the Entity and the coming doom. Sabrina did not stop the visit to each chamber that housed a biosphere of each alien race. The dwarf size leader of the forest people knew that Captain is selecting two to carry the power seed. He knew this was the last place she visits him and his people. He is honoured by the kindness and attentive nature of the silver face woman. He was not sure of the captain by his brash nature which showed to have many voices that Krell call endless noises, from a childhood memory to this adult man both with positive to negative thoughts. Yes, thought Krell these images are strange sights as well his memories of violence wash out of this strange two-legged creature. Krell grunted an elder curse. The old Captain looks down with a rueful smile and spoke telepathically.

You might have won her heart little green man. However, you must prove yourself in this coming war, by great deed, and self-sacrifice. Instead, I will watch by that murderous mind of yours when you wiped out an unknown race. Now, take the blue seed from my hand and see the truth within your living soul.

A puzzled look came over Krell. His eyes wander to the being and watch his right hand open revealing a blue gem within his grasp. He is the chosen one to hold the truth in the coming war. Without hesitation, he takes and holds the blue gem tightly in his left hand. A minor spark shot up his arm to his mind fluttering his eyes to readjust his vision. He sees Sabrina changing before him in a fog white mist. While the two fairies flutter in a circle forming brightly colour rings form above Sabrina's head. Other similar fairies join in the same fashion, but in a multitude of colours that he never saw in a million years. He tries to speak to Sabrina his throat is dry, a sudden change of silver flesh liquid flew over her head and slowly drops to reveal her inner self. *The glow is a wondrous sight* thought Krell until her head turns towards him almost blinded by the light from her eyes, he winced and covered his eyes slightly, and then he hears a voice pounding in his head.

You cannot look at me truthfully because your soul is in torment. You must face the truth behind you Krell, this is your demon and choose the path.

His eyes hurt from the brilliance of Sabrina. He turns complete around there in front of him are the six hooded figures of the hybrid race. His eye catches a diamond shaped eye peering out of the dark cloaked being. His mind washes over the unknown being. He feels something familiar within that being. A sharp pain came up his left hand, and the memory of Ru comes to him that is who she is. From deep within him, anger boils into a blind rage. He curses in an elder's cry of revenge and lunges at the hooded figure.

"I will kill you with my bare hands."

He wraps his hands around its neck choking the very life out of her. He hears the laughter and insults ringing in his ear. Then suddenly someone lift him off into the air, her eyes are deep red with rage, she floats by him. The crowds are stunned to silence, the captain rushed for his fallen comrade, shouting in his native language a wide range of insults.

"Have you not learned our laws of Azure we harm no other regardless of what happen to you in the other dimensions," Sabrina remarks in a wary tone?

"I know your laws but that is Ru and she is part of the evil that approaches your planet. She is here to kill you Sabrina," screamed Krell.

"Now let me down I have proof it is Ru."

The captain helped the fallen being off the ground. He gave a smirk and was happy that Krell failed the test. Somehow, Sabrina picks up his facial expression. Suspicion rose within her mind playing back the scene she sees the captain force a test on the little man in hopes that he will fail. She knows the powers of Krell will soon awake upon arriving back to his place of origin the solar system of Ea.

"Bring the hooded figure to me," ordered Sabrina.

"You know why they are hooded because they are disharmonious with time, great leader," muttered the captain.

"Do not force me to use my powers Captain you already now how painful it can be."

The captain's face went pale from memories, he nodded took hold of the hooded figure's arm pushing it up towards Sabrina the crowds watched the exchange. Krell floated towards his daughter. She wipes his brow to cool his forehead and with a few choices telepathic words lowers his rage.

I feel your pain father it is Ru the others of our clan also agree, but we have evolved to a new form and new beginnings please let us turn away from violence.

Yes, I know the error I made, but the pain is too deep to forgive and forget young one.

"You will stand and watch the error you have made Krell," order Sabrina.

The creature struggled with the captain to stay hidden under the dark cloak. He wraps his arm and pulls back the hood. The crowd all gasp and curse loudly. Krell curses under his breathe; it was a small human child. It had large eyes and wails for her father. The eyes of Sabrina flare over the child she stopped struggling and then stood stiffly with a stern look. On her forehead was a diamond shape birthmark, even the captain huffed in surprise. This caught Sabrina's attention and she waves the child to step closer. She looks down at the nervous expression from the child who inches forward. Sabrina eyes glowed many colours with a narrow beam striking the diamond shape. It opened slowly, and then shut quickly.

"The two of you have made this error upon my world you bring both innocent and evil thing. She is but a child that needs love and reassurance. The evil in her is frightened it wants to attack without thought at anyone who threatens it. Krell, you awoke this within her by your rage. For this Captain used her telepath abilities to invoke the rage within Krell. Now that she is here, I must decide her fate cause by you two. This child must be altering in a painful way to undo your damage," hissed Sabrina.

"No, it is KrelII that will take the punishment, the look of her makes me feel ashamed of my actions. Please, do not harm her it was my weak moment, I swore revenge against Ru and the child that cast the spell. These past few years I want to work with the children of the light to defeat the darkness."

"Humph, oh another truth that you failed to reveal to me during our debriefing indicates why our race is involved during the variant flux time is in chaos."

"I beg your pardon Sabrina the memory came out of my rage to harm Ru," hissed Krell.

"You are full of surprises little green man," Sabrina barked scornful.

Her eyes went dark completely black empty pools she turns to the other hooded beings. Suddenly loud high pitch rings struck every ones mind; many scream and drop to the ground. Only the child and the five-hooded figurer stood against the silver woman. The young girl gave a smirk as the diamond shape eye opens to face Sabrina. The child waves her hand a grey mist form and rose up from the ground that quickly filled the forest realm.

"We are the many do not fight us our goal is to shrink time to a permanent life in the dark light. The Entity is near let this existence end as we have done in the past three timelines, but this time you will never return," snorted the child.

Sabrina eyes light up to a golden colour, her silver colour changed to a blood red and she slowly drops to the ground on one knee and bows to the evil Entity. The leader of Azure kept her head down, while she struggles to send a telepathic message to the child.

We live for balance and die in chaos. You have arrived too soon to prepare for our death. You have broken protocol of our joint ritual.

The child circles Sabrina her body changing with every step she makes. Her skin turns to a bluish grey. It begins to rip open, revealing a bloated and harden body as her arms and legs stretch out. Two additional legs appear to support her larger size in both height and weight. The face of the innocent child drops to the ground. As the multi, eye with a blood red head snaps it mandibles and hissed loudly.

"I am not here for a ritual foolish child I came to end it all. This child was a tool to get excess, my poison will spread on every living creature. They shall fall at the same time as you Sabrina."

"I can see that now great leader of shadows," wailed Sabrina.

"You are right to fear me this is the time for darkness and shadows will rule all from the past to the future. The light will never return," the Entity flatly stated.

"No, you cannot do this the innocence of all life force must be released or it will die," begged Sabina. Then between her tears, Sabrina asks a strange question.

"How did you find the time crystal great shadow?"

"From these six two-legged creatures in adult form, she confronted Ru their mind gift split between them by a mechanical chip name the helix cube powers. She escapes by a rebirth spreading Ru through the genetics of her DNA expanded throughout the human race by cloning. While she travelled in many forms through time and collects the shattered pieces of the time crystal. That explains why the silly Krell shattered long ago, which gave me a new purpose to end it all. The crystal cut right through your defenses now the end has come, you cannot stop this Sabrina."

While the large creature chatted to Sabrina, the other hooded figure moved to encircle Sabrina. Each one transformed into a large insect with multi arms, large thorax, and heads with snapping mandibles. The chatter among them gave the impression that they were hungry for power. The information she received was passed on to the old ones deep under ground. The leader of the children of the light speaks softly to Katrina. Then looks up at the Entity her eyes glare with renewed energy.

"You have blundered Entity; your claim shall never be allowed to happen, the darkness in you is false, you are not the true one to challenge me, and my world," remarked Sabrina. Standing up reforming back to her natural form six-foot-tall woman holding her left hand high and raising her right arm bent across a defensive stance.

"I am and you will surrender to me now," hissed the Entity. She stomped her foot, while the others closed in on Sabrina.

"I think not little one," grunted Sabrina as she flicks her right arm a silver shield formed. After many clicks, it opens like a fan with sharp edges in a perfect circle. Her left hand snaps her figures together which appears as double edge spear with a twohanded grip. Her body also changed with a thick arm and helmet with the symbols of three circles each one a rainbow colour, red, yellow, and blue. This only angers the Entity who roars out orders to kill as all five hooded creatures attack the leader of the children of the light. Sabrina swings her double edge spear across with a slash, while her shield deflected the Entity's attack, to counter Sabrina attack and knocks her sideways into the others. Her slashes manage to cut across one of the one the attackers chest area it fell back and bleeds badly and gasp for air. Suddenly it stiffen than crumble into dust. The two fairies reappear with their weapons drawn by pulling three of the attackers off Sabrina, which left only the Entity and one warrior. They split apart to attack her on both flanks. Sabrina complains again angrily.

"What are you waiting for Katrina, now would be nice."

Katrina reappears in a burst of lightning holding a large energy pole of five feet in length. Being from the children of the light she is also a crystal being slightly smaller in stature but different in the colour of her eyes are greenish color. The attacker charged with his four arms swinging in four different directions with their large pinchers at Katrina, While the Entity charged at the legs of Sabrina. She launches high with a two-legged kick to the chest of the Entity's While Katrina somersaults using her pole to roll over the Jung zee's back. She lands on her feet and with a quick counter thrust of her pole had impale deeply into the chest of the tall attacker. He lost his balance falling backwards into the Entity. Suddenly a swarm of glowing spheres appeared from all angles in many sizes surrounding the Entity. It squealed for help the others turn to help her, but the two fairies and Sabrina kept them back. The ground rumbled as ghostly forms appear. She is much taller than Sabrina out of the ground, with her arms apart spread apart openly releasing the spheres that surround the Entity, she spoke in a deep voice.

"You are an echo of the Entity we judge you a mistake of time. Thus, you must return all souls that you have corrupted. We shall correct your path by children of the light. We shall be your guidance to a more balance life cycle. For every wrong you have done shall be undone."

"No, I am the true one," hissed the Entity. It struggled against the spheres swinging its mandibles side to side twirling backwards to escape them.

"You have dismissed the ritual, which alone is a broken agreement with the children of the light. The battle for dominance shall begin. You may leave but return all the ones you have corrupted," snorted the giant woman.

"Never, but I will give you these six children to play with. I will come with my fleet wipe you all clean from time itself," hissed the Entity.

She arches her head up and releases a black mist with the diamond shape eye glowing red floated to the same height of the giant woman, then flashes away giving off the sound of thunder, and a cold chill. All six beings lay naked and unconscious in human form. In both sexes from a child to older ages, all were at different ages. Sabrina gave a deep sigh as her appearance returned to normal. She glanced at the tall ghostly with an annoyed expression.

"You took your time to enter the fight Katrina and sister Tribeca" snorted Sabrina.

The tall woman shrank to an equal height of the leader. She slaps her hands as all the spheres reform into children. Her face shows great concern looking down at the fallen humans. She chews her lips and bent down to touch the child. It felt its sleeping thoughts, which she shared with the children of light's vision; Sabrina struggled to breath and covered her mouth to prevent the lips from uttering the name they could clearly see. The others all whispered among themselves.

"Sabrina, we have no choice but to enter their world they are the first ones, we must save them from this destruction," snapped Katrina.

"Is that why you hesitated to kill the Entity," inquired Sabrina.

Yes, I was not sure my leader; I did a mind link to tests this being when I found out she was once a human child name Helen, I immediately want to ensure it was not an innocent child. So, forgive me for not coming to rescue you."

"Katrina what did the test reveal, this quite disturbing to be intertwine with another race that we have no history but within our dreams I now that humanoid is someone from our past."

"However, the test did match our ancestors by 100% in DNA, so these beings are not another race but our true ancestors. I had no choice but to scare her off and make her release the human races," Katrina whispered sadly.

"This perplexing dilemma means we are the paradox of the future. The Entity has corrupted the human race. What should we do now," grunted Sabrina?

"I need time with Ben, he is still working on it when I left him to help you," explains Katrina.

"I had hope Krell and the other races would take the fight but now we must act to save ourselves also. Oh, dear Krell and his people are injured by my actions," hissed Sabrina.

"Calm down you know very well when we talk through our telepathic abilities it effects the other races on Azure. They will awake with a headache and see us, as we really are," grunted Katrina.

The fairies float over after they study the other three humans.

"They are quite handsome in these forms" remarked the red fairy!

"Yes, especially the young male, he looks familiar to me," quoted the blue fairy.

"Is it not times you to leave and seal this world off," inquired the red fairy.

"You did tell us that we are going back to terrain six," remarked the blue one.

Sabrina held her hand up for silence; fairies once they begin to speak never stop and can be quite annoying. Katrina moved off to check on the captain. A thought came to her head, and she decided to check out on the old man first. Since all their minds are connected through the children, everyone watches with great interest. Sabrina wanders over to Krell, she saw him against the tree with his daughter Emerald resting on his lap. The fairies flutter near by mustering all sorts of nothings. The minute the red fairy saw Emerald she swoops down close to her face studying ever feature. Her partner glides slowly beside the red fairy with curious look also at the green faced child. Sabrina was about to shoo them away. When fear washed over her and all the other children, she turns in the direction of Katrina. Her charisma is missing from the group's mind. She rushes over to another human child lying beside the captain. The little baby girl had short black hair, round face with soft complexion and bright eyes. Sabrina stepped cautiously towards the child noticed what was also wrong the captain had become younger and looked more in his thirties.

222

"Stop Sabrina do not go any nearer," came a large shout from behind her. This made her jump back by the harshness of the warning. She glares and barks his name.

"Ben, this is no way to talk to your leader. You should know your place. Something happen to Katrina; her mind is gone."

The silver being floated between the little girl and Sabrina with his arms spread to keep them apart. His eyes were a sickly green, muttered in blood tears.

"She must have read my thoughts," while he confirms it by touching the helix cube. "I just want to stop you Sabrina," Ben whispered.

"If you had touched the changeling, you would have been infecting all of us. *Katrina touches the human helix cube it absorbs her essence and reverts to a human child. Her powers are gone for now but she still has her telepath powers but in lower level that befits the time line the Captain had come from,*" remark Ben.

"I see she found a way to save us all," mumbled Sabrina. Her mind envisions "This the most dangerous act to be reborn with no memories about us, we will fall into the emotional traps of their society especially the old ones. Religion is both balance and chaos," she shakes her head no has her words bring out her faith in the Azurin race.

"How so, we have always had an open mind on all the beliefs of the other races," snapped Sabrina.

"Maybe so but their other emotions will surface within us Sabrina, hate, love and indifferent feelings for life in general plus bigotry against our own people," grunted Ben.

"We have no choice but to be reborn into the various timeline from the past to the present and even the unknown future it will represent to us. We can only hope that we can fulfill our destiny when and if we return has the children of the light. So let it be done, we shall retreat and be ready to fight another day," ordered Sabrina.

"I have a device that will hold our true self as well as awaken us in a new life form for a short time. They could help us to prepare for the battle and regain a foothold I made one for Katrina once activated the other essence from her family side will join Katrina into the present. You and I can follow Katrina after we set the other races free while we destroy our planet Azure and wipe out the entity's battlefleet. This will give us the time," claimed Ben.

"How are you going to place that on her wrist without following into its magic spell," inquired Sabrina?

The two fairies were arguing over Emerald in very loud voices that were quite annoying. Sabrina barks at the fairies to be quiet and steps over to check on Krell. He looked restful with his daughter by his side the scent of flowers rose around them this brought on a strange and sudden desire to kiss him. She shook it off immediately, and then wonders if Katrina had placed that thought in her mind. The red fairy flutters close with a plea for some help to prove the arguments between them. Sabrina eyes glowed to a deep red and both hands formed a fist. Ben touches her mind telepathically.

You are feeling emotions and look our brothers and sisters feel it too. We will be overrun and fall under the Entity. Time is reversing as we speak, Sabrina. The two fairies could help us if we can answer their question.

"Yes," Sabrina sighs for a simpler time.

Her eyes soften and her hands open slowly she takes a deep breath before inquiring what the fairies want to know. The red one is fascinated with Emerald, while the blue look is very resentful over the issue. She sat on top of Krell's hat, while the other one rested on Emerald's shoulders. Ben walked over to Sabrina and places the wrist device on her left arm; he wore his on the right arm. It sparks and pulses matching her mood and reforming her status and balance within the metal body. Sabrina chooses her words slowly to entice the two fairies with a condition.

"I will answer three questions and only three questions then you must do my request," offered Sabrina.

"There is two of us do we get each three," snorted the blue one.

"I have no more time but only three questions for the two of you," repeated Sabrina.

"I only want one and it is a request I have fought these evil shadows three times and failed. I want to be the mother of this child, feel pain, joy, and love deep within, my soul," whispered the red fairy.

"You are a silly fairy," snorted the blue fairy. You must fall in love first with your mate before a baby grows inside your belly. Besides I want to win this battle, never fight again answers that, I will ride to the moon, and straight into the sun to have this come true," grumbled the blue fairy.

"I see it is more a request then questions that will satisfy and fill each of your desires," hissed Sabrina. She went silent looking down at her bracelet then over to Katrina.

"Go over to my sister by the captain take the one person that will fill you hearts desire," Sabrina sang out a magic spell.

The two fairies reacted with enthusiasm by jumping into the air and dancing to the lyrical tune.

"Fairies of Ea. You must place these bracelets on your chosen being's left wrist to complete your requests. In addition, repeat your request only then will you receive your gifts as long as you never surrender your will to the dark shadow. These gifts will give you great joy or pain by the choices you make," remark Sabrina in a deep echoing voice."

The two fairies caught Sabrina by surprise they each took one person the red one took Emerald and the other took Krell. Sabrina gasped at first and wanted to cancel the spell, however the presence of Ben held off her in tension. His subdued thoughts express regret, which he sends openly.

We have no choice let it happen for all our family and friends must exist for the new future of the fourth generation.

Ben I need them to go in the past and face Ru and the others shadow warriors Sabrina murmured her thoughts to all her race.

They will and more so dear sister, Katrina told me all would work keep your faith in the balance of all life replied to Ben.

They watch the fairies transport the two dwarfs to Katrina the blue fairy places Krell on the stomach of the Captain Patterson. The red fairy placed the other beside Katrina. They sang the magical words and then placed each bracelet on the chosen being's left arm. The energy from the bracelet released a cascade affect. Many of Katrina's clan fell back into white spheres floated freely above her. Each sphere collected the forest dweller and then is absorbed altering their bodies into a woodland nymph. The female bodies were round and sultry. They swirl over the six humans before they would shrink smaller and faded even further as many joined the unconscious bodies. Krell melted within Captain Patterson much to the shock of the blue fairy. Only the red fairy seem to have her hopes come true. She began to grow into a full-size human female. Suddenly Emerald's eyes open with her arms reaching out and cried out mother once. The connection was made so fast it imploded within the red fairy. The red fairy panics from disappearance of Emerald as the pain struck deeply as she shrank back into a fairy.

"Screaming no, I want her back now" hissed the red fairy.

Sabrina shrugged her shoulders and turned towards the captain. The captain stood up his voice sounded harsh as he spoke. Sabrina notices his flesh starts to bubble parts of his flesh pop out and roll to the ground to reform four males at different ages. They all spoke in unison.

"You are undoing the fabric of time what will become of us."

The once evil child rose up into a young woman bowed to Sabrina and took a freshly made Captain of her choice said her farewell and stated a promise.

"I am Claudette Nightshade your lost sister of time. So, I Thank you for my release I shall redeem my honor through the children you have given me to bring peace and prosperity to all humanity."

The others also rose and stepped in line leaving behind one male. He staggers towards the blue fairy grasping her whole body within one hand. He kisses her tiny lips and mutters a name that she reacts to then he fades away to a sparkling light, which leaves his aura that flows over her. She purrs softly as the essence of energy washes over her and calls for her sister. They join hands in a loving embrace turn into a multi colour sphere and fade away. Sabrina watches this all happen around her. Like the words, the captain said aloud the fabric of time is changing to a different setting. She looks to Ben for some comforting words. He becomes a ghostly image flushing in many forms of humans, male, female and children with different colours and appearances. Swirls of white spheres swarm inward to his chest. He spoke telepathically the words sting from the many voices.

We are part of the many the whole cosmos is one, old friend. You must now set the flow, for the first time we shall have angels of mercy born from the flesh of humans. Your job is to give them passage and support for the final battle. I must warn you do not fall into the emotions of other races it will harm you, Sabrina. You must leave now I claim this world and hold it for the return of Krell. I shall await for you in the past dear sister goodbye, peace, and prosperity for all.

He crystallizes into a statue, went silent. Sabrina hears all the wild animals cry out. She steps to the portal and seals the door. Five of her clan members stand by the hallway all were weeping. Sabrina takes comfort by their presence and touches each one with her mind to ease their anguish.

No one ever dies my children we just move to the next level of existence. We have been blessed and we shall go back to the real present to save many of a cruel death. We have much to do for the first battle is about to begin, claimed Sabrina.

Sabrina and the remains of the children of the light, gather for the final prayer. The rest of her clan moves to the surface. They are gone to greet the Entity in hopes to postpone the end of time. They knew that the Entity would not settle for delays based on her secret attack within the planets core. She had done this three times and devoured all life on Azure within twenty-four hours. This time it is different all life had been seal and sent away though a time portal. The only beings left are Sabrina and fifty thousand children of the light. Sabrina decides to fight if the Entity does not compromise

The Entity memories fall back in time, has images of the 12 Galaxies and different Planets display her powers destruction that seem to wander aimless not realizing it had wiped out the light of all life until time breaks free to rewatch the beginning from the big bang. It releases the cycle of life wiping the Entity's existence away. Krell would always discuss openly with all the elders and the female Ru. Sabrina knew that Krell had the knowledge from the beginning to the end of time. Many others take care of each other, spiritual needs while they wait their turn in the next step. "Time for the final battle will happen, not here in the future or the present," quoted Sabrina. However, her thoughts turned to Ben who gave her a clue by the announcement of angels that had started the change that happened in the present.

CHAPTER 14

THE IMMORTAL WAR

Sabrina gave a strange giggle and accepted Ben's version of the battle that is about to begin the first one of the immortal wars. She looks up into the sky her thoughts wander through her pristine planet. Her mind is pulled toward outer space. There are no moons or any other planets. The planet and the red sun are surrounded by a large asteroid belt that encircles their small solar system that lies six million kilometres from the planet. Sabrina had built sensors over a million years ago that ring the outer edge of her system. *They were over-protective of their planet in the early years of developing the society shed many steps within themselves to reach the level they are now* thought the leader of Azure. All the other children join a mind link to add strength to her spiritual form boosting it to travel to the outer edge of the asteroid belt, where she would face the real Entity. The vacuum of space had no effect on her.

This is what she had done a thousand times. The beauty of her flight and the view of Azure lift all her children's spirits. She lands at the largest asteroid to engage the ancient shield. There she sees the Entity's fleet of a thousand of black ships, which reflects off the red sun light. She enters the small chamber feels the emergency from her children. A sudden chill of evil of much greater intensity then before, she hoped for a miracle from the last two children that used an old warship. Sabrina saved the last two humans that had reform into female name Stella Neptune 6 and Captain Ito Lee from another timeline. They brought them here in secret, in hopes to follow the path of the light and battle the entity from past to the final battle. Sabrina wanted them to leave a message of hope and guidance to the light, rather than self-destruct into darkness. Instead, Ben pointed and claim the fourth generation had not been reach but rewind to restart the variant flux. She wanted them back in her arms. Her mind refocuses on the job at hand. The computer room had inches of dust over the machines.

The computer lights up as the ghostly image approaches the small chamber. Sabrina spots other footprints in the dusty floor, and she became more cautious with every step. The computer spoke in a crackle of static energy to acknowledge her presence. She knows that the systems would take a few more minutes to charge up the shield generators. She realizes the neglect of the defence system by her preoccupation with other races. This reminds her next time to maintain the shields that passed on information to the children of the light. The lights in the chamber slowly rose as the air scrubbers came online. Sabrina wanders over to the view screens that light up in sequence giving a three-hundred-and-sixty-degree angle.

That is when she spots more ships of the black shape. They were transmitting an energy field that stretched out like a giant spider web. This is almost enclosing her solar system so no one can escape. The chill once again brushes pass her florescence body. The eyes of Sabrina alter the lights in the room. Tiny energy spiders were threading a web all around her preventing her to leave. Three large spiders appear at the entrance to block her escape. Three glowing eyes pulse with the same blue energy. The clock at one of the screens started a count down to shield regeneration within five minutes.

I told you Sabrina you could not escape the end of everything, whispers in her mind!

"We shall not submit to you until things have been put right you broke our agreement," grunted Sabrina.

"I have dismantled your shields little one, this chamber is your tomb. For the pain, you caused me earlier. I will have you watch me devour your world," giggled the Entity.

Before Sabrina eyes the numbers of tiny spider's increase closing in on her location narrowing the room to manoeuvre. For the first time in a million years, something trembles inside Sabrina. It was hard to express in words. She just giggles at the spiders working hard to encase her within the chamber. Somehow, the Entity was not amused and then barks an insult.

"I would not take your end so lightly," hissed the Entity then adds a few more words. "You are a small little thing of wasted life form."

"Maybe so, but I know who you really are now that makes it much clearer my end. However, it is not at this moment I will die," Sabrina boasted with a large laugh.

"You will die a slow death that is what I want to complete my revenge," snorted the Entity.

"In all aspects of the cosmos, there is always two constants balance and chaos, measured by all living creatures. You have planned this so perfectly that chaos will now be unleashed," echoed Sabrina in a loud laugh.

The Entity stunned by her words gave orders to her spiders to kill and drain the energy right out of her. They acknowledge obediently started to move towards the ghostly figure that was ignoring their approach. Suddenly a strong vibration is felt all around the large web; she spins around from the nest three black ships were on fire. Panic voices screech in her ears. The Entity barks out, "attack enemies." She spins back to see the death of Sabrina. Instead, she sees three dead spiders and the chamber on fire, with no signs of Sabrina. Anger swells inside the Entity has she releases a great roar. Her thoughts send out a message to all her ships.

Lay waste to all, kill all on Azure, and kill all that resist me.

Sabrina is still laughing when she is back in her metal form all her people circle around her not sure what will happen next. The sudden sound of thunder echo across the planet as a single ship appears overhead. It hovers then descends with the hatch opening. Two old human forms appear and wave everyone on board the ship Sabrina led the way in song to keep everyone focussed on the escape. The old couple bow low and apologize for being late. Sabrina waves their apology away and then gave them a hug with kind words.

"You have renewed my faith in chaos my children. Let us leave now and teach the Entity some manners about rituals."

"I would be honored to do the first strike for freedom for all races of the 12 galaxies," grunted the old man.

"Yes, Ito and Stella you have saved our race now we must go to alpha-prime and save earth from its doom," stated Sabrina.

"No that could alter us affecting your minds as well your own bodies," snapped Stella.

"We had no choice but to guide the new angels to the past of the ea solar system at all costs," replied Sabrina.

"Then let us not waste time on debate. The Entity might attack at any moment quoted Ito.

"Yes, let us leave our home for we shall carry it in our hearts for evermore," Sabrina replied sadly.

She steps down off the ramp and kisses the planet with glowing eyes and dug deep to take a sample of soil and press it to her body while she spoke her last words.

"I shall return to the cosmos with my friend until we meet again," with warm thoughts of farewell, sent by Sabrina.

She releases a high pitch screech which sound cuts a path, killing all the plant life in its wake. The ground quakes from the affection felt, like if to answer her loving touch and answer her farewell. She steps away never looking back. The wind swirls all round as the ship launches into space. The ground below changes colour as the atmosphere collapses. The crust of Azure opens deep into the core cascading, before it implodes scattering huge chucks deep in space.

Back around the asteroid belt, the Entity's ships are being attacked from all angles by fleet of starfighters and blast boats lead by battle cruise paint in red and gold strips. small crafts with lethal weapons. The unknown ships had a different power source that seem to outrun all her missiles and dodge all her lasers and ion cannons. The Entity roars out her rage for their failures and kills some of her attendants instantly.

"All ships attack and take control of Azure."

"We obey to the death great leader."

Hundreds of black warships race to the planet. They report another ship landing by a small forest. The commander had fired a string of multi warhead missiles hitting that location. The Entity hissed with joy of revenge. The vibrations continue though the entities web. She turns to see over eighty ships disabled and floating among immense debris are her favourite soldiers. It grumbles to hear the news of failed commander to destroy four small ships.

The rest of the entities battle fleet were engaging the four enemy's largest battle cruisers spaceships with all their weapons missing their targets. She sees them blunder they would hit their own ships because of the speed and agility of the enemy ships to pop in out of danger. The commanders of her black ships claimed they cannot lock their weapons onto these fast-moving spacecrafts. *They are too stupid to reorganize* thought the Entity then barks new instructions telepathically. She focusses on the battlecruiser and with her telepathic powers she gets a glimpse of the name that shock her, has she cries out the name of the battlecruiser the Red Witch. The entity knew and muttered, "No, I destroy them long ago near the forbidden zone. they are dead," or just a ghost came a thought has given new orders to her remaining fleet.

"All ship break for diamond formation each one cover our flanks. When the ship appears only those in range will be permitted to fire."

Yes, sounds echo of voices through her web.

She sees the quickness of her ships realign into a diamond shape formation, and then spread out along the outer rim of the Azure solar system. The results of the diamond shape proved lethal. Two ships fell into the trap and take a direct hit to their starboard side. The damage to the enemy's ships hull could be seen. However, they manage to escape into folding space. The Entity is pleased and turns back to the other attack force heading to Azure. Her mind is giddy with the smell of death all around her she muttered to herself, *the darkness shall soon be all mine.*

Her mind focuses and sees the small ship leave the planet slightly disappointed that the missiles had not reached them. Her mind tingles to the danger when a small discolouration appears on the planet surface. The Entity curses Sabrina that this creature of the light shown a different side from previous three journeys. This she learnt from the old watcher of the cosmos, he never mentions this fact. "The sudden change I must ask him again after the battle is over" whispered the Entity. Her insight finally reaches the planet and walks deep onto the surface it confirms that the life is leaving the planet.

The Entity quickly recalls her ships and retreats from the danger. The commanders only hear a faint whisper. They focussed on the small ship giving it chase and firing ion and laser cannons to capture it. The shock wave of implosion sucks the ships towards the planet's core, causing an electrical damping field. Giant pieces of Azure shot out at all angles and crush the inner fleet none survived.

"Retreat all shadow ships reassemble twenty million kilometres to section Gs 234e sector ten," orders the Entity repeatedly.

Only laughter fills her mind. She panics and turns to see the other outer fleet yanked into a black hole. None can escape it, except the Entity and her escort ships that skirt the danger and pick up speed pushing her further into the future. The multiple eyes of the Entity darken as she can only watch the destruction of her dreams fade into darkness. The red sun is swallowed into the dark hole. The inner voice of a male taunts the Entity.

You have failed dark speck to a bigger black hole the light will always be one-step ahead of you or behind you since you will travel further beyond the unknown universe, it will be two steps behind you. You must accept I gave you the killing blow that lost all your fleet of ships. I claim victory over our first battle, snarls Captain Patterson with great laughter.

I must add it ended quickly by the error of your shadow force.

He projects his image with a great smile at four different shapes, sizes, and images showing a different female. The Entity is drawn to the women the evil is pulsing through them. She sends a message; they do not respond to her orders. Each female filled with the life force of the elders. They rejected her as the laughter cuts deep in her mind. The Entity's rage boiled over in her nest killing anything that vibrated on her web. She screams orders with her mind gift.

"I will hunt you down even if it takes eternity I will feast over your blood and all of the children of the light. There is no escape from my revenge," she echoes across space. She continues to travel further away from the small ships. The four females gave orders to set courses in four different directions.

The last ship to leave the planet with the remaining survivors of Azure wept for their home. Ito had escaped the barge and the black hole that nearly destroyed them. However, their course made them travel back in time. He uses every satellite or sun that he crosses to slow the ship down. The two human's stay on the bridge, because of the over crowding. Sabrina feels the flow of time and the visions of her past flow by and erases some and gain more truths of her memories. She knows the four women must survive similar to what Ben and Katrina did in the forest realm. Sabrina now selects the twelve mothers of her clan and starts to teach them her powers to absorb the life force from the children of the light. The twelve go out to the clan members to retell the message of Sabrina in private. They explain that all shall be reborn into a human form like Ito and Stella. They mention that all will experience new life and learn earth's history. The only danger is that we may fall to the emotional side of the human minds. You must wait for the sign before you show yourself with the abilities of mind gifts, stated Sabrina they will always be the children of the light. Their renewed spirit will be reborn within humans, most accept, and freely give themselves to their new life.

Close to three thousand became wary and asked to see Sabrina in private. She had no time to explain in detail to ease their fears. With no choice, they all must submit to the plan. The disgruntle group sent out anger thoughts towards Sabrina, which deeply affected her spirit. all was finished, only the twelve remain six male and six females this Sabrina was pleased. The next step became the difficult part what to do with the two humans.

Ito called Sabrina as they approach Pluto. Stella calculated that they arrived during the beginning of the human race that lived in caves. Sabrina sets her plans in motion dropping off pairs of Azure's across the new planet. When it is all finished, she faces the two humans that had been loyal friends. Her heart sank with the dark thoughts that ran in her head. Ito and Stella could feel the tension within the leader of Azure.

"Let us live in South America there are many cultures, which I know their history and ways," offered Stella.

"You now that you will be trapped in the cycle of violence," muttered Sabrina. Stella shrugged then sighs heavily with a nod. Ito offers another suggest that seem enticing.

"Let us live on Titian moon deep within its crust. There we will establish the first city named star point before anyone arrives, the tools in this ship will give us a great advantage, and the generation we have will follow."

Sabrina agrees as she could see the merit, and then adds a condition. She knew they might refuse and expressed it as an order

"You must rejuvenate your bodies to have a fair chance to survive the planets poisonous atmosphere."

Ito face dropped as well as Stella. They look at each other with deep frowns forming across their foreheads. Sabrina felt the raw emotions from Stella although she never spoke a word. Ito gave a smirk then nodded a yes. Stella agreed with a snarled curse. Sabrina took a step towards them as her hands glowed. She touches their forehead to absorb and copy all their experiences. They both groan from the sensation. At the same time, Sabrina gave them the ability to use the metal forms to protect their bodies and passed on that skill to their generations. She changes their names so they can live a new adventure at another time to come. When all is done, Sabrina heads to South America and evolves into woman carrying a female baby. There she would preach and fill out the years and generations. Sabrina hopes to spread the seeds to the children of the light among the human races. She awaits her birth in the new world and a new name.

CHAPTER 15

THE STAR CHILD

Far into the future, somewhere among the hundred thousand galaxies of the unknown regions of space the Entity slowly recovers from the disaster of the Azure encounter. She sat quietly her legs stretched out on her energy web reviewing all what happened to her and the great fleet she had controlled. All were lost in those last seconds, when the planet blew up and the appearance of a black hole completed the destruction. All her plans made by the dark powers of ancient race, which created this hybrid creature to travel across space gathering beings from thousand of living planets to prepare the way for the end of time. She alone would rule the cosmos, all ends when Sabrina destroyed her destiny. They have gone to their deaths the doorway to rule the shadows are shut. She recalls the Azurian leaders' last words repeating them aloud.

"In all aspects of the cosmos, there is always two constants balance and chaos. For those are what we are measured by all living creatures. You have plan this so perfectly to balance that chaos will now be unleashed," came louder laugh from Sabrina.

"Yes, chaos that is what took my fleet," complained the Entity with a deep growl.

With a long hiss and fidget in her web, the echoes of laughter fuel her rage once more. Her attendants became leery but approach with food. She ignores them most of the time. When the Entity is in deep meditation, her eyes were empty black pools. She sees them approach sends them a sharp rebuttal for disturbing her.

"Get out of my chamber now, or I shall eat you and all your family."

The attendant's trip over themselves leaving the web chamber. The Entity turns back to the view screens to see the distant galaxies with only four ships at her service. She sends two to scout and find trace elements of the small ship engines her only clue to find the children of the light. The two-legged Captain interfered with challenged words that he created the black hole and claimed the first victory. His words echo often in her mind, and the images made sure they were burned into her memory and recalls his last words.

"You have failed dark speck to a bigger black hole the light will always be one-step ahead of you or behind you since you will travel further beyond the unknown universe, it will be two steps behind you. You must accept I gave you the killing blow that lost all your fleet of ships. I claimed victory over our first battle. I must add this thought, this ends quickly by the error of your shadow force."

Sudden bad taste regurgitated deep within her stomach and gushed across the floor. Many attendants rush in the chamber and began to clean the floor regardless of the fear of the Entity. She moved away from the chattering noise to her sleep chamber she wanted to make a list who she would eat first the captain or the leader Sabrina of the children of the light. She felt the change and checked her time chronometer. She had moved forward so fast that it took another thousand years to slow the ships. She travelled back to what is left of Azure with the scout's ships to find the trace of the enemy ships. She envisioned Sabrina submitting when she gets her teeth deep within the neck for another clue that the Azure knew of her origin also trouble her when the words are recall.

"Maybe so, but I know who you really are now that makes it much more clear to me my enemy that I must delay my end. However, it is not at this moment I will die."

Once inside her sleep chamber no one allowed in her private domain. An immortal being, she had collected many items in her travels. Mixture of magic potions, weapons and most important a wide collection of males from only those races that would follow her into the shadows. Mostly dead and mummified she likes to look at them and recalls the times they spent mating. They gave her everything she desires from draining their home planet resources to building her large fleet. Only one male creature still lives but he is very old. He was young when she found him almost one of the first ones she married thought the Entity. It was so far back that these memories were hard to recall. Especially since the door, shut into the shadow realm troubled her mind right now. His gift was a seer to all futures. She kept him alive like a guidepost to reach the end of time; he had advised her every step to the planet Azure. Trapped in a cocoon the Entity would feed it as long as he spoke what she wanted to hear. Still annoyed over her lost she threw water on the face of the old creature barked out a thousand curses in foreign tongue. Covered in grey fur with long stout nose, snorts and shows his large fangs growls loudly until his piercing green eyes face the Entity. He quickly changes into a whimper for mercy.

I should kill you for failing me beast of my burden, snapped the Entity.

His eyes glowed brightly to the telepathic words of the Entity. He anxiously answers with a low growl.

"Please, do I have long for my death my love? However, I must see the shadow world with my own eyes that you promised since our first pledge together long ago."

He paused and sensed a change in the air as he sniffs.

"You fail to do the ritual," howled the beast that squirmed in his cocoon.

"Quiet beast they resisted me I had to force the issue then others appear to interfere," snapped the Entity.

"You lie your thoughts tell me a different story, show me all I will not help you any further Helen."

The Entity anger roars a long hiss, and then lashes out striking the head of the beast. She lunges on top of him with her fangs pressing against his neck. She hesitated to know that she needs him to find the children of the light. By him calling saying that name, provoke her into killing the beast. She backs off but strikes his face with one of her legs. The blood dribbled slowly from his nose, he shakes the cobwebs from the blows.

"I am the Entity is all what I have never mentioned me by this other names ever again."

"Yes my mistress, I begged your forgiveness, the beast whimpered weakly.

"Now, I shall mind link and you shall find me the answers I require to find the children of the light, so I can open the gate of the shadow world. After all it is my destiny," hissed the Entity.

"You have not fed me for some time now. I am too weak from the long neglect give me some food I shall help you after."

The Entity squirms slightly from the defiant beast. She turns to give a long whistle. Two multi leg creatures walk right in the death chamber. They knew that they were the appointed sacrifice to satisfy the beasts hungry. In less then an hour the beast restored its strength. He throws the empty shells out of the entities bed chamber. While she waited for the beast to have its full, the scout's ships reported they had found ten more shadow ships with crew still alive and preparing to join in the hunt. This news perks up her spirits, has she waits to mind link soon after some time had passed.

The beast takes in all the images, his emotion reacts to the sight of familiar faces. He sees Sabrina as more of a statue then a living creature. He is intrigued, pressed on to all that is visual by the four different Captains, and crew of the enemy ships. It reveals some painful memories of his younger life. The Entity feels the pain but is unclear to what it is that seems stir in the beast. Hours go by the beast continues the mind link reviewing everything from the Entity, even repeating some scenes and interaction among the Entity and her crew. He begins to laugh she pulls away slightly annoyed and exhausted from the connection.

"Why were you laughing beast," has the Entity snarls, thumbing her six legs to shake off the extra energy pulsing within her.

"I know how much you hate criticism my love. After you promise the same oath that, I shall enter the shadow realm by your side. I will tell you what you must do to regain the entrance to the shadow realm."

The Entity hissed and danced in a circle around the beast. She knew he wanted a blood oath to protect himself from her fury. Just by this suggestion, she comes to believe that the claim from Sabrina and the Captain is true. She felt her stomach turn once again and steps outside releasing the veil liquid. She also knew that he could find them with his gift this is her only hope to reach her destiny of the shadow realm. They had sealed their fate together since the beginning of their journey a blood oath she telepathically recalls.

My oath between us will stand old beast!

No, does not, since you broke the ritual that I told you must do for the children of the light to accept you. Then you would bring all life to darkness. You placed me in deep sleep so that I could not interfere or remind you your responsibility to complete the task. You decided to use force through a balance attack and embrace chaos. This is all you are doing, snarls the beast.

The Entity paced back and forth, while listening to his words that echoes of laughter rang off in the distance of her mind. She wonders why he is more abrupt does he not now that she controls his natural life. The ship they flew the Black Scorpion has she remembers killing Marvin Patterson and turning him into slave and beast to enhance his telepathic abilities so she could conquer the Twelve galaxies and the children of the light. She then realizes his game the beast is lying and trying to provoke her anger, which was rising with every syllable. She turns her body to face him eye to eye, he winces like if prepare for her to attack him. That gave her the opening to speak through her mind gift.

"I will give you what you want old beast freely, but you must answer one question truthfully before I submit the blood oath."

The old beast twisted his head to ponder her words, they have played each other for so long that the game has lost its meaning decades ago. He shrugs his shoulders and agrees with a flat tone.

"Ask your question I have always answered honestly."

"Tell me now where they are gone the children of the light," snap the Entity.

His eyes bulge out bitterly, whimper sadly by the vision that flashes before his eyes. The Entity steps closer to mind link and share the vision. She sees what the beast sees countless stars, galaxies all flashing by until a small planet comes in view. An ice planet near a dwarf star, which changed to a red giant sun among four gas giants, and changes again to a bright yellow sun with scores of planets. The black hole appears before her mind she cannot break the link it draws her close to the beast. He bites and draws the blood from the Entity. The sudden pain along her neck, she breaks free of the last vision of Sabrina being raise high in the sky has a seer of their village. She curses the beast at first but the vision of Sabrina being reborn in a different form, gave the insight to see that he was completing his task.

"They are too far away which is neither bad nor good. I will spend the time to rebuild my fleet. Moreover, send out the black ships to destroy all ice planets in a dwarf sun. Then leave spy probes to gather information on any merging races. They will search for any signs of the children of the light," murmured the Entity to the beast.

The blood that he had taken from the Entity rejuvenated the beast his fur went to a shiny brown. His muscles swelled with strength and with a slight twist of his wrist, he broke free from the cocoon. The Entity backs away her wound closes quickly, while she watches him change the beast speaks his mind.

"You had too many mindless creatures at the controls of your ships. This is an error since they would only follow what you suggested to do next. There are no races this far out. You need a work force, we shall mate they will be smarter from what you have now and be loyal to you, my mistress."

"You are a still brash and unfeeling, but your plans have merit. Of course, you know what will happen when I mate, they are everywhere in this room," hissed the Entity pointing to all remains of all her past lovers.

"I am not afraid my spirit will live on in the next generation, and you will gain great insight on where all the children of the light," stated the beast.

"Then I agree to have star children, they will give me what I want. Since you started this ritual, I shall honour it changing my chamber into our nursery," giggled the Entity.

The Entity gave a low rumble sound. The attendants rush in like a swarm cleaning and removing all the dead bodies. They bathe both the beast, and the Entity then left the room within two hours. The Entity turns her back revealing the egg chamber the beast smells the pheromones in the air. He howls and jumps on her backside spraying the essence within the chamber. The Entity waited patiently for the signs of exhaustion; with her fore legs free, she makes another cocoon for her last mate. The moment he staggers away, she spins and bites him hard. Every ounce of his life force is within her, the Entity drinks the beast blood. It quiets down her stomach. She can feel it rushing through her blood stream and towards the egg sack. Once the beast is drained to the bone, she cracks them with her mandibles to devour the bone marrow. The echoes of his voice become clear in her mind.

We are one now and forever. Since your failure the shadow realm has pick another to find the children of the light. She comes from the ea solar system; she is a hybrid chasing the children of the light. I choose her as the messenger of Ea. You will never make it Heidi and the other Helen Nightshade. Yes, because you are the daughters of the supreme elder Krell. However, I am his equal and I hold the time crystal with my son lord Id. You are too far away from the children. Only by my essence, our descendants will follow you blindly. They may help you if you show some love which you had long ago. This is your only hope. He laughs continually in her mind.

The Entity roars in anger throwing the remains of the beast against the far wall. The blood lust boils out of her mind. Her eyes turn deep red as she storms killing and eating all in her path. The vision of Sabrina and the Captain laughing at her only fuels a deep rage. She works her way from one end to the other side of the ship. There is no escape. Many offer themselves freely. Within a week, the ship is empty of the attendants and the bridge crew. She returns to her chamber to rest bloated from the feeding frenzy to encourage the swollen egg sack to develop her new children. The only joy came from the scout ships they found the trace element to find the enemies ships, and another forty black ships have been found.

I will never give up beast hinted the Entity.

She contacts the escort ships to tow her to the rendezvous of her new fleet. She also orders that she be in quarantine, and no one allowed on board the mother ship. The commanders agree and set course. With towing lines attached to her ship, they quickly begin to move across the cosmos. The Entity calculates she is four thousand light years away from the fleet. Her children will be adults and replace her existing crew unless she used her powers to get back to the old nest. Exhausted she falls into a deep sleep and await the birth of her children. She remembers the beast's last words that love, and affection develops a strong and smarter crew. They will reach the new home of the children of the light.

EPILOGUE

THE LOST BEING

The liquid form became aware it travels aimless in darkness of deep space far from the Galaxy somewhat confuse with thoughts that he is he lost being of time. He felt weak and thought death would be his greatest release. Then the image of being name Ru pester him that he is call by other names that sound off into the deepness of space and time. Not knowing what he was made move endless between the stars. Although he had memories that puzzle him the one that haunted the creature was his body was different then his dreams. It made him feel angry and hungry to find the true meaning of life. What ease his mind was the warmth of stars and he travel to each brightly hoping to find another being that could help understand his dreams. Over and over thousand of years he never stops calling out until he heard a voice that call to him constantly spoke the unvoiced. *Come to me Krell the immortal changeling you are more then the dark liquid of the elders clan.*

It was so familiar it gave him a purpose to live on and find the being within the planets around the dwarf stars is his only clue and he had a name and its is Krell the immortal. With renew vigor he used the powers of solar winds to fly further and closer in hopes to find the planet where this voice comes from. The day came when he knew its name and mention that she is part of the children of the light. Her words are soft and sweet, "Sabrina is in a angel form told me of you. So, I wait for you Krell, you must come to me my future love for I am call Tara Whitespirt your first and I hope only wife."

Krell answer quickly, "You give me purpose I am on my way sing to me my sweet so I may follow your voice."

Tara voice hymn and whistle softly her words had many languages, somehow Krill understood her words and song reminded of his mother. Who once told his future mate is out there in the stars of many galaxies? This memory is with his mind that he must reach out and find her. It is his purpose more so than the clan of the elders and the rogue name Ru. Krell clears his mind to call out to Tara Whitespirit. "I am coming to a blue planet I now know you are my true love."

CPSIA information can be obtained
at www.ICGtesting.com
Printed in the USA
BVHW041020150223
658492BV00006B/191